Dean Koontz was born and raised in Pennsylvania. He is the author of many number one bestsellers. He lives with his wife Gerda and their dog Trixie in southern California.

LIFE EXPECTANCY

Jimmy Tock comes into the world on the very night his grandfather leaves it. As a violent storm rages outside the hospital, Rudy Tock walks the corridors between the expectant fathers' waiting room and his dying father's bedside. Suddenly, Josef Tock sits up in bed and speaks coherently for the first and last time since his stroke. What he says before he dies is that there will be five dark days in the life of his grandson — the first when Jimmy is twenty, the last when he is thirty. What terrifying events await Jimmy on these five dark days? What challenges must he survive? At each of the crisis points a mystery as dangerous as it is wondrous unfolds — a struggle against an evil so dark and pervasive only the most extraordinary of human spirits can shine through.

Books by Dean Koontz
Published by The House of Ulverscroft:

FEAR NOTHING
SEIZE THE NIGHT
FROM THE CORNER OF HIS EYE
ONE DOOR AWAY FROM HEAVEN
BY THE LIGHT OF THE MOON
ODD THOMAS
THE TAKING

DEAN KOONTZ

LIFE EXPECTANCY

Complete and Unabridged

CHARNWOOD
Leicester

First published in Great Britain in 2005 by
HarperCollins*Publishers*
London

First Charnwood Edition
published 2005
by arrangement with
HarperCollins*Publishers*
London

British Library CIP Data

Koontz, Dean R. (Dean Ray,) *1945 –*
Life expectancy.—Large print ed.—
Charnwood library series
1. Suspense fiction
2. Large type books
I. Title
813.5'4 [F]

ISBN 1–84395–912–7

uuv 15. 11. 05

Published by
F. A. Thorpe (Publishing)
Anstey, Leicestershire

Set by Words & Graphics Ltd.
Anstey, Leicestershire
Printed and bound in Great Britain by
T. J. International Ltd., Padstow, Cornwall

This book is printed on acid-free paper

To Laura Albano,
who has such a good heart.
Strange brain, but good heart.

But he that dares not grasp the thorn
Should never crave the rose.

— ANNE BRONTË, 'The Narrow Way'

Here's a sigh to those who love me,
And a smile to those who hate;
And, whatever sky's above me,
Here's a heart for every fate.

— LORD BYRON, 'To Thomas Moore'

PART ONE

WELCOME TO THE WORLD, JIMMY TOCK

1

On the night that I was born, my paternal grandfather, Josef Tock, made ten predictions that shaped my life. Then he died in the very minute that my mother gave birth to me.

Josef had never previously engaged in fortune-telling. He was a pastry chef. He made éclairs and lemon tarts, not predictions.

Some lives, conducted with grace, are beautiful arcs bridging this world to eternity. I am thirty years old and can't for certain see the course of my life, but rather than a graceful arc, my passage seems to be a herky-jerky line from one crisis to another.

I am a lummox, by which I do not mean *stupid*, only that I am biggish for my size and not always aware of where my feet are going.

This truth is not offered in a spirit of self-deprecation or even humility. Apparently, being a lummox is part of my charm, an almost winsome trait, as you will see.

No doubt I have now raised in your mind the question of what I intend to imply by 'biggish for my size.' Autobiography is proving to be a trickier task than I first imagined.

I am not as tall as people seem to think I am, in fact not tall at all by the standards of professional — or even of high school — basketball. I am neither plump nor as buff as an

3

iron-pumping fitness fanatic. At most I am somewhat husky.

Yet men taller and heavier than I am often call me 'big guy.' My nickname in school was Moose. From childhood, I have heard people joke about how astronomical our grocery bills must be.

The disconnect between my true size and many people's perception of my dimensions has always mystified me.

My wife, who is the linchpin of my life, claims that I have a presence much bigger than my physique. She says that people measure me by the impression I make on them.

I find this notion ludicrous. It is bullshit born of love.

If sometimes I make an outsized impression on people, it's as likely as not because I fell on them. Or stepped on their feet.

In Arizona, there is a place where a dropped ball appears to roll uphill in defiance of gravity. In truth, this effect is a trick of perspective in which elements of a highly unusual landscape conspire to deceive the eye.

I suspect I am a similar freak of nature. Perhaps light reflects oddly from me or bends around me in a singular fashion, so I appear to be more of a hulk than I am.

On the night I was born in Snow County Hospital, in the community of Snow Village, Colorado, my grandfather told a nurse that I would be twenty inches long and weigh eight pounds ten ounces.

The nurse was startled by this prediction not

because eight pounds ten is a huge newborn — many are larger — and not because my grandfather was a pastry chef who suddenly began acting as though he were a crystal-ball gazer. Four days previously he had suffered a massive stroke that left him paralyzed on his right side and unable to speak; yet from his bed in the intensive care unit, he began making prognostications in a clear voice, without slur or hesitation.

He also told her that I would be born at 10:46 P.M. and that I would suffer from syndactyly.

That is a word difficult to pronounce *before* a stroke, let alone after one.

Syndactyly — as the observing nurse explained to my father — is a congenital defect in which two or more fingers or toes are joined. In serious cases, the bones of adjacent digits are fused to such an extent that two fingers share a single nail.

Multiple surgeries are required to correct such a condition and to ensure that the afflicted child will grow into an adult capable of giving the F-you finger to anyone who sufficiently annoys him.

In my case, the trouble was toes. Two were fused on the left foot, three on the right.

My mother, Madelaine — whom my father affectionately calls Maddy or sometimes the Mad One — insists that they considered forgoing the surgery and, instead, christening me Flipper.

Flipper was the name of a dolphin that once

5

starred in a hit TV show — not surprisingly titled *Flipper* — in the late 1960s. My mother describes the program as 'delightfully, wonderfully, hilariously stupid.' It went off the air a few years before I was born.

Flipper, a male, was played by a trained dolphin named Suzi. This was most likely the first instance of transvestism on television.

Actually, that's not the right word because transvestism is a male dressing as a female for sexual gratification. Besides, Suzi — alias Flipper — didn't wear clothes.

So it was a program in which the female star always appeared nude and was sufficiently butch to pass for a male.

Just two nights ago at dinner, over one of my mother's infamous cheese-and-broccoli pies, she asked rhetorically if it was any wonder that such a dire collapse in broadcast standards, begun with *Flipper*, should lead to the boring freak-show shock that is contemporary television.

Playing her game, my father said, 'It actually began with *Lassie*. In every show, she was nude, too.'

'Lassie was always played by male dogs,' my mother replied.

'There you go,' Dad said, his point made.

I escaped being named Flipper when successful surgeries restored my toes to the normal condition. In my case, the fusion involved only skin, not bones. The separation was a relatively simple procedure.

Nevertheless, on that uncommonly stormy

night, my grandfather's prediction of syndactyly proved true.

If I had been born on a night of unremarkable weather, family legend would have transformed it into an eerie calm, every leaf motionless in breathless air, night birds silent with expectation. The Tock family has a proud history of self-dramatization.

Even allowing for exaggeration, the storm must have been violent enough to shake the Colorado mountains to their rocky foundations. The heavens cracked and flashed as if celestial armies were at war.

Still in the womb, I remained unaware of all the thunderclaps. And once born, I was probably distracted by my strange feet.

This was August 9, 1974, the day Richard Nixon resigned as President of the United States.

Nixon's fall has no more to do with me than the fact that John Denver's 'Annie's Song' was the number-one record in the country at the time. I mention it only to provide historical perspective.

Nixon or no Nixon, what I find most important about August 9, 1974, is my birth — and my grandfather's predictions. My sense of perspective has an egocentric taint.

Perhaps more clearly than if I had been there, because of vivid pictures painted by numerous family stories of that night, I can see my father, Rudy Tock, walking back and forth from one end of County Hospital to the other, between the maternity ward and the ICU, between joy at the prospect of his son's pending arrival and grief over his beloved father's quickening slide into death.

★ ★ ★

With blue vinyl-tile floor, pale-green wainscoting, pink walls, a yellow ceiling, and orange-and-white stork-patterned drapes, the expectant-fathers' lounge churned with the negative energy of color overload. It would have served well as the nervous-making set for a nightmare about a children's-show host who led a secret life as an ax murderer.

The chain-smoking clown didn't improve the ambience.

Rudy stood birth watch with only one other man, not a local but a performer with the circus that was playing a one-week engagement in a meadow at the Halloway Farm. He called himself Beezo. Curiously, this proved not to be his clown name but one that he'd been born with: Konrad Beezo.

Some say there is no such thing as destiny, that what happens just happens, without purpose or meaning. Konrad's surname would argue otherwise.

Beezo was married to Natalie, a trapeze artist and a member of a renowned aerialist family that qualified as circus royalty.

Neither of Natalie's parents, none of her brothers and sisters, and none of her high-flying cousins had accompanied Beezo to the hospital. This was a performance night, and as always

8

the show must go on.

Evidently the aerialists kept their distance also because they had not approved of one of their kind taking a clown for a husband. Every subculture and ethnicity has its objects of bigotry.

As Beezo waited nervously for his wife to deliver, he muttered unkind judgments of his in-laws. 'Self-satisfied,' he called them, and 'devious.'

The clown's perpetual glower, rough voice, and bitterness made Rudy uncomfortable.

Angry words plumed from him in exhalations of sour smoke: 'duplicitous' and 'scheming' and, poetically for a clown, 'blithe spirits of the air, but treacherous when the ground is under them.'

Beezo was not in full costume. Furthermore, his stage clothes were in the Emmett Kelly sad-faced tradition rather than the bright polka-dot plumage of the average Ringling Brothers clown. He cut a strange figure nonetheless.

A bright plaid patch blazed across the seat of his baggy brown suit. The sleeves of his jacket were comically short. In one lapel bloomed a fake flower the diameter of a bread plate.

Before racing to the hospital with his wife, he had traded clown shoes for sneakers and had taken off his big round red rubber nose. White greasepaint still encircled his eyes, however, and his cheeks remained heavily rouged, and he wore a rumpled porkpie hat.

Beezo's bloodshot eyes shone as scarlet as his painted cheeks, perhaps because of the acrid smoke wreathing his head, although Rudy suspected that strong drink might be involved as well.

In those days, smoking was permitted everywhere, even in many hospital waiting rooms. Expectant fathers traditionally gave out cigars by way of celebration.

When not at his dying father's bedside, poor Rudy should have been able to take refuge in that lounge. His grief should have been mitigated by the joy of his pending parenthood.

Instead, both Maddy and Natalie were long in labor. Each time that Rudy returned from the ICU, waiting for him was the glowering, muttering, bloody-eyed clown, burning through pack after pack of unfiltered Lucky Strikes.

As drumrolls of thunder shook the heavens, as reflections of lightning shuddered through the windows, Beezo made a stage of the maternity ward lounge. Restlessly circling the blue vinyl floor, from pink wall to pink wall, he smoked and fumed.

'Do you believe that snakes can fly, Rudy Tock? Of course you don't. But snakes *can* fly. I've seen them high above the center ring. They're well paid and applauded, these cobras, these diamondbacks, these copperheads, these hateful *vipers*.'

Poor Rudy responded to this vituperative rant with murmured consolation, clucks of the tongue, and sympathetic nods. He didn't want to encourage Beezo, but he sensed that a failure to commiserate would make him a target for the clown's anger.

10

Pausing at a storm-washed window, his painted face further patinated by the lightning-cast patterns of the streaming raindrops on the glass, Beezo said, 'Which are you having, Rudy Tock — a son or daughter?'

Beezo consistently addressed Rudy by his first and last names, as if the two were one: *Rudytock*.

'They have a new ultrasound scanner here,' Rudy replied, 'so they could tell us whether it's a boy or girl, but we don't want to know. We just care is the baby healthy, and it is.'

Beezo's posture straightened, and he raised his head, thrusting his face toward the window as if to bask in the pulsing storm light. 'I don't need ultrasound to tell me what I know. Natalie is giving me a son. Now the Beezo name won't die when I do. I'll call him Punchinello, after one of the first and greatest of clowns.'

Punchinello Beezo, Rudy thought. *Oh, the poor child*.

'He will be the very greatest of our kind,' said Beezo, 'the ultimate jester, harlequin, jackpudding. He will be acclaimed from coast to coast, on every continent.'

Although Rudy had just returned to the maternity ward from the ICU, he felt imprisoned by this clown whose dark energy seemed to swell each time the storm flashed in his feverish eyes.

'He will be not merely acclaimed but *immortal*.'

Rudy was hungry for news of Maddy's condition and the progress of her labor. In those days, fathers were seldom admitted to delivery rooms to witness the birth of their children.

'He will be *the* circus star of his time, Rudy Tock, and everyone who sees him perform will know Konrad Beezo is his father, patriarch of clowns.'

The ward nurses who should have regularly visited the lounge to speak with the waiting husbands were making themselves less visible than usual. No doubt they were uncomfortable in the presence of this angry bozo.

'On my father's grave, I swear my Punchinello will *never* be an aerialist,' Beezo declared.

The blast of thunder punctuating his vow was the first of two so powerful that the window-panes vibrated like drumheads, and the lights — almost extinguished — throbbed dimly.

'What do acrobatics have to do with the truth of the human condition?' Beezo demanded.

'Nothing,' Rudy said at once, for he was not an aggressive man. Indeed, he was gentle and humble, not yet a pastry chef like his father, merely a baker who, on the verge of fatherhood, wished to avoid being severely beaten by a large clown.

'Comedy and tragedy, the very tools of the clown's art — *that* is the essence of life,' Beezo declared.

'Comedy, tragedy, and the need for good bread,' Rudy said, making a little joke, including his own trade in the essence-of-life professions.

This small frivolity earned him a fierce glare, a look that seemed capable not merely of stopping clocks but of freezing time.

''Comedy, tragedy, and the need for good

bread,'' Beezo repeated, perhaps expecting Dad to admit his quip had been inane.

'Hey,' Dad said, 'that sounds just like me,' for the clown had spoken in a voice that might have passed for my father's.

''Hey, that sounds just like me,'' Beezo mocked in Dad's voice. Then he continued in his own rough growl: 'I *told* you I'm talented, Rudy Tock. In more ways than you can imagine.'

Rudy thought he could feel his chilled heart beating slower, winding down under the influence of that wintry gaze.

'My boy will never be an aerialist. The hateful snakes will hiss. Oh, how they'll hiss and thrash, but *Punchinello will never be an aerialist!*'

Another tsunami of thunder broke against the walls of the hospital, and again the lights were more than half drowned.

In that gloom, Rudy swore that the tip of Beezo's cigarette in his right hand glowed brighter, brighter, although he held it at his side, as if some phantom presence were drawing on it with eager lips.

Rudy thought, but could not swear, that Beezo's eyes briefly glowed as bright and red as the cigarette. This could not have been an inner light, of course, but a reflection of . . . something.

When the echoes of the thunder rolled away, the brownout passed. As the lights rose, so did Rudy rise from his chair.

He had only recently returned here, and although he had received no news about his wife, he was ready to flee back to the grim scene in the intensive care unit rather than experience a third doomsday peal and another dimming of lights in the company of Konrad Beezo.

When he arrived at the ICU and found two nurses at his father's bedside, Rudy feared the worst. He knew that Josef was dying, yet his throat tightened and tears welled when he thought the end loomed.

To his surprise, he discovered Josef half sitting up in bed, hands clutching the side rails, excitedly repeating the predictions that he had already made to one of the nurses. 'Twenty inches . . . eight pounds ten ounces . . . ten-forty-six tonight . . . syndactyly . . .'

When he saw his son, Josef pulled himself all the way into a sitting position, and one of the nurses raised the upper half of the bed to support him better.

He had not only regained his speech but also appeared to have overcome the partial paralysis that had followed his stroke. When he seized Rudy's right hand, his grip proved firm, even painful.

Astonished by this development, Rudy at first assumed that his father had experienced a miraculous recovery. Then, however, he recognized the desperation of a dying man with an important message to impart.

Josef's face was drawn, seemed almost shrunken, as if Death, in a sneak-thief mood, had begun days ago to steal the substance of him, ounce by ounce. By contrast his eyes appeared to be enormous. Fear sharpened his gaze when his eyes fixed on his son.

'Five days,' said Josef, his hoarse voice raw with suffering, parched because he had been taking fluids only intravenously. 'Five terrible days.'

'Easy, Dad. Don't excite yourself,' Rudy cautioned, but he saw that on the cardiac monitor, the illuminated graph of his father's heart activity revealed a fast yet regular pattern.

One of the nurses left to summon a doctor. The other stepped back from the bed, waiting to assist if the patient experienced a seizure.

First licking his cracked lips to wet the way for his whisper, he made his fifth prediction: 'James. His name will be James, but no one will call him James . . . or Jim. Everyone will call him Jimmy.'

This startled Rudy. He and Maddy had chosen James if the baby was a boy, Jennifer if it was a girl, but they had not discussed their choices with anyone.

Josef could not have known. Yet he knew.

With increasing urgency, Josef declared, 'Five days. You've got to warn him. Five terrible days.'

'Easy, Dad,' Rudy repeated. 'You'll be okay.'

His father, as pale as the cut face of a loaf of bread, grew paler, whiter than flour in a measuring cup. 'Not okay. *I'm dying*.'

'You aren't dying. Look at you. You're speaking. There's no paralysis. You're — '

'*Dying*,' Josef insisted, his rough voice rising in volume. His pulse throbbed at his temples, and on the monitor it grew more rapid as he strained to break through his son's reassurances and to seize his attention. 'Five dates. Write them down. Write them now. *NOW!*'

Confused, afraid that Josef's adamancy might trigger another stroke, Rudy mollified his father.

He borrowed a pen from the nurse. She didn't have any paper, and she wouldn't let him use the patient's chart that hung on the foot of the bed.

From his wallet, Rudy withdrew the first thing he found that offered a clean writing surface: a free pass to the very circus in which Beezo performed.

Rudy had received the pass a week ago from Huey Foster, a Snow Village police officer. They had been friends since childhood.

Huey, like Rudy, had wanted to be a pastry chef. He didn't have the talent for a career in baking. His muffins broke teeth. His lemon tarts offended the tongue.

When, by virtue of his law-enforcement job, Huey received freebies — passes to the circus, booklets of tickets for carnival rides at the county fair, sample boxes of bullets from various ammo manufacturers — he shared them with Rudy. In return, Rudy gave Huey cookies that didn't sour the appetite, cakes that didn't displease the nose, pies and strudels that didn't induce regurgitation.

Red and black lettering, illustrated with elephants and lions, crowded the face of the circus pass. The reverse was blank. Unfolded, it measured three by five inches, the size of an index card.

As hard rain beat on a nearby window, drumming up a sound like many running feet, Josef clutched again at the railings, anchoring himself, as if he feared that he might float up and

16

away. 'Nineteen ninety-four. September fifteenth. A Thursday. Write it down.'

Standing beside the bed, Rudy took dictation, using the precise printing with which he composed recipe cards: SEPT 15, 1994, THURS.

Eyes wide and wild, like those of a rabbit in the thrall of a stalking coyote, Josef stared toward a point high on the wall opposite his bed. He seemed to see more than the wall, something beyond it. Perhaps the future.

'Warn him,' the dying man said. 'For God's sake, *warn him*.'

Bewildered, Rudy said, 'Warn who?'

'Jimmy. Your son, Jimmy, my grandson.'

'He's not born yet.'

'Almost. Two minutes. *Warn him*. Nineteen ninety-eight. January nineteenth. A Monday.'

Transfixed by the ghastly expression on his father's face, Rudy stood with pen poised over paper.

'*WRITE IT DOWN!*' Josef roared. His mouth contorted so severely in the shout that his dry and peeling lower lip split. A crimson thread slowly unraveled down his chin.

'Nineteen ninety-eight,' Rudy muttered as he wrote.

'January nineteenth,' Josef repeated in a croak, his parched throat having been racked by the shout. 'A Monday. Terrible day.'

'Why?'

'Terrible, terrible.'

'Why will it be terrible?' Rudy persisted.

'Two thousand two. December twenty-third. Another Monday.'

17

Jotting down this third date, Rudy said, 'Dad, this is weird. I don't understand.'

Josef still held tight to both steel bedrails. Suddenly he shook them violently, with such uncanny strength that the railings seemed to be coming apart at their joints, raising a clatter that would have been loud in an ordinary hospital room but that was explosive in the usually hushed intensive care unit.

At first the observing nurse rushed forward, perhaps intending to calm the patient, but the electrifying combination of fury and terror that wrenched his pallid face caused her to hesitate. When waves of thunder broke against the hospital hard enough to shake dust off the acoustic ceiling tiles, the nurse retreated, almost as if she thought Josef himself had summoned that detonation.

'*WRITE IT DOWN!*' he demanded.

'I wrote, I wrote,' Rudy assured him. 'December 23, 2002, another Monday.'

'Two thousand three,' Josef said urgently. 'The twenty-sixth of November. A Wednesday. The day before Thanksgiving.'

After recording this fourth date on the back of the circus pass, just as his father stopped shaking the bedrails, Rudy looked up and saw a fresh emotion in Josef's face, in his eyes. The fury was gone, and the terror.

As tears welled, Josef said, 'Poor Jimmy, poor Rudy.'

'Dad?'

'Poor, poor Rudy. Poor Jimmy. Where is Rudy?'

18

'I'm Rudy, Dad. I'm right here.'

Josef blinked, blinked, and flicked away the tears as yet another emotion gripped him, this one not easy to define. Some would have called it astonishment. Others would have said it was wonder of the pure variety that a baby might express at the first sight of any bright marvel.

After a moment, Rudy recognized it as a state more profound than wonder. This was awe, the complete yielding of the mind to something grand and formidable.

His father's eyes shone with amazement. Across his face, expressions of delight and apprehension contested with each other.

Josef's increasingly raspy voice fell to a whisper: 'Two thousand five.'

His gaze remained fixed on another reality that apparently he found more convincing than he did this world in which he had lived for fifty-seven years.

Hand trembling now, but still printing legibly, Rudy recorded this fifth date — and waited.

'Ah,' said Joseph, as if a startling secret had been revealed.

'Dad?'

'Not this, not this,' Josef lamented.

'Dad, what's wrong?'

As curiosity outweighed her anxiety, the rattled nurse ventured closer to the bed.

A doctor entered the cubicle. 'What's going on here?'

Josef said, 'Don't trust the clown.'

The physician looked mildly offended, assuming that the patient had just questioned his medical credentials.

Leaning over the bed, trying to redirect his father's attention from his otherworldly vision, Rudy said, 'Dad, how do you know about the clown?'

'The sixteenth of April,' said Josef.

'How do you know about the clown?'

'*WRITE IT DOWN*,' Josef thundered even as the heavens crashed against the earth once more.

As the doctor went around to the other side of the bed, Rudy added APRIL 16 after 2005 to the fifth line on the back of the circus pass. He also printed SATURDAY when his father spoke it.

The doctor put a hand under Josef's chin and turned his head to have a better look at his eyes.

'He isn't who you think he is,' said Josef, not to the doctor but to his son.

'Who isn't?' Rudy asked.

'*He* isn't.'

'Who's he?'

'Now, Josef,' the physician chided, 'you know me very well. I'm Dr. Pickett.'

'Oh, the tragedy,' Josef said, voice ripe with pity, as if he were not a pastry chef but a thespian upon the Shakespearean stage.

'What tragedy?' Rudy worried.

Producing an ophthalmoscope from a pocket of his white smock, Dr. Pickett disagreed: 'No tragedy here. What I see is a remarkable recovery.'

Breaking loose of the physician's chin grip, increasingly agitated, Josef said, 'Kidneys!'

Bewildered, Rudy said, 'Kidneys?'

'Why should *kidneys* be so damned important?' Josef demanded. 'It's absurd, it's all *absurd!*'

Rudy felt his heart sink at this, for it seemed that his dad's brief clarity of mind had begun to give way to babble.

Asserting control of his patient again by once more gripping his chin, Dr. Pickett switched on the ophthalmoscope and directed the light in Josef's right eye.

As though that narrow beam were a piercing needle and his life were a balloon, Josef Tock let out an explosive breath and slumped back upon his pillow, dead.

With all the techniques and instruments available to a well-equipped hospital, attempts at resuscitation were made, but to no avail. Josef had moved on and wasn't coming back.

★　★　★

And I, James Henry Tock, arrived. The time on my grandfather's death certificate matches that on my birth certificate — 10:46 P.M.

Bereaved, Rudy understandably lingered at Josef's bedside. He had not forgotten his wife, but grief immobilized him.

Five minutes later, he received word from a nurse that Maddy had experienced a crisis in her labor and that he must go at once to her side.

Alarmed by the prospect of losing his father and his wife in the same hour, Dad fled the intensive care unit.

As he tells it, the halls of our modest county

hospital had become a white labyrinth, and at least twice he made wrong turns. Too impatient to wait for the elevator, he raced down the stairs from the third floor to the ground level before realizing that he'd passed the second floor, on which the maternity ward was located.

Dad arrived in the expectant-fathers' waiting lounge to the crack of a pistol as Konrad Beezo shot his wife's doctor.

For an instant, Dad thought Beezo had used a clown gun, some trick firearm that squirted red ink. The doctor dropped to the floor, however, not with comic flair but with hideous finality, and the smell of blood plumed thick, too real.

Beezo turned to Dad and raised the pistol.

In spite of the rumpled porkpie hat and the short-sleeved coat and the bright patch on the seat of his pants, in spite of the white greasepaint and the rouged cheeks, nothing about Konrad Beezo was clownish at that moment. His eyes were those of a jungle cat, and it was easy to imagine that the teeth bared in his snarl were tiger fangs. He loomed, the embodiment of murderous dementia, demonic.

Dad thought that he, too, would be shot, but Beezo said, 'Stay out of my way, Rudy Tock. I have no quarrel with you. You're not an aerialist.'

Beezo shouldered through the door between the lounge and the maternity ward, slammed it shut behind him.

Dad knelt beside the doctor — and discovered that a breath of life remained in him. The wounded man tried to speak, could not. Blood had pooled in his throat, and he gagged.

Gently elevating the physician's head, shoving old magazines under it to brace the man at an angle that allowed him to breathe, Dad shouted for help as the swelling storm rocked the night with doomsday peals of thunder.

Dr. Ferris MacDonald had been Maddy's physician. He had also been called upon to treat Natalie Beezo when, unexpectedly, she had been brought to the hospital in labor.

Mortally wounded, he seemed more bewildered than frightened. Able to clear his throat and breathe now, he told my father, 'She died during delivery, but it wasn't my fault.'

For a terrifying moment, my dad thought Maddy had died.

Dr. MacDonald realized this, for his last words were 'Not Maddy. The clown's wife. Maddy . . . is alive. I'm so sorry, Rudy.'

Ferris MacDonald died with my father's hand upon his heart.

As the thunder rolled toward a far horizon, Dad heard another gunshot from beyond the door through which Konrad Beezo had vanished.

Maddy lay somewhere behind that door — a woman left helpless by a difficult labor. I was back there, too — an infant who was not yet enough of a lummox to defend himself.

My father, then a baker, had never been a man of action; nor did he become one when, a few years later, he graduated to the status of pastry chef. He is of average height and weight, not physically weak but not born for the boxing ring, either. He had to that point led a charmed life,

23

without serious want, without any strife.

Nevertheless, fear for his wife and his child cast him into a strange, cold panic marked more by calculation than by hysteria. Without a weapon or a plan, but suddenly with the heart of a lion, he opened that door and went after Beezo.

Although his imagination spun a thousand bloody scenarios in mere seconds, he says that he did not anticipate what was about to happen, and of course he could not foresee how the events of that night would reverberate through the next thirty years with such terrible and astonishing consequences in his life and mine.

2

At Snow County Hospital, in the expectant-fathers' waiting room, the inner door opens to a short corridor with a supply room to the left and a bathroom to the right. Fluorescent ceiling panels, white walls, and a white ceramic-tile floor imply impeccable antibacterial procedures.

I have seen that space because my child entered the world in the same maternity ward on another unforgettable night of incomparable chaos.

On that stormy evening in 1974, with Richard Nixon gone home to California, and Beezo on a rampage, my father found a nurse sprawled in the hallway, shot point-blank.

He remembers almost being driven to his knees by pity, by despair.

The loss of Dr. MacDonald, although terrible, had not fully penetrated Dad, for it had been so sudden, so dreamlike. Mere moments later, the sight of this dead nurse — young, fair, like a fallen angel in white raiments, golden hair fanning in a halo around her eerily serene face — pierced him, and he absorbed the truth and the meaning of both deaths at once.

He tore open the storage-closet door, searching for something he might use as a weapon. He found only spare linens, bottles of antiseptic cleaner, a locked cabinet of medications . . .

Although in retrospect this moment struck him as darkly comic, at the time he thought, with grave seriousness and with the logic of desperation, that having kneaded so much dough over the past few years, his hands were dangerously strong. If only he could get past Beezo's gun, he surely would have the strength to strangle him.

No makeshift weapon could hope to be as deadly as the well-flexed hands of an angry baker. Sheer terror spawned this lunatic notion; curiously, however, terror also gave him courage.

The short hallway intersected a longer one, which led left and right. Off this new corridor, three doors served a pair of delivery rooms as well as the neonatal care unit where swaddled newborns, each in his or her bassinet, pondered their new reality of light, shadow, hunger, discontent, and taxes.

Dad sought my mother and me, but found only her. She lay in one of the delivery rooms, alone and unconscious on the birthing bed.

At first he thought that she must be dead. Darkness swooned at the edges of his vision, but before he passed out, he saw that his beloved Maddy was breathing. He clutched the edge of her bed until his vision brightened.

Gray-faced, drenched with sweat, she looked not like the vibrant woman he knew, but instead appeared to be frail and vulnerable.

Blood on the sheets suggested that she'd delivered their child, but no squalling infant was present.

Elsewhere, Beezo shouted, 'Where are you bastards?'

Reluctant to leave my mother, Dad nonetheless went in search of the conflict to see what help he could provide — as (he has always insisted) *any* baker would have done.

In the second delivery room, he found Natalie Beezo upon another birthing bed. The slender aerialist had so recently died from the complications of childbirth that her tears of suffering had not yet dried upon her cheeks.

According to Dad, even after her agony and even in death, she was ethereally beautiful. A flawless olive complexion. Raven hair. Her eyes were open, luminous green, like windows to a field in Heaven.

For Konrad Beezo, who didn't appear to be handsome under the greasepaint and who was not a man of substantial property and whose personality would surely be at least *somewhat* off-putting even under ordinary circumstances, this woman was a prize beyond all reasonable expectation. You could understand — though not excuse — his violent reaction to the loss of her.

Stepping out of the delivery room, Dad came face to face with the homicidal clown. Simultaneously Beezo flung open the door from the crèche and charged into the hall, a blanketed infant cradled in the crook of his left arm.

At this close range, the pistol in his right hand appeared to be twice the size that it had been in the waiting room, as if they were in Alice's Wonderland, where objects grew or shrank with no regard for reason or for the laws of physics.

Dad might have seized Beezo's wrist and, with his strong baker's hands, fought for possession of the gun, but he dared not act in any way that would have put the baby at risk.

With its pinched red face and furrowed brow, the infant appeared indignant, offended. Its mouth stretched open wide, as though it were trying to scream but had been shocked silent by the realization that its father was a mad clown.

Thank God for the baby, Dad has often said. *Otherwise I would have gotten myself killed. You'd have grown up fatherless, and you'd never have learned how to make a first-rate* crème brûlée.

So cradling the baby and brandishing the pistol, Beezo demanded of my father, 'Where are they, Rudy Tock?'

'Where are who?' Dad asked.

The red-eyed clown appeared to be both wrung by grief and ripped by anger. Tears streaked his makeup. His lips trembled as if he might sob uncontrollably, then skinned back from his teeth in an expression of such ferocity that a chill wound through Dad's bowels.

'Don't play dumb,' Beezo warned. 'There had to be other nurses, maybe another doctor. I want the bastards dead, all of them who failed her.'

'They ran,' my father said, certain that it would be safer to lie about having seen the medical staff escape than to insist that he had encountered no one. 'They slipped out behind your back, the way you came, through the waiting room. They're long gone.'

Feeding on his rage, Konrad Beezo appeared

to swell larger, as if anger were the food of giants. No Barnum & Bailey buffoonery brightened his face, and the poisonous hatred in his eyes was as potent as cobra venom.

Lest he become a stand-in for the medical staff no longer within Beezo's reach, Dad quickly added, with no trace of threat, as if only being helpful, 'Police are on the way. They'll want to take the baby from you.'

'My son is *mine*,' Beezo declared with such passion that the stink of stale cigarette smoke rising from his clothes might almost have been mistaken for the consequence of his fiery emotion. 'I will do *anything* to keep him from being raised by the aerialists.'

Walking a thin line between clever manipulation and obvious fawning in the interest of self-preservation, my father said, 'Your boy will be the greatest of his kind — clown, jester, harlequin, jackmuffin.'

'Jack*pudding*,' the killer corrected, but without animosity. 'Yes, he'll be the greatest. He *will*. I won't let anyone deny my son his destiny.'

With baby and pistol, Beezo pushed past my dad and hurried along the shorter hall, where he stepped over the dead nurse with no more concern for her than he'd have shown for a janitor's mop and bucket.

Feverishly trying to think of something that he could do to bring down this brute without harming the infant, Dad could only watch in frustration.

When Beezo reached the door to the expectant-fathers' lounge, he hesitated, glanced back. 'I'll never forget you, Rudy Tock. Never.'

My father could not decide whether that declaration might be an expression of misguided sentimental affection — or a threat.

Beezo pushed through the door and disappeared.

At once, Dad hurried back to the first delivery room because his primary concern understandably remained with my mother and me.

Still unattended, my mother lay on the birthing bed where Dad had moments ago discovered her. Though still gray-faced and soaked with sweat, she had regained consciousness.

She groaned with pain, blinked in confusion.

Whether she was merely disoriented or delirious is a matter of contention between my parents, but my father insists that he feared for her when she said, 'If you want Reuben sandwiches for dinner, we'll have to go to the market for cheese.'

Mom insists that she actually said, 'After this, don't think you're ever going to touch me again, you son of a bitch.'

Their love is deeper than desire, than affection, than respect, so deep that its wellspring is humor. Humor is a petal on the flower of hope, and hope blossoms on the vine of faith. They have faith in each other and faith that life has meaning, and from this faith comes their indefatigable good humor, which is their greatest gift to each other — and to me.

I grew up in a home filled with laughter. Regardless of what happens to me in the days

30

ahead, I will have had the laughter. And wonderful pastries.

In this account of my life, I will resort at every turn to amusement, for laughter is the perfect medicine for the tortured heart, the balm for misery, but I will not beguile you. I will not use laughter as a curtain to spare you the sight of horror and despair. We will laugh together, but sometimes the laughter will hurt.

So . . .

Whether my mother was delirious or sound of mind, whether she blamed my father for the pain of labor or discussed the need for cheese, they are in relative agreement about what happened next. My father found a wall-mounted phone near the door and called for help.

Because this device was more an intercom than a phone, it did not have a standard keypad, just four keys, each clearly labeled: STAFFING, PHARMACY, MAINTENANCE, SECURITY.

Dad pressed SECURITY and informed the answering officer that people had been shot, that the assailant, costumed as a clown, was even then fleeing the building, and that Maddy needed immediate medical assistance.

From the bed, clearheaded now if she had not been previously, my mother cried out, 'Where's my baby?'

Phone still to his ear, my father turned to her, astounded, alarmed. 'You don't know where it is?'

Striving unsuccessfully to sit up, grimacing with pain, Mom said, 'How would I know? I passed out or something. What do you mean someone was shot? For God's sake, who was shot? What's happening? *Where's my baby?*'

Although the delivery room had no windows, although it was surrounded by hallways and by other rooms that further insulated it from the outside world, my folks heard faint sirens rising in the distance.

Dad's memory regurgitated the suddenly nauseating image of Beezo in the hallway, the pistol in his right hand, the baby cradled in his left arm. Bitter acid burned in my father's throat, and his already harried heart raced faster.

Perhaps Beezo's wife *and* child had died at birth. Perhaps the infant in his arms hadn't been his own but had been instead little James — or Jennifer — Tock.

I thought 'kidnapped,' Dad says when he recalls the moment. I thought about the Lindbergh baby and Frank Sinatra Junior being held for ransom and Rumpelstiltskin and Tarzan being raised by apes, and though none of that makes sense, I thought it all in an instant. I wanted to scream, but I couldn't, and I felt just like that red-faced baby with its mouth open but silent, and when I thought of the baby, oh, then I just knew it had been you, not his at all, but you, my Jimmy.

Desperate now to find Beezo and stop him, Dad dropped the phone, bolted toward the open door to the hallway — and nearly collided with Charlene Coleman, a nurse who came bearing a baby in her arms.

This infant had a broader face than the one Beezo had spirited into the stormy night. Its

32

complexion was a healthy pink instead of mottled red. According to Dad, its eyes shone clear and blue, and its face glowed with wonder.

'I hid with your baby,' Charlene Coleman said. 'I hid from that awful man. I knew he would be trouble when he first showed up with his wife, him wearing that ugly hat indoors and making no apology for it.'

I wish I could verify from personal experience that, indeed, what alarmed Charlene from the get-go was not Beezo's clown makeup, not his poisonous ranting about his aerialist in-laws, not his eyes so crazy that they almost spun like pinwheels, but simply his *hat*. Unfortunately, less than one hour old, I had not yet learned English and had not even sorted out who all these people were.

3

Trembling with relief, Dad took me from Charlene Coleman and carried me to my mother.

After the nurse raised the head of the birthing bed and provided more pillows, Mom was able to take me in her arms.

Dad swears that her first words to me were these: 'You better have been worth all the pain, Little Blue Eyes, 'cause if you turn out to be an ungrateful child, I'll make your life a living hell.'

Tearful, shaken by all that had occurred, Charlene recounted recent events and explained how she'd been able to spirit me to safety when the shooting started.

Unexpectedly required to attend two women simultaneously in urgent and difficult labor, Dr. MacDonald had been unable at that hour to locate a qualified physician to assist on a timely basis. He divided his attention between the two patients, hurrying from one delivery room to the other, relying on his nurses for backup, his work complicated by the periodically dimming lights and worry about whether the hospital generator would kick in reliably if the storm knocked out electric service.

Natalie Beezo had received no prenatal care. She unknowingly suffered from preeclampsia. During labor she developed full-blown eclampsia and experienced violent convulsions that would not respond to treatment and that threatened not only her own life but the life of her unborn child.

Meanwhile, my mother endured an excruciating labor resulting largely from the failure of her cervix to dilate. Intravenous injections of synthetic oxytocin initially did not induce sufficient contractions of the uterine muscles to allow her to squeeze me into the world.

Natalie delivered first. Dr. MacDonald tried everything to save her — an endotracheal tube to assist her breathing, injections of anticonvulsants — but soaring blood pressure and convulsions led to a massive cerebral hemorrhage that killed her.

Even as the umbilical cord was tied off and cut between the Beezo baby and his dead mother, *my* mother, exhausted but still struggling to expel me, suddenly and at last experienced cervical dilation.

The Jimmy Tock show had begun.

Before undertaking the depressing task of telling Konrad Beezo that he had gained a son and lost a wife, Dr. MacDonald delivered me and, according to Charlene Coleman, announced that this solid little package would surely grow up to be a football hero.

Having successfully conveyed me from womb to wider world, my mother promptly passed out. She didn't hear the doctor's prediction and didn't see my broad, pink, wonder-filled face until my protector, Charlene, returned and presented me to my father.

After Dr. MacDonald had given me to Nurse

Coleman to be swabbed and then wrapped in a white cotton receiving cloth, and when he had satisfied himself that my mother had merely fainted and that she would come to herself in moments, with or without smelling salts, he peeled off his latex gloves, pulled down his surgical mask, and went to the expectant-fathers' lounge to console Konrad Beezo as best he could.

Almost at once, the shouting started: bitter, accusatory words, paranoid accusations, the vilest language delivered in the most furious voice imaginable.

Even in the usually serene, well-soundproofed delivery room, Nurse Coleman heard the uproar. She understood the tenor if not the specifics of Konrad Beezo's reaction to the loss of his wife.

When she left the delivery room and stepped into the hallway to hear Beezo more clearly, intuition told her to carry me with her, bundled in the thin blanket.

In the hall, she encountered Lois Hanson, another nurse, who had in her arms the Beezo baby. Lois, too, had ventured forth to hear the clown's intemperate outburst.

Lois made a fatal mistake. Against Charlene's advice, she moved toward the closed door to the waiting room, believing that the sight of his infant son would quench Beezo's hot anger and ameliorate the intense grief from which his rage had flared.

Herself a refugee from an abusive husband, Charlene had little faith that the grace of fatherhood would temper the fury of any man

36

who, even in a moment of profound loss, responded first and at once with rage and with threats of violence rather than with tears or shock, or denial. Besides, she remembered his hat, worn indoors with no regard for manners. Charlene sensed trouble coming, big trouble.

She retreated with me along the maternity ward's internal hall to the neonatal care unit. As that door was swinging shut behind us, she heard the gunshot that killed Dr. MacDonald.

This room contained rows of bassinets in which newborns were nestled, most dreaming, a few cooing, none yet crying. An enormous view window occupied the better part of one long wall, but no proud fathers or grandparents were currently standing on the other side of it.

With the infants were two crèche nurses. They had heard the shouting, then the shot, and they were more receptive to Charlene's advice than Lois had been.

Presciently, Nurse Coleman assured them the gunman wouldn't hurt the babies but warned he would surely kill every member of the hospital staff that he could find.

Nevertheless, before fleeing, each nurse scooped up an infant — and fretted about those they were forced to leave behind. Frightened by a second shot, they followed Charlene through a door beside the view window, out of the maternity ward into the main corridor.

The three, with their charges, took refuge in a room where an elderly man slept on unaware.

A low-wattage night-light did little to press back the gloom, and the flickering storm at the window only made the shadows jitter with insectile energy.

Quiet, hardly daring to breathe, the three nurses huddled together until Charlene heard sirens in the distance. This welcome wail drew her to the window, which provided a view of the parking lot in front of the hospital; she hoped to see police cars.

Instead, from that second-story room, she saw Beezo with his baby, crossing the rain-washed blacktop. He looked, she said, like a figure in a foul dream, scuttling and strange, like something you might see on the night that the world ended and cracks opened in the foundations of the earth to let loose the angry legions of the damned.

Charlene is a transplanted Mississippian and a Baptist whose soul is filled with the poetry of the South.

Beezo had parked at such a distance that through the screen of rain and under the yellow pall of the sodium-vapor lamps, the make, model, and true color of his car could not be discerned. Charlene watched him drive away, hoping the police would intercept him before he reached the nearby county road, but his taillights dwindled into the drizzling darkness.

With the threat removed, she returned to the delivery room just as Dad's thoughts were flashing from the Lindbergh baby tragedy to Rumpelstiltskin to Tarzan raised by apes, in time to assure him that I had not been kidnapped by a homicidal clown.

Later my father would confirm that the

38

minute of my birth, my length, and my weight precisely fulfilled the predictions made by my grandfather on his deathbed. His first proof, however, that the events in the intensive care unit were not just extraordinary but supernatural came when, as my mother held me, he folded back the receiving blanket, exposing my feet, and found that my toes were fused as Josef had predicted.

'Syndactyly,' Dad said.

'It can be fixed,' Charlene assured him. Then her eyes widened with surprise. 'How do you know such a doctorish word?'

My father only repeated, 'Syndactyly,' as he gently, lovingly, and with amazement fingered my fused toes.

4

Syndactyly is not merely the name of the affliction with which I was born but also the theme of my life for thirty years now. Things often prove to be fused in unanticipated ways. Moments separated by many years are unexpectedly joined, as if the space-time continuum has been folded by some power with either a peculiar sense of humor or an agenda arguably worthwhile but so complex as to be mystifying. People unknown to one another discover that they are bonded by fate as completely as two toes sharing a single sheath of skin.

Surgeons repaired my feet so long ago that I have no slightest memory of the procedures. I walk, I run when I must, I dance but not well.

With all due respect for the memory of Dr. Ferris MacDonald, I never became a football hero and never wished to be one. My family has never had an interest in sports.

We are fans, instead, of puffs, éclairs, tarts, tortes, cakes, trifles, and fans as well of the infamous cheese-and-broccoli pies and the Reuben sandwiches and all the fabulous dishes of table-cracking weight that my mother produces. We will trade the thrills and glory of all the games and tournaments mankind has ever invented for a dinner together and for the conversation and the laughter that runs like a fast tide from the unfolding of our napkins to the final sip of coffee.

Over the years, I have grown from twenty inches to six feet. My weight has increased from eight pounds ten ounces to one hundred eighty-eight pounds, which should prove my contention that I am at most husky, not as large as I appear to be to most people.

The fifth of my grandfather's ten predictions — that everyone would call me *Jimmy* — has also proved true.

Even on first meeting me, people seem to think that James is too formal to fit and that Jim is too earnest or otherwise inappropriate. Even if I introduce myself as *James*, and with emphasis, they at once begin addressing me as Jimmy, with complete comfort and familiarity, as though they have known me since my face was postpartum pink and my toes were fused.

As I make these tape recordings with the hope that I may survive to transcribe and edit them, I have lived through four of the five terrible days about which Grandpa Josef warned my father. They were terrible both in the same and in different ways, each day filled with the unexpected and with terror, some marked by tragedy, but they were days filled with much else, as well. Much else.

And now . . . one more to go.

★   ★   ★

41

My dad, my mom, and I spent twenty years pretending that the accuracy of Josef's first five predictions did not necessarily mean that the next five would be fulfilled. My childhood and teenage years passed uneventfully, presenting no evidence whatsoever that my life was a yo-yo on the string of fate.

Nevertheless, as the first of those five days relentlessly approached — Thursday, September 15, 1994 — we worried.

Mom's coffee consumption went from ten cups a day to twenty.

She has a curious relationship with caffeine. Instead of fraying her nerves, the brew soothes them.

If she fails to drink her usual three cups during the morning, by noon she will be as fidgety as a frustrated fly buzzing against a windowpane. If she doesn't pour down eight by bedtime, she lies awake, so mentally active that she not only counts sheep by the thousand but also names them and develops an elaborate life story for each.

Dad believes that Maddy's topsy-turvy metabolism is a direct result of the fact that her father was a long-haul trucker who ate Nō-Dōz caffeine tablets as if they were candy.

Maybe so, Mom sometimes answers my father, *but what are you complaining about? When we were dating all you had to do was get five or six cheap coffees into me, and I was as pliable as a rubber band.*

As September 15, 1994, drew near, my father's worry expressed itself in fallen cakes, curdled custard, rubbery pie crusts, and *crème brûlée* that had a sandy texture. He could not concentrate on his recipes or his ovens.

I believe that I handled the anticipation reasonably well. In the last two days leading up to the first of those five ominous dates, I might have walked into more closed doors than usual, might have tripped more often than is customary for me when climbing the stairs. And I do admit to dropping a hammer on Grandma Rowena's foot while trying to hang a picture for her. But it was her foot, not her head, and the one instance when a trip led to a fall, I only tumbled down a single flight of steps and didn't break anything.

Our worry was kept somewhat in check by the fact that Grandpa Josef had given Dad five 'terrible days' in my life, not just one. Obviously, regardless of how grim September 15 might be, I would not die on that day.

'Yes, but there's always the possibility of severed limbs and mutilation,' Grandma Rowena cautioned. 'And paralysis and brain damage.'

She is a sweet woman, my maternal grandmother, but one with too sharp a sense of the fragility of life.

As a child, I had dreaded those occasions when she insisted on reading me to sleep. Even when she didn't revise the classic stories, which she often did, even when the Big Bad Wolf was defeated, as he should have been, Grandma paused at key points in the narrative to muse aloud on the many gruesome things that *might* have happened to the three little pigs if their defenses had not held or if their strategies had proved faulty. Being ground up for sausages was the least of it.

And so, less than six weeks after my twentieth birthday, came the first of my five ordeals . . .

PART TWO

MIGHT AS WELL DIE
IF I CAN'T FLY

5

At nine o'clock on the evening of Wednesday, September 14, my parents and I met in their dining room to have as heavy a dinner as we might be able to stand up from without our knees buckling.

We were also gathered to discuss once more the wisest strategies for getting through the fateful day that lay just three hours ahead of me. We hoped that in a prepared and cautious state of mind, I might reach September 16 as unscathed as the three little pigs after their encounter with the wolf.

Grandma Rowena joined us to speak from the point of view of the wolf. That is, she would play the devil's advocate and relate to us what flaws she saw in our precautions.

As always, we took dinner on gold-rimmed Raynaud Limoges china, using sterling-silver flatware by Buccellati.

In spite of what the table setting suggests, my parents are not wealthy, just securely middle class. Although my father makes a fine salary as a pastry chef, stock options and corporate jets don't come with his position.

My mother earns a modest income working part-time from home, painting pet portraits on commission: mostly cats and dogs, but also rabbits, parakeets, and once a milk snake that came to pose and didn't want to leave.

Their small Victorian house would be called humble if it weren't so cozy that it feels sumptuous. The ceilings are not high and the proportions of the rooms are not grand, but they have been furnished with great care and with an eye to comfort.

You can't blame Earl for taking refuge behind the living-room sofa, under the claw-foot tub in the upstairs bath, in a clothes hamper, in the pantry potato basket, and elsewhere during the three interesting weeks that he adopted us. Earl was the milk snake, and the home from which he'd come was a sterile place with stainless-steel-and-black-leather furniture, abstract art, and cactuses for houseplants.

Of all the charming corners in this small house where you might read a book, listen to music, or gaze out a many-paned window at a bejeweled winter day, none is as welcoming as the dining room. This is because to the Tock family, food — and the conviviality that marks our every meal — is the hub that turns the spokes that spin the wheel of life.

Therefore, the luxury of Limoges and Buccellati.

Considering that we are incapable of pulling up a chair to any dinner with less than five courses and that we regard the first four, in which we fully indulge, as mere preparation for the fifth, it is miraculous that none of us is overweight.

Dad once discovered that his best wool suit had grown tight in the waist. He merely skipped lunch three days, and the pants were then loose on him.

Mom's caffeine tolerance is not the most significant curiosity regarding our unusual relationship to food. Both sides of the family, the Tock side and the Greenwich side (Greenwich being my mother's maiden name), have metabolisms as efficient as that of a hummingbird, a creature which can eat three times its body weight each day and remain light enough to fly.

Mom once suggested that she and my father had been instantly attracted to each other in part because of a subliminal perception that they were metabolic royalty.

The dining room features a coffered mahogany ceiling, mahogany wainscoting, and a mahogany floor. Silk moiré walls and a Persian carpet soften all the wood.

There is a blown-glass chandelier with pendant crystals, but dinner is always served by candlelight.

On this special night in September of 1994, the candles were numerous and squat, set in small but not shallow cut-crystal bowls, some clear and others ruby-red, which fractured the light into soft prismatic patterns on the linen tablecloth, on the walls, and on our faces. Candles were placed not only on the table but also on the sideboards.

Had you glanced in through a window, you might have thought not that we were at dinner but that we were conducting a séance, with food provided to keep us entertained until at last the ghosts showed up.

Although my parents had prepared my favorite

49

dishes, I tried not to think of it as the condemned man's last meal.

Five properly presented courses cannot be eaten on the same schedule as a McDonald's Happy Meal, especially not with carefully chosen wines. We were prepared for a long evening together.

Dad is the head pastry chef for the world-famous Snow Village Resort, a position he inherited from his father, Josef. Because all breads and pastries must be fresh each day, he goes to work at one o'clock in the morning at least five and often six days a week. By eight, with the baking for the entire day complete, he comes home for breakfast with Mom, then sleeps until three in the afternoon.

That September, I also worked those hours because I had been an apprentice baker for two years at the same resort. The Tock family believes in nepotism.

Dad says it's not really nepotism if your talent is real. Give me a good oven, and I am a wicked competitor.

Funny, but I am never clumsy in a kitchen. When baking, I am Gene Kelly, I am Fred Astaire, I am grace personified.

Dad would be going from our late dinner to work, but I would not. In preparation for the first of the five days in Grandpa Josef's prediction, I had taken a week's vacation.

Our starter course was *sou bourek*, an Armenian dish. Numerous paper-thin layers of pasta are separated by equally thin layers of butter and cheese, finished with a golden crust.

I still lived with my folks in those days, so Dad said, 'You should stay home from midnight to midnight. Hide out. Nap, read, watch a little TV.'

'Then what'll happen,' Grandma Rowena imagined, 'is that he'll fall down the stairs and break his neck.'

'Don't use the stairs,' Mom advised. 'Stay in your room, honey. I can bring your meals to you.'

'So then the house will burn down,' Rowena said.

'Now, Weena, the house won't burn down,' Dad assured her. 'The electrical wiring is sound, the furnace is brand new, both fireplace chimneys were recently cleaned, there's a grounded lightning rod on the roof, and Jimmy doesn't play with matches.'

Rowena was seventy-seven in 1994, twenty-four years a widow and past her grief, a happy woman but opinionated. She'd been asked to play the devil's advocate, and she was adamant in her role.

'If not a fire, then a gas explosion,' she declared.

'Gee, I don't want to be responsible for destroying the house,' I said.

'Weena,' Dad reasoned, 'there hasn't been a house-destroying gas explosion in the entire history of Snow Village.'

'So an airliner will crash into the place.'

'Oh, and that happens weekly around here,' my father said.

'There's a first time for everything,' Rowena asserted.

'If there's a first time for an airliner to crash into our house, then there's a first time for vampires to move in next door, but I'm not going to start wearing a garlic necklace.'

'If not an airliner, one of those Federal Express planes full of packages,' Rowena said.

Dad gaped at her, shook his head. 'Federal Express.'

Mom interpreted: 'What Mother means is that surely if fate has something planned for our Jimmy, he can't hide from it. Fate is fate. It'll find him.'

'Maybe a United Parcel Service plane,' said Rowena.

Over steaming bowls of pureed cauliflower soup enlivened with white beans and tarragon, we agreed that the wisest course for me would be to proceed as I would on any ordinary day off work — though always with caution.

'On the other hand,' Grandma Rowena said, 'caution could get him killed.'

'Now, Weena, how could *caution* get a person killed?' my father wondered.

Grandma finished a spoonful of soup and smacked her lips as she had never done until she had turned seventy-five, two years previously. She smacked them with relish, repeatedly.

Halfway between her seventh and eighth decades, she had decided that longevity had earned her the right to indulge in certain small pleasures she had never previously allowed herself. These were pretty much limited to smacking her lips, blowing her nose as noisily as she wished (though never at the table), and

52

leaving her spoon and/or fork turned useful side up on the plate at the end of each course, instead of useful side down as her mother, a true Victorian and a stickler for etiquette, had instructed her always to do in order properly to indicate that she had finished.

She smacked her lips again and explained why caution could be dangerous: 'Say Jimmy's going to cross the street, but he worries that a bus might hit him — '

'Or a garbage truck,' Mom suggested. 'Those great lumbering things on these hilly streets — why, if the brakes let go, what's to stop them? They'd go right *through* a house.'

'Bus, garbage truck, might even be a speeding hearse,' Grandma allowed.

'What reason would a hearse have to speed?' Dad asked.

'Speeding or not, if it *was* a hearse,' said Grandma, 'wouldn't that be ironic — run down by a hearse? God knows, life is often ironic in a way it's never shown on television.'

'The viewing public could never handle it,' Mom said. 'Their capacity for genuine irony is exhausted halfway through an episode of *Murder, She Wrote*.'

'What passes for irony on TV these days,' my dad noted, 'is just poor plotting.'

I said, 'I'm less spooked by garbage trucks than by those huge concrete mixers they drive to construction sites. I'm always sure the part that revolves is suddenly going to work loose of the truck, roll down the street, and flatten me.'

'All right,' Grandma Rowena said, 'so it's a

concrete mixer Jimmy's afraid of meeting up with.'

'Not afraid exactly,' I said. 'Just leery.'

'So he stands on the sidewalk, looks left, then looks right, then looks left again, being cautious, taking his time — and because he delays there on the curb too long, he's hit by a falling safe.'

In the interest of a healthy debate, my father was willing to entertain some rather exotic speculations, but this stretched his patience too far. 'A falling safe? Where would it fall *from?*'

'From a tall building, of course,' Grandma said.

'There aren't any tall buildings in Snow Village,' Dad gently protested.

'Rudy, dear,' Mom said, 'I think you're forgetting the Alpine Hotel.'

'That's only four stories.'

'A safe dropped four stories would obliterate Jimmy,' Grandma insisted. To me, in a concerned tone, she said, 'I'm sorry. Is this upsetting you, sweetheart?'

'Not at all, Grandma.'

'It's the simple truth, I'm afraid.'

'I know, Grandma.'

'It would obliterate you.'

'Totally,' I agreed.

'But it's such a final word — *obliterate.*'

'It sure does focus the mind.'

'I should've thought before I spoke. I should've said *crushed.*'

In lambent red candlelight, Weena had a Mona Lisa smile.

54

I reached across the table and patted her hand.

Being a pastry chef, required to mix many ingredients in precise measure, my father has a greater respect for mathematics and reason than do my mother and grandmother, who are more artistic in their temperaments and less slavishly devoted to logic than he is. 'Why,' he asked, 'would anyone raise a safe to the top of the Alpine Hotel?'

'Well, of course, to keep their valuables in,' said Grandma.

'Whose valuables?'

'The hotel's valuables.'

Although Dad never triumphs in exchanges of this nature, he always remains hopeful that if only he persists, reason will prevail.

'Why,' he asked, 'wouldn't they put a big heavy safe on the ground floor? Why go to all the trouble of craning it to the roof?'

My mother said, 'Because no doubt their valuables were on the top floor.'

In moments like these, I have never been quite sure if Mom shares more than a little of Weena's cockeyed perspective on the world or if she's playing with my father.

Her face is guileless. Her eyes are never evasive, and always limpid. She is by nature a straightforward woman. Her emotions are too clear for misinterpretation, and her intentions are never ambiguous.

Yet as Dad says, for a person so admirably open and direct by nature, she can turn inscrutable when it tickles her to, just as easily as

55

throwing a light switch.

That's one of the things he loves about her.

Our conversation continued through an endive salad with pears, walnuts, and crumbled blue cheese, followed by filet mignon on a bed of potato-and-onion pancakes, with asparagus on the side.

Before Dad got up to roll the dessert cart in from the kitchen, we had agreed that, for the momentous day ahead, I should keep to my usual vacation routine. With caution. But not too much caution.

Midnight arrived.

September 15 began.

Nothing happened right away.

'Maybe nothing will,' Mom said.

'Something will,' Grandma disagreed, and smacked her lips. 'Something will.'

If I had not been obliterated or even badly crushed by nine o'clock the next evening, we would meet here for dinner again. Together, we would break bread while remaining alert for the whiff of natural gas and the drone of a descending airliner.

Now, after demidessert, followed by a full dessert, followed by petits fours, all accompanied by oceans of coffee, Dad went off to work, and I helped with the kitchen cleanup.

Then at one-thirty in the morning, I retired to the living room to read a new book for which I had high expectations. I have a great fondness for murder mysteries.

On the first page, a victim was found chopped up and packed in a trunk. His name was Jim.

I put that book aside, selected another from the stack on the coffee table, and returned to my armchair.

A beautiful dead blonde stared from the book jacket, strangled with an antique Japanese obi knotted colorfully around her throat.

The first victim was named Delores. With a sigh of contentment, I settled down in my chair.

Grandma sat on the sofa, busy with a needlepoint pillow. She had been a master of decorative stitching since her teenage years.

Since she had moved in with Mom and Dad almost two decades ago, she had kept baker's hours, sewing elaborate patterns through the night. My mother and I kept that schedule, too. Mom had home-schooled me because our family lived by night.

Recently, Grandma's preferred embroidery motifs were insects. Her butterfly wall hanging and even her ladybug chair cushions were charming, but I did not care for the spider-festooned antimacassars on my armchair or for the cockroach pillow.

In an adjacent alcove, which Mom had outfitted as her studio, she worked happily on a pet portrait. The subject was a glittery-eyed Gila monster named Killer.

Because Killer was hostile toward strangers and not housebroken, the proud owners had provided a series of photos from which Mom could work. A hissing, biting, pooping Gila monster can really spoil an otherwise pleasant evening.

The living room is small and the shallow art

alcove is separated from it only by silk curtains in a wide archway. The curtains were open, so Mom could keep an eye on me and could be ready to move fast in case she recognized, say, signs of impending spontaneous human combustion.

For perhaps an hour, we were silent, immersed in our various pursuits, and then Mom said, 'Sometimes I worry that we're becoming the Addams family.'

★ ★ ★

The initial eight hours of my first terrible day passed without a disturbing incident.

At 8:15, his eyebrows white with flour, Dad came home from work. 'I couldn't make a good *crème plombières* to save my ass. I'll be glad when we've got through this day and I can focus again.'

We had breakfast together at the kitchen table. By 9:00 A.M., after more than the usual day's-end hugs, we went to our bedrooms and hid beneath the sheets.

Perhaps the rest of my family wasn't hiding, but I pretty much was. I believed in my grandfather's predictions more than I cared to admit to the rest of them, and my nerves tightened with every tick of the clock.

Going to bed at an hour when most people are beginning their workday, I required blackout blinds overlaid by heavy drapes that absorbed both light and sound. My room was quiet and dead black.

After a few minutes, I urgently needed to turn on a bedside lamp. Not since early childhood had I been this disturbed by the dark.

From my nightstand drawer I withdrew a plastic sleeve in which was preserved the free pass to the circus that Officer Huey Foster had given to my father more than twenty years ago. The three-by-five card appeared newly printed, marred only by the crease through the middle, where Dad had folded it to fit in his wallet.

On the blank reverse, Dad had taken dictation from Josef on his deathbed. The five dates.

The front of the pass featured lions and elephants. ADMIT TWO it directed in black letters, and in red blazed the promise FREE.

Toward the bottom were four words I had read uncounted times over the years: PREPARE TO BE ENCHANTED.

Depending on my mood, sometimes that sentence seemed to betoken forthcoming adventure and wonder. At other times, I drew from it a more threatening interpretation: PREPARE TO BE SCARED SHITLESS.

After returning the pass to the drawer, I lay awake for a while. I didn't think I would sleep. Then I slept.

Three hours later, I sat up in bed, instantly awake and alert. Trembling with fear.

To the best of my knowledge, I hadn't been awakened by a bad dream. No nightmare images lingered in memory.

Nevertheless, I woke with a completely formed and terrifying thought so oppressive that my heart felt as if it were being squeezed in a vise, and I could draw only quick shallow breaths.

If there were to be five terrible days in my life, I would not die on this one. In her inimitable way, however, Weena had pointed out that an exemption from death this September did not rule out severed limbs, mutilation, paralysis, and brain damage.

Neither could I rule out the death of someone else. Someone dear to me. My father, my mother, my grandmother . . .

If this were to be a terrible day because one of them would suffer a painful and violent death that would haunt me for the rest of my life, then I might wish that I had been the one to die.

I sat on the edge of the bed, glad that I had gone to sleep with the nightstand lamp aglow. My hands were slick with sweat and shaking so badly that I might not have been able either to find the switch or to turn it.

A close and loving family is a blessing. But the more people we love and the more deeply we love them, the more vulnerable we are to loss and grief and loneliness.

I was finished with sleep.

The bedside clock reported 1:30 P.M.

Less than half the day remained, only ten and a half hours until midnight.

In that time, however, a life could be taken, a world could end — and hope.

6

Millions of years before the Travel Channel existed to report the change, storms inside the earth had raised the land into serried waves, like a monsoon seascape, so any voyager in this territory is nearly always moving up or down, seldom on the horizontal.

Evergreen forests — pine and fir and spruce — navigate the waves of soil and rock, docking along every shore of Snow Village, but also finding harbors deep within town limits.

Fourteen thousand full-time residents live here. Most make their living directly or indirectly from nature as surely as do those who dwell in fishing ports in lower, balmier lands.

Snow Village Resort and Spa, and its world-famous network of ski runs, along with other area hotels and winter-sport facilities, draw so many vacationers that the town's population increases sixty percent from mid-October through March. Camping, hiking, boating, and white-water rafting pull in almost as many the rest of the year.

Autumn weather arrives early in the Rocky Mountains; but that day in September was not one of our refreshingly crisp afternoons. Pleasantly warm air, as still as the greatly compressed fathoms at the bottom of an ocean, conspired with golden afternoon sunlight to give Snow Village the look of a community petrified in amber.

Because my parents' house is in a perimeter neighborhood, I drove rather than walked into the heart of town, where I had a few errands to undertake.

In those days I owned a seven-year-old Dodge Daytona Shelby Z. Other than my mother and grandmother, I'd not yet met a woman I could love as much as I loved that sporty little coupe.

I have no mechanical skills, and I lack the talent to acquire any. The workings of an engine are as mysterious to me as is the enduring popularity of the tuna casserole.

I loved that peppy little Dodge sheerly for its form: the sleek lines, the black paint job, the harvest-moon-yellow racing stripes. That car was a piece of the night, driven down from the sky, with evidence of a lunar sideswipe on its flanks.

Generally speaking, I do not romanticize inanimate objects unless they can be eaten. The Dodge was a rare exception.

Arriving downtown, thus far having been spared from a head-on collision with an ironic speeding hearse, I passed several minutes in a search for the perfect parking spot.

Much of Alpine Avenue, our main street, features angle-to-the-curb parking, which I avoided in those days. The doors of flanking vehicles, if opened carelessly, could dent my Shelby Z and chip its paint. I took its every injury as a personal wound.

I much preferred to parallel park, and found a suitable place across the street from Center Square Park, which is in fact square and in the center of town. We Rocky Mountain types sometimes are as plainspoken as our magnificent scenery is ornate.

I curbed the Shelby Z behind a yellow panel van, in front of the Snow Mansion, a landmark open to the public eleven months of the year but closed here in September, which falls between the two main tourist seasons.

Ordinarily, of course, I would have stepped from the car on the driver's side. As I was about to exit, a pickup truck exploded past, dangerously close and at twice the posted speed. Had I opened the door seconds sooner and started to get out, I would have spent the autumn hospitalized and would have met the winter with fewer limbs.

On any other day, I might have muttered to myself about the driver's recklessness and then opened the door in his wake. Not this time.

Being cautious — but I hoped not too cautious — I slid over the console into the passenger's seat and got out on the curb side.

At once I looked up. No falling safe. So far, so good.

Founded in 1872 with gold-mining and railroad money, much of Snow Village is an alfresco museum of Victorian architecture, especially on the town square, where an active preservation society has been most successful. Brick and limestone were the favored building materials in the four blocks surrounding the park, with carved or molded pediments over doors and windows, and ornate iron railings.

Here the street trees are larches: tall, conical,

and old. They had not yet traded their green summer wardrobe for autumn gold.

I had business at the dry cleaner's, at the bank, and at the library. None of those establishments was on the side of the park where I'd found a suitable place for my car.

Of the three, the bank most concerned me. Occasionally people robbed banks. Bystanders were sometimes shot.

Prudence suggested that I wait until the following day to do my banking.

On the other hand, though no dry cleaner has ever been charged with causing a catastrophe in the course of Martinizing a three-piece wool suit, I was pretty sure they used caustic, toxic, perhaps even explosive chemicals.

Likewise, with all the narrow aisles between wooden shelves packed full of highly combustible books, libraries are potential firetraps.

Halted by indecision, I stood on the sidewalk, dappled with larch shadows and sunlight.

Because Grandpa Josef's predictions of five terrible days lacked specificity, I had not been able to plan defensively for any of them. All my life, however, I had been preparing psychologically.

Yet all that preparation afforded me no comfort. My imagination had hatched a crawling dread that crept down my spine and into every extremity.

As long as I had not ventured out of the house, the comfort of home and the courage of family had insulated me from fear. Now I felt exposed, vulnerable, *targeted*.

Paranoia may be an occupational hazard of spies, politicians, drug dealers, and big-city cops, but bakers rarely suffer from it. Weevils in the flour and a shortage of bitter chocolate in the pantry do not at once strike us as evidence of cunning adversaries and vast conspiracies.

Having led a fortunate, cozy, and — after the night of my birth — happily uneventful life, I had made no enemies of whom I was aware. Yet I surveyed the second- and third-story windows overlooking the town square, convinced I would spot a sniper drawing a bead on me.

Until that moment, my assumption had always been that whatever misfortune befell me on the five days would be impersonal, an act of nature: lightning strike, snakebite, cerebral thrombosis, incoming meteorite. Or otherwise it might be an accident resulting from the fallibility of my fellow human beings: a runaway concrete truck, a runaway train, a faultily constructed propane tank.

Even stumbling into the middle of a bank robbery and being shot would be a kind of accident, considering that I could have delayed my banking errand by taking a walk in the park, feeding squirrels, getting bitten, and contracting rabies.

Now I was paralyzed by the possibility of *intent*, by the realization that an unknown person might consciously select me as the object upon which to visit mayhem and misery.

He didn't have to be anyone I knew. Most likely he would be a crazed loner. Some homicidal stranger with a grudge against life, a rifle, plenty of hollow-point ammunition, and a supply of tasty high-protein power bars to keep him alert during a long standoff with the police.

Many windowpanes blazed with orange reflections of the afternoon sun. Others were dark, at angles that didn't take the solar image; any of those might have been open, the gunman lurking in the shadows beyond.

In my paralysis I became convinced that I possessed the talent for precognition that Grandpa Josef had displayed on his deathbed. The sniper was not just a possibility; he was *here*, finger on the trigger. I had not imagined him, but had sensed him clairvoyantly, him and my bullet-riddled future.

I tried to continue forward and then attempted to retreat, but I couldn't move. I felt that a step in the wrong direction would take me into the path of a bullet.

Of course as long as I stood motionless, I made a perfect target. Rational argument, however, couldn't dispel the paralysis.

My gaze rose from windows to rooftops, which might provide an even more likely roost for a sniper.

So intense was my concentration that I heard but didn't respond to the question until he repeated it: 'I said — are you all right?'

I lowered my attention from the search for a sniper to the young man standing on the sidewalk in front of me. Dark-haired, green-eyed, he was handsome enough to be a movie star.

For a moment I felt disoriented, as though I

had briefly stepped outside the flow of time and now, stepping in again, could not adjust to the pace of life.

He glanced toward the rooftops that had concerned me, then fixed me with those remarkable eyes. 'You don't look well.'

My tongue felt thick. 'I . . . just . . . I thought I saw something over there.'

This statement was peculiar enough to tweak an uncertain smile from him. 'You mean something in the sky?'

I couldn't explain that my focus had been on rooftops, because it seemed this would lead me inexorably to the revelation that I had been mesmerized by the possibility of a sniper.

Instead, I said, 'Yes, uh, in the sky, something . . . odd,' and at once realized that this statement made me seem no less peculiar than talk of a sniper would have done.

'UFO, you mean?' he asked, revealing a lopsided smile as winning as that of Tom Cruise at his most insouciant.

He might in fact have been a well-known actor, a rising star. Many entertainment figures vacationed in Snow Village.

Even if he had been famous, I wouldn't have recognized him. I didn't have that much interest in movies, being too busy with baking and family and life.

The only film I'd seen that year had been *Forrest Gump*. Now I supposed that I must appear to have the IQ of the title character.

Heat blossomed in my face, and I said with some embarrassment, 'Maybe a UFO thing.

Probably not. I don't know. It's gone now.'

'Are you all right?' he repeated.

'Yeah, sure, I'm fine, just the sky thing, gone now,' I said, embarrassed to hear myself babbling.

His amused scrutiny broke my paralysis. I wished him a good day, walked away, tripped on a fault in the sidewalk, and almost fell.

When I regained my balance, I didn't look back. I knew he would be watching me, his face alight with that million-dollar smile.

I couldn't understand how I had so completely given myself to an irrational fear. Being shot by a sniper was no more likely than being abducted by extraterrestrials.

Grimly determined to get a grip on myself, I went directly to the bank.

What would be would be. If a ruthless holdup gang crippled me with a shot to the spine, that might be preferable to being horribly disfigured in a library fire or to spending the rest of my life on an artificial-lung machine after inhaling toxic fumes in a catastrophic dry-cleaning accident.

The bank would be closing in minutes; consequently, there were few customers, but everyone looked suspicious to me. I tried not to turn my back on any of them.

I didn't even trust the eighty-year-old lady whose head bobbed with palsy. Some professional thieves were masters of disguise; the tremors might prove to be a brilliant bit of acting. But her chin wart sure looked real.

In the nineteenth century, they expected banks

to be impressive. The lobby had a granite floor, granite walls, fluted columns, and a lot of bronze work.

When a bank employee, crossing the room, dropped a ledger book, the report, ricocheting off the walls, sounded quite like a gunshot. I twitched but didn't soil my pants.

After depositing a paycheck and taking back a little cash, I departed without incident. The revolving door felt confining, but it brought me safely into the warm afternoon.

I needed to pick up several garments at the dry cleaner's, so I left that task for last, and went to the library.

The Cornelius Rutherford Snow Library is much bigger than one would expect for a town as small as ours, a handsome limestone structure. Flanking the main entry are stone lions on plinths in the shape of books.

The lions are not frozen in a roar. Neither are they posed with heads raised and alert. Curiously, both are shown asleep, as if they have been reading a politician's autobiography and have been thus sedated.

Cornelius, whose money built the library, didn't have a great deal of interest in books but thought that he should. Funding a handsome library was, to his way of reasoning, as broadening of the spirit and as edifying to the mind as actually having pored through hundreds of tomes. When the building was complete, he thereafter thought of himself as a well-read man.

Our town isn't named after the form in which

most of its annual precipitation falls. It honors instead the railroad-and-mining magnate whose pre-income-tax fortune founded it: Cornelius Rutherford Snow.

Just inside the front doors of the library hangs a portrait of Cornelius. He is all steely eyes, mustache, muttonchops, and pride.

When I entered, no one sat at any of the reading tables. The only patron in sight was at the main desk, leaning casually against the high counter, in a hushed conversation with Lionel Davis, the head librarian.

As I drew near the elevated desk, I recognized the patron. His green eyes brightened at the sight of me, and his big-screen smile was friendly, not mocking, though he said to Lionel, 'I think this gentleman will be wanting a book on flying saucers.'

I'd known Lionel Davis forever. He'd made a life of books to the same extent that I had made a life of baking. He was warm-hearted, kind, with enthusiasms ranging from Egyptian history to hard-boiled detective novels.

He had the worn yet perpetually childlike countenance of a kindly blacksmith or a sincere vicar in a Dickens novel. I knew his face well, but I had never seen on it an expression quite like the one that currently occupied it.

His smile was broad but his eyes were narrow. A tic at the left corner of his mouth suggested that the eyes more truly revealed his state of mind than did the smile.

If I had recognized the warning in his face, I could not have done anything to save myself or him. The handsome fellow with the porcelain-white teeth had already decided on a course of action the moment I entered.

First, he shot Lionel Davis in the head.

7

The pistol made a hard flat noise not half as loud as I would have expected.

Crazily, I thought how in the movies they didn't fire real bullets, but blanks, so this sound would have to be enhanced in post-production.

I almost looked around for the cameras, the crew. The shooter was movie-star handsome, the gunshot didn't sound right, and no one would have any reason to kill a sweet man like Lionel Davis, which must mean that all this had been scripted and that the finished film would be in theaters nationwide next summer.

'How many flies do you swallow on the average day, standing around with your mouth hanging open?' asked the killer. 'Is your mouth ever *not* hanging open?'

He appeared to be amused by me, to have already forgotten Lionel, as if killing the librarian had been an act of no more consequence than stepping on an ant.

I heard my voice turn hollow with stunned incomprehension, brittle with anger: 'What did he ever do to you?'

'Who?'

Though you will think his perplexity must have been an act, tough-guy bravura meant to impress me with his cruelty, I assure you that it was not. I knew at once that he didn't relate my

72

question to the man whom he had just murdered.

The word *insane* did not entirely describe him, but it was a good adjective with which to begin.

Surprised that fear remained absent from my voice even as more anger crowded into it, I said, 'Lionel. He was a good man, gentle.'

'Oh, him.'

'Lionel Davis. He had a name, you know. He had a life, friends, he was somebody.'

Genuinely puzzled, his smile turning uneasy, he said, 'Wasn't he just a librarian?'

'You sick son of a bitch.'

As the smile stiffened, his features grew pale, grew hard, as though flesh might transform into a plaster death mask. He raised the pistol, pointed it at my chest, and said with utmost seriousness, 'Don't you dare insult my mother.'

The offense he took at my language, so out of proportion to the indifference with which he committed murder, struck me as darkly funny. If a laugh, even one of shocked disbelief, had escaped me then, I'm sure he would have killed me.

Confronted by the muzzle of the handgun, I felt fear enter the halls of my mind, but I didn't give it the keys to every room.

Earlier in the street, the prospect of a sniper had paralyzed me with dread. I realized now that I'd not been afraid of a rifleman in some high concealment but that I'd been petrified because I did not know if the sniper was real or if instead the mortal threat might be any of a thousand other things. When danger can be sensed but not identified, then everyone and everything becomes a source of concern; the world from horizon to horizon seems hostile.

Fear of the unknown is the most purely distilled and potent terror.

Now I had identified my enemy. Although he might be a sociopath capable of any atrocity, I felt some relief because I knew his face. The uncountable threats in my imagination had evaporated, replaced by this one real danger.

His hard expression softened. He lowered the pistol.

With perhaps fifteen feet between us, I didn't dare rush him. I could only repeat, 'What did he ever do to you?'

He smiled and shrugged. 'I wouldn't have shot him if you hadn't come in.'

Like a slowly turning auger, the pain of Lionel's death drilled deeper into me. The tremor in my voice was grief, not fear. 'What're you talking about?'

'By myself, I can't manage two hostages. He was here alone. The assistant librarian is out sick. There were no patrons at the moment. He was going to lock the doors — then you came in.'

'Don't tell me I'm responsible.'

'Oh, no, not at all,' he assured me with what sounded like genuine concern for my feelings. 'Not your fault. It was just one of those things.'

'Just one of those things,' I repeated with some astonishment, unable to comprehend a mind that could be so casual about murder.

'I might have shot you instead,' he said, 'but

having met you earlier in the street, I figured you'd be more interesting company than a boring old librarian.'

'What do you need a hostage for?'

'In case things go wrong.'

'What things?'

'You'll see.'

His sport coat was cut stylishly full. From one of the roomy interior pockets he withdrew a pair of handcuffs. 'I'm going to throw these to you.'

'I don't want them.'

He smiled. 'You *are* going to be fun. Catch them. Lock one cuff around your right wrist. Then lie on the floor with both hands behind your back, so I can finish the job.'

When he threw the cuffs, I sidestepped them. They rattled off a reading table, clattered to the floor.

He'd been holding the pistol at his side. He aimed at me again.

Although I'd stared down that muzzle before, I didn't find it any less disconcerting the second time.

I'd never held a handgun, let alone fired one. In my line of work, the closest thing to a weapon is a cake knife. Maybe a rolling pin. We bakers, however, tend not to carry rolling pins in shoulder holsters and are therefore defenseless in situations like this.

'Pick them up, big fella.'

Big fella. He was approximately my size.

'Pick them up, or I'll do a Lionel on you and just wait for another hostage to walk through that door.'

I had been using my grief and my anger over Lionel's death to suppress my terror. Fear could diminish and defeat me, but now I realized that fearlessness could get me killed.

Wisely giving recognition to the coward in me, I stooped, picked up the cuffs, and clamped one steel circlet around my right wrist.

Snaring a set of keys off the librarian's desk, he said, 'Don't lie down yet. Stay on your feet where I can see you while I lock the door.'

When he was halfway between the main desk and the portrait of Cornelius Rutherford Snow, the door opened. A young woman, a stranger to me, entered with a stack of books.

She was prettier than a *gâteau à l'orange* with chocolate-butter icing decorated with candied orange peel and cherries.

I wouldn't be able to endure seeing her shot, not her.

8

She was prettier than a *soufflé au chocolat* drizzled with *crème anglaise* flavored by apricots, served in a Limoges cup on a Limoges plate on a silver charger, by candlelight.

The door had swung shut behind her and she had taken a few steps into the room before she realized that this was not a typical library tableau. She couldn't see the dead man behind the desk, but she spotted the handcuffs dangling from my right wrist.

When she spoke, she had a wonderfully throaty voice, the effect of which was heightened by the fact that she addressed the killer in a stage whisper: 'Is that a gun?'

'Doesn't it look like a gun?'

'Well, it might be a toy,' she said. 'I mean, is it a real gun?'

Gesturing at me with the weapon, he said, 'You want to see me shoot him with it?'

I sensed that I'd just become the least desirable of available hostages.

'Gee,' she said, 'that seems a little extreme.'

'I only need one hostage.'

'Nevertheless,' she said with an aplomb that dazzled me, 'maybe you could just fire a shot into the ceiling.'

The killer smiled at her with all the expansive good humor that he had directed toward me earlier, in the street. In fact it was a warmer and even more adorable smile than the one I'd received.

'Why are you whispering?' he asked.

'It's a library,' she whispered.

'The usual rules have been suspended.'

'Are you the librarian?' she asked him.

'Me — a librarian? No. In fact — '

'Then you can't possibly have the authority to suspend the rules,' she said, speaking softly but no longer in a whisper.

'This gives me the authority,' he declared, and fired a round into the ceiling.

She glanced at the front windows, where the street was visible only in a succession of wedges between the half-closed Venetian blinds. When she looked next at me, I saw that she was disappointed, as I had been, by the pathetic volume of the shot. The walls, padded by books, absorbed the sound. Outside, it might have been not much louder than a muffled cough.

Giving no indication that his casual gunfire rattled her, she said, 'May I put these books down somewhere? They're quite an armful.'

With the pistol, he indicated a reading table. 'There.'

As the woman put down the books, the killer went to the door and locked it, always keeping an eye on us.

'I don't mean to criticize,' the woman said, 'and I'm sure you know your business better than I do, but you're wrong about needing only one hostage.'

She was so dangerously appealing to the eye that under other circumstances, she could have reduced any guy to his most deeply stupid state of desire. Already, however, I found myself more interested in what she had to say than I was in her figure, more fascinated by her chutzpah than by her radiant face.

The maniac seemed to share my fascination. By his expression, anyone could see that she had charmed him. His killer smile became more luminous.

When he spoke to her, his voice had no bite to it, no trace of sarcasm: 'You have a theory or something about hostages?'

She shook her head. 'Not a theory. Just a practical observation. If you wind up in a showdown with the police and you have only one hostage, how are you going to convince them you would actually kill the person, that you're not bluffing?'

'How?' he and I asked simultaneously.

'You *couldn't* make them believe you,' she said. 'Not beyond a shadow of a doubt. So they might try to rush you, in which case both you *and* the hostage wind up dead.'

'I can be pretty convincing,' he assured her in a mellower tone that suggested he might be thinking of asking her for a date.

'If I was a cop, I wouldn't believe you for a minute. You're too cute to be a killer.' To me, she said, 'Isn't he too cute?'

I almost said I didn't think he was that cute, so you can see what I mean by her bringing out the deeply stupid in a guy.

'But if you had *two* hostages,' she continued, 'you could kill one to prove the sincerity of your

79

threat, and after that the second would be a reliable shield. No cop would dare test you twice.'

He stared at her for a moment. 'You're some piece of work,' he said at last, and clearly meant to compliment her.

'Well,' she replied, indicating the stack of books that she had just returned, 'I'm a reader and a thinker, that's all.'

'What's your name?' he asked.

'Lorrie.'

'Lorrie what?'

'Lorrie Lynn Hicks,' she said. 'And you are?'

He opened his mouth, almost told her his name, then smiled and said, 'I'm a man of mystery.'

'And a man with a mission, by the look of it.'

'I've already killed the librarian,' he told her, as if murder were a resumé enhancement.

'I was sort of afraid you had,' she said.

I cleared my throat. 'My name is James.'

'Hi, Jimmy,' she said, and though she smiled, I saw in her eyes a terrible sadness and desperate calculation.

'Go stand beside him,' the maniac ordered.

Lorrie came to me. She smelled as good as she looked: fresh, clean, lemony.

'Cuff yourself to him.'

As she locked the empty ring around her left wrist, thereby linking our fates, I felt I should say something to comfort her, in response to the desperation I'd glimpsed in her eyes. Wit failed me, and I could only say, 'You smell like lemons.'

'I've spent the day making homemade lemon

80

marmalade. I intended to have the first of it tonight, on toasted English muffins.'

'I'll brew a pot of bittersweet hot chocolate with a dash of cinnamon,' I told her. 'That and your marmalade muffins will be the perfect thing to celebrate.'

Clearly she appreciated my confident assertion of our survival, but her eyes were no less troubled.

Checking his wristwatch, the maniac said, 'This has taken too much time. I've got a lot of research to do before the explosions start.'

9

All our yesterdays neatly shelved, time cata-
logued in drawers: News grows brittle and yellow
under the library, in catacombs of paper.

The killer had learned that the *Snow County
Gazette* had for more than a century stored their
dead issues here in the subbasement, two stories
under the town square. They called it a 'priceless
archive of local history.' Preserved for the ages in
the *Gazette* morgue were the details of Girl
Scout bake sales, school-board elections, and
zoning battles over the intent of Sugar Time
Donuts to expand the size of its operation.

Every issue from 1950 forward could be
viewed on microfiche. When your research led
you to earlier dates, you were supposed to fill out
a requisition form for hard copies of the *Gazette;*
a staff member would oversee your perusal of the
newspaper.

If you were a person who shot librarians for no
reason, standard procedures were of no concern
to you. The maniac prowled the archives and
took what he wanted to a study table. He
handled the yellowing newsprint with no more
consideration for its preservation than he would
have shown for the most current edition of *USA
Today.*

He had parked Lorrie Lynn Hicks and me in a
pair of chairs at the farther end of the enormous
room in which he worked. We were not close

enough to see what articles in the *Gazette* interested him.

We sat under a barrel-vaulted ceiling, under a double row of inverted torchieres that cast a dusty light acceptable only to those scholars who had lived in a time when electricity was new and the memory of oil lamps still fresh from childhood.

With another set of handcuffs, our captor had linked our wrist shackles to a backrail of one of the chairs on which we were perched.

Because not all the archives were contained in this one room, he paid repeated visits to an adjacent chamber, leaving us alone at times. His absences afforded us no chance to escape. Chained together and dragging a chair, we could move neither quickly nor quietly.

'I've got a nail file in my purse,' Lorrie whispered.

I glanced down at her cuffed hand next to mine. A strong but graceful hand. Elegant fingers. 'Your nails look fine,' I assured her.

'Are you serious?'

'Absolutely. I like the shade of your polish. Looks like candied cherries.'

'It's called *Glaçage de Framboise*.'

'Then it's misnamed. It's not a shade of any raspberries I've ever worked with.'

'You work with raspberries?'

'I'm a baker, going to be a pastry chef.'

She sounded slightly disappointed. 'You look more dangerous than a pastry chef.'

'Well, I'm biggish for my size.'

'Is that what it is?'

'And bakers tend to have strong hands.'

'No,' she said, 'it's your eyes. There's something dangerous about your eyes.'

This was adolescent with fulfillment of the purest kind: being told by a beautiful woman that you have dangerous eyes.

She said, 'They're direct, a nice shade of blue — but then there's something lunatic about them.'

Lunatic eyes are dangerous eyes, all right, but not *romantic* dangerous. James Bond has dangerous eyes. Charles Manson has lunatic eyes. Charles Manson, Osama bin Laden, Wile E. Coyote. Women stand in line for James Bond, but Wile E. Coyote can't get a date.

She said, 'The reason I mentioned the nail file in my purse is because it's a metal file, sharp enough at one end to be a weapon.'

'Oh.' I felt inane, and I couldn't blame my dunderheadedness entirely on her stupidity-inducing good looks. 'He took your purse,' I noted.

'Maybe I can get it back.'

Her handbag stood on the table where he sat reading old issues of the *Snow County Gazette*.

The next time he left the room, we could stand as erect as a chair on our backs would allow and hobble in tandem and as fast as possible toward her purse. The noise would most likely draw him back before we reached our goal.

Or we could make our way across the room with stealth foremost in mind, which would require us to move as slowly as Siamese twins negotiating a minefield. Judging by the average

84

length of time that he had thus far been absent when extracting additional issues from the files, we would not reach the purse before he returned.

As if my thoughts were as clear to her as the lunacy in my eyes, she said, 'That's not what I had in mind. I'm thinking if I claim a female emergency, he'll let me have my purse.'

Female emergency.

Maybe it was the shock of living out my grandfather's prediction or maybe it was the persistent memory of the librarian being shot, but I couldn't get my mind around the meaning of those two words.

Aware of my befuddlement, as she seemed to be aware of every electrical current leaping across every synapse in my brain, Lorrie said, 'If I tell him I'm having my period and I desperately need a tampon, I'm sure he'll do the gentlemanly thing and give me my purse.'

'He's a murderer,' I reminded her.

'But he doesn't seem to be a particularly rude murderer.'

'He shot Lionel Davis in the head.'

'That doesn't mean he's incapable of courtesy.'

'I wouldn't bet the bank on it,' I said.

She squinched her face in annoyance and still looked darned good. 'I hope to God you're not a congenital pessimist. That would be just too much — held hostage by a librarian killer *and* shackled to a congenital pessimist.'

I didn't want to be disagreeable. I wanted her to like me. Every guy wants a good-looking woman to like him. Nevertheless, I could not accept her characterization of me.

'I'm not a pessimist. I'm a realist.'

She sighed. 'That's what every pessimist says.'

'You'll see,' I said lamely. 'I'm not a pessimist.'

'I'm an indefatigable optimist,' she informed me. 'Do you know what that means — indefatigable?'

'The words *baker* and *illiterate* aren't synonyms,' I assured her. 'You're not the only reader and thinker in Snow Village.'

'So what does it mean — indefatigable?'

'Incapable of being fatigued. Persistent.'

'*Tireless*,' she stressed. 'I'm a tireless optimist.'

'It's a fine line between an optimist and a Pollyanna.'

Fifty feet away, having left the room earlier, the killer returned to his table with an armload of yellowing newspapers.

Lorrie eyed him with predatory calculation. 'When the moment's right,' she whispered, 'I'm going to tell him I've got a female emergency and need my purse.'

'Sharp or not, a nail file isn't much use against a gun,' I protested.

'There you go again. Congenital pessimism. That can't be a good thing even in a baker. If you expect all your cakes to fall, they will.'

'My cakes never fall.'

She raised one eyebrow. 'So you say.'

'You think you can stab him in the heart and just stop him like a clock?' I asked with enough disdain to get my point across but not sarcastically enough to alienate her from the possibility that we could have dinner together if we survived the day.

'Stop his heart? Of course not. Second best would be to go for the neck, sever the carotid artery. *First* choice would be to put out an eye.'

She looked like a dream and talked like a nightmare.

I was probably guilty of gaping again. I know I sputtered: 'Put out an eye?'

'Drive it deep enough, and you might even damage the brain,' she said, nodding as if in somber agreement with herself. 'He'd have an instant convulsion, drop the gun, and if he didn't drop it, he'd be so devastated, we could easily just take the pistol out of his hand.'

'Oh my God, you're going to get us killed.'

'There you go again,' she said.

'Listen,' I tried to reason with her, 'when the crunch came, you wouldn't have the stomach to do something like that.'

'I certainly would, to save my life.'

Alarmed by her calm conviction, I insisted, 'You'd flinch at the last moment.'

'I never flinch from anything.'

'Have you ever stabbed someone in the eye before?'

'No. But I can clearly picture myself doing it.'

I couldn't suppress the sarcasm any longer: 'What are you, a professional assassin or something?'

She frowned. 'Keep your voice down. I'm a dance instructor.'

'And teaching ballet prepares you to put out a man's eye?'

'Of course not, silly. I don't teach ballet. I give ballroom-dancing lessons. Fox-trot, waltz, rumba, tango, cha-cha, swing, you name it.'

Just my luck: to be cuffed to a beautiful woman who turns out to be a ballroom-dance instructor, and me a lummox.

'You'll flinch,' I insisted, 'and you'll miss his eye, and he'll shoot us dead.'

'Even if I flub it,' she said, 'which I won't, but even if I do, he won't shoot us dead. Haven't you been paying attention? *He needs hostages.*'

I disagreed. 'He doesn't need hostages *who try to stab him in the eye.*'

She raised her eyes as if imploring the heavens beyond the ceiling: 'Please tell me I'm not shackled to a pessimist *and* a coward.'

'I'm not a coward. I'm just responsibly cautious.'

'That's what every coward says.'

'That's also what every responsibly cautious person says,' I replied, wishing I didn't sound so defensive.

At the far end of the room, the maniac began to pound one fist against the newspaper he was reading. Then both fists. Pounding and pounding like a baby in a tantrum.

Face contorted fearsomely, he made inarticulate noises of rage. Some rough Neanderthal consciousness, remnant in his genes, seemed to break free from the chains of time and DNA.

Fury informed his voice, then frustration, then what might have been a wild grief, then fury once more and escalating. This was the performance of an animal howling with loss, its

88

rage rooted in the black soil of misery.

He pushed his chair back from the table, picked up his pistol. He emptied the remaining eight rounds in the magazine, aiming at the newspaper he had been reading.

The hard report of each shot boomed off the vaulted ceiling, rang off the brass shades of the inverted torchieres, and crashed back and forth between the metal filing cabinets. I felt echoes of each concussion humming in my teeth.

Cut loose two floors underground, the barrage would be at most a faint crackle at street level.

Splinters of the old oak refectory table sprayed and scraps of paper spun and a couple bullets ricocheted through the air, some fragments trailing threads of smoke. The fragrance of aging newsprint was seasoned with the more acrid scent of gunfire and with a raw wood smell liberated from the table's wounds.

For a moment, as he repeatedly squeezed the trigger without effect, I rejoiced that he had depleted his ammunition. But of course he had a spare magazine, perhaps several.

While he reloaded the weapon, he seemed intent on delivering ten more rounds to the hated newspaper. Instead, with the fresh magazine installed, his rage abruptly abated. He began to weep. Wretched sobs racked him.

He collapsed into his chair once more and put down the gun. He leaned over the table and seemed to want to piece together the pages that he had ripped and riddled with gunfire, as if some story therein was precious to him.

Still lemony enough to sweeten the air that

had been soured by gunfire, Lorrie Lynn Hicks tilted her head toward me and whispered, 'You see? He's vulnerable.'

I wondered if excessive optimism could ever qualify as a form of madness.

Gazing into her eyes, I saw, as previously, the fear that she adamantly refused to express. She winked.

Her stubborn resistance to terror scared me because it seemed so reckless, so irrational — and yet I loved her for it.

Whidding through me, like the spirit of Death's black horse, came a premonition that she would be shot. Despair followed this dark precognitive flash, and I was desperate to protect her.

In time, the premonition eventually proved true, and nothing I did was able to alter the trajectory of the bullet.

10

Tears damp on his cheeks, green eyes washed clear of bitter emotions, and clear of doubts as well, the maniac had the look of a pilgrim who has been to the mountaintop and knows his destiny, his purpose.

He freed me and Lorrie from the chairs but left us tethered to each other.

'Are you both locals?' he asked as we rose to our feet.

After his violent display and flamboyant emotional outburst, I found it difficult to believe that he now wished to engage in pleasant chitchat. The question had a purpose more important than the words themselves conveyed, which meant our answers might have consequences we could not foresee.

Wary, I hesitated to reply, and the same logic led Lorrie to remain silent as well.

He persisted. 'What about it, Jimmy? This is the county library, so people come here from all around. Do you live in town or outside somewhere?'

Although I didn't know which answer he would regard favorably, I sensed that silence would earn me a bullet. He had shot Lionel Davis for less, for no reason at all.

'I live in Snow Village,' I said.

'How long have you been here?'

'All my life.'

91

'Do you like it here?'

'Not handcuffed in the subcellar of the library,' I said, 'but I like most other places in town, yeah.'

His smile was uncannily appealing, and I couldn't figure out how anyone's eyes could twinkle so constantly as his unless implanted in them were motorized prisms that ceaselessly tracked environmental light sources. Surely no other maniacal killer could make you want to like him just by cocking his head and favoring you with a crooked smile.

He said, 'You're a funny guy, Jimmy.'

'I don't mean to be,' I said apologetically, shuffling my feet on the honed limestone floor. Then I added, 'Unless, of course, you want me to be.'

'In spite of everything I've been through, I have a sense of humor,' he said.

'I could tell.'

'What about you?' he asked Lorrie.

'I have a sense of humor, too,' she said.

'For sure. You're way funnier than Jimmy.'

'Way,' she agreed.

'But what I meant,' he clarified, 'is do you live here in town?'

As I had answered the same question positively and had not been immediately shot, she dared to say, 'Yeah. Two blocks from here.'

'You lived here all your life?'

'No. Just a year.'

This explained how I could have missed seeing her for twenty years. In a community of fourteen thousand, you can pass a long life and never

92

speak to ninety percent of the population.

If I had just once *glimpsed* her turning a corner, however, I would never have forgotten her face. I would have spent long anxious nights awake, wondering who she was, where she'd gone, how I could find her.

She said, 'I grew up in Los Angeles. Nineteen years in L.A. and I wasn't totally bug-eyed crazy yet, so I knew I had almost no time left to get out.'

'Do you like it here in Snow Village?' he asked.

'So far, yeah. It's nice.'

Still smiling, still twinkly-eyed, with his charm in full gear and none of the insane-guy edge to his voice, he nevertheless said, 'Snow Village is an evil place.'

'Well,' Lorrie said, 'sure, it's evil, but parts of it are also kind of nice.'

'Like Morelli's Restaurant,' I said.

Lorrie said, 'They have fabulous chicken all' Alba. And the Bijou is a terrific place.'

Delighted that we shared these favorite places, I said, 'Imagine a movie theater actually called the Bijou.'

'All those cute Art Deco details,' she said. 'And they use real butter on the popcorn.'

'I like Center Square Park,' I said.

The maniac disagreed: 'No, that's an evil place. I sat there earlier, watching the birds crap on the statue of Cornelius Randolph Snow.'

'What's evil about that?' Lorrie wondered. 'If he was half as pompous as the statue makes him look, the birds have got it right.'

'I don't mean the birds are evil,' the maniac

93

explained with sunny good humor. 'Although they might be. What I mean is the park is evil, the *ground*, all the ground this town is built on.'

I wanted to talk to Lorrie about more things we liked, attitudes we might have in common, and I was pretty sure she wanted to have that conversation, too, but we felt we had to listen to the smiley guy because he had the gun.

'So . . . did they build the town on an Indian burial ground or something?' Lorrie wondered.

He shook his head. 'No, no. The earth itself was good once long ago, but it was corrupted because of evil things that evil people did here.'

'Fortunately,' Lorrie said, 'I don't own any real estate. I'm a renter.'

'I live with my folks,' I told him, hoping this fact would exempt me from complicity with the evil earth.

'The time has come,' he said, 'for payback.'

As if to emphasize his threat, a spider suddenly appeared and slowly descended on a silken thread from within the shade of one of the overhead lamps. Projected by the cone of light, the eight-legged shadow on the floor between us and the maniac was the size of a dinner plate, distorted and squirming.

'Answering evil with evil just means everyone loses,' Lorrie said.

'I'm not answering evil with evil,' he replied not angrily but with exasperation. 'I'm answering evil with justice.'

'Well, that's very different,' Lorrie said.

'If I were you,' I told the maniac, 'I'd wonder how to know for sure that something I'm doing

94

is justice and not just more evil. I mean, the thing about evil is it's slippery. My mom says the devil knows how to mislead us into thinking we're doing the right thing when what we're really doing is the devil's work.'

'Your mother sounds like a caring person,' he said.

Sensing I'd made a connection with him, I said, 'She is. When I was growing up, she even ironed my socks.'

This revelation drew from Lorrie a look of troubled speculation.

Concerned that she might think I was an eccentric or, worse, a momma's boy, I quickly added: 'I've been doing my own ironing since I was seventeen. And I never iron my socks.'

Lorrie's expression didn't change.

'I don't mean that my mother still irons them,' I hastened to assure her. 'Nobody irons my socks anymore. Only an idiot irons socks.'

Lorrie frowned.

'Not that I mean my mother is an idiot,' I clarified. 'She's a wonderful woman. She's not an idiot, she's just caring. I mean *other* people who iron their socks are idiots.'

At once I saw that with the language skills of a lummox, I had talked myself into a corner.

'If either of you irons your socks,' I said, 'I don't mean that you're idiots. I'm sure you're just caring people, like my mom.'

With disturbingly similar expressions, Lorrie and the maniac stared at me as though I had just walked down the debarkation ramp from a flying saucer.

95

I thought that being shackled to me suddenly creeped her out, and I figured the maniac would decide that a single hostage was plenty of insurance, after all.

The descending spider still hung over our heads, but its shadow on the floor was smaller, now the size of a salad plate, and blurry.

To my surprise, the killer's eyes grew misty. 'That was very touching — the socks. Very sweet.'

My sock story didn't seem to have struck a sentimental chord in Lorrie. She stared at me with squint-eyed intensity.

The maniac said, 'You're a very lucky man, Jimmy.'

'I am,' I agreed, although my only bit of luck — being cuffed to Lorrie Lynn Hicks instead of to a diseased wino — seemed to be turning sour.

'To have a caring mother,' the maniac mused. 'What must that be like?'

'Good,' I said, 'it's good,' but I didn't trust myself to say more.

Spinning gossamer from its innards, the spider unreeled a longer umbilical, finally dangling in front of our faces.

With dreamy-voiced eloquence, the killer said, 'To have a caring mother who makes you hot cocoa each evening, tucks you in bed every night, kisses you on the cheek, reads you to sleep . . . '

Before I myself could read, I was almost always read to sleep because ours is a bookish family. More often than not, however, the reader had been my Grandma Rowena.

Sometimes the story was about a Snow White whose seven dwarf friends suffered fatal accidents and diseases until it was Snow alone against the evil queen. Come to think of it, a two-ton safe fell on Happy once. That was a lot cleaner than what happened to poor Sneezy. Or maybe Weena would read the one about Cinderella — the dangerous glass slippers splintering painfully around Cindy's feet, the pumpkin coach plunging off the road into the ravine.

I was a grown man before I discovered that in Arnold Lobel's charming Frog and Toad books, there was *not* always a scene in which one or the other of the title characters had a foot gnawed off by another meadowland creature.

'I didn't have a caring mother,' the maniac said, a disturbing note of whiny distress entering his voice. 'My childhood was hard, cold, and loveless.'

Now occurred an unexpected turn of events: My fear of being shot to death took second place to the dread that this guy would harangue us with a droning account of his victimization. Beaten with wire coathangers. Forced to wear girly clothes until he was six. Sent to bed without his porridge.

I didn't need to get kidnapped, cuffed, and held at gunpoint to be subjected to a pityfest. I could have stayed home and watched daytime-TV talk shows.

Fortunately, he bit his lip, stiffened his spine, and said, 'It's a waste of time to dwell on the past. What's done is done.'

97

*Un*fortunately, the glimmer of teary self-pity in his eyes was not replaced by that charming twinkle, but instead by a fanatical gleam.

The spider had not continued its descent. It hung in front of our faces, perhaps freaked out by the sight of us and frozen in fear.

As though he were a vintner plucking a grape from a vine, the maniac pinched the fat spider between the thumb and forefinger of his left hand, crushed it, and brought the mangled remains to his nose to savor the scent.

I hoped he wouldn't offer me a sniff. I have a highly refined sense of smell, which is one reason that I'm a natural-born baker.

Fortunately, he had no intention of sharing the heady fragrance.

*Un*fortunately, he brought the morsel to his mouth and delicately licked the arachnid paste. He savored this strange fruit, decided it was not sufficiently ripe, and wiped his fingers on the sleeve of his jacket.

Here was a graduate of Hannibal Lecter University, ready for a career in hospitality services as the new manager of the Bates Motel.

This spider-sampling had not been a performance for our benefit. The entire incident had been as unconscious as shooing away a fly, except the opposite.

Now, quite unaware of the effect his culinary curiosity had on us, he said, 'Anyway, the time for talking is long past. It's time for action now, for justice.'

'And how will that justice be achieved?' Lorrie wondered. For the moment, anyway, she was no longer able to maintain a sprightly, let alone flippant, let alone devil-may-care tone of voice.

In spite of his adult baritone, he sounded uncannily like an angry little boy: 'I'm going to blow up a lot of stuff and kill a bunch of people and make this town sorry.'

'Sounds pretty ambitious,' she said.

'I've been planning this all my life.'

Having changed my mind, I said, 'Actually, I'd really like to hear about the coathangers.'

'What coathangers?' he asked.

Before I could talk my way into a bullet between the eyes, Lorrie said, 'Do you think I could have my purse?'

He frowned. 'Why?'

'It's a female emergency.'

I couldn't believe she was going to do this. I knew I hadn't won the argument, but I assumed that I'd put enough doubt in her mind to give her second thoughts.

'Female emergency?' the maniac asked. 'What's that mean?'

'You know,' she said coyly.

For a guy who looked like a babe magnet able to draw swooning women like iron filings from a hundred-mile radius, he proved surprisingly obtuse in this matter. 'How would I know?'

'It's that time of month,' she said.

He claimed bafflement. 'The middle?'

As if it were infectious, Lorrie caught his bewilderment: 'The middle?'

'It's the middle of the month,' he reminded her. 'The fifteenth of September. So what?'

'It's *my* time of month,' she elucidated.

He just stared at her, befuddled.

'*I'm having my period*,' she declared impatiently.

The furrows in his brow were smoothed away by understanding. 'Ah. A female emergency.'

'Yes. That's right. Hallelujah. Now may I have my purse?'

'Why?'

If she ever got her hands on that nail file, she would plunge it into him with enthusiasm.

'I need a tampon,' she said.

'You're saying there's a tampon in your purse?'

'Yes.'

'And you need it now, you can't wait?'

'No, I absolutely can't wait,' she confirmed. Then she played to his compassionate side, which he hadn't shown to the head-shot librarian, but which she seemed to think must be there, considering that he had not been actually *rude*: 'I'm sorry, gee, this is so embarrassing.'

Regarding matters female, he might be a bit thick, but regarding Machiavellian schemes, he smelled a rat instantly: 'What's really in your purse — a gun?'

Admitting that she had been caught out, Lorrie shrugged. 'No gun. Just a pointy metal nail file.'

'You were going to — what? — stab me in the carotid artery?'

'Only if I couldn't get one of your eyes,' she said.

He raised his pistol, and though he pointed it at her, I figured that once he started blasting away, he'd drill me, too. I'd seen what he'd done to the newspaper.

'I should kill you dead right here,' he said, although without any animosity in his voice.

'You should,' she agreed. 'I would if I were you.'

He grinned and shook his head. 'What a piece of work.'

'Right back at ya,' she said, and matched his grin.

My teeth were revealed molar to molar, as well, though my grin was so tight with anxiety that it hurt my face.

'All these years, planning for this day,' the maniac said, 'I expected it to be gratifying in a savage sort of way, even thrilling, but I never thought it would be as much *fun* as this.'

Lorrie said, 'A party can never be better than the guests you invite.'

The lunatic killer considered this as if Lorrie had quoted one of the most complex philosophical propositions of Schopenhauer. He nodded solemnly, rolled his tongue over his teeth, uppers and lowers, as though he could *taste* the brilliance of those words, and finally he said, 'How true. How very true.'

I realized that I wasn't holding up my end of the conversation. I didn't want him to get the idea that a party of two might be more fun than three.

When I opened my mouth — no doubt to say something even more inappropriate than my stupid coathangers line, something that would bring me closer to a bullet in the groin — a great hollow peal tolled through the vaulted subcellar.

101

King Kong pounded his mighty fists one, two, three times against the giant door in the massive wall that separated his half of the island from the half where the nervous natives lived.

The maniac brightened at the sound. 'That'll be Honker and Crinkles. You'll like them. They have the explosives.'

11

As it turned out, Cornelius Randolph Snow not only had a keen appreciation for fine Victorian architecture but also for Victorian hugger-mugger of the kind that flourished in melodramas of the period and that Sir Arthur Conan Doyle had used with singular effect in his immortal Sherlock Holmes yarns: concealed doors, hidden rooms, blind staircases, secret passageways.

Hand in hand but only because of the steel cuffs, quickly but only because of the gun prodding us in the back, Lorrie and I went to the end of the room where the maniac had brutally shot the old newspaper.

Shelves spanned the width of that wall, rose from floor to ceiling. Stored thereon were periodicals in labeled slipcases.

The maniac studied several shelves, up and down, back and forth, maybe looking for the 1952 run of *Life* magazine, maybe hoping to spot a juicier spider.

Nope, neither. He was searching for a hidden switch. He found it, and a section of bookshelves pivoted open, revealing an alcove behind them.

At the back of the alcove, a stone wall embraced an iron-banded oak door. In an age that demanded harsher punishment for patrons with overdue books, they might have kept a tardy Jane Austen reader here until solitary confinement and a short ration of gruel brought the miscreant to remorse and contrition.

The maniac pounded one fist three times on the door — obviously an answering signal.

From the farther side came two knocks, hollow and loud.

After the maniac responded with two, a single knock came from the space beyond. He answered with one thump.

This seemed to be an unnecessarily complicated passcode, but the maniac was delighted by the ritual. He beamed happily at us.

His toothy smile no longer had quite the endearing quality that had marked it previously. He was an adorable-looking fellow, and against your better judgment, you still wanted to be charmed by him, but you kept scanning for dark hairy bits of spider on his lips and tongue.

A moment after the last knock, the buzz of a small high-speed motor arose from the farther side of the door. Then metal shrieked on metal.

A diamond-point steel drill bit thrust through the keyhole. The spinning shaft chewed up the lock mechanism and spat metal shavings on the floor.

Our host raised his voice and reported with boyish enthusiasm: 'We tortured a member of the Snow Village Historical Preservation Society, but we couldn't get keys out of him. I'm sure he'd have given them to us if he'd known where to get them, but it was our bad luck — and his — that we chose the wrong person to torture. So we've had to resort to this.'

104

Lorrie's cuffed hand sought my cuffed hand and held it tight.

I wished that we had met under different circumstances. Like at a town picnic or even at a tea dance.

The drill withdrew from the lock plate, fell silent. The broken lock assembly rattled, clinked, twanged, and gave way as the door opened into the alcove.

I had a glimpse of what appeared to be an eerily lit tunnel beyond the door.

A dour man came through, out of the alcove, past the pivoted section of bookcase, into the library's subcellar. A similar specimen followed him, pulling a handcart.

The first newcomer was about fifty, totally bald, with black eyebrows so shaggy that you could have knitted a child's sweater from them. He wore khakis, a green Ban Lon shirt, and a shoulder holster with gun.

'Excellent, excellent. You're right on time, Honker,' said the maniac.

I had no way of knowing whether the new guy's name was, say, Bob Honker, or whether this was a nickname inspired by the size of his nose. He had an enormous nose. Once it must have been straight and proud, but time had rendered it a spongy lump, ruddy with a fine webbing of burst capillaries — the nose of a serious drinker.

Honker appeared to be sober now, but brooding and suspicious.

He scowled at me, at Lorrie, and said gruffly, 'Who're the bitch and Bigfoot?'

'Hostages,' the maniac explained.

'What the hell we need hostages for?'

'If something goes wrong.'

'You think something'll go wrong?'

'No,' the maniac said, 'but they entertain me.'

The second newcomer stepped away from the handcart to join the discussion. He resembled Art Garfunkel, the singer: a decadent choirboy's face, electroshocked hair.

He wore a zippered nylon windbreaker over a T-shirt, but I could see the bulk of a holster and weapon beneath it.

'Whether something goes wrong or not,' he said, 'we'll have to waste them.'

'Of course,' the maniac said.

'It'd be a shame to off the bitch without using it,' said the choirboy.

More than their casual talk of murdering us, this reference to Lorrie as 'it' chilled me.

Her hand gripped mine so tightly that my knuckles ached.

The maniac said, 'Put her out of your mind, Crinkles. That isn't going to happen.'

Whether this was the guy's legal name or nickname, you might expect someone called Crinkles either to have a well-creased face or to be wonderfully amusing. His face looked as smooth as a hard-boiled egg, and he was about as amusing as antibiotic-resistant streptococcus infection.

To the maniac, Crinkles said, 'Why's she off limits? She belong to you?'

'She belongs to nobody,' our host replied with some annoyance. 'We didn't come all this way

106

just to score some quiff. If we don't stay focused on the main objective, the whole operation will fall apart.'

I felt that I ought to say something to the effect that if they wanted to get at Lorrie, they would have to come through me. But the truth was, armed and crazy, they could come through me as easily as the blades of a kitchen mixer churning through cake batter.

The prospect of dying didn't distress me nearly as much as the realization that I was helpless to defend her.

I hadn't made pastry chef yet, but in my mind I had *always* been a hero — or could be in a crisis. As a kid, I often fantasized about whipping up *soufflés au chocolat* fit for kings while at the same time battling the evil minions of Darth Vader.

Now reality set in. These violent lunatics would eat Darth Vader in a pita pocket and pick their teeth with his light saber.

'Whether something goes wrong or not,' Crinkles repeated, 'we'll have to burn them.'

'We've already gone over this,' the maniac said impatiently.

'Because they've seen our faces,' Crinkles persisted, 'we'll have to whack them both.'

'I *understand*,' the maniac assured him.

Crinkles had eyes the color of brandy. They grew pale when he said, 'The time comes, I want to be the one gets to ice the bitch.'

Waste, off, burn, whack, ice. This guy was a walking thesaurus when it came to synonyms for *kill*.

Maybe this meant he had croaked so many people that he found discussion of murder boring and therefore needed richer language to maintain his interest. Or, conversely, he might be a hit-man wannabe, all boast and jargon, with no guts when it came to doing the dirty deed.

Considering that Crinkles hung out with a madman who shot librarians for no reason and who saw no difference between spiders and bonbons, I decided that the wisest course was not to doubt his sincerity.

'You can whack her when we won't need hostages anymore,' the maniac promised Crinkles. 'I don't have a problem with that.'

'Hell, you can whack both of them,' Honker said. 'Means nothing to me.'

'Thanks,' Crinkles said. 'I appreciate that.'

'*De nada*,' said Honker.

The maniac guided us to another pair of wooden chairs. Although he had backup now, he nevertheless secured our cuffs to one of the backrails, as he had done previously.

The two newcomers began to unload the cargo on the handcart. There were at least a hundred one-kilo bricks of a gray substance wrapped in what appeared to be greasy, translucent paper.

I'm not a demolitions expert, not even a demolitions dabbler, but I figured these were the explosives of which the maniac had spoken.

Honker and Crinkles were physically the same type: burly and thick-necked but quick on their feet. They reminded me of the Beagle Boys.

In the Scrooge McDuck comic books that I

108

loved as a child, a group of criminal brothers were perpetually scheming to raid Uncle Scrooge's enormous money bin, where he swam through his fortune as if it were an ocean and occasionally recontoured the acres of gold coins with a bull-dozer. These felons were blunt-faced, round-shouldered, barrel-chested, doglike creatures that stood erect in the manner of human beings, had hands instead of paws, and owned a signature wardrobe of prison-stripe shirts.

Although Honker and Crinkles chose not to advertise their villainy by the outfits they wore, they were body doubles for those comic-book villains. The Beagle Boys, however, were more handsome than Honker and a lot less scary-looking than Crinkles.

These two worked quickly, tirelessly. They were obviously happy to be occupied in useful criminal activity.

While his associates distributed bricks of plastic explosives to all points of the subcellar, in this room and others, the maniac sat at the study table. He carefully synchronized the clocks on more than a dozen detonators.

He hunched over his work, concentrating intensely. He pinched his tongue gently between his teeth. His dark hair fell across his forehead, and he kept brushing it back, out of his eyes.

If you squinted, blurring the scene just a little, he looked like a twelve-year-old hobbyist assembling a plastic model of a Navy fighter jet.

Lorrie and I were far enough away from him that we could talk privately if we kept our voices low.

Leaning close, she said conspiratorially, 'If we're in the room alone with Crinkles, I'm going to tell him I'm having a female emergency.'

Being in the hands of three psychotics instead of one, hearing herself referred to as *it*, listening to them discuss our execution with no more emotion than if they had been deciding who should take out the trash: I had thought all of that would surely give her second thoughts about reckless actions based on wildly exuberant optimism. To Lorrie Lynn, three psychotics just meant two more opportunities to bamboozle someone with the female-emergency story, get her hands on the nail file, and stab her way to freedom.

'You're going to get us killed,' I warned again.

'That's lame. They're going to kill us anyway. Weren't you listening?'

'But you'll get us killed *sooner*,' I said, managing to make a whisper surprisingly shrill, and realized that I sounded as if I had a university degree in wimp.

What had happened to the kid who'd been pumped for intergalactic warfare? Wasn't he still inside me somewhere?

Lorrie couldn't get her hand out of the cuffs, but she could slip her hand out of mine. She looked as if she wanted to wash it. In carbolic acid.

When it comes to romance, I'd had some success, but I wasn't a reincarnation of Rudolph Valentino. In fact, I didn't need a little black book to record the phone numbers of all my conquests. I didn't even need a page from a little black book. A Post-it note would do. One of the half-size Post-its you stick to the fridge as a reminder: just room enough to print BUY CARROTS FOR DINNER.

Here I had the clearest shot that Cupid was ever likely to give me — *chained* to the most beautiful woman I'd ever met — and I couldn't take advantage of the moment, couldn't woo her and win her, for the stupid reason that I wanted to live.

'We'll get an opportunity,' I told her, 'and when it comes, we'll take it. But it's got to be something a lot better than the female-emergency gimmick.'

'Like what?'

'Something that'll give us an edge.'

'Such as?'

'Something. I don't know. Something.'

'We can't just wait,' she said.

'Yeah, we can.'

'We're just waiting to die.'

'No,' I said, pretending I was analyzing the situation, seeking advantages, instead of vamping in hope of a miracle. 'I'm waiting for the right opportunity.'

'*You're* going to get us killed,' she predicted.

I threw some withering scorn at her: 'What happened to the indefatigable optimist?'

'You're smothering her.'

She had lobbed the scorn back at me so fast that my face was flushed and burning with it before I fully realized I'd taken the hit.

12

Sitting two stories under the evil streets and surrounded by the evil earth of Snow Village, we watched Honker, Crinkles, and the nameless maniac plant explosives at key structural points and plug timers into the charges.

You might think that our terror sharpened by the minute. I speak from much experience when I say that it isn't possible to sustain terror at a peak for long periods of time.

If monstrous misfortune can be called a disease, terror is a symptom of it. Like any symptom, it is not expressed continuously to the same degree, but waxes and wanes. Sick with the flu, you don't vomit every minute of the day and are not in the throes of diarrhea from dawn to dusk.

That may be a disgusting analogy, but it's apt and vivid. I'm glad I didn't think of it while chained to those chairs with Lorrie, because in my eagerness to patch things up with her and break the frigid silence between us, I probably would have blurted it out just to have something to say.

I soon discovered that Lorrie wasn't one to gild an offense or nurse her anger. In perhaps two minutes, she broke the silence and became my chum and co-conspirator once more.

'Crinkles is the weak link,' she said softly.

I loved her throaty voice, but I wished that she

would use it to say something that made sense.

At that moment Crinkles was packing plastic explosives around the base of a ceiling-support column. He handled the boom clay with no more trepidation than a child playing with Silly Putty.

'He doesn't look like a weak link, but maybe you're right,' I said by way of conciliation.

'Trust me, he is.'

Now with both hands busy shaping explosives, Crinkles held a detonator in his teeth.

'Do you know why he's the weak link?' Lorrie asked.

'I'm eager to hear.'

'He likes me.'

I counted to five before replying, the better to ensure that my voice was free of an argumentative tone. 'He wants to kill you.'

'Before that.'

'Before what?'

'Before he asked the grinning feeb if he could kill me, he very distinctly expressed a romantic interest.'

This time I counted to seven. 'The way I remember it,' I said in a tone that I hoped might be taken for cheerful reminiscence, 'he wanted to rape you.'

'You don't rape someone you don't find attractive.'

'Actually, you do. It happens all the time.'

'Maybe *you* would,' she said, 'but not most men.'

'Rape isn't about sex,' I explained. 'It's about power.'

113

She frowned at me. 'Why do you find it so hard to believe that Crinkles might think I'm cute?'

Only after I got to *ten* did I say, 'You *are* cute. You're beyond cute. You're gorgeous. But Crinkles isn't the kind of guy who falls in love.'

'Do you mean that?'

'Absolutely. Crinkles is the kind of guy who falls in *hate*.'

'No, I mean the other part.'

'What other part?'

'The cute-beyond-cute-gorgeous part.'

'You're the most amazing-looking person I've ever seen. But you've got to — '

'That's so sweet,' she said. 'But I'm not sensitive about my looks, and though I like compliments as much as any girl does, I prefer honesty in the long run. I'm aware of my nose, for instance.'

Honker lumbered in from the adjacent room, slouched to the explosives-laden handcart, looking like nothing so much as a troll brooding over whether he'd added enough sage and butter to the child currently cooking in his oven.

Still holding the detonator in his teeth, Crinkles blew his nose in his hand and wiped his hand on the sleeve of his jacket.

The maniac prepared the last of the detonators. When he noticed me looking at him, he waved.

'My nose is pinched,' Lorrie said.

'It's not pinched,' I assured her because in truth it was no more pinched than the nose of a goddess.

'It's pinched,' she insisted.

'All right, maybe it's pinched,' I agreed, to avoid an argument, 'but it's pinched in a totally perfect way.'

'Then there's the problem with my teeth.'

I was tempted to seize her wonderfully full lips, pull them apart, inspect her choppers as a vet might examine a racehorse, and declare them fit in no uncertain terms.

Instead, I smiled and kept my voice calm. 'There's nothing wrong with your teeth. They're white and even, as flawless as pearls.'

'Exactly,' she said. 'They don't look real. People must think I have false teeth.'

'No one will think a woman as young as you has false teeth.'

'There's Chilson Strawberry.'

No matter how often I put it through the mill wheels of my mind, that statement wouldn't process. 'What is Chilson Strawberry?'

'She's a friend of mine, my age exactly, she does bungee tours.'

'Bungee tours?'

'She puts together travel packages, takes groups of people all over the world to bungee jump off bridges and stuff.'

'I wouldn't have dreamed you could make a living packaging bungee tours.'

'She does quite well,' Lorrie assured me. 'Though I don't like to think what all that taunting of gravity is going to do to her breasts in ten years.'

I didn't know what to say to that. I took some pride in having found *something* to say

115

throughout the conversation so far, regardless of its mystifying turns. I figured I had earned a time-out.

Barely pausing for breath, Lorrie said, 'Chilson lost every one of her teeth.'

Interested in spite of myself, I said, 'How did she do that — did a bungee break?'

'No, it wasn't work-related. She screwed up on her motorcycle, flipped, rolled, smacked her face into a bridge abutment.'

My teeth throbbed with sympathy pain so bad that for a moment I couldn't speak.

'When they rebuilt her jaw,' Lorrie said, 'they extracted what teeth hadn't been broken out in the accident. Later they implanted fabrications. She can crack walnuts with them.'

'Considering that she's a friend of yours,' I said with complete sincerity, 'I'm wondering what happened to the bridge abutment.'

'Not as much as you might think. They had to hose the blood off. There were a few chips, a little crack.'

Her face was guileless. Her limpid eyes were not evasive. If she was putting me on, she gave no clue of it.

'You've got to meet my family,' I said.

'Uh-oh,' she said. 'Something's happening.'

Blinking, mildly disoriented, I looked around, as though coming out of a trance. I had all but forgotten about Honker, Crinkles, and the grinning feeb.

Although at least half the bricks of plastic explosive remained on the handcart, Honker pulled it out of the room, through the alcove

116

door, into the tunnel by which he had arrived.

Having synchronized the final detonator, the nameless maniac presented it to Crinkles, along with the handcuff key, and gave him instructions: 'When you've finished here, bring the babe and the ox with you.'

Ox. The feeb was *my* size, and I'm sure that he didn't think of himself as an ox.

He followed Honker into the tunnel.

We were alone with Crinkles, which was like being alone with Satan in the sadomasochism wing of Hell.

Lorrie waited a minute to be sure those in the tunnel had gone too far to hear, and then she said, 'Oh, Mr. Crinkles?'

'Don't do this,' I pleaded.

Crinkles had gone to the distant end of the room to insert the last detonator in the charge that he had packed around another column. He appeared not to have heard Lorrie.

'Even if he thinks you're cute,' I said, 'he's the kind of guy who'd be as happy to rape you *after* he's killed you as before, and how does that help us?'

'Necrophilia? That's a terrible thing to say about a person.'

'He's not a person. He's a Morlock.'

She brightened. 'H. G. Wells. *The Time Machine*. You really are a reader. Of course you could have seen the movie.'

'Crinkles isn't a person. He's Grendel.'

'*Beowulf*,' she said, naming the work in which the monster Grendel lurked.

'He's Tom Ripley.'

117

'That's the psychopath in some books by Patricia Highsmith.'

'Five books,' I said. 'Tom Ripley is the essential Hannibal Lecter thirty years before anyone had heard of Hannibal.'

Having finished his work at the distant end of the long room, Crinkles returned to us.

As our Grendel approached, I expected Lorrie to tell him she had a female emergency. She smiled at him and batted her eyelashes, but hesitated to speak.

Crinkles's mouth was puckered strangely. He appeared to be rolling something on his tongue as he unlocked the second set of handcuffs that secured our cuffs to the chair.

As we got to our feet, still tethered to each other, Lorrie tossed her head to fluff her hair. With her free hand, she undid a button at the top of her blouse to better reveal her lovely throat.

Trouble.

She was making herself look more seductive before announcing that she had a female emergency.

Being seductive with Crinkles made no more sense than trying to unwind a coiled rattlesnake by kissing it. He would see through her even quicker than had the nameless maniac, and he would be so pissed by her attempt to manipulate him that he'd put the nail file through *her* eye.

Apparently, my credentials as a reader and the analogies I had drawn between Crinkles and various monstrous fictional characters gave her reason to pause. She glanced at me, hesitated.

Before she could speak, Crinkles spat into his hand the object he had been rolling on his tongue. It was round, the size of a large gumball, gray and glistening with saliva.

The ominous glob might have been something other than a wad of the plastic explosive, but that's sure what it appeared to be.

Maybe he got a thrill from holding in his mouth a couple ounces of concentrated death so potent that if detonated it would turn his head into a spray of mush.

Or maybe this was a good-luck ritual, the equivalent of kissing the dice before throwing them across the craps table.

Or maybe he just liked the taste. After all, some people enjoy creamed Spam. He might really have a festival of flavor if he first rolled the round treat in crushed spiders.

Without a comment about it, he put the gray wad on the chair in which I had been sitting, and he said, 'Let's get out of here. Move it.'

On our way to the alcove that waited behind the secret door in the bookshelves, we walked by the table on which stood Lorrie's purse.

She boldly picked it up as we passed.

Behind us, Crinkles raised no objection.

13

About eight feet in width, the limestone-clad tunnel featured a low barrel-vaulted ceiling but straight walls. Underfoot, the rectangular paving stones had been laid in a herringbone pattern.

Cast off by fat yellow candles in bronze sconces, draft-stirred light shimmered lambently along the walls and, with shadows, wove an everchanging tapestry across the curve of the ceiling.

This forbidding passageway appeared to be long, dwindling into a confusion of shadows and sinuous sylphs of light before an end could be glimpsed.

I would not have been surprised to encounter Edgar Allan Poe, but there was no sign of him, nor of Honker and the nameless maniac.

Although the cool — but not damp — air smelled surprisingly clean and free of moldy malodors, scented by nothing but raw limestone and hot candle wax, I expected bats, rats, roaches, scuttling mysteries, but at the moment we had only Crinkles.

We had proceeded hesitantly ten or fifteen feet when he said, 'Stop there a minute.'

While we waited, he closed the secret door in the bookshelves from this side and then shut the ironbound oak door to the alcove. Perhaps the intention was to minimize the effect of the blast on the tunnel if the library explosion occurred

120

prematurely, before we had reached absolute safety.

While Crinkles closed things behind us, Lorrie zippered open her purse and rummaged through it. She found the steel nail file.

To her shock, with my free left hand, I snatched it from her.

She expected me to throw it away, and when I didn't, she said, 'Gimme.'

'I pulled this Excalibur from the stone, and only I have the power to use it,' I whispered, going totally literary on her with the hope that this would charm her into acceptance.

She looked like she wanted to take a swing at me. I suspected her punch would pack one hell of a wallop.

Rejoining us, moving past us, so arrogant and so sure of our timidity that he *actually turned his back on us*, Crinkles led the way. 'Come on, come on, and don't think I haven't got eyes in the back of my head.'

He probably did. Everyone had back-of-the-head eyes on his native planet.

'Where are we?' I asked as we followed him.

The core of him was such a tightly wound ball of psychopathic fury that he could make a direct and simple answer sound fraught with anger: 'Going under Center Square Park about now.'

'I mean the tunnel. What is it?'

'What the hell do you mean *what is it?* It's a tunnel, you shit-for-brains moron.'

Taking no offense, I asked, 'When was it built, by who?'

'Back in the 1800s, before anything else.

Cornelius Snow had it constructed — the greedy, grasping bastard.'

'Why?'

'So he'd be able to get around town secretly.'

'What was he, a Victorian Batman or something?'

'The tunnels connect four of his major holdings around the square — the belly-crawling capitalist pig.'

Throughout this conversation, Lorrie cast meaningful looks my way, wanting me at once to attack Crinkles with Excalibur.

As enchanted swords go, the nail file left a lot to be desired. Mostly hidden in my hand, the flat length of steel felt stiff but not as thick as a knife. The point wasn't sharp enough to prick my thumb.

If Lorrie had been wearing spike-heeled shoes instead of white tennies, I'd have preferred to go at Crinkles with one of those.

I responded to her increasingly exasperated looks with the broad expressions of a bad mime, telling her not to be impatient, not to be rash, just to give me time to find the right opportunity for nail-file mayhem.

'So . . . what four major holdings do the tunnels connect?' I asked Crinkles as we moved forward through wafting candlelight and clinging shadows.

He listed them with increasing venom: 'His mansion, that pile of gaudy excess. His library, which is nothing but a temple to decadent Western so-called literature. His courthouse, that nest of poisonous judges who oppressed the masses for him. And the bank, where he stole from the poor and foreclosed on widows.'

'He owned his own bank?' I asked. 'How cool.'

Crinkles said, 'He owned most of some things and some of just about everything — the blood-sucking, black-hearted, running dog. If a hundred men had divided his possessions, every one of them would have been too rich to be allowed to live. Wish I'd been alive back then. I'd have cut the imperialist swine's head off and played kickball with it.'

Even in the inconstant candlelight, I could see that Lorrie's face was red and taut with barely contained — one might almost say *hysterical* — frustration. I didn't need a facial-language specialist to interpret her expression for me: *Go, Jimmy, go, Jimmy, go, go, go! Stab the bastard, stab the bastard! Siss-boom-bah!*

I chose instead to bide my time.

She was probably wishing she had worn those spike-heeled shoes so she could take them off and tattoo my head.

A moment later we came to an intersection with another tunnel. A still gentle but stronger draft moved here. To the left and right, more sconces with additional fat yellow candles threw rippling curtains of light into a crawling darkness.

I should have realized that a cross of passageways must underlie the town square, because each of the four holdings that Crinkles had bitterly enumerated was in a different block from the others: north, south, east, and west of the park.

Nevertheless, I could not help but be impressed by the abruptly revealed complication of this subterranean structure. Looking left, right, back, forward, I thought of the stone corridors and torchlit chambers in old movies about a mummy's tomb, and in spite of our perilous circumstances, a thrill of adventure shivered through me.

Crinkles said, 'This way,' and turned left.

Before we followed him, Lorrie put her purse on the floor. She tucked it in shadows close to the wall, in the length of corridor along which we had walked from the library.

If the nameless grinning feeb saw her with the handbag, the jig would be up — if you're willing to allow that our pathetic nail-file scheme qualified as anything so grand as a jig.

She seemed reluctant to leave the purse. No doubt she considered it an arsenal of makeshift weapons. We might be able to suffocate Crinkles with a powder puff. If she had a hairbrush, we could spank him severely.

As we trailed after our guide once more, I said, 'Why all the candles?'

Crinkles grew less patient with me by the minute. 'So we can see in the dark, you freaking idiot.'

'But it's not very efficient.'

'This is all they had back in the 1870s, candles and oil lamps, you drooling imbecile.'

Once more Lorrie began signaling me, by fantastical contortions of her face and a mad-horse rolling of the eyes, that the time had come to stab him.

Crinkles had declined so drastically in my affections that, against my better judgment, I was almost ready to carve him like scrimshaw.

I said, 'Yes, but we aren't in the 1870s. You could use flashlights, battery-powered lanterns, those sparkless chemical-tube flares.'

'Don't you think we know that, you brain-dead jackass? But then the ambience wouldn't be authentic.'

We proceeded several steps in silence before I could no longer resist asking: 'Why does the ambience need to be authentic?'

'The boss wants it that way.'

I assumed the boss must be the nameless maniac, unless there was a Mr. Big whom we had not yet encountered.

At some date long after the initial construction, the last ten feet of this corridor had been walled off. They had used a double width of concrete blocks with embedded steel rebar.

Recently half the blocks had been broken out. The rebar had been cut with an acetylene torch. To one side of the corridor lay a pile of rubble.

We followed Crinkles through the gap in this partition, into the last portion of the corridor. Another ironbound oak door stood open at the end of the passageway.

Beyond, electric light from more ceiling fixtures, added decades after the original construction, revealed a large stone-walled room with massive columns and herringbone floor. Two stone staircases with stately ornamental iron railings climbed opposite walls to doors of brushed stainless steel. But for the stainless steel, there was a feeling of an occult temple about the place.

Half the space stood empty. The other half contained rows of green filing cabinets with aisles between.

Honker and the killer of librarians stood beside the handcart with its depleted load of explosives, in murmured conversation.

Concerned that the brighter light would reveal too much, I surreptitiously slipped the nail file into my pants pocket.

Beaming at the sight of Lorrie and me, as if we were old friends arriving at a cocktail party, our smiley host came to us, indicating the encompassing architecture with a sweep of one arm. 'Some place, huh? The institution's historical records are stored on this level.'

'What institution?' I asked.

'We're under the bank.'

Lorrie said, 'I'll be damned. You're going to rob it, aren't you?'

He shrugged. 'Isn't that what banks are for?'

The Beagle Boys were already planting explosive charges at two of the columns.

14

Pleased with himself, the maniac pointed to a hulking piece of equipment in a corner of the room. 'Do you know what that is?'

Lorrie guessed, 'A time machine?'

Having come from a family in which non sequiturs were as common in conversation as adverbs, I had adapted to the young Ms. Hicks's style in short order.

Although the maniac was intrigued by her, he wasn't always able to dance with her as I could, metaphorically speaking. His green eyes glazed, and his smile slightly rounded into puzzlement.

'How could it be a time machine?' he asked.

'At the fantastic pace science is progressing,' she said, 'space shuttles and CAT scans, heart transplants and computerized toaster ovens, now cell phones you can carry anywhere and lipstick that won't smear . . . Well, I mean, at this rate, sooner than later there's going to be a time machine, so if there has to be one, why not here and now?'

He stared at Lorrie for a moment, then looked at the equipment in the corner as though wondering whether he had misidentified it and whether it might in fact be a time machine.

Had I made that same speech, he would have decided that I was either a headcase or a mocking smart-ass. Annoyed or offended, he would have shot me.

127

A beautiful woman, on the other hand, can say just about any damn thing, and men will seriously consider it.

Her guileless face, pellucid eyes, and sincere smile prevented me from determining whether the time-machine comment — or any other off-the-wall business that came out of her — was offered with total sincerity or in a spirit of fun.

Most people don't have fun while being held hostage and being threatened with death by the likes of Crinkles. I suspected, however, that Lorrie Lynn Hicks might be capable of it.

I couldn't wait for her to meet my family.

A lot of people don't actually have fun even when they're at a party having fun. That's because they don't have a sense of humor. Everyone claims to have a sense of humor, but some of them are lying and a significant number are fooling themselves.

This explains the success of most TV sitcoms and movie comedies. These shows can be entirely humorless, but scads of people will laugh uproariously at them because they come with a label that says FUNNY. The congenitally humor-challenged audience knows it's safe to laugh, that it's even expected.

This part of the entertainment business serves the community of the humorless in much the way that a manufacturer of prosthetic limbs serves those unfortunates who have lost arms or legs. Their work may be more important than feeding the poor.

My family has always *insisted* on fun not only during the sunny times of life but also during times of adversity, even in the face of loss and tragedy (though right now they must be sick with worry regarding my whereabouts). Maybe we inherited an acutely sensitive funny-recognition gene. Or maybe we're just on a permanent sugar high from all the baked goods we eat.

'No,' said the nameless maniac, 'it's not a time machine. It's the bank's emergency generator.'

'Too bad,' Lorrie lamented. 'I'd rather it had been a time machine.'

Gazing wistfully at the generator, the maniac sighed. 'Yeah. I know what you mean.'

'So you've disabled the bank's emergency generator,' I said.

My statement harried him out of his time-travel fantasy. 'How did you know?'

I pointed. 'The parts scattered there on the floor were a clue.'

'You're quick,' he said with admiration.

'In my line of work, we have to be.'

He didn't ask what job I held. As I've learned over the past ten years, psychopaths are routinely self-absorbed.

'The bank closed an hour ago,' he said, clearly proud of his elaborate plan and gratified to have an opportunity to share it. 'The tellers' drawers have been reconciled, and they've gone home. The vault will have been closed ten minutes ago. By routine, the manager and the two security guards were the last to leave.'

'Somewhere,' Lorrie guessed, 'you've rigged a power-company transformer to blow, cutting electrical service to the town square.'

'When the power goes,' I said, 'the generator

129

won't cut in, and the vault will be vulnerable.'

'You're *both* very quick,' he said approvingly. 'What's the story with you two? Have you planned a heist before?'

'Not in this reincarnation,' Lorrie replied. 'But that's another story.'

He indicated the farther staircase. 'That leads to the half of the bank's upper basement where they fill coin rolls, bundle cash, verify incoming money shipments, and prepare outgoing transfers. The front door to the vault is also in that area.'

'The vault has a back door?' I asked with a note of disbelief that amused him.

He grinned, nodded, and pointed to the nearer staircase. 'The door at the top goes directly into the vault.'

This detail seemed to belong entirely in the maniac's distorted view of reality and not at all in the real world that I inhabited.

Pleased by my amazement, he said, 'Cornelius Snow was the sole stockholder in the bank when he built it. He arranged things for his convenience.'

'Are we talking skullduggery here?' Lorrie wondered, and seemed to be delighted that there might be some.

'Not at all,' he assured her. 'From every indication, Cornelius Snow was an honest, civic-minded man.'

'He was an insatiable greedy drooling pig,' Crinkles angrily disagreed as he worked on another explosive charge.

'He didn't need to misappropriate any

depositor's funds because eighty percent of the deposits were his to begin with.'

Crinkles had no interest in these facts of accounting, only in emotion: 'I would have roasted him on a spit and fed him to dogs.'

'In the 1870s,' the maniac said, 'there wasn't anything remotely like the complex web of regulation and oversight by which banks operate these days.'

'Except dogs would have the good sense not to eat the venomous bastard,' Crinkles added in a voice bitter enough to curdle milk.

'Shortly past the turn of the century, that simpler world began to fade away.'

'Even inbred, starving sewer rats wouldn't have eaten the avaricious creep if you'd basted him in bacon grease,' Crinkles elaborated.

'After Cornelius died, when the bulk of his estate was left to a charitable trust, the section of tunnel leading to the bank's subterranean entrance was walled shut.'

I recalled the breach in the wall that we had passed through en route. The Beagle Boys had been busy.

'The steel door at the head of those stairs to the vault isn't actually operable,' the nameless maniac continued. 'The old oak door was replaced with steel in the 1930s, then welded shut. And on the other side is a reinforced concrete-block wall. But we can get through all of that in maybe two hours, once we've dealt with the alarm.'

'I'm surprised this room right here isn't alarmed,' Lorrie said. 'Though I suppose if that was really a time machine, it would be.'

'Nobody saw the need. To all appearances, it's not a major bank, not worth knocking over. Besides, after 1902, when they sealed off the underground approach, there *wasn't* a back entrance anymore. And in respect of the bank's security, the charitable trust that owns the Snow Mansion agreed not to disclose Cornelius's tunnels. A few people in the historical society have seen them, but only after signing a nondisclosure agreement with teeth.'

Earlier he had mentioned torturing a member of the historical society, who was no doubt now as dead as the librarian. No matter how tightly a lawyer constructs a nondisclosure clause, there are ways around it.

I won't say that I was thunderstruck by these revelations, but I was certainly flabbergasted, however fine a point that might be. Although born and raised in Snow Village, and although I loved my picturesque hometown and was steeped in its history, I'd never heard so much as a rumor about secret passageways under the town square.

When I expressed my amazement to the maniac, the warm twinkle in his eyes crystalized into a colder glitter that I recognized from the eyes of Killer the Gila monster and Earl the milk snake.

'You can't deeply, fully *know* a town,' he said, 'if you love it. Loving it, you're charmed by surfaces. To deeply, fully know a town, you've got to hate it, *loathe* it, loathe it with an unquenchable fiery passion. You've got to be

132

consumed by a need to learn all its rotten shameful secrets and use them against it, find its hidden cancers and feed them until they metastasize into apocalyptic tumors. You've got to *live* for the day when its every stone and stick will be wiped forever from the face of the earth.'

I assumed that once upon a time something bad had happened to him in our little tourist mecca. Something more traumatic than being given a lesser hotel room when he had reserved a suite or being unable to buy a ski-lift pass on a busy winter weekend.

'But when you come right down to it,' Lorrie said (somewhat riskily, it seemed to me), 'this whole escapade isn't about hate or about justice, like you said earlier. It's about bank robbery. It's just about money.'

The maniac's face turned so livid that from hairline to chin and from ear to ear it looked like one big bruise. His smile went flatline.

'I don't care about money,' he said so tightly that the words seemed to escape him without parting his fiercely compressed lips.

'You're not breaking into a produce market to steal a lot of carrots and snow peas,' Lorrie said. 'You're robbing a bank.'

'I'm destroying the bank to break the town.'

'Money, money, money,' she persisted.

'This is about *vengeance*. Well-deserved, long-overdue vengeance. And that's close enough to justice for me.'

'Not for me, it isn't,' Crinkles interjected, leaving his work with the explosives to contribute to the conversation more directly. 'This *is* about money because wealth isn't just wealth but also the root and stalk and flower of power, and power liberates the powerful while it oppresses the powerless, so to crush what crushes, those who are oppressed must oppress the oppressors.'

I made no attempt to rerun that sentence through my memory banks. I was afraid that by trying to untangle it, my brain would crash. This was Karl Marx filtered through the lens of Abbott and Costello.

Aware from our expressions that his point had been too blunt to penetrate, Crinkles stated his philosophy more succinctly: 'Some of that filthy stinking pig's money belongs to me and to lots of other people he exploited to get it.'

'Gee whiz, take a rest from stupid for a moment,' Lorrie told Crinkles. 'Cornelius Snow never exploited you. He died long before you were born.'

She was on a roll now, insulting everyone who had the power and the motivation to kill us.

I shook my cuffed hand, thereby shaking hers, to remind her that any spray of bullets she invited was likely to leave me dead, as well.

Crinkles's mass of wiry hair seemed to stiffen until he less resembled Art Garfunkel than he did the bride of Frankenstein.

'What we're doing here is making a *political* statement,' he insisted.

Thus far phlegmatic compared to his companions, Honker joined them, so exacerbated by all this talk of vengeance and politics that his caterpillar eyebrows twitched as if jolts of an electric current enlivened them.

'Cash,' he said. 'That's all it's about for me. Cold cash. I'm here to take the money and run. If there wasn't a bank, I wouldn't have signed up for this, the rest of it doesn't matter to me, and if you guys don't shut up *and get the job done* — then I'm out of here, and you're on your own.'

Honker must have had skills essential to the heist, because his threat quieted his partners.

Their fury, however, did not abate. They looked like thwarted attack dogs, held back on choke chains, faces dark with unspent rage, eyes hot with violent passion that would not cool until they had been allowed to bite.

I wished that I had some cookies to give them, maybe German *lebkuchen* or nice crisp Scotch shortbread. Or chocolate pecan tarts. The poet William Congreve wrote, 'Music has charms to soothe the savage breast,' but I suspect good muffins are more effective.

As if aware that his associates' submission to a threat did not constitute teamwork, Honker threw a bone to each man's mania, beginning with Crinkles: 'There's a clock running and we've got a lot to do. That's all I'm saying. And if we just do the job, your political statement will be made, loud and clear.'

Crinkles bit his lower lip in a manner reminiscent of our young president. Reluctantly he nodded agreement.

To the green-eyed maniac, Honker said, 'You planned this caper 'cause you want justice for your mother's death. So let's do the job and *get* that justice.'

The librarian-killer's eyes grew misty, as they had done when his heartstrings had been strummed by my revelation that my mother used to iron my socks.

'I found the issues of the newspaper that carried the story,' he told Honker.

'They must have been hard to read,' Honker sympathized.

'I felt like my heart was being ripped out. I could hardly . . . force myself through them.' His voice thickened with emotion. 'But then I got so angry.'

'Understandable,' Honker commiserated. 'Each of us only gets one mother.'

'It wasn't just her being murdered. It was the lies, Honker. Almost everything in the newspaper was a *lie*.'

Glancing at his wristwatch, Honker shrugged and said, 'Well, what do you expect from newspapers?'

'Capitalist lapdogs is all they are,' Crinkles observed.

'They said my mother died in childbirth and Dad shot the doctor in a mad rage, as if *that* makes any sense.'

The nameless maniac could have been my age. To the day? To the hour? Almost to the minute? If he'd gotten his good looks and green eyes from his mother . . .

Astonished, without thinking, I said, 'Punchinello?'

When Honker furrowed his forehead, his push-broom eyebrows swept shadows of suspicion over his eyes.

136

Crinkles slipped his right hand inside his windbreaker, touching the butt of his holstered pistol.

The shooter of newspapers took a step back, startled that I knew his name.

I said, 'Punchinello Beezo?'

15

The three clowns placed the last of the explosives and inserted synchronized detonators.

Clowns they were, though not in costume. *Honker, Crinkles:* stage names that would seem entirely appropriate when they were cavorting in size 58 shoes, baggy polka-dot pants, and bright orange wigs. Maybe Punchinello used his real name as his stage name, or perhaps under the big top he was known as Squiggles or Slappy.

Either in the center ring or out here in the world of rubes, the name Nutsy also would have suited him.

Lorrie and I sat on the stone floor, our backs against a row of green filing cabinets filled with the historical records of the bank's first hundred years. Judging by the preparations being made around us, the building would implode seventy-eight years short of its second century.

I was in a mood.

Although I wasn't yet gripped by terror, which overwhelms the will and paralyzes, my condition was well north of mere misgiving.

Combined with my anxiety was a sense that fate had not dealt with me fairly. No family of good, kind-hearted bakers should have to be afflicted with two generations of Beezos. It would be like after Churchill wins World War II, a week later a woman moves in next door with twenty-six cats, and it's Hitler's batty sister.

138

All right, that's not a brilliant analogy or maybe not even one that makes any sense, but it expresses how I felt. Put-upon. Cruelly victimized. The innocent whipping boy for a universe gone mad.

In addition to anxiety and a keen sense of injustice, I was tormented by a formless determination. Formless because determination requires the setting of limits within which one must act, but I did not know what those limits should be, didn't know what to do, when to do it, or how.

I felt like throwing my head back and screaming in frustration. The only thing preventing me from doing so was the unnerving concern that when I screamed, Honker and Crinkles and Punchinello would scream wildly with me, honk horns, blow whistles, and squeeze rubber bladders that made a farting sound.

Until that moment, I had never suffered from harlequinaphobia, which is a fear of clowns. Too often to count, I had heard the story of the night I was born, the tale of the murderous chain-smoking fugitive from a circus, but never had Konrad Beezo's homicidal acts instilled in me an uneasiness about *all* clowns.

In less than two hours, the lunatic son had achieved what the father could not. I watched him and his two subordinate merry-andrews at work with the explosives, and they seemed to me to be *alien* in the most troubling sense — like the pod people from *Invasion of the Body Snatchers* — passing for human beings but with an ultimate agenda so dark and so strange that it lay beyond human comprehension.

Like I said, I was in a mood.

The Tock family's exquisitely sensitive funny-recognition gene was still functioning. I remained aware of the screwball nature of the situation, but I did not *feel* in the least amused.

Insanity is not evil, but all evil is insane. Evil itself is never funny, but insanity sometimes can be. We need to laugh at the irrationality of evil, for in doing so we deny evil's power over us, diminish its influence in the world, and tarnish the allure it has for some people.

There in the subcellar of the bank, I failed in my duty to deny, diminish, and tarnish. I was offended by fate, anxious, angry, and even Lorrie Lynn Hicks in all her glory could not lift my spirits.

She had a lot of questions, as you might imagine. Usually I enjoyed recounting the story of the night of my birth, but not this time. Nevertheless, she got out of me the stuff about Konrad Beezo. She is indefatigable.

I didn't mention my grandfather's predictions. If I brought up that subject, I'd almost inevitably also tell her that back in the newspaper morgue at the library, I'd experienced a semi-precognitive moment of my own, a premonition — sharper than a hunch but fuzzy on the details — that she would be shot.

I didn't see anything to be gained by alarming her, especially since my sudden sixth sense might be nothing but hooey, just a flare from an over-heated imagination.

140

Finished preparing explosives, the out-of-uniform motley fools lit and placed a series of Coleman lanterns to illuminate the chamber when the power failed. They didn't have enough of them to brighten the entire big room, just the end in which they would be working on the vault.

Lorrie and I were left sitting at a distance. When the electric lights went off, we would be in shadows.

Having absorbed my story, Lorrie brooded for a moment and then said, 'Are all clowns so angry?'

'I don't know a lot of clowns.'

'You know these three. And Konrad Beezo.'

'I never met Konrad Beezo. I was like five minutes old when our paths crossed.'

'I count it as a meet. So regarding clowns and anger, that's four for four. I'm bummed. It's like you meet the real Santa Claus and he turns out to have a drinking problem. You do still have the shiv?'

'The what?' I asked.

'The shiv.'

'You mean the nail file?'

'If that's what you want to call it,' she said.

'That's what it is.'

'Whatever you say. When are you gonna make your move?'

'When the time's right,' I said patiently.

'Let's hope that's before rather than after we're blown to smithereens.'

They had finished placing the five gas lanterns. One stood at the foot of the stairs, one

141

at the middle of the long flight, and a third on the wide landing at the top, outside the back door to the vault.

From a couple of large suitcases, Punchinello unpacked tools, welder's masks, and other items I couldn't identify from a distance.

Honker and Crinkles muscled a wheeled tank of acetylene up the stairs to the landing.

Lorrie said, 'What kind of name is Punchinello?'

'His father named him after a famous clown. You know, like Punch and Judy.'

'Punch and Judy are puppets.'

'Yes,' I said, 'but Punch is also a clown.'

'I didn't realize that.'

'He wears a sort of jester hat.'

She said, 'I thought Punch was a car salesman.'

'Where did you get that idea?'

'It's just always the impression I've had.'

'Punch and Judy shows go all the way back to the nineteenth century, maybe the eighteenth,' I said. 'There weren't cars then.'

'Well, who would want the same job for two centuries? Back then, before cars, he was probably a candlemaker or a blacksmith.'

She is an enchantress. She casts a spell over you, and you find yourself wanting to see the world from her perspective.

That's why I heard myself replying as if Punch were as real as she and I were: 'He's not a candlemaking, blacksmithing sort of guy. That's just not *him*. He wouldn't be fulfilled in that kind of work. Besides, he wears a jester's hat.'

'The hat doesn't prove anything. He could have been a hip sort of blacksmith with a funky style.' She frowned. 'He's always going berserk and beating up Judy, isn't he? So that makes five.'

'Five what?'

'Five angry clowns and no happy ones at all.'

'To be fair,' I said, 'Judy's always beating the crap out of him, too.'

'Is she a clown?'

'I don't know. Maybe.'

'Well, Punch is her husband, so at the very least she's a clown by marriage. So that makes six of them, all angry. This is quite a revelation.'

Elsewhere in town, the transformer blew up. It must have been housed in an underground vault, for the rumble of the muffled blast seemed to translate laterally through the walls of the bank's subcellar.

Instantly the electric lights went off. The farther end of the room glowed with lantern light, while Lorrie and I sat in gloom.

16

On the spacious landing at the top of the stairs, Honker and Crinkles stood in welder's masks, full-body fireproof aprons, and flared-cuff asbestos gloves. With the acetylene torch, Honker cut open the sealed perimeter of the steel door.

Smiling, shaking his head, Punchinello dropped to one knee in front of Lorrie and me. 'You're really Jimmy Tock?'

'James,' I said.

'Son of Rudy Tock.'

'That's right.'

'My father says Rudy Tock saved his life.'

I said, 'Dad might be surprised to hear that.'

'Well, Rudy Tock is a modest man as well as a man of courage,' Punchinello declared. 'But when that phony nurse, with a poisoned dagger in her fist, was sneaking up behind the great Konrad Beezo, my father, he would have been a goner if your dad hadn't shot her dead.'

As I sat in stupefaction, Lorrie said, 'I hadn't heard this part.'

To me, Punchinello said, 'You haven't told her?'

'He's just as modest as his father,' Lorrie told Punchinello.

As the smell of hot steel and molten welding compound spread through the room, Lorrie said, 'What about the phony nurse?'

144

Settling all the way to the floor, cross-legged in front of us, Punchinello said, 'She was dispatched to the hospital to murder the great Konrad Beezo, my mother, and me.'

'Who dispatched her?' Lorrie wondered.

Even in the shadows, I could see a fever of hatred flare in his remarkable eyes as he said through clenched teeth: 'Virgilio Vivacemente.'

Under the pressurized circumstances, I heard his reply — which he delivered with more sibilants than the words actually contained — as just an ear-pleasing series of meaningless syllables.

Apparently Lorrie made no more of it than I did because she said, '*Gesundheit*.'

'The hateful aerialists,' he said acidly. 'The world-famous Flying Vivacementes. Trapeze artists, high-wire walkers, overpaid prima donnas. The most arrogant, most pompous, most conceited, most overrated of them all is Virgilio, the paterfamilias, my mother's father. Virgilio Vivacemente, swine of swines.'

'Now, now,' Lorrie said, 'that's not a nice thing to say about your *grandfather*.'

This admonition triggered a rush of rejection from Punchinello: 'I deny his right to be my grandfather, I refuse him, renounce him, I *repudiate* that old preening pile of crap!'

'That sounds terribly final,' Lorrie said. 'Personally, I'd pretty much always give a grandparent one more chance.'

Leaning toward her, eager to explain, Punchinello said, 'When my mother married my father, her family was shocked, *furious*. That a

145

Flying Vivacemente should marry a clown! To them, aerialists are not merely the royalty of the circus but demigods, while clowns are to them a lower life-form, the scum of the big top.'

'Maybe if clowns were less angry,' Lorrie said, 'other circus people would like them more.'

He seemed not to hear her, so determined was he to make the case against his mother's family.

'When Mother married the great Konrad Beezo, the aerialists first shunned her, then scorned her, then disinherited and disowned her. Because she married for love, married a man they considered to be beneath her class, she was not their daughter anymore, she was *dirt* to them!'

'So,' Lorrie said, 'let me get this straight. They were all in the same circus, your mom living on the clown end of the encampment with your father, the Vivacemente family living in the upper-class neighborhood, on the road together but apart. The tension must have been uncomfortable.'

'You can't know! Every performance, the Vivacementes prayed to Jesus that the great Beezo would break his spine and be paralyzed for life when he was shot out of a cannon, and every performance my father prayed to Jesus that their entire family would fall as one from their high trapezes and die horribly on impact with the center ring.'

Glancing at me, Lorrie said, 'Wouldn't you like to have seen Jesus's face when he read *their* e-mail?'

Breathless with the momentum of his story,

Punchinello said, 'On the night that I was born here in Snow Village, Virgilio hired an assassin who came to the hospital disguised as a nurse.'

'He would know where to find an assassin-for-hire on a moment's notice?' she asked.

Punchinello's voice wavered between the most caustic hatred and abject fear: 'Virgilio Vivacemente, that animated sewage that calls itself a man . . . he is *connected*, he sits at the center of a web of evil. He plucks a strand, and criminals half a world away feel the vibrations and answer them at once. He is a pompous charlatan and a fool . . . but he is also a venomous centipede, quick and vicious, supremely dangerous. He arranged to have us murdered, while he and his devious family were performing — an airtight alibi.'

This was the story of the night of my birth as reimagined by a drunken lunatic.

Punchinello had been nurtured on it instead of on mother's milk and love. Having heard the tale a thousand times, having been raised in an atmosphere of paranoid fantasy and hatred, he believed in this absurd history as idol worshippers once believed in the consciousness and divinity of solid-gold calves and slabs of stone.

'And in the expectant-fathers' lounge,' he said, 'when the hired killer crept up on my father from behind, Rudy Tock entered at that very moment, saw the fiend, drew his pistol, and shot her before she could carry out Virgilio's orders.'

Poor Lois Hanson, young and dedicated, murdered by a psychotic clown, had been transformed by that same clown from a nurse

147

into a combination Ninja assassin and baby-killing agent of King Herod.

Patting my knee to snap me out of a trance of astonishment, Lorrie said, 'Your dad carried a pistol, did he? I thought he was a simple pastry chef.'

'Back then he was just a baker,' I said.

'Wow. What's he packing now that he's become a pastry chef — a submachine gun?'

Compelled to tell his woeful tale, Punchinello impatiently pressed on: 'Saved by Rudy Tock, my father realized that my mother and I, too, were in great danger. He rushed into the maternity ward, located the delivery room, and arrived as the doctor was suffocating me — *me*, an innocent newborn!'

'The *doctor* was a phony, too?' Lorrie asked.

'No. MacDonald was a real doctor, but he had been corrupted by Virgilio Vivacemente, that worm from the bowels of a syphilitic weasel.'

'Weasels can get syphilis?' Lorrie wondered.

He chose to consider this a rhetorical question, and continued: 'Dr. MacDonald was paid an enormous sum, a fortune, to make it appear that my mother died in childbirth and that I was stillborn. Virgilio — may he be cast into hell *tonight* — believed that the oh-so-precious Vivacemente blood had been polluted by the great Konrad Beezo and that my mother and me, being tainted, must be eradicated.'

'What a vile man,' Lorrie said as if she actually believed any of this.

'I *told* you!' Punchinello cried. 'He is lower than a festering canker on Satan's ass.'

148

'That *is* low,' Lorrie agreed.

'Konrad Beezo shot Dr. MacDonald as he tried to suffocate me. My mother, my beautiful mother, was already dead.'

'That's some story,' I said, for I was concerned that I might be seen as one of Virgilio's minions if I drew attention to any of the numerous absurdities in this Nuthouse Theater version of those long-ago events.

'But Virgilio Vivacemente, that spawn of a witch's toilet — '

'Oh, I like that one,' Lorrie interrupted.

' — that animated dog vomit knew how corrupt this town was, how easily he could conceal the truth. He bribed the police, the local journalists. The official story is the outrageous concoction of lies reported in the *Gazette*.'

I managed to sound sympathetic to his version: 'Seems like such a *transparent* concoction when you know the truth.'

He nodded vigorously. 'Rudy Tock must have been frustrated to have silence imposed on him all these years.'

'Dad took no money from Virgilio,' I hastened to assure him, fearing that he might later take a spin across town to gun down Dad, Mom, and Weena. 'Not a penny.'

'No, no, of course he didn't,' Punchinello said, and apologized effusively if I had inferred such an accusation. 'Konrad Beezo, my father, has impressed on me what a courageous man of integrity Rudy Tock is. I know they must have silenced him in some brutal fashion.'

Understanding Punchinello's psychology well

enough to suspect that only wild exaggeration and flamboyant lies had the ring of truth to him, I said, 'They beat Dad once a week for years.'

'This *evil* town.'

'But that alone wouldn't have silenced him,' I added. 'They threatened to kill my Grandma Rowena if he talked.'

'They beat her, too,' said Lorrie.

Whether she intended to be helpful or mischievous, I could not tell.

'But they only beat her once,' I said.

Summoning a credible note of outrage, Lorrie revealed, 'They knocked out her teeth.'

'Only two teeth,' I hastened to correct, concerned that we might overplay the lie.

'They tore off her ear.'

'Not her ear,' I said quickly. 'Her hat.'

'I thought it was her ear,' Lorrie said.

'It was her *hat*,' I insisted in a tone of voice that said *enough is enough*. 'They tore off her hat and stomped on it.'

Punchinello Beezo buried his face in his hands, muffling his voice: 'Tore off an old lady's hat. An old lady's hat. We've all suffered at the hands of these monsters.'

Before Lorrie could claim that Virgilio's henchmen had cut off Grandma Rowena's thumbs, I said, 'Where has your father been these past twenty years?'

Dropping his mask of fingers, he said, 'On the run, always moving, two steps ahead of the law but barely one step ahead of Vivacemente's private detectives. He raised me in a dozen different places. He was forced to give up the big

150

career. The great Konrad Beezo . . . reduced to taking clown positions with smaller shows and demeaning jobs like children's-party clown, car-wash clown, dunk-the-clown in a carnival. Living under false names — Cheeso, Giggles, Clappo, Saucy.'

'Saucy?' Lorrie asked.

Blushing, Punchinello said, 'For a while he was a clown MC in a strip club. He was so humiliated. The men who go to those places, they didn't appreciate his genius. All they cared about were boobs and butts.'

'Philistines,' I sympathized.

'Grieving, despairing, in a constant seething fury, terrified that an agent of the Vivacementes would find him at any moment, he was as good a father as he could be under the circumstances, though Konrad Beezo had lost all capacity to love when he lost my mother.'

'Hollywood could make a great tearjerker out of this,' Lorrie said.

Punchinello agreed. 'My father thinks Charles Bronson should play him.'

'The absolute king of tearjerkers,' Lorrie said.

'My childhood was cold, loveless, but there were compensations. By the time I was ten, for instance, in preparation for the day that I might have to stalk and destroy Virgilio Vivacemente, I'd learned an enormous amount about guns, knives, and poisons.'

'Other ten-year-old boys have nothing useful in their heads,' Lorrie said. 'Just baseball, video games, and collecting Pokémon cards.'

'I didn't get love, but at least he kept me safe

151

from the vicious Virgilio . . . and he did his best to teach me all the craft and the technique that had made him a legend in his profession.'

A hard clang, like the toll of a tuneless bell, pealed through the room.

At the top of the stairs, having torched open the steel door, Honker and Crinkles torqued it from its frame and dropped it on the landing.

'I've got to do my part now,' Punchinello said. His anger and hatred dimmed as if on a rheostat, while warmth and what passed for affection brightened his face. 'But don't worry. When this is done, Jimmy, I'll protect you. I know we can trust you not to rat us out. Nothing will happen to the son of Rudy Tock.'

'What about me?' Lorrie asked.

'You'll have to be killed,' he said without hesitation, his smile fading into a bland robotic expression, his eyes abruptly empty of compassion.

While all evil is insane and while some insanity can be funny from a comfortable distance, few insane people have a sense of humor. If Punchinello had one, it wasn't wry enough to produce a line like that. I knew at once that he was serious. He would release me but kill Lorrie.

As he rose to his feet and moved away, shock briefly silenced me. Then I called out, 'Punch, wait! I've got a secret to tell you.'

He turned to me. His dark emotions became light as rapidly as a flock of birds radically altering its flight path to catch a sudden change of wind. The robot had vanished, and the cold stare. Now he was all glamor and fellowship:

152

good looks, great hair, twinkling best-friend eyes.

'Lorrie,' I told him, 'is my fiancée.'

He paid out one of those million-dollar smiles. 'Fantastic! You make a perfect couple.'

Not sure he got the point, I said, 'We're going to be married in November. We'd like you to come to the wedding if that's possible. But there can't be a wedding if you kill her.'

Smiling, nodding, he considered this as I held my breath. And considered it. Finally he said, 'I want only happiness for the son of Rudy Tock, my father's savior and mine. This will be tricky with Honker and Crinkles, but we'll work it out.'

The 'thank you' came out of me on an explosive exhalation.

He left us and proceeded to the stairs.

However reluctant she might have been to show weakness, Lorrie could not repress a shudder of relief that chattered her teeth.

When Punchinello was out of earshot, she said, 'Let's get one thing straight, baker boy. I'm not naming the first kid either Konrad or Beezo.'

17

Punchinello swung the sledge and broke blocks. Honker cut the rebar as it was uncovered. Crinkles moved the debris to the bottom of the stairs and out of the way. They were remarkably efficient and coordinated for a trio of clowns.

Each time that Punchinello paused to rest, allowing Honker to use the acetylene torch, he stepped as far away from his companion as possible, to avoid the sparks showering off the rebar. And each time he consulted his wristwatch.

Obviously, they had calculated the time that the power company would need to repair the transformer and were confident with their conclusion. They didn't appear to be nervous. Crazy, yes, but not in the least anxious.

My watch was on my left wrist, so I could check it without disturbing Lorrie, who was shackled to my right arm.

Not that she took a nap as we leaned back against the cozy metal filing cabinets. She was wide awake and — I'm sure this will be no surprise to you — talking.

'I wish my father had been a clown,' she said wistfully.

'Why would you want to live with such *anger* every day?'

'My father wouldn't be an angry clown. He's a

154

sweet-tempered man, just irresponsible.'

'He wasn't around much, huh?'

'Always off chasing tornadoes,' she said.

I decided to ask: 'Why?'

'He's a storm chaser. That's how he makes his living, traveling the Midwest in his souped-up Suburban.'

This was 1994. The movie *Twister* would not be released until 1996. I had never imagined chasing tornadoes could be a career.

Assuming that this had to be a put-on, I played along: 'Has he ever caught one?'

'Oh, dozens.'

'What's he do with them?'

'Sells them, of course.'

'So once he's caught a tornado, it's his? He has a right to sell it?'

'Of course. It's copyrighted.'

'So he sees a tornado, and he chases after it, and when he gets close enough — '

'They're fearless,' she said, 'they get right *in* there.'

'So he gets right *in* there and then he — what? — you can't just shoot a tornado as if it were a lion on the veldt.'

'Sure you can,' she said. 'It's pretty much exactly the same.'

This was beginning to seem less like a put-on than like a kind of madness that Punchinello might embrace.

'Would your father sell to me?'

'If you had the money.'

'I don't think I could afford an entire tornado. They must be expensive.'

'Well,' she said, 'it depends on what you want to use it for.'

'I was thinking I could threaten Chicago with it, demand ten million, maybe twenty million, or else.'

She regarded me with clear impatience and with what might have been pity. 'Like I haven't heard *that* lame joke a million times.'

I began to suspect that I was missing something. 'I'm sorry. I want to know. Really.'

'Well, partly he charges by how much video you want to buy — a minute, two minutes, ten.'

Video. Film. Of course. He wasn't out there *lassoing* tornadoes. I had become so accustomed to her cockeyed conversation that when she said her father chased tornadoes, I hadn't been able to believe that she meant exactly what she said.

'If you're a scientist,' she continued, 'he charges you a lower rate than he'd charge a television network or a movie studio.'

'Geez, that really *is* dangerous work.'

'Yeah, but it seems now like even if he *had* been a clown, that wouldn't have been a cakewalk, either.' She sighed. 'I just wish he'd been around more when I was a kid.'

'The tornado season doesn't last all year.'

'No, it doesn't. But he also chases hurricanes.'

'I guess he figures he's already geared up for it.'

'That's exactly what he figures. When one season ends, the other is beginning, so then he's tracking weather reports along the Gulf Coast and the Atlantic seaboard.'

At the top of the stairs, the three larcenous

jackpuddings had opened a hole large enough to afford them entrance to the vault.

With flashlights, Punchinello and Crinkles disappeared through the broken masonry. Honker stayed behind, keeping a watch on us from the landing.

'When the generator didn't come on after the power went off,' Lorrie said, 'maybe an automatic alarm went out over the phone line, and the police are in the bank right now.'

Although I hoped her unshakable optimism would prove justified, I said, 'These guys would've covered that. They seem to have thought of everything.'

She fell silent. So did I.

I suspected that our thoughts were occupied with the same worry: Would Punchinello keep his promise to let us go?

His cohorts were going to be the problem. Neither of them seemed tightly wrapped, but they weren't insane in the way that the son of the great Konrad Beezo was insane. Their feet were more solidly on the ground than his. Honker was motivated by greed, Crinkles by greed and envy. They would not be in the least sentimental about the son of Rudy Tock.

Silence sucked. Worry thrived in it.

I felt better just hearing Lorrie talk, so I tried to start her up again. 'I'm surprised your mother and you didn't travel with your father. If I were married to a storm chaser who was away from home all the time, I'd want to be with him. Well, her.'

'Mom has her own successful business. She

loves it, and if she left L.A., she'd have to give it up.'

'What business is she in?' I asked.

'She's a snake handler.'

This seemed promising.

Lorrie said, 'Having a mother who's a snake handler isn't as much fun as you'd think.'

'Really? I think it would be a delight.'

'Sometimes, yeah. But she worked out of our home. Snakes — they aren't as easy to train as puppies.'

'You can housebreak a snake?'

'I'm not talking potty training. I mean tricks. Dogs love to learn stuff, but snakes get bored easily. When they're bored, they try to slither away, and sometimes they can move *fast*.'

Punchinello and Crinkles came out of the vault, onto the high landing where Honker waited for them. They were carrying boxes which they put down and from which they removed the lids.

Honker whooped when he saw the contents. The three men laughed and high-fived one another.

I figured the boxes contained something more exciting than either snakes or pastries.

18

They brought sixteen boxes out of the vault, carried them down the stairs, and loaded them on the handcart that had previously held the explosives. These were cardboard cartons with removable lids, similar to the kind in which movers pack books.

'Over three million in cash,' Punchinello said when he urged Lorrie and me to our feet and led us to the loot.

I remembered something he'd said earlier: *To all appearances, it's not a major bank, not worth knocking over.*

'There wouldn't be this much cash on hand in most big-city banks,' Punchinello said. 'This is a Treasury Department collection center for what's called 'fatigued currency.' All banks cull worn currency from circulation. Those in a twelve-county district send it here on a weekly basis for retirement, and in return they receive freshly printed bills.'

'Two thirds of this,' Honker said, 'is fatigued currency, and the other million is new and crisp. Don't matter. It'll all spend the same.'

'We just drained some blood out of a capitalist leech,' said Crinkles, but his weak metaphor reflected his physical exhaustion. His explosion of wiry hair had gone limp with sweat.

Consulting his watch, Punchinello said, 'We're going to have to shake ass to beat the fireworks.'

Crinkles and Honker exited the bank's subcellar first, one pulling and the other pushing the handcart. Lorrie and I followed, with Punchinello close behind us.

In Cornelius Snow's secret subterranean corridors, half the fat yellow candles were guttering in the sconces. The quivering flames illuminated the passageway less well than they had done previously. Sinuous figures of light and clawing shadows contested silently on a battle-field of limestone walls and ceiling, like spirits in a war between good and evil.

This was one of those places where you wouldn't be surprised if Leatherface, from *The Texas Chainsaw Massacre*, turned a corner and fired up his trademark weapon. He might have met his match in the killer clowns.

'Tonight,' Punchinello said as we approached the intersection where a right turn would take us to the library, 'I will finally make my father proud, after failing him in everything else.'

'Oh, honey,' Lorrie said, 'don't be so hard on yourself. You seem to be a whiz on all the gun-knife-poison stuff.'

'That wasn't what mattered to him. All he wanted was for me to be a clown, the greatest clown of all time, a star, but I have no talent for it.'

'You're still young,' Lorrie assured him. 'Plenty of time to learn.'

'No, he's right,' Honker said with apparent earnestness. 'The boy has no talent for it. It's a genuine tragedy. His father's *the* Konrad Beezo, so he learned from the greatest, but he can't

160

even do a good pratfall. I love you, Punch, but it's true.'

'No offense, Honker. I faced the truth long ago.'

At the intersection, we turned neither left nor right. I had my bearings now. Straight ahead would be the Snow Mansion, in front of which I had parked my Shelby Z, directly across the town square from the bank.

Crinkles said, 'I've been in the ring with Punch, done the exploding clown-car routine with him, the foot-in-the-bucket hokum, the rain-from-under-the-umbrella skit, even the mouse-in-the-pants number, which *nobody* can screw up —'

'But I screw them all up,' Punchinello said morosely.

'The audience laughs at him,' Honker revealed.

'Aren't they supposed to laugh at a clown?' Lorrie asked.

'This isn't good laughter,' Punchinello said.

'Really, miss, it's mean,' Honker told Lorrie. 'It's laughing *at*, not *with*.'

'How can you tell the difference?' she wondered.

'Oh, lady,' said Crinkles, 'if you're a clown, you *know*.'

As we proceeded under Center Square Park, I was struck by these two men's change in attitude. They seemed less hostile toward us, positively chatty. Lorrie was now *miss* and *lady* instead of *it*.

Maybe the three million dollars put them in a

161

better mood. Maybe Punchinello had spoken to them, explained who I was; they might see us not as hostages any longer but as honorary clowns.

Or perhaps they intended to waste us in the next few minutes and preferred to shoot people with whom they had formed a bond. Trying to think like a psychopath, I asked myself, *What fun can it be, really, to shoot a virtual stranger?*

In a mood to flagellate himself, Punchinello revealed, 'Instead of getting my foot stuck in the bucket, I once got my *head* stuck in the damn thing.'

'That sounds pretty funny,' Lorrie said.

'Not the way *he* did it,' Honker assured her.

'They booed,' Punchinello said. 'They booed me out of the big top that night.'

In front of the handcart, pulling as Honker pushed, wheezing, Crinkles said, 'You're a good boy, Punch. That's what matters. I'd be proud if you were my son.'

'That's nice, Crinkles. That's really nice.'

Honker said, 'What's so great about being a clown, anyway? Even when rubes *are* laughing with you, they're also laughing at you, and the fringe benefits suck.'

At the end of the passageway, we arrived at another formidable oak door with iron banding. Beyond lay the subcellar of the Snow Mansion.

The three men produced powerful flashlights with which they revealed this space. The most salient details were the explosive charges set strategically around the enormous room, at the bases of support columns, detonators already inserted.

I assumed the fourth key point in the town square — the county courthouse — was likewise wired to blow. Quiet little Snow Village was going to be big news.

Bakers are a curious bunch, especially when something in a recipe doesn't seem right, so I asked Punchinello, 'Why flashlights here but candles in the tunnels?'

'Candles were so authentic out there,' he explained. 'I am a connoisseur of the authentic wherever it can be found, which is less often every day in this increasingly plastic, polyester world.'

'I don't understand.'

He regarded me with what might have been pity when he said, 'You don't understand because you're not an artist.'

That didn't clarify anything for me, but we were already moving on to a spacious nineteenth-century dumbwaiter with a folding brass gate instead of a door. Driven by pulleys and counterweights, it had the capacity and leverage to accommodate the handcart with all the boxes of cash.

We climbed four flights of stairs to the kitchen at the back of the house, on the main floor. The flashlight beams flared off white ceramic-tile counters, polished copper, and the beveled glass in French-pane cabinet doors.

I spotted a large polished-granite insert in one tile counter, the perfect surface on which to work dough for pies and tarts. Even if Cornelius had been the greedy, exploiting, blood-sucking, black-hearted, running-dog, drooling, baby-eating pig

163

that Crinkles had described, he could not have been all bad if he'd had a particular liking for pastries.

Honker said, 'Look at this great old iron stove.'

Crinkles said, 'Food tasted *real* coming out of that baby.'

'Because it was *authentic*,' Punchinello said.

Honker put his flashlight on a counter and worked the crank that operated the dumbwaiter cable drive, bringing the proceeds of the bank robbery to the kitchen.

Crinkles set his flashlight aside, too, folded open the brass gate, and pulled the cart into the kitchen.

Punchinello shot Honker in the chest, Crinkles in the back, then pumped two more rounds into each of them as they thrashed, screaming, on the floor.

19

The unexpectedness and ferocity of these murders shocked silence into Lorrie, but I think that I screamed. I can't be sure because the screams of the victims, although brief, were ghastly and louder than whatever half-throttled screech might or might not have escaped me.

I *do* know that I almost threw up. Nausea rolled through me, and a sudden flood of bitter saliva insulated my mouth against the acidic rush from my stomach.

Clenching my teeth, taking deep rapid breaths, I swallowed hard and quelled the nausea largely by opening the tap of anger.

These killings sickened, frightened, and enraged me even more than did the murder of Lionel Davis, our librarian. I cannot say with any certainty why this should be the case.

I was physically closer to these victims than to Lionel, who had collapsed out of sight behind his desk instantly upon being shot. Maybe that was it: a proximity that forced upon me the very smell of death, not just the subtle odor of blood but also the reek of one victim's bowels loosened in his final agonized spasms.

Or perhaps I was so powerfully affected because the killer and his two accomplices had been conversing with evident mutual affection such a short time before he had blown them away.

The victims were men of low character, no question about that, but so was Punchinello. No matter what breed of miserable lost soul you might be, you deserved at least the safe community of your own kind.

Wolves do not kill wolves. Vipers don't attack vipers.

Only in the various communities of human beings must brother be on guard against brother.

That lesson had been so vividly delivered with six bullets that I felt hammered by cold truth. As the shock knocked the wind out of my lungs, another exhalation escaped my spirit, leaving me two kinds of breathless.

Ejecting the magazine that now contained four rounds, inserting a fresh one in the pistol, Punchinello misread our reactions. He grinned, pleased with himself, assuming that we also were pleased with him.

'Surprised you, huh? Bet you thought I'd clip them only when we were loaded in the van and out of town with the money. But trust me, this was the best moment.'

Perhaps if Lorrie and I had never stumbled into this caper, he would have murdered his companions at this very place. Three million dollars is a powerful motivator.

If he could so coldly execute these men who had seemed like uncles to him, however, betraying his promise to us would trouble him no more than jaywalking.

'My wedding gift to you,' he said, as if he had given us a toaster oven or a tea set and would, in due course, expect a handwritten thank-you note.

166

To have called him mad or evil, to have registered revulsion or anger at his ruthlessness, might have invited instant execution. When balancing a bottle of nitroglycerin on the point of a sword, never complicate the task by trying to tap dance.

Although I realized that he might read the truth of our feelings in our silence, I could find neither my voice nor anything to say.

Not for the first time and certainly not for the last, Lorrie saved our skin: 'Would it even begin to be an adequate expression of our gratitude if we named our first son Konrad?'

I thought this offer would strike him as pure sycophancy and that he would be offended by her obvious attempt to manipulate him. I was wrong. She had struck the perfect note.

In the backwash of the flashlight beams, Punchinello's eyes visibly misted with emotion. He bit his lower lip.

'That's so sweet,' he said. 'So kind. I can't think of anything that would please my father, the great Konrad Beezo, more than to know that the grandson of Rudy Tock was named after him.'

Lorrie greeted this response with a radiant smile that Leonardo da Vinci would have given his left foot to paint. 'Then all that remains to make me and Jimmy happy is if you would agree to be our baby's godfather.'

When in the presence of a prince of madness, safety lies, if anywhere, in presenting yourself as a member of that same royal family.

More lip biting preceded his emotional reply:

'I understand the obligation. I'll be little Konrad's protector. Anyone who ever wrongs him will answer to me.'

'You can't know,' Lorrie told him, 'what comfort that gives to a mother.'

Not as though issuing an order, more as though he were a friend seeking help, he asked us to take the handcart through the rambling historical mansion to the front door. I pushed the cart, and Lorrie picked out the route with a flashlight.

Punchinello followed us with a flashlight in one hand and the pistol in the other.

I didn't want him behind my back. I had no choice. If I had hesitated, he might have accelerated through one of his hairpin mood turns.

'You know what's ironic?' he asked.

'Yeah — that I was worried about going to the *dry cleaner.*'

He had no interest in *my* irony: 'What's ironic is that as bad as I am at clowncraft, I'm that *good* at walking a wire, and I'm *at home* on a trapeze.'

Lorrie said, 'You inherited your mother's talent.'

'And secretly took some training,' he admitted as we passed from the kitchen through a butler's pantry into a grand dining room. 'If I could have put half the time into those instructions as I put into clowning, I'd have been a star.'

'You're still young,' Lorrie said. 'It's not too late.'

'No. Even if I sold my soul for the chance, I

could not become one of *them*, never an aerialist. Virgilio Vivacemente is the living god of aerialists and knows them all. If I performed, he would hear of me. He would come to see me. He would recognize my mother's face in mine, and he would kill me.'

'Maybe he'd embrace you,' Lorrie suggested.

'Never. To him, my blood is tainted. He would kill me, dismember me, marinate my remains in gasoline, burn them, urinate on the ashes, put the wet ashes in a bucket, take them to a farm, and stir them into the muddy wallow in the corner of a pigpen.'

'Maybe you're overestimating his villainy,' I suggested as we followed a narrow hall to a wider one.

'He's done that very thing before,' Punchinello assured me. 'He is an arrogant *beast*. He claims that he is descended from Caligula, the mad emperor of ancient Rome.'

Having seen Punchinello in action, I couldn't argue against the proposition that he might come from such lineage.

He sighed. 'That's why I've decided to throw my life away in a frenzy of vengeance. Might as well die if I can't fly.'

A grand staircase swept up into gloom from the lavishly detailed foyer. An inlaid black granite and terra-cotta floor depicted toga-clad figures and mythological beings reminiscent of images on ancient Grecian urns.

Our sweeping flashlight beams imparted an illusion of movement to the scenes and the processions underfoot, as if these populations

169

lived in a two-dimensional world as real as our realm of three.

A brief dizziness spiraled through me, related less to the patterned floor, I suspect, than to a further delayed reaction to the murders of the two men in the kitchen. In addition, I felt unsteady because I recalled my premonition that Lorrie would be shot, and I wondered if this might be the place where the trigger would be pulled.

My mouth was dry. My hands were clammy. I wanted a good éclair.

Lorrie gripped my right hand, held it tight. Her elegant fingers were icy.

At one of the windows that flanked the pair of tall entry doors, Punchinello extinguished his flashlight, parted the brocade drapery, and scanned the night. 'No lights anywhere around the square.'

The detonators in the subcellar of the mansion were ticking toward zero. I wondered how long until everything under us erupted in a blast wave and fire.

As if reading my mind, Punchinello turned from the window and said, 'We could use more than seven minutes, but that's all we have.'

He switched on his light, put it on the floor, fished a handcuff key from a coat pocket, and approached me. 'I'd like you to roll the handcart down the front steps and across the sidewalk to the back of a yellow van parked at the curb.'

'Sure, no problem,' I said, and cringed at the submissive note in my voice. But I certainly wasn't going to say, *Do it yourself, clown boy.*

As he keyed open my cuff, I considered trying to wrench the pistol out of his hand. Something about his body language told me that he expected such a move and would counter it brutally and effectively.

If Lorrie was shot, an ill-considered action on my part might be the thing that precipitated her death. Prudence seemed wise, and I didn't go for the gun.

I expected him to release her, as well, but in a magician-quick maneuver, he cuffed himself to her and switched the pistol from his right hand to his left. He held the weapon with such assurance that he appeared to be ambidextrous.

20

He had cuffed himself to Lorrie.

I saw it happen, yet I needed a moment to accept the reality. I didn't want to believe that our hopes for survival had so abruptly and so drastically diminished.

Cuffed together, Lorrie and I might have tried to break for freedom once we were in the open air. Now she was his hostage not only for the purpose of holding the police at bay if they should stumble upon us but also to keep me docile.

And as for me . . . Punchinello had decided that if his situation soured in any way, I would be expendable.

To question why he cuffed himself to Lorrie would be to question the sincerity of his promise to spare us. Then things might get ugly sooner rather than later.

Consequently, neither Lorrie nor I indicated that his behavior struck us as odd. This required us to appear as naive as newborns.

We were grinning as if we were, gosh, just having the best time.

Her smile was fixed like the smiles on Miss America contestants during the personality competition when the host asked a particularly tricky question: *Miss Ohio, if you saw a puppy and a kitten playing on railroad tracks, and a train was coming, and you had only time enough to save one or the other, which would you let die a horrible death — the puppy or the kitten?*

My face seemed to have been starched, and my lips felt as if they had been stretched on a clothesline and pinned at both ends: another Miss Ohio smile.

I opened one of the two front doors and pushed the handcart onto the porch.

Cool evergreen-scented air chilled the sweat on the back of my neck.

The moon had not yet risen. A skin of clouds let through only prickles of starlight.

No lights glowed in the park, and the streetlamps had failed. Around the square, the buildings stood dark and silent.

The enormous larches between the sidewalk and the curb screened much of the town from view. Nevertheless, between their branches I could see flashing yellow lights and power-company repair trucks on Alpine Avenue, half a block north of the square.

No traffic in the street at the moment. No pedestrians on the sidewalk as far as the overhanging trees would allow me to see.

Punchinello and Lorrie followed me onto the porch.

He had left his flashlight inside. In these layered shadows, I could not clearly see his face.

That was probably for the good. If I had been able to see him better, I'd have read one crazy intention or another in his face — and wouldn't have known what to do about it.

I wished I could more clearly see Lorrie. I could tell that her smile had faded. So had mine.

173

The ten steps led between limestone balusters to the public sidewalk. They looked steep.

I said, 'I'll have to carry the boxes one or two at a time to the van. The bottom of the handcart's going to get hung up on these steps.'

'No, it won't,' he assured me. 'That's why we bought one with big tires. It'll roll down smooth and easy.'

'But — '

'Less than six minutes,' he warned. 'Don't let the cart get away from you and spill the money. That would be . . . stupid.'

His admonition was a taunt to the lummox in me, virtually guaranteeing that I would wind up flat on my back on the sidewalk with three million dollars tumbled atop me.

I got in front of the handcart and pulled it onto the steps, letting gravity drive it, using my body to prevent it from gaining momentum. Miraculously, I reached the sidewalk without catastrophe.

Punchinello and Lorrie descended after me.

I didn't know whether to pray that pedestrians would appear or that we would be left alone. He was so delicately balanced that even an innocent encounter might lead to more murder.

Where was a judiciously aimed falling safe when you really, really needed one?

I pushed the cart to the back of the van.

Just eight feet away stood my Dodge Daytona Shelby Z. A sweet car — and vulnerable.

'The van doors are unlocked,' he said, following me, stopping short of the curb. 'Load the boxes in the back. And hurry.'

174

Although I understood everything about the effects of yeast and about the chemical process by which eggs raised a soufflé, I had neglected my studies of high explosives. I didn't know exactly what would happen when the boom plastic went off.

Yanking open the doors on the back of the van, I imagined the entire front of Snow Mansion collapsing on us, burying us under tons of brick and limestone.

Moving boxes from the handcart to the cargo hold of the van, I also imagined the force of the blast tearing us limb from limb in an instant.

Six boxes, eight boxes, ten boxes . . .

In my mind's eye, I saw myself being battered and lacerated and set afire by a storm of blast-propelled debris, blinded and blood-soaked, running along the street with my hair ablaze.

Thank you, Grandma Rowena.

As I shoved the last of the boxes into the van, Punchinello said, 'Leave those doors open for now. We'll ride in back with the money. You can drive.'

When we got wherever we were going and I parked the van, he would be behind me, in a perfect position to shoot me in the back of the head. I knew he would do it.

The way this guy was behaving, we were going to have to find someone else to be little Konrad's godfather.

'Catch,' he said.

When I realized he was going to throw the keys to me, I cried out, 'No! Wait. If I miss them, they might go down the street drain, and then we're screwed.'

Between us lay a four-foot-by-three-foot steel grille with inch-wide gaps between the bars. Walking across it I caught the faint scent of brackish water below.

He held out the keys, and even though the pistol wasn't pointed at me as I approached him, I had the feeling that he would shoot me when I reached for them.

Most likely, this apprehension arose from my queasy ambiguity about what I intended to do. As I took the keys with my left hand, I swung my right fist in a low-origin arc hard into his crotch, driving the nail file deep and no doubt pinning the parts of his male package into an unprecedented arrangement.

In the dark, I could not see the blood drain from his face, but I could almost hear it.

Surprising myself with a ruthlessness that I had never exhibited — or required — in a bakery kitchen, I twisted the nail file.

Dimly I recalled that Jack had done something like this to the giant at the foot of the beanstalk, except that he used a pitchfork.

Letting go of the shiv, I grabbed at once for the pistol.

As he had taken in the nail file, he had let out his breath with a high-pitched sound, half wheeze, half squeal. The file stayed in him, the breath stayed out, and he made dry strangulation sounds as he tried to inhale.

I expected him to drop the gun or to have had his grip weakened by shock, but he clutched the weapon with grim determination.

As she twisted her body and shuffled her feet in a graceless dance, trying to stay out of the line of fire, Lorrie hit Punchinello in the face with her free hand, hit him again, again, grunting with each blow, exhibiting the machine determination of a figure swinging a hammer at a bell in an animated Swiss clock.

We fought over the pistol, my two hands prying at his one. Muzzle flashed, shot cracked, and a slug ricocheted off the sidewalk, spraying chips of concrete that tattooed my face, clanged off metal, maybe the van, maybe my sweet Shelby Z.

I almost had the weapon, but he managed to squeeze the trigger again, and in spite of all that my father had done for his father, the ingrate shot me. Twice.

21

If an ax had cleaved my leg, the pain could not have been worse than this.

In movies, the hero takes a bullet and keeps on coming, for God, for love of country, for the sake of his woman. A bullet might make him wince, but often it just pisses him off and drives him to even greater heroics.

As I said earlier, since childhood I had thought of myself as having the potential to be a hero if put to the test. Now I realized that I lacked at least one essential requirement for the job: a really high pain threshold.

Screaming, I fell off the curb and onto the pavement, between the van and the Shelby Z. My head rattled the drainage grille, or maybe the grille rattled my head.

I was terrified that he would shoot me in the face — until I realized I had possession of the pistol.

Reaching between his legs, he tried to pull the nail file out of his crotch, but merely touching it caused him to squeal more pitifully than a pig catching sight of the butcher's blade. Agony knocked him to his knees. Then he went all the way down, onto his side, pulling Lorrie with him.

We lay there screaming, Punchinello and I, like two teenage girls who had just found a severed head in an old Jamie Lee Curtis movie.

I heard Lorrie shouting my name and something about time.

Unable to focus through the pain, undoubtedly slightly delirious, I found myself imagining what she might be saying:

Time waits for no man. Time and the river, how quickly they go by. Time bears away all things.

Even in my condition, I quickly realized that she would not be waxing philosophical at a moment like this. When I recognized the note of urgency in her voice, I also knew the essence of what she must be saying: *Time is running out. The bombs!*

The pain in my left leg churned with fiery exuberance, and I was surprised to see that flames weren't eating through the flesh. I could also feel something bristling in the meat of it, perhaps shattered bones. I could not, however, move it.

How odd to be terrified but at the same time weary to the point of sleepiness. Wracked by pain yet capable of taking a nap. Pillowy now, the pavement. Bedding with a faint fragrance of tar.

This tempting slumber was, of course, the sleep of death, which I recognized and resisted.

Making no attempt to stand, dragging the useless leg after me as if I were Sisyphus and it were my stone, I scaled the towering curb. I crawled to Lorrie.

Lying on his side, one arm behind him, Punchinello remained cuffed to Lorrie. With his free hand, he plucked the nail file out of his crotch — and promptly threw up on himself.

I was gratified by this evidence that he felt worse than I did.

During the past few hours, I had come to believe in the reality of Evil for the first time in my twenty years. I believed suddenly not merely in evil as a necessary antagonist in movies and books — bad guys and boogeymen — not merely in evil as the consequence of parental rejection or parental indulgence or social injustice, but in Evil as a presence alive in the world.

It is a presence that tirelessly romances and beguiles, but it cannot consummate a relationship until invited to do so. Punchinello might have been raised by an evil man, might have been instructed in the linguistics of evil, but ultimately the choice of how to live was his alone.

My gratification at the sight of his suffering might have been unwholesome, corrupting, but I don't believe that it was itself a small evil. At the time it felt — and even now feels — like righteous satisfaction prompted by this proof that evil has a price to extract from those who embrace it and that resistance to it, while costly, might have a lower cost than acquiescence.

Funny how so much windy philosophy could be inspired by a little puke.

One man's regurgitation, even if it might give rise in him to some remorse, couldn't stop the ticking of a single detonator. We must have had at most a minute or two until the works of Cornelius Rutherford Snow fell into ruin nearly as complete as the empire of Ozymandias.

'Gimme,' Lorrie said.

180

'What?'

'The gun.'

I hadn't realized I still had the pistol.

'Why?' I asked.

'I don't know which pocket he put the key in.'

We didn't have time to search the pockets in his pants, coat, and shirt. Considering the vomit, we didn't have the inclination, either.

I failed to understand what the gun had to do with the handcuff key. I worried that she would hurt herself, so I decided not to give her the pistol.

Then I realized that she had already taken it out of my hand.

'You've already taken it out of my hand,' I said, and my voice sounded slurred.

'Better turn your face away,' she warned, 'there might be shrapnel.'

'I think I like shrapnel,' I replied, unable to remember what the word meant.

She fumbled with the gun, squinting at it in the dark.

'I don't think I hurt as much as I used to hurt,' I told her. 'Now I'm mostly cold.'

'That's bad,' she said worriedly.

'I've been cold before,' I assured her.

Punchinello groaned, shuddered, and began to upchuck on himself again.

'Have we been drinking?' I wondered.

'Turn your face away,' Lorrie repeated, this time sharply.

'Don't talk so mean to me. I love you.'

'Yeah, well, we always hurt the one we love,'

181

she said, grabbing a fistful of my hair and *pulling* my face away from the handcuffs.

'That's sad,' I said, meaning that we always hurt the one we love, and then I discovered I was lying on the sidewalk and must have fallen. 'Lummox.'

A gun boomed, and I didn't realize until later that she'd put the muzzle of the pistol against the links of chain that connected one handcuff to the other, and had freed herself from Punchinello with that shot.

'On your feet,' she urged me. 'Come on, come on.'

'I'll lay here till I'm sober.'

'You'll lay there till you're dead.'

'No, that's too long.'

She cajoled me, she cursed me, she commanded me, pushed and yanked and pulled, and the next thing I knew, I was on my feet, leaning on her, moving between the van and my Shelby Z, into the street, away from the mansion.

'How is your leg?'

'What leg?'

'I mean what about the pain?'

'I think we left him back there on the sidewalk.'

'God, you're a hulk,' she said.

'I'm a little husky, that's all.'

'It's all right, it's okay. Lean on me. Come on.'

In a voice now as thick as English custard, I said, 'Are we going to the park?'

'That's right.'

'Picnic?'

'That's right. And we're late, let's hurry.'

I peered past Lorrie, toward the sound of an approaching engine. Headlights washed across us. An array of revolving blue and yellow beacons on the roof indicated that it was either a police cruiser or an intergalactic vehicle.

The car slid to a halt, doors flew open, and two men got out about fifteen feet away. One of them said, 'What's going on here?'

'This man is shot,' Lorrie told them. I wondered who she was talking about. Before I could ask she said, 'We need an ambulance.'

The cops approached warily. 'Where's the shooter?'

'Over there on the sidewalk. He's hurt, doesn't have a gun anymore.' When the officers moved toward Punchinello, Lorrie shouted, 'No! Stay back. The building's going to blow.'

In my condition, her warning was mystifying; it didn't seem to make sense to the police, either. They hurried toward Punchinello, who lay half revealed in the backwash of the squad-car lights.

With single-minded determination, Lorrie kept me moving toward the park.

'Too cold for a picnic,' I said. 'So cold.'

'We'll build a bonfire. Just *move*.'

My teeth chattered, and words shivered out of me: 'Will there be p-p-potato salad?'

'Yes. Plenty of potato salad.'

'The p-p-pickly kind?'

'Yes, that's right, keep moving.'

'I hate the p-pickly k-k-kind.'

'We have both kinds.'

183

Another curb almost defeated me. The sidewalk looked soft and inviting.

'It's too c-c-cold for a picnic,' I said, 'and too d-dark.'

An instant later it was also too *noisy*.

22

The four virtually simultaneous explosions — mansion, bank, courthouse, library — purged confusion from my mind. For a moment I could think too clearly.

As the ground rocked, as the evergreens in the park swayed and shook off dead needles, as the initial blasts gave way to the mad-gods-bowling clatter of stone structures collapsing, I remembered being shot twice and not enjoying it either time.

The pain didn't return with the memory, and now I was clearheaded enough to understand that being unable to feel my leg *at all* was worse than the fiery agony that I had first endured. The utter lack of feeling suggested that the leg was damaged beyond repair, already dead, amputated, gone.

Exhausted, I stumbled when the ground rocked. Lorrie helped me lower myself to the grass, where I leaned against the trunk of a sycamore, even as the final blasts quaked through the town square.

With the memory of being shot came a nightmare montage of the three murders that Punchinello had committed in front of me. These bloody images were more vivid in recollection than at the time of the killings, perhaps because then I had been so concerned with my own and Lorrie's survival that I dared

185

not consciously consider the hideous details for fear of being paralyzed by terror.

Sickened, I tried to repress those memories, but they tormented me. All my life, I had been comfortable inside my own head; but now that interior landscape was bloodstained and darkened by an ominous eclipse.

When I wished for the comforting return of the haze to which I had earlier succumbed, it came immediately in a great gray wave — drowning the lights of the police car in the street, then seething through the trees as might rich billows of wind-driven fog, which was curious on a windless night.

Dust.

The turbulent mass proved to be neither fog nor mental haze but thick clouds of fine dust expelled from Cornelius Snow's mansion as it crashed down from imposing edifice to shattered ruin. Pulverized limestone, powdered brick, crushed plaster: In a thousand scents and flavors, dust rolled over us.

Pale as it approached, the cloud brought darkness when it fell upon us, a gloom deeper than the lightless night itself. I eased away from the sycamore and rolled onto my right side, closing my eyes, pulling my shirt up to mask my nose and mouth against the choking dust.

I reached down with one hand to touch my numb left leg, to reassure myself that it was still there. My hand came away slick with warm blood.

In what seemed but an instant, dust caked the

blood and formed a grisly plaster around my hand.

At first I thought that Lorrie must have dropped to the grass beside me, covering her face against the suffocating pall. Then I heard her voice above me and knew that she remained on her feet. She called for an ambulance, coughing, wheezing, ceaselessly shouting for help, help, a man's been shot.

I wanted to reach for her, pull her down, but I had no strength to raise my arm. A fearsome weakness had overcome me.

The comforting mental haze that I had wished for now returned. Frantic about Lorrie, I no longer wanted this escape, but resistance was impossible.

My thoughts wove an incoherent narrative of hidden doors, candlelit tunnels, dead faces, gunshots, snake handlers, tornadoes, clowns . . . Soon I must have been unconscious and dreaming, for I had become an aerialist, walking the high wire, using a long pole for balance, progressing tentatively and precariously toward a platform on which Lorrie waited.

When I glanced behind to see what distance I'd already traveled, I found Punchinello Beezo in pursuit of me. He carried a balancing pole, too, but each end of it terminated in a wickedly sharp blade. He was smiling, confident, and faster than I was. He said, '*I could have been a star, Jimmy Tock. I could have been a star.*'

Occasionally I drifted up from big-top dreams and from secret passageways in my soul, and realized that I was being moved. Carried in a litter. Then strapped on a gurney in a rollicking ambulance.

When I tried to open my eyes but could not, I told myself that they were simply glued shut by dust and tears. I knew this to be a lie, but I took comfort from it, anyway.

Eventually someone said, 'The leg can't be saved.'

I didn't know if he was a person in a dream or a real doctor, but I responded in a voice that sounded like me if I had been a frog prince: 'I need both legs. I'm a storm chaser.'

Thereafter, I sank uncounted fathoms into an abyss where the dreams were too real to be dreams, where mysterious behemoths stood guard over me but always at the periphery of vision, and where the air smelled of cherry tart flambé.

23

Six weeks later, Lorrie Lynn Hicks came to dinner. She looked prettier than *pommes à la Sévillane*. Never at any meal previously had I spent so little time admiring the food on my plate.

Candles in ruby-red, cut-crystal chimneys cast soft trembling geometrics on the silk moiré walls and shimmering amber circles on the coffered mahogany ceiling.

She outshone the candlelight.

Over the appetizer — sesame-baked crab — my father said, 'I've never known anyone whose mother is a snake handler.'

'A lot of women take it up because it sounds fun,' Lorrie said, 'but it's a lot harder than they think. Eventually they give it up.'

'But surely it's still fun,' my mother said.

'Oh, yes! Snakes are great. They don't bark, claw the furniture, and you'll never have a rodent problem.'

'And you don't have to walk them,' Mom added.

'Well, you can if you want, but it freaks out the neighbors. Maddy, this crab is fabulous.'

'How does a snake handler make money from it?' Dad wondered.

'Mom has developed three primary revenue streams. She provides a variety of snakes to movie and TV productions. There for a while, it seemed every music video used snakes.'

My mother was delighted: 'So she rents out the snakes.'

Dad asked, 'By the hour, the day, the week?'

'Usually by the day. Even a snake-heavy movie only needs them for maybe four, five days.'

'There isn't a movie these days that wouldn't be improved by a lively bunch of snakes,' Grandma Rowena declared. 'Especially that last Dustin Hoffman thing.'

'People who rent snakes by the hour,' Lorrie said somberly, 'are for the most part not reputable.'

This intrigued me. 'I've never heard of a disreputable snake-rental company.'

'Oh, they're around, all right.' Lorrie grimaced. 'Very tacky outfits. They rent to individuals by the hour, no questions asked.'

Dad, Mom, and I exchanged baffled looks, but Weena knew the score: 'For erotic purposes.'

Dad said, 'Yuch,' and Mom said, 'Creepy,' and I said, 'Grandma, sometimes you scare me.'

Lorrie wanted to make one thing clear: 'My mother *never* rents snakes to individuals.'

'When I was a child,' Weena said, 'Little Ned Yarnel, the boy next door, was bit by a rattlesnake.'

'A free snake or a rented one?' Dad asked.

'Free. Little Ned didn't die but he got gangrene. They had to amputate — first a thumb and finger, then everything to the wrist.'

'Jimmy, dear,' Mom said, 'I'm so glad we didn't have to cut your leg off.'

'Me too.'

Dad raised his wineglass. 'Let's drink to our Jimmy not being an amputee.'

After the toast, Weena said, 'Little Ned grew up to be the only one-handed bow-and-arrow champion ever to compete in the Olympics.'

Amazed, Lorrie said, 'That isn't possible.'

'Dear girl,' Weena said, 'if you think there were lots of one-handed Olympic bow-and-arrow champions, you can't know much about the sport.'

'Of course, he didn't win gold,' Dad clarified.

'A silver medal,' Grandma admitted. 'But he'd have won the gold if he'd had two eyes.'

Putting down her fork to punctuate her astonishment, Lorrie said, 'He was a cyclops?'

'No,' my mother said, 'he had two eyes. He just couldn't see out of one of them.'

'But don't you need depth perception to be good at something like the bow and arrow?' Lorrie wondered.

Proud of her childhood friend, Weena said, 'Little Ned had something better than depth perception. He had spunk. Nothing could keep Little Ned down.'

Picking up her fork again, taking the last morsel of crab from her plate, Lorrie said, 'I'm fascinated to know if Little Ned might also have been a dwarf.'

'What a peculiar but somehow charming idea,' my mother said.

'Just peculiar in my book,' Grandma disagreed. 'Little Ned was six feet tall by his eleventh birthday, wound up six feet four — a big lug like our Jimmy.'

No matter what my grandmother thinks, I am inches shorter than Little Ned. I probably weigh a lot less than he did, too — except if the comparison is limited to hand weight, in which case I would have a considerable advantage over him.

Comparing my own two legs, my left weighs more than the right by virtue of the two steel plates and the numerous screws that now hold the femur together, plus the single steel plate in the tibia. The leg required considerable vascular surgery, as well, but that didn't add an ounce.

At dinner there in early November 1994, the wound drains were no longer in place, which improved the way I smelled, but I still wore a fiberglass cast. I sat at the end of the table, stiff leg thrust out to one side, as if I hoped to trip Grandma.

Weena finished her crab, smacked her lips in the flamboyant manner that she believes is a right of anyone her age, and said, 'You mentioned your mama makes snake money three ways.'

Lorrie patted her wonderfully full lips on her napkin. 'She also milks rattlesnakes.'

Appalled, my dad said, 'What kind of supermarket from hell would sell such stuff?'

'We had a cute little milk snake lived with us for a while,' Mom told Lorrie. 'His name was Earl, but I always thought Bernard would suit him better.'

'He looked like a Ralph to me,' Grandma Rowena disagreed.

'Earl was a male,' Mom said, 'or at least we

always assumed so. If he'd been a female, should we have milked him? After all, if you don't milk a cow, it can end up in terrible distress.'

The evening was off to a splendid start. I hardly had to say anything.

I looked at Dad. He smiled at me. I could tell he was having a wonderful time.

'There's not actually milk in a milk snake,' Lorrie said. 'None in a rattler, either. What my mother milks out of them is venom. She gets a grip behind the head and massages the poison glands. The venom squirts out of the fangs, which are hypodermic in rattlers, and into a collection beaker.'

Because he considers the dining room to be a temple, Dad rarely puts an elbow on the table. He put one on it now, and rested his chin in his hand, as though settling in for a long listen. 'So your mother has a rattlesnake ranch.'

'*Ranch* is too grand a word, Rudy. So is *farm*, for that matter. It's more of a garden with just the one crop.'

My grandmother let out a satisfying belch and said, 'Who does she sell this venom to — assassins, or maybe those pygmies with blowguns?'

'Drug companies need it to make antivenin. And it has a few other medical uses.'

'You mentioned a third revenue stream,' my father reminded her.

'My mother's a real ham,' Lorrie said with affection. 'So she takes party bookings. She has this fantastic act with the snakes.'

'Who would book such an act?' my father wondered.

'Who *wouldn't?*' my mother asked, probably already thinking ahead to their anniversary party and Weena's birthday.

'Exactly,' Lorrie said. 'All kinds of corporate affairs like retirement parties, Christmas parties. Bar mitzvahs, the American Library Association, you name it.'

Mom and Dad removed the appetizer plates. They served bowls of chicken corn soup with cheddar crisps on the side.

'I love corn,' Grandma said, 'but it gives me flatulence. I used to care, but I'm not obliged to anymore. The golden years rock.'

Raising a toast not with wine but with his first spoonful of soup, Dad said, 'Here's hoping that bugger won't weasel out of a trial. Here's hoping he fries.'

The bugger, of course, was Punchinello Beezo. The following morning, he would attend a preliminary hearing to determine if he was mentally fit to stand trial.

He had gunned down Lionel Davis, Honker, Crinkles, and Byron Metcalf, a longtime leader of the town's preservation society, whom he had tortured to obtain information about access to the passageways under the town square.

In addition, the explosions had killed two members of a cleaning crew at work in the courthouse and a hobo assessing the treasures of a Dumpster behind the library. Martha Faye Jeeter, an elderly widow living in an apartment in the building next door to the courthouse, had also perished.

Eight is a heavy toll in human life, but considering the extent of the destruction, scores of victims might have been expected. Lives were spared because the explosions were two stories underground, and some of the force vented into the subterranean tunnels. The library, the mansion, and the bank imploded, crashing down into their cellars and subcellars as though brought to ruin by the precise formulations of a demolitions expert.

The courthouse largely imploded, as well, but its bell tower toppled into the building next door, bringing sudden fury into the quiet life of the Widow Jeeter.

Her two cats also were squashed. Some citizens of Snow Village seemed to be angrier about this outrage than about either the human or the architectural losses.

Punchinello had expressed regret that hundreds hadn't died. He told police that if he could do it all over again, he would add packages of napalm to ensure a firestorm that would devastate many square blocks.

Portions of the street and the park subsided into Cornelius Snow's secret passageways. My fine black sporty coupe with yellow racing stripes had been swallowed by one of these sinkholes.

Remember when I said that I hadn't met a young woman whom I could love as much as I loved that seven-year-old Dodge Daytona Shelby Z? Funny thing — I didn't mourn the loss of it, not for a minute.

Although Lorrie would have looked good in

the Shelby Z, she would look even better in a 1986 Pontiac Trans Am, not black but maybe red or silver, a color to match her exuberant spirit. Or a 1988 Chevy Camaro IROC-Z convertible.

My problem, however, was one that any young baker on a bread-and-cake wage could appreciate. There were men in the world who, upon getting one look at her, would buy Lorrie a Rolls-Royce for every day of the week. And not all of them would look like trolls.

'You don't think they'll send the bugger to some asylum and let him off the hook?' Dad asked.

'He doesn't want that himself,' I said. 'He's saying he knew exactly what he was doing, and it was all about revenge.'

'He's crazy in his way,' Lorrie said. 'But he knows right from wrong as sure as I do. Maddy, Rudy — this soup is fantastic even if it causes flatulence.'

Grandma Rowena had a relevant story: 'Hector Sanchez, lived over near Bright Falls, killed himself with a fart.'

The rationalist in my father was stirred by Grandma's assertion. 'Weena, that's just not possible.'

'Hector worked in the hair-oil industry,' Grandma recalled. 'He had beautiful hair but not much common sense. This was fifty-six years ago, back in '38, before the war.'

'Even *then* it wasn't possible,' Dad declared.

'You weren't even born yet, Maddy, neither, so don't tell me what wasn't possible. I saw it with my own eyes.'

'You've never mentioned this before,' Dad said, suspecting a fabrication but not ready to make the accusation. 'Jimmy, has she ever mentioned this before?'

'No,' I confirmed. 'I remember Grandma telling us about a Harry Ramirez who boiled himself to death, but not this Hector Sanchez.'

'Maddy, do you remember ever hearing this before?'

'No, honey,' my mother admitted, 'but what does that prove? I'm sure it just slipped Mother's mind until now.'

'Seeing a man fart himself to death doesn't just slip your mind.' To Lorrie, Dad said, 'I'm sorry, dear. Our table talk isn't usually this low.'

'You don't know what low is until you're eating canned ravioli while listening to stories about snake cankers and the smell of a tornado that's sucked up the contents of a sewage-processing plant.'

Impatiently, Grandma said, 'Hector Sanchez never slipped my mind. This is just the first time we've been in a conversation where the subject came up naturally.'

'What was Hector's job in the hair-oil industry?' Mom asked.

'If he blew himself up with a fart fifty-six years ago,' Dad said, 'who cares what he did in hair oil?'

'I'm sure his family cared,' Weena said. 'It put food on their table. Anyway, he didn't blow himself up. That isn't possible.'

'Case closed,' my father said triumphantly.

'I turned twenty-one, and my husband, Sam,

took me to a tavern for the first time. We were in a booth. Hector was on a bar stool. I ordered a Pink Squirrel. Do you like Pink Squirrels, Lorrie?'

Lorrie said yes, and Dad said, 'You're driving me so crazy with this, I'm seeing pink squirrels right now, crawling on the ceiling.'

'Hector was drinking beer with lime slices, sitting just one stool away from this bodybuilder. He had biceps the size of hams and the prettiest tattoo of a snarling bulldog on his arm.'

'Hector or the bodybuilder?' my mother asked.

'Hector didn't have any tattoos, at least not in any place that was visible. But he had a pet monkey named Pancho.'

My mother said, 'Was Pancho also drinking beer?'

'The monkey wasn't there.'

'Where was he?'

'Home with the family. He wasn't one of those monkeys that likes running around to gin mills. Pancho was family oriented.'

Mom patted Dad on the shoulder. 'That's my kind of monkey.'

'So Hector, sitting on the bar stool, he cuts a ripe one — '

'At last,' my father said.

' — and the bodybuilder takes offense at the smell. Hector tells him to buzz off, though he doesn't say *buzz*.'

'How big was this Hector?' Lorrie wondered.

'I'd say about five feet seven, a hundred thirty pounds.'

'He sure could have used the monkey for

backup,' Lorrie said.

'So the bodybuilder punches him twice, grabs him by the hair, and smashes his face into the bar three times. Hector falls off the stool, dead, and the bodybuilder orders another boilermaker spiked with two fresh eggs for the protein.'

My father glowed with vindication. 'So I was right. Passing gas didn't kill him. The drunken *bodybuilder* killed him.'

'If he hadn't farted, he wouldn't have been killed,' Grandma insisted.

Finishing her soup, Lorrie said, 'So how did Harry Ramirez boil himself to death?'

Next came the entree — roast chicken with chestnut-and-sausage stuffing, polenta, and snap peas — followed by celery-root salad.

When, past midnight, Dad rolled in the dessert cart from the kitchen, Lorrie couldn't make up her mind between a tangerine cream tart and a slice of genoise; she took both. She sampled the *coeur à la crème*, the *budino di ricotta*, and the *Mont Blanc aux marrons*, then chose four items from the three-tiered cookie tray.

She ate a *springerle* cookie with intense concentration until she realized that everyone at the table had fallen silent. When she looked up, all of us were smiling at her.

'Delicious,' she said.

We smiled.

'What?' she asked.

'Nothing, dear,' my mother said. 'It just seems like you've always been here.'

Lorrie left at one in the morning, which was

early for the Tock family but late for her. At nine in the morning, she had to teach two angry Hungarians to dance.

The angry Hungarians are a story unto themselves. I'll save them for another book if I live to write one.

At the front door, as I stood with the aid of a walker, Lorrie kissed me. This would have been the perfect end to the evening . . . if she hadn't kissed me just on the cheek and if my entire family had not been two feet away, watching and smiling and, in one case, indulging in too much lip-smacking.

Then she also kissed my grandmother, my mother, and my father, which didn't make me feel so special anymore.

She returned to me, kissed me on the cheek again, and that made me feel somewhat better.

When she breezed out of the house and into the night, she seemed to take most of the oxygen with her. In her absence, breathing hurt a little.

Dad was late leaving for work at the resort. He had delayed in order to see Lorrie off.

Before he left, he said, 'Son, no self-respecting baker would let that one get away.'

While Mom and Grandma cleared the dinner table and loaded the two dishwashers, I settled into a living-room armchair and leaned my head back against the spider-pattern antimacassar. With my stomach pleasantly full and my castbound leg raised on a footstool, I felt beached.

I tried to read a mystery novel, one in a series about a private detective with neurofibromatosis, the disease made famous by the Elephant Man. He traveled from end to end of San Francisco in his investigations, always wearing a hooded cloak to conceal his deformed features. I couldn't get into the story.

With dinner cleanup completed, Grandma returned to the sofa and to her needlepoint. She had begun a centipede pillow.

Mom sat at the easel in her alcove and worked on a portrait of a collie whose owner wanted it portrayed in a checkered neck scarf and cowboy hat.

Considering my life and the dinner just enjoyed, I naturally gave some thought to eccentricity. As I write about the Tock clan, its members seem odd and singular. Which they are. Which is one reason why I love them.

Every family is eccentric in its own way, however, as is each human being. Like the Tocks, they have their tics.

Eccentric means off or aside from the ordinary, off or aside from what is considered normal. As a civilization, through consensus, we agree on what is normal, but this consensus is as wide as a river, not as narrow as the high wire above a big top.

Even so, not one of us lives a perfectly normal, ordinary life in every regard. We are, after all, human beings, each of us unique to an extent that no member of any other species is different from others of its kind.

We have instinct but we are not ruled by it. We feel the pull of the mindless herd, the allure of the pack, but we resist the extreme effects of this influence — and when we do not, we drag our societies down into the bloody wreckage of failed utopias, led by Hitler or Lenin, or Mao Tsetung. And the wreckage reminds us that God gave us our individualism and that to surrender it is to follow a dark path.

When we fail to see the eccentricities in ourselves and to be amused by them, we become monsters of self-regard. Each in its own way, every family is as eccentric as mine. I guarantee it. Opening your eyes to this truth is to open your heart to humanity.

Read Dickens; he knew.

Those in my family don't wish to be anyone but who they are. They will not edit themselves to impress others.

They find meaning in their quiet faith, in one another, and in the little miracles of their daily lives. They don't need ideologies or philosophies to define themselves. They are defined by living, with all senses engaged, with hope, and with a laugh ever ready.

Almost from the moment I had met her in the library, I had known that Lorrie Lynn Hicks knew everything that Dickens knew, whether she had read him or not. Her beauty lay less in her physical appearance than in the fact that she wasn't a Freudian automaton and would never allow herself to be defined by those terms; she was nobody's victim, nobody's fool. She was motivated not by what others had done to her, not by envy, not by a conviction of moral superiority, but by life's *possibilities*.

I put aside the novel featuring the Elephant

Man detective, and I levered myself up from the armchair, into the walker. The wheels squeaked faintly.

In the kitchen, I closed the door behind myself and went to the wall phone.

For a while I stood there, blotting my damp palms on my shirt. Trembling. This nervousness was less acute but more profound than anything I'd felt while under Punchinello's gun.

This was the trepidation of a climber who wishes to scale the world's highest mountain in record time, who knows that for a certain window of his life he will have the skills and the physical resources to achieve his dream, but who fears that bureaucrats or storms, or fate, will foil him until his window closes. And then who will he be, what will he become?

During the six weeks since the night of the clowns, we had spoken by phone many times. I had committed her number to memory.

I keyed in three digits, hung up.

My mouth had gone dry. I squeaked to a cabinet, got a drinking glass, squeaked to the sink. I drew chilled and filtered water from the special tap.

Eight ounces heavier but still with a dry mouth, I returned to the phone.

I keyed in five digits, hung up.

I didn't trust my voice. I practiced: 'Hi, it's Jimmy.'

Even I had given up calling myself James. When you realize you're fighting a fundamental law of the universe, it's best to surrender to nature.

'Hi, it's Jimmy. I'm sorry if I woke you.'

My voice had grown shaky and had risen two octaves. I had not sounded like this since I was thirteen.

I cleared my throat, tried again, and might have passed for fifteen.

After keying six digits, I started to hang up. Then with reckless abandon, I punched in the seventh.

Lorrie answered on the first ring, as if she had been sitting by the phone.

'Hi, it's Jimmy,' I said. 'I'm sorry if I woke you.'

'I only got home fifteen minutes ago. I'm not in bed yet.'

'I had fun tonight.'

'Me too,' she said. 'I love your family.'

'Listen, this isn't something that should be done by phone, but if I don't do it, I won't sleep. I'll lie awake worrying that my window is closing and that I'm missing my last chance at the mountain.'

'All right,' she said, 'but if you're going to be this cryptic, I better take notes so later I'll have a chance of puzzling out what the hell you were talking about. Okay, I've got pen and paper.'

'First of all, I'm not much to look at.'

'Who says?'

'Mirror, mirror, on the wall. And I'm a lummox.'

'So you keep saying, but I haven't seen a whole lot of evidence of it — except in moments like this.'

'I couldn't dance *before* I had these steel

plates holding my leg together. Now I'll have about as much ballroom grace as Dr. Frankenstein's firstmade.'

'All you need is the right teacher. I once taught a blind couple to dance.'

'And anyway, I'm a baker, and maybe one day a pastry chef, and that means I'll never be a millionaire.'

'Do you *want* to be a millionaire?' she asked.

'Not particularly. I'd be worried all the time about how not to lose the money. I *should* want to be a millionaire, I guess. Some people say I don't have enough ambition.'

'Who?'

'What?'

'Who says you don't have enough ambition?'

'Probably everybody. Another thing, I'm not much of a traveller. Most people want to see the world, but I'm a homebody. I think you can see the whole world in one square mile, if you know how to look. I'm never going to have great adventures in China or the Republic of Tonga.'

'Where's the Republic of Tonga?'

'I don't have a clue. I'll never see Tonga. I'll probably never see Paris or London, either. Some people would say that's tragic.'

'Who?'

In a rush of self-judgment, I said, 'And I am utterly without sophistication.'

'Not utterly.'

'Some people think so.'

'Them again,' she said.

'Who?'

' 'Some people,' ' she said.

205

'We live in one of the most famous ski resorts in the world,' I plunged on, 'and I don't ski. Never cared to learn.'

'Is that a crime?'

'It reveals a lack of adventurousness.'

'Some people absolutely *must* have adventure,' she said.

'Not me. And everyone's into hiking, running marathons, pumping iron. I'll never be in that loop. I like books, long dinners full of talk, long walks full of talk. You can't talk going fifty miles an hour down a ski slope. You can't talk when you're running a marathon. Some people say I talk too much.'

'They're very opinionated, aren't they?'

'Who?'

'"Some people." Do you care what anyone thinks of you, outside your family?'

'Not really. And that's strange, don't you think? I mean, only sociopathic maniacs don't care what anyone thinks of them.'

'Do you think you're a sociopathic maniac?' she asked.

'Maybe I could be.'

'I don't think you could be,' she disagreed.

'You're probably right. You have to be adventurous to be a good sociopathic maniac. You have to like danger and change and taking risks, and none of that's me. I'm dull. I'm boring.'

'And this is what you called to tell me — that you're a dull, boring, talkative, unadventurous, failed sociopath?'

'Well, yes, but all that's preamble.'

'To what?'

'To something I shouldn't ask over the telephone, something I should ask in person, something that I'm probably asking *way* too soon, but I've worked myself up into this weird terrifying conviction that if I don't ask you tonight, I'll be foiled by fate or storms, and my window of opportunity will close, so the question is . . . Lorrie Lynn Hicks, will you marry me?'

I thought her silence meant she was speechless with surprise, and then I thought it meant she was teasing me, and then I thought it might mean something darker, and then she said, 'I'm in love with someone else.'

PART THREE

WELCOME TO THE WORLD, ANNIE TOCK

24

The events of September 15, 1994 — when a significant portion of the town square was blown up — encouraged me to take seriously the rest of Grandpa Josef's predictions.

I survived the first of my five 'terrible days.' But survival came at a price.

Being in your early twenties with a leg full of metal and an occasional limp might be romantic if you're carrying around shrapnel acquired while serving with the Marines. There is no glory in being shot while struggling with a clown for possession of a pistol.

Even if he's a failed clown and a bank robber, he's still enough of a clown to rob your story of heroics. And render it absurd.

People say things like *So you got the gun away from him, but did he manage to hold on to the seltzer bottle?*

During the preceding eight or ten months, we brooded about and planned for the second day in the list of five, which came more than three years after the first: Monday, January 19, 1998.

As part of my preparations, I had bought a 9mm pistol. I don't much like guns, but I'm even less fond of being defenseless.

I discouraged my family from putting their lives on the line by tying my fate to theirs. Nevertheless, Mom, Dad, and Grandma insisted they would be with me all twenty-four hours of the fateful day.

Their primary argument seemed to be that Punchinello Beezo would not have taken me hostage in the library if he'd also had to take the three of them hostage with me. Safety in numbers.

My response was that he would have shot the three of them dead and taken just me hostage.

This elicited from them the weakest possible counterargument, but they always felt that they won the debate with their forcibly expressed interjections: '*Nonsense! Fiddlesticks! Baloney! Phoo! Poo! Poppycock! Bah! Twaddle! Don't be silly! My eye! In your hat! That's pure applesauce!*'

You can't really argue with my family. They are like the mighty Mississippi River: They just keep rollin', and pretty soon you find yourself in the Delta, drifting along, dazed by the sunshine and the lazy movement of the water.

Over many dinners, over uncounted pots of coffee, we debated whether we would be wise to hunker down behind four walls, lock the doors and windows, and defend the homestead against all clowns and whatever other agents of chaos came calling.

Mom felt we should spend the day in a public space filled with people. Since there's nowhere in Snow Village where crowds gather around the clock, she proposed flying to Las Vegas and camping out in a casino for two circuits of the clock.

Dad preferred to be in the middle of an

enormous field with a clear view for a mile in every direction.

Grandma warned that a meteorite, smashing down out of the sky, would be just as dangerous if we were in an open field as if we were at home with the doors locked or in Vegas.

'Nothing like that would happen in Vegas,' Mom insisted, drawing conviction from a mug of coffee half as big as her head. 'Remember, the mob still runs the place. They have the situation controlled.'

'The mob!' my father said exasperatedly. 'Maddy, the mob can't control meteorites.'

'I'm sure they can,' my mother said. 'They're very determined, ruthless, and clever.'

'Definitely,' Grandma agreed. 'I read in a magazine that two thousand years ago, a spaceship landed in Sicily. Aliens interbred with the Sicilians — which is why they're so tough.'

'What stupid magazine would publish such twaddle?' Dad asked.

Grandma replied, '*Newsweek*.'

'Never in a million years would *Newsweek* publish such nonsense!'

'Well,' Grandma assured him, 'they did.'

'You read it in one of your crazy tabloids.'

'*Newsweek*.'

Smiling, I drifted in the Delta as I listened.

Days passed, weeks, months, and it remained clear, as it had always been, that you can't scheme to defeat destiny.

The situation was complicated by the fact that we were pregnant.

Yes, I'm aware that some find it arrogant for a

man to say 'we,' considering that he shares the pleasure of conception and the delight of parenthood but *none* of the pain between. The previous spring, my wife, who is the linchpin of my life, had happily announced to the family, 'We're pregnant.' Once she had given me license to use the plural pronoun, I embraced it.

Because we were able to deduce the date of conception, our family doctor had told us that the most likely forty-eight-hour window for delivery would be January 18 and 19.

We were at once convinced that our first child would enter the world on the day about which Grandpa Josef had long ago warned my father: Monday the nineteenth.

The stakes were suddenly so high that we wanted out of the game. When you're playing poker with the devil, however, no one leaves the table before he does.

Although we all tried not to show it, we were scared to the extent that we needed no laxatives. As time swept us toward that rendezvous with the unknown, the hope and the strength that Lorrie and I took from family mattered more than ever.

25

My beloved wife is capable of jerking my chain
— 'I'm in love with someone else' — and
therefore I jerked yours.

Remember: I have learned the structure of
story from a family that delights in narrative and
understands in its bones the magical realism of
life. I know the routines, the tricks; I might be
clumsy in other ways, but in writing of my life, I
will try my best not to get my head stuck in the
bucket, and if the mouse-in-the-pants number
comes up, I'm pretty sure I won't be booed out
of the big top.

In other words, hold on. What looks tragic
might be comic on second consideration, and
what is comic might bring tears in time. Like life.

So, flashing back for a moment, there I stood
in my parents' kitchen, that night in November
of 1994, leaning against the counter to avoid
putting weight on my castbound leg, explaining
to Lorrie that although I wasn't much to look at,
although I might be dull and boring and talkative
and unadventurous, I hoped she would be
thrilled to marry me. And she said, 'I'm in love
with someone else.'

I could have wished her a good life. I could
have squeaked out of the kitchen with my
walker, lurched up the stairs, taken refuge in
my bedroom, and smothered myself to death
with a pillow.

That would have meant never seeing her again in this life or in the next. I found that prospect intolerable.

Besides, I hadn't yet eaten enough pastries to be willing to trade this world for one in which the existence of sugar is not guaranteed by theologians.

Keeping my voice steady, determined to sound like a stoic loser who wouldn't *think* of smothering himself, I said, 'Someone else?'

'He's a baker,' she said. 'What are the odds — huh?'

Snow Village was markedly smaller than New York City. If she loved another baker, surely I knew the guy.

'I must know him,' I said.

'You do. He's very talented. He creates pieces of Heaven in his kitchen. He's the best.'

I could not tolerate losing the love of my life *and* my rightful place in the bakers' hierarchy of Snow County. 'Well, I'm sure he's a nice guy, you know, but the fact is that around these parts, only my dad's a better baker than me, and I'm closing on him fast.'

'*There* he is,' she said.

'Who?'

'The someone I'm in love with.'

'He's there now? Put him on the line.'

'Why?'

'I want to find out if he even knows how to make a decent *pâte sablée*.'

'What's that?'

'If he's such a hotshot, he'll *know* what it is. Listen, Lorrie, the world is full of guys who'll claim they have the stuff to be a baker to kings, but they're all talk. Make this guy put his muffins where his mouth is. Put him on the line.'

'He's already on the line,' she said. 'That weird *other* Jimmy — the one that kept putting himself down, telling me how plain and dull and unworthy he was — I hope *he's* gone forever.'

Oh.

'*My* Jimmy,' she continued, 'isn't a braggart, but he knows his worth. And *my* Jimmy will never stop till he gets what he wants.'

'So,' I said, no longer able to keep the tremor out of my voice, 'will you marry your Jimmy?'

'You saved my life, didn't you?'

'But then you saved mine.'

'Why would we have gone to all that trouble and then not get married?' she asked.

Two Saturdays before Christmas, we were wed.

My father stood as my best man.

Chilson Strawberry flew in from a bungee-jumping tour of New Zealand to be maid of honor. Looking at her, you would never have known that she once crashed face-first into a bridge abutment.

Lorrie's dad, Bailey, took a break from storm chasing to give the bride away. He arrived looking windblown, looked windblown in his rented tux, and left looking windblown, marked by his profession.

Alysa Hicks, Lorrie's mother, proved to be lovely and charming. She disappointed us, however, by arriving without a single snake.

In the three years following our wedding, I

became a pastry chef. Lorrie changed careers from ballroom-dance instructor to website designer, so she could work baker's hours.

We bought a house. Nothing fancy. Two stories, two bedrooms, two baths. A place to start a life together.

We caught colds. Got well. Made plans. Made love. Had raccoon trouble. Played lots of pinochle with Mom and Dad.

And we got pregnant.

At noon Monday, January 12, after three hours of sleep, Lorrie woke with pain in the lower abdomen and groin. She lay for a while, timing the contractions. They were irregular and widely separated.

Because this was exactly one week prior to her most likely delivery date, she assumed that she was experiencing false labor.

She'd had a similar episode three days previously. We had gone to the hospital — and come home with the baby still in the oven.

The spasms were sufficiently painful to prevent her from falling back into sleep. Careful not to wake me, she slipped out of bed, took a bath, dressed, and went to the kitchen.

In spite of the periodic abdominal pain, she was hungry. At the kitchen table, reading a mystery that I had recommended, she ate a slice of chocolate cherry cake, then two slices of caraway *kugelhopf.*

For a few hours, the contractions did not become more painful or less irregular.

Beyond the windows, the white wings of the sky were molting. Snow descended silently and feathered the trees, the yard.

Lorrie gave little thought to the snow at first. In an ordinary January, snow fell as many days as not.

I woke shortly after four in the afternoon, showered, shaved, and went into the kitchen as the day slowly faded into an early winter twilight.

Still at the table, immersed in the final chapter of the mystery novel, Lorrie returned my kiss when I bent to her, taking her eyes from the page for only a moment.

Then: 'Hey, pastry god, would you get me a slice of *streusel*?'

During her pregnancy, she had developed numerous food cravings, but at the top of the list were *streusel* coffee cake and various kinds of *kugelhopf.*

'This baby's going to be born speaking German,' I predicted.

Before getting the cake, I glanced through the window in the back door and saw that about six inches of fresh powder covered the porch steps.

'Looks like the weatherman was wrong again,' I said. 'This is more than flurries.'

Enchanted by the book, Lorrie had failed to notice that the lazy snow-fall had turned into an intense if windless storm.

'Beautiful,' she said of the ermine view. Then half a minute later, she stiffened in her chair. 'Uh-oh.'

As I began to slice the *streusel*, I thought her *uh-oh* referred to a tense development in the story that she was reading.

With a hiss, she sucked breath through her

teeth, groaned, and let the book fall from her hands onto the table.

I turned from the cake to the sight of her suddenly as pale as the snow-mantled world beyond the window.

'What's wrong?'

'I thought it was false labor again.'

I went to the table. 'When did it start?'

'About noon.'

'*Five hours ago?* And you didn't wake me?'

'The pain was just in the lower abdomen and the groin, like before,' she said. 'But now . . . '

'Across the entire abdomen?'

'Yeah.'

'All the way around your back?'

'Oh, yeah.'

That specific topography of pain signified genuine labor.

I clutched, but only for a moment. Fear gave way to excitement as I considered my impending fatherhood.

Fear would have abided with me if I'd known that our house was being watched and that a sensitive surveillance device, planted in our kitchen, had just transmitted our conversation to a listener no more than two hundred yards away.

26

For a woman carrying her first baby, the initial stage of labor lasts twelve hours on average. We had plenty of time. The hospital lay only six miles away.

'I'll pack the SUV,' I said. 'You finish the novel.'

'Gimme the *streusel*.'

'Should you eat during first-stage labor?'

'What're you talking about? I'm starved. I intend to eat all the way through the delivery.'

After giving her the slice of *streusel* that I'd just cut, I went upstairs to fetch the bag that we had prepacked for her. I climbed the steps with caution and descended with something like paranoia. If there is ever a good time to fall and break a leg, this wasn't it.

During three years of marriage, I had become markedly less of a lummox than before we'd taken our vows. I seemed to have absorbed some of her grace as if by osmosis.

Nevertheless, I took no chances as I carried the suitcase into the garage and quickly loaded it in the back of our Ford Explorer.

We also had a 1986 Pontiac Trans Am. Candy-apple red with black interior. Lorrie looked fabulous in it.

After raising the automatic garage door a few inches to provide ventilation, I started the Explorer and left the engine running. I wanted the interior to be warm by the time that Lorrie got aboard.

Following a lesser storm four days previously, I'd put snow chains on the tires. I had decided to leave them on.

Now I felt prescient, competent, and in charge. I figured this was going to be a milk run, thanks to my foresight.

Under Lorrie's mellowing influence, I'd become an indefatigable optimist. Before the night was out, I'd pay a price for my optimism.

In the mud room between garage and kitchen, I kicked off my shoes and hurriedly put on ski boots. I snared my Gore-Tex/Thermolite parka from a wall hook and shrugged into it.

I took a similar parka into the kitchen for Lorrie and found her standing near the refrigerator, groaning.

'The pain's worse when I'm moving than when I'm standing still or sitting down,' she said.

'Then all the moving you're going to do is out to the Explorer. At the hospital, we'll get you in a wheelchair.'

After I'd assisted her into the front passenger's seat and got the safety harness around her, I returned to the mud room. I switched off the house lights. Pulled shut the door, locked it.

I had not forgotten the 9mm pistol. I just didn't think that I would need it.

My second of five terrible days was still a week in the future. Considering Grandpa Josef's track record, it didn't occur to me that he might have gotten the second date wrong — or that he

222

might have predicted only five of *six* terrible days.

When I got behind the wheel of the Explorer, Lorrie said, 'I love you more than all the *streusel* and *kugelhopf* in the world.'

I said right back at her: 'I love you more than *crème brûlée* and *tarte aux limettes*.'

'Do you love me more than mungo-bean custard?' she asked.

'Twice as much.'

'I'm a lucky woman.' As the segmented garage door rumbled upward, Lorrie winced with a contraction. 'I think it's a boy.'

She had undergone an ultrasound scan to be sure the baby was healthy, but we hadn't wanted to know the gender. I'm all for modern technology, but not if it robs life of one of its sweetest surprises.

I pulled into the driveway and discovered that the storm had worked up a little wind. Though only a breeze, it harried the dense snow through the headlights, masking the night with billowing veils.

Our house stood along Hawksbill Road, two lanes of blacktop that link Snow Village itself with the resort of the same name. The resort, where Dad and I work, is a mile and a half to the north, and the outskirts of town lie five miles to the south.

At the moment, the highway was deserted in both directions. Only road crews, reckless fools, and the pregnant would be out in weather this bad.

Not many houses have been built along

223

Hawksbill Road. For most of its length, the rocky and angular terrain flanking the highway is not conducive to construction.

In the pocket of more hospitable territory where we live, five houses stand on large properties: three on our side of the highway, two on the east side of the blacktop.

We know and are friendly with the neighbors in four of those houses. In the fifth, directly across Hawksbill Road from us, lived Nedra Lamm, who had been a local character for decades.

In Nedra's front lawn stood half a dozen eight-foot-tall totems that she carved from deadwood and accessorized with deer antlers. These grotesque figures faced the highway, threatening a rain of hoodoo violence on unwelcome visitors.

Nedra Lamm was a recluse with a sense of humor. The greeting on the mat at her front door did not say WELCOME but commanded GO AWAY.

Through the falling snow, I could barely see her house, a pale shape in a paler landscape.

As I followed our driveway to the county road, movement at the Lamm place caught my attention. From the dark hole of her open garage came a rushing shape that at a distance first appeared to be a large pickup truck with headlights off.

For more than thirty-eight years, Nedra had driven a 1960 Plymouth Valiant, arguably the ugliest car ever produced by Detroit, which she maintained in pristine showroom condition, as if it were a classic of automotive design.

As the oncoming vehicle reached the end of her driveway and raced onto Hawksbill Road, parting the veils of snow, I identified it as a black Hummer, the civilian version of the military Humvee. Big, fast, with four-wheel drive, undeterred by snow and ice, the Hummer turned neither left nor right but, lightless, crossed the highway toward us.

'What's he doing?' Lorrie wondered.

Fearing a collision, I braked, halted.

The Hummer slid to a stop at an angle across the driveway, blocking our exit.

The driver's door flew open. A man got out. He had a rifle.

27

Tall, broad shouldered, given additional bulk by a fleece-lined thigh-length leather coat, the man wore a toboggan cap pulled down over his ears and low on his forehead.

I noticed no additional fashion details because I fixated on the rifle, which looked less like a hunter's gun than like a military piece, with an extended magazine. Stepping in front of the Hummer, only fifteen feet from the Explorer, he raised the weapon either to intimidate or to kill.

The average baker might have been confused and paralyzed by this development, but I was primed for action.

As he brought up the rifle, I jammed my right foot on the accelerator. He had started this, not me, so I had no compunction about responding with overwhelming force. I intended to crush him between the vehicles.

Instantly realizing that he might place a bullet between my eyes but could not stop the Explorer, he dropped the rifle and scrambled onto the hood of the Hummer with an alacrity suggesting significant monkey blood in his family tree.

As he reached up toward the rack of spotlights above the windshield, perhaps intending to pull himself onto the roof, I cut hard to the right, to avoid a now-pointless collision. The Explorer's bumper roughly kissed the Hummer, offended metal shrieked, dancing sparks lived briefly in the descending snow, and we were out of there.

I angled across the front yard, grateful that the ground under the snow had weeks ago frozen almost as hard as pavement and would not be churned into sucking mud.

'What was *that* about?' Lorrie asked.

'Beats me.'

'You know him?'

'I don't think so. But I didn't get a really good look at his face.'

'I don't *want* a really good look at his face.'

The drooping boughs of the immense deodar cedar were laden with snow, rendering it a looming white form against a white background. Cataracts of falling snow further obscured it. With not a second to spare, I pulled the wheel hard left, barely avoiding taking a header into the tree trunk.

For a moment I thought the Explorer would roll, but it didn't. We thrashed through the perimeter of the cedar. Branches scraped the roof and the passenger's side, and cascades of snow poured off the boughs, across the windshield, blinding me.

Most likely, even as we'd roared past him, the gunman would have rolled off the Hummer and snatched up the rifle. I wouldn't even hear the high-powered round if it smashed out the rear window, punched through the headrest, and blew open my skull. Or Lorrie's.

My heart seemed to clench into a fist and thrust into my throat, beating there with such force that I had trouble swallowing.

I switched on the wipers, front and back, and the blades swept the snow away, swept the night into place once more, as we reached the highway. We crossed the drainage swale with a jolt and swung right into the southbound lane.

'You okay?' I asked.

'Watch the road. I'm fine.'

'The baby?'

'He's pissed — someone tryin' to shoot his mama.'

Turning in the passenger's seat as far as her safety harness and her condition would allow, Lorrie squinted back toward the house.

I could see nothing in my mirrors other than empty highway directly behind us and a tumult of snow whipped into horizontal spirals by our wake wind, reflecting our taillights.

'See anything?' I asked.

'He's coming.'

'We'll outrun him.'

'Can we?'

The Hummer had a more powerful engine than the Explorer. Because he didn't have a pregnant woman aboard, the gunman would be quicker to take risks, to push his vehicle to its limits.

'Call 911,' I said.

The cell phone was plugged into the cigarette lighter, nestled in a console cupholder.

She plucked it up, switched it on, made an impatient wordless sound as she waited for the phone-company logo and the preliminary data to fade.

Headlights appeared in my rearview mirror.

They were higher off the pavement than the lights of the average SUV. The Hummer.

Lorrie keyed in 911. She waited, listened, pressed END, and entered the three digits again.

Cell phone service in some rural areas wasn't as good in 1998 as it is now, just seven years later. Complicating matters, the storm chopped the signal.

The Hummer had gained on us: about twenty yards back, a vehicle with a personality, beetle-browed and belligerent.

I had to weigh which risk was worse for mother and baby: pushing the Explorer faster in terrible weather, or waiting to see if the Hummer could catch us.

We were already doing forty, too fast for these conditions. Accumulated snow concealed the lane markings. I couldn't easily tell where the pavement ended and the shoulder of the road began.

Having often traveled this highway, I knew in some places the westside shoulder was wide, in other places narrow. Guardrails edged the steepest drop-offs; but some of the unprotected slopes beyond the shoulder were abrupt enough to tip us into a roll if I went more than two feet off the pavement.

I accelerated to fifty, and like a ghost ship fading into haunted fog, the Hummer receded into thickening snow.

'Damn phone,' Lorrie said.

'Keep trying.'

The night abruptly grew blustery. Rugged land looms over Hawksbill Road in the east. In

229

certain storms, the wind comes down off those slopes and builds velocity on its way into the lowlands, scourging the highway.

Higher-profile vehicles — big rigs and motor homes — are sometimes blown over along this route if their drivers ignore wind advisories from the highway patrol. Fierce gusts hammered us, hampering my best efforts to keep the Explorer in what I perceived to be the southbound lane.

Feverishly I wracked my brain for a better strategy than this headlong flight. I couldn't think of one.

Lorrie groaned louder than before, sucked breath between her clenched teeth. 'Oh, baby,' she told our unborn, 'please take your time. No rush, baby, no hurry.'

Out of the glittering white murk, the Hummer reappeared behind us: black, big, blazing, like a demon-possessed vehicle in a bad horror movie.

We hadn't gone a mile. The outskirts of Snow Village still lay over four miles away.

The tire chains made a bell song on exposed blacktop, churned with much crunching and creaking across ice. In spite of the chains and the SUV's four-wheel drive, any speed above fifty invited catastrophe.

Headlights flared in the rearview mirror.

Lorrie was having no success with the phone. She made a rude suggestion to our service provider, and I seconded her sentiments.

For the first time in this pursuit, I detected the growl of the Hummer's engine separate from the roar of the Explorer. It was just a machine, not capable of intention, not evil, yet it sounded sinister.

Regardless of the risks of speed, I couldn't let the gunman ram us from behind. On this snowy pavement, we would spin out of control, tip over, and roll along the road or off it.

I pushed the Ford to fifty-five. Sixty. When we came to the next descending stretch of roadway, it would feel as though I had driven onto a bobsled chute.

The Hummer dwindled in the mirror as I accelerated, then almost at once began to gain on us again.

In a blizzard as daunting as this, sheriff's deputies sometimes cruise Hawksbill Road in Suburbans equipped with plows and winches and multiple thermoses of hot coffee, searching for motorists in trouble. With luck, we wouldn't have to get all the way to town to find help. I prayed for a police storm patrol.

Behind us, the spotlights on the Hummer's roof rack suddenly blazed, filling the Explorer, illuminating us no less brightly than we would have been if we'd been performing on a stage.

He couldn't possibly drive and use the rifle at the same time. Nevertheless, the back of my neck crawled.

Time-smoothed rock formations along the west side of the highway formed an effective block to the banshee wind that howled out of the east. Snow had drifted against that barrier, forming a mound that diminished from west to east but remained formidable across the width of the roadway.

Trickster to the eye, the storm deceived with every device at its command. The thick falling snow half blinded but also imparted the false impression of a tilt to the landscape. White on white, in white, the drift had been sculpted as if by a master of camouflage, so that it appeared to be a smooth rise in the pavement.

A soft wall, three feet high, met us before I could brake, and we plowed into it, losing a third of our speed in an instant.

Lorrie cried out as we were thrown forward in our harnesses, and I hoped to God she'd taken most of the jolt with the shoulder restraint, not with the lap belt.

Once into the drift, the front wheels chewed at it, tried to crawl over it. Compacted snow scraped the undercarriage. Although rapidly losing more speed, we struggled forward, one tire spinning, three taking grip, and I thought we would make it, but then the engine stalled.

28

The engine never stalls when you're enjoying a lazy drive in the country and have ample time to assess and deal with the problem. No, the engine stalls when you're rushing your pregnant wife to the hospital in a blizzard with a gunman chasing you in an SUV the size of a battleship.

This proves something. Maybe that life has a design, though one that's hard to understand. Maybe that fate exists. Maybe that when your wife is expecting, you should live next to a hospital.

Sometimes, as I'm writing about my life, I get the weird feeling that someone is *writing my life as I write about it.*

If God is an author and the universe is the biggest novel ever written, I may feel as if I'm the lead character in the story, but like every man and woman on Earth, I am a supporting player in one of billions of subplots. You know what happens to supporting players. Too often they are killed off in chapter three or in chapter ten, or in chapter thirty-five. A supporting player always has to be looking over his shoulder.

When I looked over my shoulder there on Hawksbill Road, I saw that the Hummer had come to a stop no more than fifteen feet behind us. The driver did not immediately get out.

Lorrie said, 'We leave the Explorer, he shoots us.'

'Probably.'

I twisted the key in the ignition, pumped the accelerator. The grinding of the starter and the complaint of the engine didn't inspire hope.

She said, 'We stay here, he shoots us.'

'Probably.'

'Shit.'

'Deep,' I agreed.

The Hummer drifted closer. The array of spotlights on the roof now shone over the Explorer, both dazzling and darkling the highway ahead.

Worried that I would flood the engine, I gave it a rest.

'I forgot my purse,' Lorrie said.

'We aren't going back for it.'

'I'm just saying — I don't even have a nail file this time.'

As the Hummer came forward, it began to arc around us, into the northbound lane.

Focusing on the hand in which I held the key, trying the engine again, I didn't dare look up, not because I dreaded the Hummer but because the sight of the ceaselessly falling snowflakes in their millions resonated with me in a troubling way. I felt borne on a wind, as they were, subject to every changing current, helpless to chart my own course.

'What's he doing?' Lorrie asked.

I didn't know what he was doing, so I stayed focused on the key, and the engine almost caught.

'Jimmy, get us out of here,' she urged.

Don't flood it, I warned myself. Don't force it.

Let it find the spark.

'*Jimmy!*'

The engine caught, roared.

The Hummer had pulled beside us, not parallel but at a forty-five-degree angle. Its front bumper gleamed inches from my door, as high as the bottom of my window, allowing me no exit.

Close up, it appeared huge, in part because it stood on enormous tires that added a foot to its showroom height, as though the driver intended to compete in a monster-truck rally.

The Explorer churned forward, not fast but doggedly, tearing at the drift, climbing over it, but the Hummer paced us, angled into us. The metallic clunk of impact was followed by a shriek of tortured sheet metal.

With advantages of size and power, the Hummer began to shove the Explorer sideways toward the rock formation along the western shoulder even as both vehicles continued crawling forward.

I glanced out of my side window, up at the Hummer, trying to see the crazy bastard's face behind the windshield, as though something in his expression might explain *why*. Through the glare of headlights and roof-rack spotlights, I couldn't get a glimpse of him.

One of our snow chains broke but continued to cling to the spinning tire, flailing loose links against the wheel wells and the undercarriage, rattling out a series of hard knocks reminiscent of gunfire.

I couldn't negotiate the impeding wall of snow and at the same time attempt to accelerate around the Hummer.

As I despaired of escaping him, an abrupt diminishment of resistance indicated that we were through the drift, and suddenly I had hope again.

From his higher vantage point, our attacker must have seen what had been about to happen and must have tramped his accelerator at the penultimate moment. Instantly, as we lurched forward, so did the Hummer, jamming harder against us.

To the west, the anomalous rock formation was gone, and the land dropped off into a woodland.

Lorrie had bad news: 'There's no guardrail.'

The Explorer slid far enough sideways that it must surely have been off the pavement, on the shoulder. As I tried to power past the Hummer and regain the roadway, we were forced counterclockwise. When we turned far enough, we would plummet backward down whatever slope lay beyond — a terrifying prospect.

Lorrie made a sound half gasp, half whimper, either because a contraction wrenched her or because the thought of a backward plunge into unknown territory didn't appeal quite as much as did a roller-coaster ride.

I let up on the accelerator. This changed the physics equation, and the Explorer shifted clockwise, straightened up.

Too late. The right front end dropped sharply, and I knew we had been pressed to the outer edge of the highway shoulder. With the Hummer pushing relentlessly, the Explorer would roll, tumble side over side into whatever lay below.

Counter to instinct, I pulled the steering wheel hard right, into the drop, which Lorrie must have thought was suicidal, but I hoped to use the Hummer instead of continuing to fight it. We turned ninety degrees as we hung on the brink, away from our attacker, until we were facing down a long snowy slope — neither gentle nor impossibly steep — stippled with pine trees receding into a wintry gloom that the headlights could not dispel.

We started down, and I stood at once on the brake pedal, holding us at the crest of the incline. We could see where we were headed now, but I still didn't want to go there.

The Hummer shifted into reverse, backed away from us, no doubt with the intention of ramming us from behind. At our angle, canted sharply forward, he might be able to tip us end over end into the forest below.

I had no choice. Before he could ram us, I let up on the brake.

'Hold on,' I told Lorrie.

The idling engine and gravity pulled us off the crest and down.

29

To put distance between ourselves and the rifleman, we had nowhere to go but down. Judiciously, I pumped the brakes, trying to keep our descent under control.

The broken chain tore loose from the tire. Other than engine noise and the faint clink of the other chains, the only sound was the *shush* of parting snow.

This was a section of old-growth forest, the trees so immense, the high branches so densely interlaced into a sheltering canopy, that the accumulated winter snow was only twelve inches deep, less in some places. Likewise, so little sunlight reached the floor of these woods that undergrowth posed no obstruction, and the lowest limbs were far above us.

Trees numbered fewer here than in a younger and more competitive evergreen forest. The enormous spreading elders, greedy for sunlight, had repressed new individuals, which withered as saplings.

Consequently, the pines — and interleaving stands of firs — were more widely separated than they might have been elsewhere. Their impressive trunks — straight, with fissured bark — reminded me of fluted columns supporting the many-vaulted ceiling of a cathedral, though this cathedral offered no warmth to body or spirit and listed like a sinking ship.

As long as I could control our speed, I would be able to steer between the trees. Eventually we would find a bottom, a valley, or perhaps only a narrow defile. I could then turn north or south and hope to find a forestry-service road that would provide a route out of the wilderness.

We would not make it back up the slope that we were descending. A four-wheel-drive vehicle might cope with the snow and the terrain, but the severe angle of incline would defeat it sooner than later, in part because the high altitude would starve a laboring engine.

Our hope of escape and survival depended entirely on reaching the bottom intact. As long as the Explorer remained drivable, we would have a chance.

Although I had never learned to ski, I had to think like a skier in a slalom event as I piloted the Explorer in a serpentine course, weaving through the maze of trees. I dared not turn as sharply as a skier tucking close to a marker flag, because I would surely roll the SUV. Smooth wide easy turns were the trick, which necessitated quick decisions about each new configuration of obstacles but also required that I comprehend the oncoming forest in dimension, holistically, in order to be considering the *next* maneuver even as I executed the current one.

This proved to be markedly more difficult than cooking a custard to precisely the right consistency.

'Jimmy, boulders!'

'I see 'em.'

'Deadwood!'

'Goin' left.'

'Trees!'

'Yeah.'

'The gap's too narrow!'

'We'll make it.'

We did.

'Nice move,' she said.

'Except I wet my pants.'

'Where'd you learn to drive?'

'Old Steve McQueen movies.'

I couldn't avoid this controlled plunge by simply turning across the face of the slope, because in places the incline seemed too steep to allow the Explorer to remain upright while navigating laterally. So I took what little comfort I could from the word *controlled*.

If the vehicle were damaged and we were forced to abandon it, our situation would become almost untenable.

In her condition, Lorrie would not be able to walk miles, not even on more friendly ground. She wasn't wearing boots, either, just athletic shoes.

Our parkas offered considerable protection, but neither of us wore insulated underwear. I had a pair of unlined leather gloves in a coat pocket; she'd brought no gloves at all.

The temperature was at best twenty degrees above zero. When rescuers found us — if they did before spring — we would be frozen as solid as mastodons in polar ice.

'Jimmy, rocks!'

'You bet I do.'

I arced around the stone formation.

'Swale!' she warned.

She wasn't usually a backseat driver. Maybe this compulsion to direct my driving reflected her time as a ballroom-dance teacher, when she called out the steps of a fox-trot to her students.

The depression — the swale — measured about twenty feet wide, six deep. We traversed it, scraped bottom coming out, and so narrowly avoided a head-on collision with the trunk of a fir tree that the passenger-side mirror was torn off.

As the Explorer bounced across uneven ground, dervish shadows whirled and swooped from the slashing headlight beams. I found it dangerously easy to mistake some of these phantoms for real figures, and to be distracted by the movement.

'Deer!' Lorrie exclaimed.

Seven white-tailed deer were dead-center in our path, all adults, no fawns at this time of year. The herd leader, an imposing buck with a magnificent rack of antlers, had frozen at our approach, head raised, eyes as bright yellow as the reflective plastic of embedded highway lane dividers.

I figured to swing left, go wide around them, and I spotted a passage through the trees beyond the herd.

As I steered the Explorer in that direction, however, the old buck startled. He blew twin plumes of frosted breath and sprang forward, followed at once by the rest of the herd.

I couldn't turn back to the right sharply enough to avoid them. When I tramped the

241

brakes perhaps too hard, the Explorer dug in, finding some traction in the blanket of dead needles and fallen cones immediately under the snow. We slowed for a moment, then encountered ice. The wheels alternately locked and stuttered as we slid toward the herd.

The deer were beautiful, limber, graceful. They seemed to travel without quite touching hooves to ground, as though they were spirits in a dream.

I desperately hoped to avoid them, not only because the thought of killing them sickened me but also because they weighed hundreds of pounds. Hitting one of them would devastate the Explorer no less than would driving it into a wall.

The encounter unfolded as though the deer moved in different universes from ours, as if we were briefly visible to each other through some window between our realities. Having no substance in each other's realm, the SUV slid through the herd, and the frightened herd bounded past the SUV, and we didn't collide with any of them, although we must have missed more than one by a fraction of an inch.

Although the deer were gone, the wheels remained locked. I could neither steer nor brake.

The descent continued uncontrolled, a glissade over snow that had compacted into a brittle crust of dirty ice. This mantle cracked and popped under us, and our speed increased.

I saw more deadwood in our path. A fallen tree. It had been down so long that all the foliage and most of the smaller branches had moldered

242

away, leaving a four-foot-diameter log that would be mottled with lichen and festooned with fungus during warmer months but that was not ornamented now, nestled into the forest loam.

Lorrie must have seen it, too, but did not cry out, only braced herself.

We struck the log. The impact did the Explorer no good, but didn't rack it up as bad as I expected, either. We were lifted from our seats, tested the safety harnesses, but with less violence than we had experienced when we plowed into the snowdrift on the highway.

The fallen tree had been hollowed out by worms and beetles and decomposition. It was largely a shell, and what wood remained under the bark was rotten.

The collision didn't turn the Explorer to junk, merely slowed it down. Sheets of bark and cambium wrapped the front axle, snared throughout the undercarriage, causing friction, slowing us further.

We began to turn as we descended. The wheel spun through my hands, useless. Then we were proceeding backward, headlights aimed upslope, gliding blindly into the ravine, the very fate that had terrified me when the Hummer had been pushing us toward the brink.

30

Fortunately, we didn't slide far enough to build speed again. The left rear bumper clipped a tree. We ricocheted sideways into a flanking tree, and then the back of the Explorer wedged between the two. We were at a full stop.

'Well done,' Lorrie said dryly.

'You okay?'

'Pregnant.'

'Contractions?'

'Tolerable.'

'Still irregular?'

She nodded. 'Thank God.'

I switched off the headlights. The trail we had left would be easy to follow, but I saw no point in helping our mysterious assailant find us sooner.

Here under the canopy of evergreens, the darkness pooled deep. Although we had descended perhaps four hundred yards, it seemed that we must be thousands of fathoms from the highway and even farther from any hope of surfacing to the sight of the sky again.

Although I couldn't smell gasoline and had to conclude that neither the tank nor the fuel lines had sustained damage, and though keeping the car as warm as possible had to be a priority, I switched off the engine. Without our headlights to guide him, the gunman might have tried to track us by the engine noise.

I wanted him to be forced to use a light of his

own and thereby reveal his position as he descended.

He would have to come on foot. If he drove down, even the Hummer wouldn't reliably climb back up such a slope, not in the thinner air of this altitude. He wouldn't risk it.

I said, 'Lock the doors after me.'

'Where you going?'

'Surprise him.'

'No. Let's run.'

'You can't.'

She looked stricken. 'This blows.'

My reassuring smile must have been ghastly. 'Gotta go.'

'Love you.'

'More than mung-bean custard,' I said.

As I climbed out, the ceiling light was a minor betrayal, quickly extinguished when I closed the driver's door as quietly as possible.

Lorrie reached to the console and pressed the master-lock button among the power controls.

I took a moment to assure myself that the trees blocked the Explorer from further descent. Neither rear door could be opened. The SUV would not slip loose and roll backward.

The darkness seemed to be more than just an absence of light, seemed to have a texture, as though billions of sooty spoors were sifting out of the trees. The humidity, the cold, and most of all my fear conspired to invest this particular darkness with a special substance.

Holding my breath, I listened but heard only the clicks and creaks of the Explorer cooling in the bitter air and the solemn wind lamenting in the highest reaches of the trees. Nothing that suggested an approaching enemy.

The rifleman might still be standing far above us, on the shoulder of Hawksbill Road, mulling over his next move. I suspected, however, that he was a guy who acted quickly and wouldn't spend much time brooding about alternatives.

I didn't waste time wondering who he was, rummaging my mind for explanations. If he killed me, I'd never know. If I got the better of him, I'd have answers. In either case, speculation was fruitless.

Leaving Lorrie alone in the locked car felt like abandonment, although without leaving her, I could not hope to save her and our baby.

Gradually my eyes became dark-adapted, but I couldn't wait for full night vision.

I eased around the trunk of one of the trees between which we had become lodged, and moved to the back of the Explorer.

The forest floor laid clever traps. A crust of hardened snow gave me less trouble than the detritus scattered across it: masses of slippery dead fir needles and cones that rolled treacherously underfoot.

From the rifleman's perspective at the top of the incline, the landscape down here had no profile; the dynamic forest congealed into a black murk. I knew he could not see me as I moved south across the slope, but I nonetheless vividly imagined the crosshairs of a sniper scope scoring my face as he lined up a head shot.

The snow cover wasn't uniform in these sheltered depths, two or three inches in some places, a foot in others, with numerous patches of bare ground. As my night vision improved, I saw the rising land as a crazy quilt of vaguely luminous white swatches stitched in a random pattern with scraps of dark fabric.

I quickly learned how to move more stealthily, but the nature of the terrain made silent progress impossible.

Every few steps, I stopped and listened for any indication that our attacker might be descending. I heard nothing other than the soughing of wind in the highest needled boughs and a menacing — almost subliminal — low droning that seemed to arise from the earth itself but that must have been an echo of the wind.

When I had gone about forty feet, I turned east and began to climb parallel to the tracks we had left in our plunge. I stayed low to the ground, grabbing at rock formations, exposed roots, and other hand-holds to steady myself, ascending in monkey fashion though not with monkey agility.

I hoped to get half or two thirds of the way up the slope before spotting the rifleman on the way down. Then I could lie low, wait for him to pass, move north across the slope, and attempt to creep up behind him.

This plan was fully insane. I wasn't James Bond. Or even Maxwell Smart. As a man of action, I preferred kneading dough to knocking heads, mixers to submachine guns.

Unable to conceive of an alternative that might be any less insane, I continued climbing, feeling more like a monkey the higher I went.

My hands grew cold. The unlined gloves in one of the parka pockets would provide a small measure of warmth, but they would also interfere with my sense of touch and the flexibility of my grip. I preferred to bring my hands to my mouth and warm them with my breath.

Worse than chilled hands, my left leg began to ache, throbbing like the root of an abscessed tooth. In warmer weather, I'm never aware that surgical steel accessorizes my leg bones, but sometimes in the winter, I am able to discern the location and precise shape of every plate and screw.

When I figured I was two thirds of the way up the slope and had not seen a flashlight or any other indication of a man on his way down, I paused. Certain that my footing was secure, I rose to full height, the better to survey the crest of the slope, which still lay over a hundred yards above me.

Even if the Hummer were parked along the shoulder, I didn't expect to see it at this severe an angle. I thought I might detect the aurora of its headlights or parking lights, but the crest was defined only by the faint gray ambient glow of the open snow-filled sky over the highway.

I didn't believe that the attacker would have left the scene. After being so determined to stop us, he would never have driven casually away. And if his intention had been to kill us, he wouldn't trust in that steep but negotiable hill to have done the job.

Patience is required of a good pastry chef, but occasionally mine was short even in the kitchen.

Standing there, waiting for our assailant to reveal himself, I grew as irritated as I sometimes did when making *crème anglaise* from egg yolks, sugar, and milk, which requires steady stirring with a wire whip and low heat so that the yolks won't scramble.

My yolks were starting to scramble, in a manner of speaking, when a rushing sound came from overhead. This was not merely a quickening of the wind but something formidable plummeting from the high canopy of branches.

Considering that as a student I'd had no head for history, Greek or otherwise, I thought it strange that I should think of the razor-sharp sword suspended by a hair over the head of Damocles.

I looked up.

31

Pale, cutting the air with a *whoosh*, many blades descended in an arc, but softer than steel: pinions forming a six-foot wingspan. I saw luminous round eyes and the sharpness of a beak, heard its familiar question — 'Who?' — and knew it was an owl. Nevertheless I cried out in surprise as it passed over me.

Scouting for forest rodents, the great bird swooped north-northwest, descending with the slope, gliding soundlessly now. It crossed the trail that the Explorer had made on its downward journey — and sailed past a man whose presence had until then not registered with me.

Even to dark-adapted eyes, visibility was poor in those woods. The patchwork of bare earth and faintly luminous snow had the eerie quality of a dreamscape, seemed always to be shifting, as if it were a black-and-white mosaic at the bottom of a slowly, slowly turning kaleidoscope.

He stood thirty feet north of me, maybe twenty feet downslope, visible between trees. In mutual stealth, we had passed each other, unaware.

Although brief and not loud, my cry had revealed me to him, and the owl had drawn my eyes to his silhouette. I could see no details of him, not even the fleecy collar of his leather coat, just an unmistakably human form.

I had expected him to reveal his position with

a flashlight. He couldn't possibly have followed the Explorer's tracks such a distance in gloom as deep and deceptive as this unaided by a lamp.

I wondered if he could see me at least as well as I saw him. I dared not move in case he hadn't yet pinpointed the source of the cry that had alerted him.

He opened fire.

Back at our house, when he had first gotten out of the Hummer, the weapon had resembled military ordnance. Now the distinctive *acketta-acketta-acketta* of an assault rifle confirmed the initial impression.

Louder than whip cracks, high-powered rounds lashed trees to the left and right of me.

Astonished that the spray of bullets between those two hits had all missed me, I took no comfort that this was not one of the five terrible days on Grandpa Josef's list.

I stood rooted like one of the evergreens. For a moment it seemed that Jimmy Tock, man of action, would do no more than dump an abundance of biological end products in his pants.

Then I ran.

Racing all but blindly south across the slope, I wished the majestic trees grew closer together. I weaved among the huge trunks, seeking what cover they might give, chased by another extended burst of gunfire, a death-drum paradiddle in which any beat could mark a bullet in my back.

I heard the *thock* when a tree was wounded, the *zing* of a ricochet off a rock. Something whined past my head, and I knew that it wasn't a bee.

The profligate use of ammunition might be a mistake. Even an extended magazine would quickly run dry at the rate he was tapping it.

If he emptied the rifle without bringing me down, he would have to pause to reload. When he paused, I'd keep moving. He'd lose track of me.

Having lost track of me, he might go directly to the Explorer and kill Lorrie.

That thought tripped me. I fell over the unthinkable and landed hard on one shoulder, face in the cold reality of snow prickled with evergreen needles.

I rolled, not by choice, propelled by the momentum of the fall. Tumbling downhill, I knocked knees and elbows against stones, surface roots, and frozen earth.

Although I had fallen into this tactic, staying low and in motion seemed to be smart. After a few revolutions, however, I realized that if I rolled into a tree at the wrong angle, I might break my neck.

The clumps of undergrowth were sparse and widely separated, but if I thrashed through one, a stiff dead stick could put out an eye. Thereafter, I'd be half as likely to see that plummeting safe when at last it dropped on me.

I came out of the roll, grabbed at tufts of dead bunch-grass, at a tangle of withered ivy, at rocks, at anything that might slow me down. Scrambled to my hands and knees. Got to my feet. Ran in a crouch for a distance until I wondered if I needed to run anymore, and stopped.

Disoriented, I scanned the woods, found the colorless landscape as deceiving to the eye as ever, and tried to quiet my breathing. I didn't know how far I'd come: most likely far enough to have escaped him for the moment.

I couldn't see him, which I figured meant he couldn't see me, either.

Wrong. I heard him running toward me.

Without glancing back, I hurried south once more, across the face of the slope, following a serpentine path through the trees, repeatedly stumbling, skidding, recovering my balance, staggering from side to side, hurtling forward.

When he didn't at once open fire, I assumed he was either out of ammunition altogether or hadn't taken time to reload. If he no longer had the advantage of the weapon, it might be smart to turn and charge him. He wouldn't expect such boldness.

A sudden field of loose stones provided bad footing but gave me an idea. If we were going to wind up in hand-to-hand combat, he might have a knife or a lot of training. I needed an equalizer. Among the stones underfoot were larger rocks.

I stopped, stooped, at once put my hand around a rock the size of a small grapefruit. But as I stooped, another burst of gunfire shattered my fragile plan.

Even as those whistling whispers of death spoke inches above me, I left the rock where I'd found it, crabbed in a crouch across the shifting stones, slipped between two trees, dodged left, dared to stand in order to gain speed, and ran off the edge of a cliff.

32

Cliff is an exaggeration, but that's what it felt like when my right foot met empty air, and then my left. Falling, I cried out in shock and dropped about fifteen feet into a bristling yet soft mound. On impact, I recognized the sound of rushing water, saw surging torrents laced with phosphorescent foam, and realized where I was. And knew what I must do.

The assault rifle had been cutting the night when I stepped off the brink, and if the gunman had heard my shout, he might have thought I'd been hit. To encourage that misperception, I screamed once, as horribly as I could, then again, weaker and with what I hoped sounded like agony.

At once I sprang up and, staying close to the bank, hurried ten feet uphill.

Goldmine Run, which is bigger than a stream and smaller than a river, originates from a hot artesian well that forms a steaming volcanic lake in the mountains to the east. Hawksbill Road bridges it; this western slope receives it.

The channel is narrow, no more than twenty feet wide, forcing a deep stream twelve to fourteen feet across. By the time it gets here, the water is no longer warm, but because the bed of the run is so steep, the rapid currents resist freezing even in an unusually cold winter. An almost whimsical fresco of ice, formed from

254

spray, appears only along the edges of the run.

A gunshot man, falling into those waters, would be swiftly swept into the valley below, tumbled and battered en route.

The banks did not slope down to Goldmine Run but were concave, a pair of bracketing parentheses. An embedded web of tree roots prevented the overhang from collapsing.

Ten feet upstream from where I'd fallen, I sheltered under that earthen cowl, knee deep in a wind-deposited pile of decaying leaves and evergreen needles like the mound into which I'd fallen. I pressed my back to the bank, with my feet buried in mulch, confident that I could not be seen from above.

Even in this frigid night, here the crisp air had a faint scent of moldering vegetation, thin threads of foul odor that would be much riper in spring and early summer.

I longed for my work kitchen, the aroma of baking pie crusts, the comfort of meringue.

I didn't try to quiet my breathing. The splash and chuckle of the rampant water would mask those sounds.

No sooner had I taken cover than immediately to my right, a foot from my face, a drizzle of dirt, small stones, and dead leaves fell past me. The rifleman must have dislodged them as he stepped to the brink above.

I hoped that he would see the force of the tumbling water and assume that, badly wounded, I had fallen into Goldmine Run and been swept downstream, either to bleed to death or to drown, or to die of exposure.

If he descended into the water-carved channel to search the narrow shore, I would be as exposed as a single decorative cherry perched atop a chocolate cake.

Another dribble of soil and pebbles suggested that he either had shifted his weight or might be on the move.

In truth, I doubted that he would clamber down the bank for a closer inspection of the channel. From his higher perspective, he probably wouldn't realize that under his feet lay a concavity just sufficiently deep to shelter a man, and he would figure that he could see well enough from his superior position.

At this point, I *did* expect him to produce a flashlight and sweep the channel, but the seconds ticked past with no disturbance of the darkness.

This seemed peculiar to me. Even from down here, when I studied the plunging torrents, I could see pale rock formations along the shore and others midstream that might have been the slumped form of a wounded man, or a corpse. You would think that such a determined gunman would want to know for certain whether his target had been eliminated or merely wounded.

My sense of time might have been distorted. Terror plays havoc with your inner clock. I hadn't been counting the seconds, but I felt as though I had been hiding there for a minute, perhaps longer.

I quickly grew impatient. Maybe I was not a genuine, certified man of action, but I wasn't a man of inertia, either.

If I came out of hiding too soon and

discovered him gazing down at me, I'd be shot in the face. Although a certain stubbornness is in my lineage, I'm not as obstinate as Grandma Rowena. In my case, there was no chance whatsoever that, meeting at high velocity, a bullet would fare worse than my skull.

On the other hand, if I waited too long, the gunman might get too much of a head start for the Explorer. Lorrie hadn't been with me, so if he knew that she was pregnant, he would expect to find her in the SUV.

Call it a premonition or just a hunch, but I suspected that I was of peripheral interest to him, an annoying fly to be swatted, and Lorrie was the primary object of his interest. I didn't know why. I just *knew*.

When I stepped away from the bank, out of the knee-high compost and from under the overhang, I half expected a sudden light, a cruel laugh, a shot.

Rush of water, brush of wind, shrouds of darkness, deep forest waiting . . .

No shadowy form stood at the brink above.

Cautious because I feared stumbling and falling into the violent current so near at hand, I moved downslope along the bank, searching anxiously for an easy way up, preferably an escalator.

My left leg had taken a lot of punishment. The implanted steel seemed to throb. I limped.

Like gray bones, knobs of bedrock thrust from a section of the bank, entangled by the exposed roots of a tree. Even with my aching leg, ropes and a ladder could not have served me better.

At the top, I crouched, scanned the murky woods. No deer, no owls, no sociopathic gunman.

Instinct told me that I was alone. Instinct serves me well when I'm creating new recipes; therefore, I decided to trust it also in these circumstances.

Although forced to limp, I could move fast. I set off through the trees.

I had gone some distance when I began to feel confused as to direction. The contours of this higher land seemed to have shifted while I'd been below.

The highway lay uphill, of course, to the east. Consequently, west lay directly downhill. Goldmine Run lay south, behind me. The Explorer waited west of Hawksbill Road and north of my position.

Clear enough.

Yet when I rounded another tree and weaved between two more, I found myself back at the stream and almost plunged off the bank again. Knowing where all four points of the compass were, I had nevertheless wandered in a circle — and in no time at all.

Having lived in the mountains all my life, in a town besieged by forest, I had heard stories of even experienced outdoorsmen going lost in bright daylight and good weather. Wilderness-rescue teams searched for and extracted these bewildered and embarrassed hikers on a regular basis.

Some poor souls were neither bewildered nor embarrassed. They were dead. Mortally dehydrated, starved, bear-bitten, cougar-slashed, broken in a fall ... In Mother Nature's gruesome collection, the instruments of death were numberless.

Any six acres of wilderness could be a thwarting maze. Every year or two, the *Snow County Gazette* carried a front-page story about a hiker hopelessly lost for days, though he had always been within a half mile of a highway.

I have never been an intrepid woodsman. I love civilization, the warmth of a hearth, the coziness of a kitchen.

Turning away from the wordless prattle of racing water, I strove frantically to comprehend the primeval patterns of the wildwood. I ventured forth hesitantly, then with greater haste, though with more trepidation than conviction.

Alone and imperiled, Lorrie needed Davy Crockett. Instead, all she had was me — a hairy-chested Julia Child.

33

This I did not see but have been told: Locked alone in the Explorer, Lorrie turned in her seat as best she could to watch me set out into the forest. Considering the depth of the gloom, this took fifteen seconds, after which she was free to contemplate her mortality.

She opened the cell phone and keyed in 911 again. As before, she could not get service.

Her wristwatch had clocked off just half a minute, and she had already run out of options to pass time. These weren't circumstances conducive to singing 'Ninety-nine Bottles of Beer on the Wall.'

Although I had saved her life (and she mine) on the night of the day we had met, she wasn't entirely confident in my ability to sneak up on the rifleman and overpower him barehanded.

She later told me, *No offense, muffin man, but I figured you had gone off to be killed and I would wind up being the bride of Big Foot or worse.*

Sharp anxiety at once scraped her nerves raw — not so much worry for herself, she says, as for me, which I believe because that is quintessential Lorrie. She seldom puts herself first in anything.

Our unborn baby was equal to me in her thoughts. Her inability to protect her child in any meaningful way elicited alternate floods of anger and anxiety.

Awash in strong emotions, she felt that if she just sat there waiting, if she didn't take some positive action, frustration and fear would gnaw at the seams of her mind, loosening the stitches a little.

A plan occurred to her. If the ground under the Explorer allowed and if her distended belly didn't get in the way, perhaps she should slip out of the SUV, squirm beneath it, and wait there, out of sight.

If I returned triumphant, she could call to me from her hiding place. If instead the rifleman showed up, he might think she had fled either with me or, later, on her own.

She popped the locks and opened her door. She felt the cold air suck all the color from her face in an instant.

The winter night was a vampire, its wings the darkness and its fangs the cold.

Under the Explorer, she would be lying on frozen ground. There would be welcome heat from the cooling engine, but not much and not for long.

A sharp contraction made her gasp. She pulled the door shut and engaged the locks once more.

Never in her life had she felt so helpless. Helplessness fed her frustration, fear, and anger.

Eventually, she thought she heard shots being fired.

She turned the ignition key, not far enough to start the engine, just to be able to power down her window a few inches.

Another volley confirmed that she had heard

the bark of an automatic weapon. Her gut clenched, not with a contraction this time but with dread, for she thought she might be a widow.

Curiously, a third burst of gunfire reminded her that she was an indefatigable optimist. *If our adversary had failed to kill me with the first two barrages, maybe he wasn't such a great shot or maybe I wasn't easy to kill.*

When she had opened the door, she had let out a lot of heat. Now the cold night insinuated itself through the gap in the window, and she shivered.

After putting the window up, she switched off the ignition and searched for a weapon, first in the map pocket on her door. A little soft black vinyl trash container half full of used tissues. A plastic bottle of hand lotion.

She fared no better in the glove box. A pack of chewing gum, Life Savers. A tube of lip balm. A change purse full of quarters for parking meters and newspaper dispensers.

If you'll spare my life and my baby's, I'll give you two dollars and seventy-five cents.

The console storage compartment contained a box of Kleenex. Two foil packets of moist towelettes.

Although it wasn't easy in her condition, she managed to lean forward and feel under her seat, hoping to find something, anything, a screwdriver. If a screwdriver, why not a revolver? If a revolver, why not a magic wand with which to turn the rifleman into a toad?

She found no wand, no revolver, no

screwdriver, no anything, no something. Zip, zero.

A man appeared out of the darkness in front of the Explorer, breath smoking from his open mouth. He carried an assault rifle, and he wasn't me.

Her heart swelled painfully, and hot tears rose in her eyes, for the arrival of this gunman seemed to suggest that I must be dead or at best badly wounded.

Superstition gripped her, and she thought that if she simply refused to grieve, then I would not be dead, after all. Only when she accepted the loss of me would that loss become true and real. Call it the Tinkerbell-resurrection strategy.

She fought back the tears. Her vision cleared.

As he drew closer, Lorrie saw that he wore a pair of peculiar goggles. She guessed, correctly as it turned out, that these were night-vision goggles.

He stripped them off and stuffed them in a coat pocket as he approached the front passenger's door.

When he tried the door, he found it locked. He smiled at her through the window, gave her a little wave, and rapped his knuckles on the glass.

He had a broad, bold-featured face, like a clay model for a new Muppet. She didn't think she had ever seen him before, yet something about him was familiar.

Leaning close, voice muffled by the glass but easily understood, he said with a friendly lilt, 'Hello there.'

As a young girl searching for order in a world

of snakes and tornadoes, Lorrie had read Emily Post's famous book on etiquette, but nothing in that thick volume had prepared her for this bizarre encounter.

He rapped on the glass again. 'Missy?'

Intuition told her that she should not speak to him. He needed to be handled in the same way that children were taught to deal with strange men offering candy: Don't talk, turn away, run. She couldn't run, but she could refuse to be engaged in conversation.

'Please open the door, missy.'

She faced front, looked away from him, remained silent.

'Little lady, I've traveled a long way to see you.'

Her hands had fisted so tightly that her fingernails gouged her palms.

'Is the baby coming?' he asked.

At the mention of our baby, Lorrie's heart broke from a canter into a full gallop.

'I don't want to harm you,' he assured her.

She searched the gloom in front of the Explorer, hoping that I would appear, but I did not.

'I don't want anything from you except the baby,' he said. 'I want the baby.'

34

Trash container, hand lotion, chewing gum, Life Savers, lip balm, change purse, Kleenex, packets of moist towelettes . . .

Even seized by a passionate, urgent desire to become a killing machine, Lorrie could not see any previously overlooked deadly edge to any of the items through which she had earlier sorted. A simple length of rope could double as a garrote. A fork could serve either as an eating utensil or as a weapon. But she didn't have rope or a fork, and she couldn't lip-balm a man to death.

At the window, the rifleman's voice sounded neither accusing nor hateful, nor hostile in any way. He was twinkle-eyed and smiling, and he spoke in a teasing, you're-naughty-and-you-know-it tone: 'You owe me one bouncy baby, one cute itsy little baby.'

Although he was not a dwarf, he was deformed in mind and spirit, which caused Lorrie to think *Rumpelstiltskin*. He'd come to collect her end of some monstrous bargain.

When she didn't answer him, he started toward the front of the Explorer, and she knew he would go around to the driver's door.

This Rumpelstiltskin had never taught her how to spin flax into gold, so there was no way in hell the son of a bitch would get her firstborn.

Leaning across the console between the seats,

she switched on the headlights.

Thus illuminated, the steeply ascending forest, stark black trunks and silhouetted foliage, seemed as unreal and as stylized as a stage setting.

Brightened by the beams, Rumpelstiltskin paused in front of the Explorer and peered at her through the windshield. He smiled. He waved.

Flurries of snow found their way through the thick canopy of interleaved branches. They swirled like celebratory confetti around the grinning, waving man.

Never had Death looked so festive.

Lorrie didn't know whether the headlights could be seen all the way up on Hawksbill Road. Probably not in the storm, perhaps not even on a clear night.

Still leaning toward the steering wheel, she blew the horn. One long blast. Then another.

Rumpelstiltskin shook his head sadly, as if he were disappointed in her. He sighed out a long plume of breath and continued around the Explorer to the driver's door.

Lorrie blew the horn again, again.

When she saw him draw back the assault rifle, she let up on the horn, turned away, and protected her face.

He smashed the driver's-door window with the butt of the weapon. Wads of gummy, prickly safety glass sprayed over Lorrie.

He popped the lock and settled in behind the wheel, leaving the door open.

'This sure hasn't gone anything like I planned,' he said. 'It's one of those cursed days

266

makes a man believe in bad mojo and the evil eye.'

He switched off the headlights.

When he put down the assault rifle, laying it across both the console and Lorrie's lap, she twitched with fear and tried to shrink from the weapon.

'Relax, little lady. Relax. Didn't I already say I wouldn't do you any harm?'

In spite of having spent time in the cleansing wind and the freshening cold, he reeked of unwholesome things: whiskey, cigarette smoke, gunpowder, and gum disease.

Switching on an interior light, he said, 'For the first time in a long while, I've got hope in my heart. It feels good.'

Reluctantly, she looked at him.

He had a kindly and happy expression, but it was so utterly unrelated to the torment in his eyes that the smile might as well have been painted on his face. Anguish issued from his every pore, and chronic anxiety was the underlying smell of him. His eyes were those of a trapped animal, full of throttled fear and yearning that he strove to conceal.

Sensing that she saw the suffering at the heart of him, he let his expression falter, but then painted it on twice as thick. His wide smile grew impossibly wider.

She would have pitied him if he hadn't terrified her.

'Just because it's on your lap,' he said, 'don't make a move for the gun. You don't know how to use it. You'd hurt yourself. Besides, I don't want to have to punch you in the face — you being the mother of my boy.'

Lorrie's maternal alarm had gone off when this man had first spoken of the baby through the closed window. Now her mind filled with uncountable steeples full of bells ringing out a tocsin.

'What are you talking about?' she demanded, dismayed to hear a tremor in her voice.

When only her own life was at risk, she could maintain a pose of fearlessness. Now she carried in her womb a hostage to fortune, and she could not hide her fear for that innocent.

From a coat pocket, he extracted a small black leather case and worked the zipper around three sides of it.

'You took my son from me, my only child,' he said, 'and I'm certain that if you search your heart, you'll be the first to admit that now you owe me yours.'

'Your son? I don't know your son.'

In a voice of reason and sweet good will, he said, 'You sent him to prison for life. And your husband, the ungrateful progeny of Rudy Tock, rendered him . . . unable to procreate.'

Stunned, Lorrie said, 'You're . . . Konrad Beezo?'

'The one and only, for many years on the run and often denied a spotlight to display my talents, but still a clown at heart and full of glory.'

He opened the black case. It contained two hypodermic syringes and a vial of amber fluid.

Although he had seemed familiar to her, he

didn't much resemble the photos in the newspapers that Rudy had kept from August 1974.

'You don't look like you,' she said.

Smiling, nodding, his voice chirrupy with inexplicable bonhomie, he said, 'Ah, well, twenty-four years takes a toll of any man. And as a fugitive of some notoriety, I spent a long holiday in South America with my little Punchinello, where I had just enough plastic surgery to restore anonymity.'

He unwrapped one of the hypodermic syringes. The point of the needle gleamed with unnerving brightness in the dim light.

Although Lorrie knew that reasoning with this man would be no more fruitful than discussing the music of Mozart with a deaf horse, she said, 'You can't blame us for what happened to Punchinello.'

'Blame is such a harsh word,' he said with great geniality. 'We don't need to talk of guilt and blame. Life is too short for that. A thing was done, for whatever reason, and now in all fairness a price must be paid.'

'*For whatever reason?*'

Smiling, nodding, insistently cordial, Beezo said, 'Yes, yes, we all have our reasons, and surely you had yours. And who am I to say that you were wrong? There's no need for judgmentalism, nothing to be gained by ugly accusations. There's always two sides to every story, and sometimes ten. It's just that a thing was done, my son was taken from me and rendered incapable of giving me grandchildren, heirs to the Beezo talent, and therefore it's only fair that I be compensated.'

'*Your Punchinello killed a bunch of people and would have killed me and Jimmy, too,*' Lorrie declared, stressing every word, unable to match Beezo's unshakable cheerfulness.

'So the story goes,' Beezo said, and winked. 'But let me assure you, missy, nothing you read in a newspaper can be trusted. The truth never makes it into print.'

'I didn't read about it, I *lived* it,' she said.

Beezo smiled and nodded, winked, smiled and nodded, let out a little laugh, nodded, and returned his attention to the hypodermic.

Lorrie realized that his fragile self-control depended upon maintaining an air of cheerful amiability, regardless of the fact that it was patently insincere. If that facade slipped at all, it would collapse entirely; his repressed self-pity and rage would then explode. Unable to control himself, he would kill her *and* the baby that he so much wanted.

Under these smiles and chuckles was not a lovelorn Pagliacci but a homicidal bozo.

Eyeing the contents of the vial, she asked, 'What is that?'

'Just a mild sedative, a little dream juice.'

His hands were large, rough, but dexterous. With the practiced efficiency of a physician, he tapped the vial and filled the syringe.

'I can't take that,' she protested. 'I'm in labor.'

'Oh, worry not, dear, it's very mild. It won't much delay the baby.'

'No. No, no.'

'Dear girl, you're only in first-stage labor and

270

you will be for hours yet.'

'How do you know that?'

With a mischievous chuckle and a wink and a twitch of his nose, he said, 'Darling, I must confess to being just a little bit naughty. A week ago, I planted a listening device in your kitchen, another in your living room, and I've been monitoring them ever since from Nedra Lamm's house across the highway.'

Lorrie felt dizzy. 'You know Nedra?'

'I knew her for a few minutes, the poor dear,' Beezo revealed. 'What are those totems with antlers all about, anyway?'

Wondering whether Nedra lay at rest among the cords of dry pine in her woodshed or in her basement freezer, Lorrie put one hand on the assault rifle.

'That's not friendly, missy.'

She took her hand off the weapon.

Beezo put the open hypodermic kit on the dashboard, placed the prepared syringe atop it. 'Be a lamb and take off your parka, roll up a sleeve, and let me find a vein.'

Instead of obeying, she said, 'What are you going to do to me?'

He surprised her by affectionately pinching her cheek as if he were a maiden aunt and she were a favorite niece. 'You fret too much, missy. Too much worry only makes the most-feared thing come true. I'm going to sedate you a little to make you cooperative and pliable.'

'And then?'

'I'll cut the lap and shoulder belts from this vehicle, fashion them into a sling, and pull you

271

up this slope to Hawksbill Road.'

'I'm *pregnant*.'

'As anyone but a blind man can see,' Beezo replied, and winked. 'There you go worrying again. I won't secure the sling in any way that would harm you or the baby. I can't carry you up that incline. Too hard. And dangerous.'

'And when we reach the top?'

'I'll load you in the Hummer and drive to a nice cozy private place. When the time comes, I'll deliver your adorable baby.'

Appalled, she said, 'You're not a doctor.'

'Don't you concern yourself. I know the procedure.'

'How would you know?'

'I've read an entire book about it,' he said cheerily. 'I've got all the necessary supplies and instruments.'

'Oh my God.'

'There you go, fretting again,' he said. 'You really do need a better attitude, dear. Attitude is the secret to a happy life. I can recommend some excellent books on the subject.' He patted her shoulder. 'I'll tie everything off just right and leave you where you'll be safe until you're found. Then the boy and I will be away on our great adventure.'

Speechless with horror, she stared at him.

'I will teach him everything I know, and though he doesn't have Beezo blood in his veins, he will become the most acclaimed clown of his century.' An ironic laugh bubbled from him like gas from a swamp. 'I learned with my Punchinello that talent doesn't always travel

272

from generation to generation. But I have so very much to share and such a passion for sharing it that I have no doubt I will make him a *star!*'

'It's going to be a girl,' she said.

Smiling, always smiling, he wagged a finger at her in gentle admonishment. 'Remember, I've been listening for a week. You didn't want the doctor to tell you the sex of the baby.'

'But what if it *is* a girl?'

'It'll be a boy,' he insisted, winking, winking, winking again until he realized that the wink was about to become an uncontrollable tic. 'It will be a boy because I *need* a boy.'

She was afraid to look away from him but could barely tolerate the rage and misery in his eyes. 'Why? Oh. Because no girl has ever been a famous clown.'

'There are female clowns,' he acknowledged, 'but none of great merit. The merry kingdom of the big top is ruled by men.'

If her baby was a girl, he would kill them both.

'It's cold in here now,' Beezo said, 'and getting very late. Be a sweet thing and take off your parka, roll up your sleeve.'

'No.'

His smile grew fixed, then sagged. He forced the curve back into his lips. 'It would grieve me to have to knock you unconscious with a punch or two. But I will if you give me no choice. A thing was done, for whatever reasons, and in your heart you know fairness requires that I be compensated. You can always have another baby.'

35

The door hung open. I had a rock the size of a small grapefruit in my right hand. I leaned into the Explorer, and as the rifleman became aware of me and turned his head, I slammed the rock into his left temple, hard but not as hard as I would have liked.

He regarded me with the surprise that anyone might have shown at the sight of a shot-and-drowned pastry chef miraculously returned to life.

For an instant I thought I would have to hit him with the rock again. Then he slumped into the steering wheel, blowing the horn with his face.

Pushing him back against the headrest, silencing the horn, I looked past him at Lorrie, inexpressibly relieved to see that she appeared to be unharmed.

She said, 'I never again want to hear that song 'Send in the Clowns.''

Not for the first time, I stood uncomprehending before her.

Indicating the man slumped in the driver's seat beside her, Lorrie said, 'Punchinello's daddy.'

Amazed, leaning into the SUV, I pulled off his toboggan cap to examine him. 'I guess he looks a *little* like Konrad Beezo . . . '

'Twenty-four years and plastic surgery,' she explained.

I put my chilled fingertips to his throat, feeling

for a pulse. His heart-beat was slow and steady.

'What's he doing here?' I asked.

'Soliciting donations for UNICEF. Plus he wanted our baby.'

My heart dropped, my stomach turned, something seemed to be wringing my bladder: a major rearrangement of internal organs. 'The baby?'

'I'll tell you later. Jimmy, the contractions aren't more frequent but they sure are a lot more painful, and I'm way cold.'

Her words scared me more than gunfire. Beezo had been subdued; but we were a long way from a hospital delivery room.

'I'll shackle him with the tow cable, put him in the backseat,' I told her.

'Can we drive out of here?'

'I don't think so.'

'Neither do I. But we've got to try, don't we?'

'Yeah.'

She probably wouldn't make it to the top on foot. Too far, too steep. In her condition, if she slipped and took a bad fall, she'd probably start to hemorrhage.

'If we're going to drive,' she said, 'I don't want him in here with us.'

'He'll be restrained.'

'Famous last words. He's not just your ordinary maniac. If he was your ordinary maniac, he could sit on my lap and I'd feed him Life Savers. But he's the great Beezo. I don't want him in here.'

I could sympathize with her position. 'All right, I'll shackle him to a tree.'

'Good.'

'As soon as we reach the hospital, I'll inform the police, and they can come back here for him. But it's awful cold, and maybe he's had a concussion, so he might not survive.'

Staring at the unconscious Beezo with a ferocity I hoped never to see directed at me, Lorrie said, 'Baby, if I had a nail gun, I'd *crucify* him to the tree and never tell anyone.'

Here was an important lesson for villains who hoped for a long career in lawbreaking. The maternal instinct to protect offspring is an awesome thing. Never threaten an expectant mother with the theft of her precious child, especially not if she is the daughter of a snake handler.

I took the assault rifle to the back of the Explorer, opened the tailgate, and put the weapon inside.

The toolbox contained the coiled tow cable. Each end featured a snaplink with a locking sleeve.

Up front, Lorrie cried out urgently, 'Jimmy! He's waking up.'

When I hurried around to the open driver's door, I found Beezo groaning, rolling his head back and forth.

He muttered fearfully, 'Vivacemente.'

Earlier, feeling for his pulse, I had put the rock on the seat beside him. I picked it up and tapped him solidly on the forehead.

His right hand fluttered up from his side, fumbling feebly against his face, and he mumbled, 'Syphilitic weasel, swine of swines . . . '

276

The first tap I had administered had been too restrained. I rapped him harder with the rock, and he slumped unconscious once more.

Having been reluctantly pushed to violence by Punchinello more than four years previously, my ruthlessness didn't surprise me, but I was disturbed to find I enjoyed it. A warm satisfaction flushed my winter-bitten face, and I was tempted to smack him again, though I did not.

My restraint seemed admirable and a consequence of the wholesome values with which I had been raised, but a part of me believed then — and still believes — that a restrained response to evil is not moral. Revenge and justice are twin braids in a line as thin as the high wire that an aerialist must walk, and if you can't keep your balance, then you are doomed — and damned — regardless of whether you fall to the left or to the right of the line.

I hauled Konrad Beezo out of the Explorer and dragged him to a suitable pine tree. He was a difficult package to handle, but that was even more true when he was conscious.

After propping him against the pine, I opened his coat, quickly fed the tow cable up the left sleeve, across his chest, and down the right sleeve. Then I buttoned the coat to his throat.

One at a time, I took the ends of the cable around to the farther side of the tree and hooked one snaplink through the other. I screwed the locking metal sleeves over the snap gates.

Little slack remained in the cable. He would not be able to get his hands in front of himself to try to strip off the coat. He had been essentially straitjacketed, which seemed appropriate.

I checked the pulse in his throat once more. The artery throbbed strong and steady.

For a while in those days, we had a saying in our family: *The only way to kill a clown is to beat him to death with a mime.*

Returning to the Explorer, I put on my leather gloves. I brushed the crumbles of safety glass off the driver's seat, got in behind the wheel, and pulled the door shut.

Huddled in the passenger's seat, Lorrie pressed her hands to her rounded abdomen, alternately hissing through her clenched teeth and groaning.

'Worse?' I asked.

'You remember the chest-burster scene in *Alien*?'

On the dashboard lay a small black leather drug kit with two hypodermics.

'He wanted to shoot me up to make me cooperative and 'pliable,'' she revealed.

Rage flared in me, but nothing would be gained by letting it build into an all-consuming fire.

As I carefully returned the filled syringe to its niche and then zipped the kit shut, setting it aside as evidence, I said, 'Domestic bliss through modern chemistry. Why didn't I think of that? I'm all for pliability in a wife.'

'If you were, you'd never have married me.'

I kissed her quickly on the cheek. 'For sure.'

'I've had enough adventure for tonight. Get me to an epidural.'

Hesitating to turn the key in the ignition, I worried that the engine wouldn't start, that the pinching trees wouldn't release us.

She said, 'Beezo was going to make a sling out of the lap and shoulder belts and haul me up to the highway like a hunter dragging a deer carcass.'

I wanted to get out of the Explorer and kill him. And I prayed that we wouldn't be reduced to implementing his plan.

36

On the second try, the engine turned over and caught. I switched on the headlights. Lorrie cranked up the heater to compensate for the icy air pouring through the broken window.

The gap between the ancient firs that bracketed the SUV had been narrow enough to halt our backward slide; but those trees might not have us in a sufficiently tight grip to resist the forward thrust of the engine.

I eased down on the accelerator, and the engine growled. Tires spun, stuttered, spun. The Explorer creaked, protesting the hard embrace of the trees.

Pressed for more power, the engine shrieked. The tires squealed, and the creaking increased, augmented by a phantom rattle the source of which I could not place.

The Explorer began to shudder like a terrified horse with a leg trapped in a rockfall.

A hard metallic grinding arose. I didn't like the sound of it.

When I eased off the accelerator, the Explorer settled backward an inch or two. I had not been aware of gaining that ground when the SUV had been straining forward.

I established a rhythmic application of the gas pedal. The Explorer rocked gently back and forth, abrading the bark on the fir trees.

Turning the steering wheel slightly to the right

had no effect. When I turned it slightly to the left, we jolted forward four or five inches before getting hung up again.

I eased the wheel back to the right, pumped the pedal. A loud *twang*! reverberated around us as if we were in the hollow of a bell, and suddenly we were free.

Lorrie said, 'I hope the baby comes out that easy.'

'Anything changes, I want to know right away.'

'Changes?'

'Like if your water breaks.'

'Oh, honey, if my water breaks, you'll know it without being told. You'll be ankle deep in it.'

Because of the altitude, I didn't think that the Explorer would get far in a direct assault on the slope. Still, I had to give it a try.

The incline wasn't as steep down here as it became higher up, and we powered forward farther than I expected, deviating from a straight ascent only to ease around trees and the rare knob of rock. We had gone perhaps a hundred yards before the way grew steeper and the air-starved engine began to cough.

From that point on, I intended to pursue a switchback ascent, thereby demanding less of the vehicle. Proceeding due north or due south, crossing the slope at ninety degrees to the gradient, would be suicide; the way was too steep, and the Explorer would sooner or later roll. But tacking left and right at cautious angles, we might neither stall out nor roll, and wend our way up as if following the architecture of a staircase.

This strategy required caution and intense concentration. Each time that we switchbacked, I had to calculate, by sheer instinct, the angle of ascent that would gain us the most ground while putting us at the least risk.

The terrain proved wildly irregular. Frequently, if I pressed forward the slightest bit too hastily, the Explorer began to rock side to side on the corrugated land, bouncing us roughly in our seats, gathering lateral momentum that on this hillside might topple it. More than once in my mind's eye, we went crashing to the bottom of the ravine, caroming from tree to tree like a pinball bouncing off flippers and bumpers.

Sometimes I slowed to let the vehicle stabilize. At other times I stopped altogether, frightened by the way the steering wheel pulled in my hands. Pausing, I studied the forbidding landscape revealed by the headlights, making small adjustments in our route.

When we passed the midpoint of our journey, I dared to believe that we would make it.

Lorrie's confidence must have improved, too, for she broke the tense silence in which we had thus far ascended: 'There's something I would have regretted never having told you if we died here tonight.'

'That I'm a love god?'

'Guys who think they're love gods are arrogant twits. You . . . you're a snuggle puppy, but if I'd died without telling you that, I wouldn't have had any regrets.'

'If I'd died without hearing it, I'd have been okay, too.'

'You know,' she said, 'parents and children and love come in some strange combinations. I mean, your parents can love you and you can *know* they love you, and you can love them, and still grow up so lonely that you feel . . . hollow.'

I hadn't expected a revelation this serious. I knew it was a genuine revelation because I understood what her next words inevitably must be.

She said, 'Love isn't enough. Your parents have to know how to relate to you, and to each other. They have to want to be with you more than with anyone else. They have to love being home more than anywhere in the world, and they have to be more interested in you than in . . . '

'Snakes and tornadoes,' I suggested.

'God, I love them. They're nice, Jimmy, they really are, and they *mean* well. But they live inside themselves more than not, and they keep their doors closed. You see them mostly through windows.'

The tremor in her voice grew as she spoke, and when she paused, I said, 'You are a treasure, Lorrie Lynn.'

'You grew up with everything I wanted so bad, everything that I dreamed of having. Your folks *live* for you and for each other, for family. So does Weena in her own way. It's bliss, Jimmy. And I'm so damned grateful that you all let me in.'

Under her admirable toughness, under the armor of her beauty and her wit, my wife is a tender spirit and might have been a shy wallflower if she had not chosen, instead, to make herself into a survivor, and a survivor with *style*.

Under my less than tough exterior, I am mushy. Mucho mushy. I have been known to cry at the sight of roadkill.

Her words rendered me incapable of speech. If I had tried to talk, I would have teared up. Piloting the Explorer toward the crest, I dared not risk blurred vision.

Fortunately, she picked up her next thread of thought and, with firmer voice, continued to weave the conversation without me. 'You can't know what a joy it's going to be for me, Jimmy, to raise our kids the way that you were raised, to give them the gift of Maddy and Rudy and Weena, to bring them up in a family so close that they can find in it the deepest meaning of their lives.'

We were two or three switchbacks from the summit.

She said, 'We've never discussed how many children we're going to have. Right now I'm thinking maybe five. What about you — are you thinking five?'

I found my voice. 'I always thought three, but after that little speech, I'm thinking twenty.'

'Let's make the decision five at a time.'

'Deal,' I said. 'One almost out of the oven, four left to bake.'

'Two girls and three boys,' she wondered, 'or three girls and two boys?'

'Is that really our decision?'

'I believe we shape our own reality by positive thinking. I'm sure we could positive-think ourselves any combination we wanted, although for ideal balance we should have two girls, two boys, and one hermaphrodite.'

'That might be taking balance too far.'

'Oh, Jimmy, no kids will ever have been loved more than these are going to be loved.'

'But they won't be spoiled,' I said.

'Damn right they won't, the little brats. Their Great-Grandma Rowena can read them fairy tales. *That'll* keep them on the straight and narrow.'

She talked and talked, and soon I saw that she had wisely talked us through the dread and the danger of the climb, to the top of the slope and Hawksbill Road.

37

We arrived on Hawksbill Road twenty feet in front of the parked Hummer. We churned across a recently compacted high curb of snow, onto the southbound lane, which had been scraped almost to the bare blacktop.

Immediately to the south of us, a highway department crew in two vehicles was carving a passage to town through the storm. A road grader on immense knobby tires, fitted with an angled plow, led the way, trailed by a truck spreading salt and cinders in its wake.

I followed the truck at a safe distance. A police escort could have gotten us to town no quicker in this mean weather.

The night sky hid behind the shedding snow, and the wind was revealed only by the white shrouds that it wound about itself and whirled, and flapped, and billowed.

Also unseen but not for long, the baby made known its impatience to be free from nine months of confinement. Lorrie's contractions had become regular. By her wristwatch, she timed them, and by her groans and louder cries, I knew the intervals and *willed* the road crew to move faster.

Suffering people frequently curse their pain. For some reason we seem to believe that acute agony can be managed by injections of obscenities. Lorrie allowed not one such word to cross her lips that night.

I can testify that in ordinary times she is capable of treating a cut or a contusion with a verbal blue streak more astringent than iodine. Birth night was not an ordinary time.

She said that she didn't curse the pain because the baby, as it made its entrance, might think it wasn't wanted in the world.

That our child might be born with advanced language skills had not crossed my mind. I accepted her concern as legitimate — and loved her for it.

When groans and grunts and wordless cries did not satisfy her urge to express the effect of her pangs, she resorted for the baby's sake to words that described some of the world's beauty and bounty.

'Strawberries, sunflowers, seashells,' she said, hissing out the sibilants with such vehemence that someone who spoke no English would have been convinced that she had wished pestilence, disease, and damnation on a hated enemy.

By the time that we reached town and then Snow County Hospital, Lorrie's water had not yet broken, but it seemed instead to be coming out of her through every pore. This labor, as surely as chopping wood or digging a trench, wrung rivers of sweat from her. She unzipped her parka, then stripped it off. She was soaked.

I parked at the emergency entrance, rushed inside, and returned in a minute with an orderly and a wheelchair.

The orderly, a freckled young man named Cory, thought Lorrie had descended into delirium when, trading Explorer for wheelchair, she snarled in rapid succession, 'Geraniums, Coca-Cola, kittens, snow geese, *Christmas cakes and cookies*,' with such fervency that she scared him.

On the way inside I explained to him about welcoming the baby to the world by trading curses for words of beauty and bounty, but I think I only succeeded in making him a little afraid of me, too.

I couldn't accompany Lorrie directly to the maternity ward in part because I had to present our insurance card to the clerk at the admissions desk at the back of the ER waiting lounge. I kissed her, and she squeezed my hand hard enough to crack my knuckles and said, 'Maybe not twenty.'

A nurse joined the orderly, and together they wheeled Lorrie toward the elevators.

As they rolled her out of sight, I heard her say with singular intensity, '*Crêpes Suzette, clafouti, gâteau à l'orange, soufflé au chocolat*.'

I supposed that if our baby might be born with a command of English, it might also know French and might already anticipate a career as a pastry chef.

While the admissions clerk Xeroxed my insurance card and began to fill out two pounds of registration forms, I used her phone to call Huey Foster. He was my father's friend from childhood, the failed baker who had become a cop.

From Huey, Dad had received the free pass to the circus on the back of which he had written the five terrible days in my life. We didn't hold that against Huey.

He worked nights, and I caught him at the station house. When I told him about Konrad Beezo, fugitive murderer and would-be baby bandit, shackled to a tree in the woods about three to four hundred yards downhill and west of his parked Hummer, Huey said, 'That's state trooper jurisdiction. I'll get 'em right on it. I'll go with 'em. After all these years, I want to personally put the cuffs on that crazy bastard.'

Next I called my folks to tell them only that we were at the hospital and that Lorrie was in labor.

'I'm painting a potbelly pig,' Mom said, 'but that can wait. We'll be there quick as we can.'

'It's not necessary for you to come in this weather.'

'Sweetie, if it was raining scorpions and cow pies, we'd still come, though we wouldn't like it much. It'll take us a while because we first have to get Weena into her snowsuit. You know what an ordeal she'll make of that, but we'll be there.'

I was still a relatively young man when the admissions clerk finished filling out forms for me to sign, and from her desk I went up to the maternity ward.

The expectant-fathers' lounge had been remodeled since the night that I gave my mother such a hard time being born. The flamboyance of cheerful clashing colors had been replaced by gray carpet, pale-gray walls, and black leatherette chairs, as though the hospital directors had reached a consensus that in the intervening

289

twenty-four years, all the joy had gone out of parenthood.

The admissions clerk had phoned ahead to advise that I was en route. A nurse showed me to a lavatory, where I washed up according to instructions and changed into hospital greens; then I was taken to my wife.

Lorrie's water had not yet broken, but all the signs pointed to an impending birth. Therefore, and because no other pregnant women had been reckless enough to go into labor in a blizzard, she had been prepared quickly in her assigned room and conveyed to Delivery.

When I entered, a heavyset red-haired nurse was taking Lorrie's blood pressure, and Dr. Mello Melodeon, our physician, was listening to her heart through a stethoscope.

Mello is as solid as any football fullback, as personable as a popular tavern owner whose charm keeps the bar stools filled, and a mensch. Judging by his fine name, his skin the color of raisins, his relaxed manner, and his mellifluous voice, you might think he had once been a Jamaican Rastafarian who had traded dreadlocks and reggae for a career in medicine. Instead, he'd been born in Atlanta and came from a family of professional gospel singers.

Finished with the stethoscope, he said, 'Jimmy, how come when Rachel makes your chocolate apple lattice tart, it doesn't *taste* like yours?'

Rachel was his wife.

I said, 'Where'd she get the recipe?'

'The resort gives it out if you ask. We ate at the restaurant out there last week.'

290

'She should have asked me. That's the original resort recipe, but I've modified it. Mainly, I've added a tablespoon of vanilla and another of nutmeg.'

'The nutmeg I understand, but vanilla in a chocolate tart?'

'That's the secret,' I guaranteed him.

'Yoo-hoo, I'm here,' Lorrie reminded us.

I took her hand. 'And you're not snarling about *crêpes Suzette* and *clafouti*.'

'Because of an even more beautiful word,' she said. '*Epidural*. Isn't that a beautiful word?'

'So let me get this straight — you just add vanilla to the filling?' Mello asked.

'It's not in the filling. It's in the dough.'

'In the *dough*,' he repeated, nodding sagely.

Lorrie said, 'Anybody want a website designed? That's what *I* do. I design websites. And make babies.'

'Website design is interesting, dear,' Mello Melodeon assured her, 'but it'll never be as interesting as what Jimmy does. You can't eat a website.'

'You can't eat a baby, either,' she said, 'but I'd rather have one than a chocolate apple lattice tart.'

'I don't see why you can't have both,' Mello said, 'although not simultaneously.'

Grimacing, clutching two handfuls of the sheet that was draped over her, she said, 'I need more epidural.'

'As your doctor, I'll make that determination. It's to relieve the pain, not eliminate it entirely.'

To me, she said, 'I knew we should have

291

gotten a *real* doctor.'

To me, Mello said, 'So do you add the vanilla to the ingredients the same time you add the cocoa?'

'No. That's too early. Add it right before the egg yolks.'

'Before the egg *yolks*,' he repeated, impressed by this culinary tactic.

And so the conversation went until Lorrie's water broke. Then she was unquestionably the center of attention.

Lorrie and I had agreed: no video camera. She thought filming the blessed event would be tacky. I thought it would be beyond my mechanical abilities.

Nevertheless, I wanted to be present in part to share the joy and to welcome our firstborn, but also to prove to Grandma Rowena that I would not pass out, fall on my face, and break my nose, as she insisted that I would.

No sooner had Lorrie's water broken, however, than a nurse in squeaky shoes entered the delivery room as if with a chorus of mice, to announce there was an important telephone call for me. Captain Huey Foster, of the Snow Village Police Department, urgently needed to speak with me.

'I'll be back in a minute,' I told Lorrie. 'Hold everything.'

'Yeah, right.'

I took the call on the phone at the nurses' station. 'What's up, Huey?'

'He's gone.'

'Who?'

'Who do you think? Beezo.'

'He *can't* be gone. You haven't found the right tree.'

'Excuse me, Jimmy, but I'd bet you my left ass cheek there's not more than one tree out there decorated with a tow cable and a torn-up coat with sheepskin lining.'

Add up all the times my heart had sunk that night, and you were at the depth of the *Titanic*.

'He couldn't use his hands,' I said. 'They were behind him. I had him trussed up tight. What the hell did he do — chew his way out of the coat?'

'Almost looks like it.'

The black Hummer had been parked along Hawksbill Road exactly where I had told them to look for it.

'By the way,' Huey said, 'we already learned it was stolen twelve days ago in Las Vegas.'

A police search team had descended through the woods, following the Explorer's original trail. When they discovered that Beezo had escaped, they had considered calling in a bloodhound team; but the weather argued against it.

'He won't get far in this cold without a coat,' Huey predicted. 'After the spring thaw, we'll find him as dead as the dinosaurs.'

'Not this one,' I said shakily. 'This one is ... different. He's like the clown in a jack-in-the-box, he just keeps popping up.'

'He ain't supernatural.'

'I wouldn't take that side of the argument,' I said.

Huey sighed. 'I'm half of the same conclusion,' he admitted. 'I just called up four off-duty men.

293

They'll be coming around to the hospital just in case.'

'How long till they get here?'

'Ten minutes. Maybe fifteen. Meanwhile, you better watch out for Lorrie. I don't think it'll come to that, but it might. She have the baby yet?'

'It's on the way right now. Huey, listen, he camped out in Nedra Lamm's house to keep a watch on us.'

'Nedra's a pill, but she wouldn't allow that.'

'I don't think she had a choice. It's maybe not too far for him to get back to her place. If he thinks the Hummer's now too hot to drive, she has a car he might want.'

'That hideous old Plymouth Valiant.'

'It's in showroom shape, and she keeps snow chains on it.'

'We'll check it out,' Huey promised. 'Now you better get back to that special girl of yours and don't let anything happen to her till my men arrive.'

I hung up. My palms were slick with sweat. I blotted them on my hospital greens.

Beezo was coming. I knew it in my bones. More than twenty-four years after his first visit, he was returning to the Snow County Hospital maternity ward. This time, the baby he wanted was ours.

38

I didn't want Lorrie to learn about the situation. As it was, she had her hands full. Well, not her *hands*, but she was otherwise fully occupied, and it couldn't be good for her to know that Beezo was loose.

If I returned to the delivery room, no matter how distracted Lorrie was, she would at first glance read the fear in me. I would not be able to lie to her even for her own good. I would be butter to her hot knife, and she would spread me on toast in six seconds flat.

Besides, Dr. Mcllo Melodeon would have more questions about my chocolate apple lattice tart, and I didn't have time for that.

I hurried to the expectant-fathers' lounge where, in different decor, Dr. Ferris MacDonald had been shot to death. From this room, Beezo had burst into the maternity ward, shooting Nurse Hanson.

If criminals really did like to return to the scenes of their crimes, he might come after our baby by this route.

Might.

I wasn't willing to hang the fate of my wife and baby on a *might* or a *maybe*.

Blotting my hands on my greens again, I stepped into the main corridor that served the second floor.

The place was unnaturally quiet, hushed, even

for a hospital, as though the heavy snowfall exerted a muffling influence through the walls.

Farther to my right, on this side of the hall, were four doors that evidently led into various departments of the maternity ward. Beyond the doors lay the long window that provided a view into the neonatal care unit where newborns were cradled in bassinets.

At the end of the hall, a lighted red EXIT sign marked the door to the emergency stairs.

Beezo could come up the stairs and choose any entrance to the ward. I wouldn't see him from the expectant-fathers' lounge, so I'd have to stand guard here in the corridor.

Ding! Soft but instantly identifiable, the chime issued from the elevator alcove that branched off the midpoint of this main corridor. Someone had arrived on the second floor.

Lately I'd gotten so much practice holding my breath that I would soon be ready for a career in pearl diving.

A doctor in a white lab coat came out of the alcove, carrying a clipboard, chatting with a nurse who was too small and too female to be Konrad Beezo. They headed toward the farther end of the hall.

I thought I should go to the emergency stairwell and listen for ascending footsteps, but I didn't want to turn my back on the hallway.

Where were Huey Foster's men? Surely they should have arrived by now.

Consulting my watch, I discovered that only two minutes had passed since I'd hung up the phone. Huey's men were still putting on their shoes.

Time doesn't pass a fraction as fast when you're waiting for a killer as it does when you're having fun in the kitchen.

The hospital had a single security guard stationed in the lobby on the ground floor. I considered calling him up here to help cover the territory.

His name was Vernon Tibbit. Sixty-eight years old, pot-bellied, near-sighted, Vernon didn't have a gun. Basically his job entailed giving directions to visitors, assisting patients in wheelchairs, getting coffee for the lady at the information desk, and polishing his badge.

I didn't want to get Vernon killed and leave the info lady with no one to fetch her java.

If Konrad Beezo didn't actually drive a tank through the walls of the hospital, he would at least arrive with a formidable weapon. I had the distinct impression that he didn't go anywhere without heat.

I didn't have a gun. I didn't have a knife. I didn't have a club. I didn't have a spitball.

When I remembered the assault rifle that I had taken from Beezo and that now lay in the back of the Explorer, a thrill coursed up my spine. He had changed the magazine in the woods, and surely he hadn't emptied the second one. I succumbed to a spasm of macho stupidity, envisioning myself as Rambo, except markedly more buff than Sylvester Stallone.

Then I realized I couldn't charge through a hospital, blithely firing an assault rifle. I wasn't a staff member, and visiting hours were over.

In fear of being shot, worried about Lorrie in labor, worried about my unborn child, worried that my aching left leg — having taken so much punishment — would fail me at a crucial moment, I was further distracted by the hospital greens. I wasn't comfortable in them.

After taking off the elasticized cloth booties that covered my shoes, I didn't feel much better. I felt as though I were decked out for a masquerade party.

Halloween had arrived nine months early this year. At any moment, a maniac clown would come trick-or-treating, out of costume but scary as hell nonetheless.

Ding!

I swallowed my Adam's apple, which bounced around inside my stomach.

Following the chime, the second floor seemed more hushed than ever. This was the high-noon stillness of a dusty street in a small Western town, with every citizen gone to ground and the gunfighters about to appear.

Instead of a gunfighter, out of the elevator alcove came Dad, Mom, and Grandma Rowena.

I was stunned that they had gotten here so soon, half an hour before I expected them. Their presence lifted my heart and renewed my courage.

As they started toward me, waving, I moved to meet them, eager to have a hug fest.

Then I realized that everyone I most loved — Mom, Dad, Grandma, Lorrie, and my baby — were gathered in the same place. Beezo could kill all of them in one bloody spree.

39

Outdoors in winter, Grandma only wore full-body snowsuits, which she sewed from quilted fabrics. Having no tolerance for cold weather, she believed that she had been Hawaiian in a previous life. Occasionally she enjoyed dreams in which she wore puka-shell necklaces and a grass skirt, and danced at the foot of a volcano.

She and everyone in her village had been killed in a volcanic eruption. You might think this would lead to a fear of fire. But she suspected that in yet another and more recent previous life, she had been an Eskimo who died with her dogsled team in a furious blizzard through which they were unable to find their way back to the igloo.

In a puffy white snowsuit with a closely fitted hood zippered snugly under her chin, leaving only her face revealed, Weena toddled toward me, arms wide in anticipation of an embrace. I couldn't decide whether she looked more like a three-year-old togged out for play in the snow or like the Michelin Tire Man.

Neither Mom nor Dad had a taste for flamboyant couture — or if they did, they never indulged it, because they knew there were times when Grandma was determined to be the center of attention.

They were full of questions. With all the

hugging and the excitement about the baby, I needed a minute to get their attention and make them understand that Beezo was back. Then they formed up around me with the steely determination of the Praetorian Guard, as though they had plenty of practice taking down would-be assassins.

This scared me more than if they had quaked with fear. I was greatly relieved when a few minutes later the first of Huey Foster's officers arrived, uniformed and armed.

Soon a deputy had stationed himself in the stairwell. Two others covered the corridor that provided all access to the maternity ward, and the fourth took up a post in the elevator alcove.

The last of these men brought word that Nedra Lamm had been murdered in her home. Preliminary examination of the body indicated that she had been strangled.

By the time I settled my folks in the expectant-fathers' lounge, a nurse brought me word that Lorrie was still in labor and that Huey Foster was on the phone for me.

Leaving Mom, Dad, and Grandma in the care of the deputies, I took the call at the nurses' station, as before.

Huey was by nature an ebullient guy. Even a small-town cop sees more grisly sights than the average citizen; the consequences of catastrophic car crashes alone ensure that he will be familiar with bloody deaths. But Huey Foster had never allowed his work to twist him through an emotional wringer.

Until now. He sounded grim, angry, and

sickened, all at once. Several times he had to stop and collect himself before he could continue.

Nedra Lamm had been strangled, as Officer Paolini reported, but no one could yet determine at what point in her ordeal she had been murdered.

As proudly self-sufficient as she was cranky, Nedra had been a deer hunter with an enormous freezer full of venison. Konrad Beezo piled the packaged deer meat on the back porch and stored Nedra in the Amana.

Before he consigned her to the big chill, he had stripped her naked. Then he painted her entire body — front and back, neck to toes — in the brightly striped and polka-dotted patterns of a traditional clown costume.

She might have been alive for this.

With what appeared to be stage makeup, he had greasepainted her face to resemble that of a clown. He blackened three of her teeth and colored her tongue green.

In a kitchen drawer, he had found a turkey-basting syringe. He removed from it the rubber squeeze bulb, which he painted red and glued over Nedra's nose.

The makeup had not been applied in a slapdash manner. Judging by appearances, Beezo spent hours at the task, paying meticulous attention to detail.

Whether she had been alive for all of that, she had certainly been dead by the time he used a needle and thread to sew shut her eyelids. Then he painted stars over them.

Finally, he selected a set of deer antlers from the collection in Nedra's garage, and he tied them to her head. To get her into the freezer with the antlers, in a position that assured her face would be turned up to greet whoever found her, he had to break her legs in several places, a task he accomplished with a sledgehammer.

Huey Foster said, 'Jimmy, I swear, he did this 'cause he thought it was funny. He thought someone would open that freezer and laugh, that we'd all be snickering about Nedra in her clown getup for years to come, talking about what a joker that Beezo was.'

Standing there at the nurses' station, I was colder than I had been in the woods, in the blizzard.

'Well, the crazy sick son of a bitch didn't get any laughs from us,' Huey said. 'Not one smile. This young state trooper, he bolted from the house and threw up in the backyard.'

'Where is Beezo, Huey?'

'Freezing to death in the woods, I hope.'

'He didn't go back there for Nedra's Plymouth?'

'It's still in the garage.'

'He's not in the woods, Huey.'

'Maybe not,' he admitted.

'If he made it back up to Hawksbill Road and someone came along, he could have hitched a ride.'

'Who would be dumb enough to pick him up?'

'What ordinary decent person *wouldn't* pick him up on a night like this? You see a guy not dressed for the weather, maybe standing by the

302

Hummer, you think he broke down. If you don't pick him up, he's likely to freeze. You don't say to yourself, *Better not pick him up, he looks like a murderous clown.*'

'If he got a ride, he probably took the car.'

'And the guy who gave him the ride is dead in the trunk.'

'Hasn't been a murder in this town in thirty years that this creep and his son didn't commit.'

'What now?'

'State police are thinking roadblocks. There's only five routes out of the county, and the snow already helps us.'

'He won't leave tonight,' I predicted. 'He has unfinished business.'

'I sure hope you're wrong about that.'

'I have a built-in oven timer,' I told him.

'You what?'

'When I've got something in the oven, I always check it five seconds before the timer goes off. Always. I instinctively know when something's finished baking — and when it's not. Beezo isn't done.'

'You get that from your dad. He could have been a cop as easy as a baker. You too, maybe. Me, I had no choice.'

'I'm scared, Huey.'

'Yeah. Me too.'

As I hung up the phone, a nurse arrived to inform me that Lorrie had given birth. 'No complications,' she said.

Boy, could I have given her an earful.

In the delivery room, the red-haired nurse was

at a basin in the corner, cleaning off our little miracle.

Mello Melodeon was waiting for Lorrie to expel the afterbirth, gently massaging her abdomen to control the flow of blood.

Whether or not I could have been a cop as easily as a baker, I could never have been a doctor. I'm not even a good patient.

The only thing preventing me from passing out and breaking my nose against the floor was the certainty that Grandma Rowena would toddle in here and take a picture of me. She would have a disposable camera tucked in a pocket of that snowsuit.

Using the photo as a pattern, she would needlepoint the scene of my humiliation on a pillow and give it a place of honor on the living-room sofa.

The head of the birthing bed had been elevated, so Lorrie was half sitting. She looked sweaty, sore, exhausted — and radiant.

'Well, there you are,' she said. 'I thought maybe you went off to have dinner.'

Licking my lips, patting my belly, I said, 'New York steak, baked potato, creamed corn, pepper slaw, and a slab of chocolate fudge *gâteau*.'

'When you make chocolate fudge *gâteau*,' Mello Melodeon asked, 'do you always have to use ground almonds, or can you substitute hazelnuts?'

Lorrie said, 'Good Lord, what does a girl have to do around here to be a *star*?'

Just then she expelled the afterbirth. There's some spectacle involved in this final bit of business, but it's not the stuff of stardom.

On my feet at her bedside, swaying, I gripped her hand, and she said, 'You can lean on me, big guy,' and I sincerely said, 'Thanks.'

When the red-haired nurse brought the baby, it was washed and pink and swaddled in a soft white cloth. 'Mr. Tock, say hello to your daughter.'

Lorrie held the precious bundle, while I stood paralyzed and speechless. For nine months, I had known where this was leading, but it nevertheless seemed impossible.

We had chosen the name Andy if it was a boy, Anne if it was a girl.

Anne had fine golden hair. Her nose was perfect. Her eyes, too, and her chin, and her tiny little hands, all perfect.

I thought of Nedra Lamm in the freezer, Punchinello in prison, Konrad Beezo out there somewhere in the winter night, and I wondered how I dared to bring a vulnerable child into a world as dark as ours, and getting darker year by year.

On days when the universe seems cruel or at least indifferent, my dad has a saying that he relies on to cheer him up. I have heard it a thousand times: *Where there's cake, there's hope. And there's always cake.*

In spite of Konrad Beezo and all my concerns, my eyes filled with tears of joy, and I said, 'Welcome to the world, Annie Tock.'

40

As you might remember, Annie came to us on Monday night, January 12, 1998, exactly seven days before the second of the five terrible dates foreseen by Grandpa Josef.

The following week was the longest week of my life. Waiting for the other big clown shoe to drop.

The storm passed. The sky became that hard pale blue familiar to those who live at high altitudes, such a clean and steely and sharp shade of blue that you felt you could reach up and cut your hand on it.

With Beezo loose and the fateful day ahead of us, our house on Hawksbill Road seemed dangerously isolated. We stayed in town with my folks.

Naturally, our worst fear was that Annie, with whom we had been so recently blessed, would be taken from us — one way or another.

We were prepared to die rather than let that happen.

Because Huey Foster knew all about my grandfather's predictions and their unsettling accuracy, the Snow Village Police assigned an officer to my parents' house around the clock, beginning Wednesday morning, when I brought Lorrie and Annie home. Indeed, we were driven from the hospital in a squad car.

Each officer came for an eight-hour shift. He

patrolled the house every hour, checking door and window locks, studying the neighboring residences and the street.

Dad went to work, but I took time off and stayed home. Of course when the tension made me crazy, I baked.

Each of the cops chose the kitchen table as his post, and by Thursday all of them agreed that they had never eaten so well in their lives.

In times of loss and trouble of all kinds, neighbors usually express their concern and solidarity by bringing food. In our case, the neighbors were too intimidated to offer the usual casseroles and homebaked pies.

Instead, they brought DVDs. I don't know whether independently each of them arrived at the conclusion that in this media-drenched era, DVDs were an acceptable substitute for consoling gifts of food, or if they had a community meeting to debate the issue. By Friday our home-entertainment needs for the next two years were covered.

Grandma Rowena snatched up all the Schwarzenegger movies and watched them on the TV in her bedroom, with the door closed.

We put the rest of the DVDs in a box in the corner of the living room and forgot about them for the duration.

Mom finished painting the potbelly pig and started work on a portrait of the baby. Perhaps she had restricted herself to animal subjects for too many years, because on her new canvas, our sweet little girl had a weird resemblance to a bunny rabbit.

Annie didn't keep us as busy as I expected. She was a perfect baby. She didn't cry. She hardly fussed. She slept through the night — baker's night, from nine in the morning until four o'clock in the afternoon — better than any of us.

I almost wished she would turn cranky just to distract me from thoughts of the fugitive Beezo.

Even with a police officer in the house at all times, I was glad that I had a pistol of my own and that I had taken instruction in its proper use.

I noticed that Lorrie always kept a sharp knife close at hand — and an apple that she said she intended to peel and eat 'in a little while.' By Saturday morning, the apple had withered somewhat, and she exchanged it for a pear.

Usually you peel fruit with a paring knife. Lorrie preferred the blade named for the butcher.

Dad, bless his heart, came home with two baseball bats. They weren't those modern aluminum kind, but solid-wood Louisville Sluggers. He'd never had an interest in guns and had no time to learn. He gave one bat to Mom.

No one asked him why he hadn't bought a third bat for Grandma. With no strain at all, each of us could conjure up a vivid mind movie to explain his decision.

Finally the terrible day came.

Monday was a day off for Dad, and from midnight Sunday until dawn on January 19, the six of us gathered in the dining room. We fortified ourselves with cookies and *kugelhopf* and *streusel* and pots of black coffee.

We kept the drapes tight shut. The conversation was as fluent as ever, but we spoke in softer voices than usual, and from time to time we all fell silent, heads cocked, listening to the settling noises of the house and to the snuffling wind in the eaves.

Dawn came without a clown.

The sky had aged again, gray and bearded.

Our police guards changed shifts. The officer leaving took a bag of cookies with him; the new arrival brought an empty bag with him.

As the rest of the world went to work, our bedtime came. Only Grandma and the baby were able to sleep.

Monday morning waned without incident.

Noon came, and afternoon.

Guards changed again at four o'clock, and little more than an hour later, the early winter twilight descended.

The uneventfulness of the day did not reassure me. Quite the opposite. As we came to the last six hours, every nerve in my body wound tighter than an efficiency expert's watch spring.

In that condition, I would most likely use my pistol only to shoot myself in the foot. Another moment of family history worthy of a needle-point pillow.

At seven o'clock, Huey Foster called to inform me that our house on Hawksbill Road was ablaze. Firemen reported that the intensity of the flames indicated arson.

My first impulse was to race out to the fire, be there, *do* something.

Officer Paolini — who happened to be our bodyguard that shift — made a convincing case that Beezo might have set the fire with the purpose of drawing me out in the open. I stayed with my wife, my daughter, my well-armed family.

By eight o'clock, we learned that our house had burned to the ground with such fury that nothing remained but hot coals. Evidently the interior had been liberally doused with gasoline before the match had been struck.

No furniture could be salvaged. No kitchen utensils, no clothes. No mementoes.

We returned to the dining-room table, this time for dinner, no less worried, no less alert. When ten o'clock came without further activity, however, we began to wonder if the worst that would happen had already passed.

Losing your house and all of your possessions in a fire is not a good thing, granted, but it's a lot better than being shot twice in the leg and immeasurably better than having your beautiful infant daughter kidnapped by a maniac.

We were prepared to make this bargain with fate: Take the house and all our possessions, no hard feelings, as long as we know we'll be safe until the *third* of Grandpa Josef's terrible days — Monday, December 23, 2002. That price for nearly four years of peace seemed cheap.

By eleven o'clock, the six of us — and even Officer Paolini, who diligently set out on another patrol through the house — suspected that fate had accepted our offer. A tentative celebratory mood began to color our conversation.

Huey called with news that seemed to give us closure, but it didn't inspire us to raise champagne toasts.

As the firemen had been mopping up the scene and stowing their hoses, one of them noticed that the drop door on our roadside mailbox was hanging open. In the mailbox, he found a mason jar. In the mason jar, a folded slip of paper.

The paper had a message for us in neat handwriting that police later matched to Konrad Beezo's penmanship on the admission forms he had filled out when he'd brought his wife, Natalie, to the hospital on the night of my birth. More than a message, it constituted a promise: IF YOU EVER HAVE A BABY BOY, I'LL BE BACK FOR HIM.

PART FOUR

ALL I EVER WANTED WAS IMMORTALITY

41

No one's life should be rooted in fear. We are born for wonder, for joy, for hope, for love, to marvel at the mystery of existence, to be ravished by the beauty of the world, to seek truth and meaning, to acquire wisdom, and by our treatment of others to brighten the corner where we are.

Simply by existing, unseen and in some distant redoubt, Konrad Beezo made the world a darker place, but we lived in light, not in his shadow.

No one can grant you happiness. Happiness is a choice we all have the power to make. There is always cake.

Following the destruction of our house in January 1998, Lorrie and Annie and I moved in with my parents for several weeks.

Huey Foster's estimation, the night of the fire, that nothing whatsoever could be salvaged from our house proved correct as to furniture, housewares, books, and clothes.

Three items that qualified as mementoes, however, were raked from the ashes in acceptable condition. A cameo pendant that I had bought for Lorrie. A crystal Christmas-tree ornament that she had purchased at a gift shop in Carmel, California, on our honeymoon. And the free pass to the circus on the back of which my father had written five dates.

The face of that card had been singed and water-spotted. The words ADMIT TWO and the word FREE had vaporized entirely. Only a few fragments of the beautifully rendered lions and elephants survived as ghost images, glimpsed between mottling scorches, embedded soot, and water stains.

Curiously, at the bottom of the free pass, the words PREPARE TO BE ENCHANTED were almost as bright and clear as they had ever been. In this new context, that line struck me as vaguely ominous, as it had never done before, as though it were not a promise of delight but a subtle threat.

More curiously still, the reverse of the circus pass appeared all but untouched by heat and water. On that side, the paper had been only slightly yellowed; the five dates in my father's printing were easy to read.

The card smelled of smoke. I cannot say truthfully that it smelled also of brimstone.

In early March, we began looking for a place in town, preferably in my parents' neighborhood. By the end of that month, the house next door to theirs came on the market.

We know an omen when we see one. We made an offer the sellers couldn't refuse, and closed escrow on May 15.

If we had been rich, we could have bought a compound of houses encircled by a wall, entered by a single gate, guarded around the clock. A house next door to my folks, however, was as close as we could get to living like the Corleone family.

Our lives after Annie's arrival went on pretty much as before, except with greater focus on poop and pee. I chafe at the injustice of the Nobel Prize Committee awarding peace prizes to the likes of Yasir Arafat while failing year after year to honor the person who invented the Velcro-sealed disposable diaper.

Annie didn't need to be weaned from breast-feeding. At five months, she turned adamantly away from an offered breast and insisted on culinary diversity.

Something of a smartie, she spoke her first word shortly before Christmas that year. If you believe Lorrie and my mother, it happened on the twenty-second of December, and the word was *mama*. If instead you believe my father, it happened on the twenty-*first*, and she spoke not one word but two: *chocolate zabaglione*.

On Christmas Day, she said *dada*. I don't remember any other gifts I received that year.

For a while, Grandma produced needlepoint images of bunnies, kittens, puppies, and other creatures that would charm a child. She soon grew bored, however, and switched to reptiles.

On March 21, 1999, when Annie was fourteen months old, I drove Lorrie to the hospital in good weather and without incident, and she delivered Lucy Jean.

When the afterbirth issued only moments after Mello Melodeon had tied and cut the umbilical, he complimented Lorrie: 'Smoother than last time. Why, that was as effortlessness as an experienced broodmare dropping a colt.'

'As soon as you pull the wagon home,' I

317

promised her, 'I'll give you a nice bag of oats.'

'Better laugh while you can,' she said. ''Cause now you're a lone man in a house of three women. There's enough of us to form a coven.'

'I'm not afraid. What more could happen to me? I'm *already* bewitched.'

Perhaps Konrad Beezo had some long-distance means of keeping tabs on us — which seemed to be the case, considering his timely visit prior to Annie's birth. If so, he had chosen not to risk exposure this time until the baby's gender was known.

Although I wanted a son someday, I would happily raise five daughters — or ten! — with no regrets if that would thwart Beezo's thirst for vengeance and keep him at bay.

Just in case fate graced us with a band of sisters, I would have to get serious about the ballroom-dance instructions to which Lorrie periodically subjected me. With five daughters to chaperone and to give away in marriage, I'd miss out on too many memories if I couldn't fox-trot.

Consequently, I learned to trip the light fantastic better than I had imagined that I could, considering that I'm biggish for my size and something of a gimp. The legend of Fred Astaire is in no danger of being eclipsed, but if you let me spin you around the floor either to a bit of Strauss or Benny Goodman, I can make you forget all about Bruno the dancing bear.

On July 14, 2000, after I'd gone to the trouble of learning to dance, fate in a single stroke pulled out from under me the rug that I was cutting, granting my desire to have a son and challenging the mad clown to keep the dark promise in the mason jar.

Fresh from his mother, little Andy did not respond to Mello Melodeon's slap on the butt with the usual birth cry full of shock and dismay. He issued a sharp yelp unmistakably expressing offense, followed by a perfect tongue-between-the-lips raspberry.

At once I had a concern I could not help but relate to Mello. 'Gee, he's got such . . . a tiny one.'

'Tiny what?'

'Peepee.'

'You call it a peepee?'

'What — they use a fancier word at medical school?'

'His willy is the usual size,' Mello assured me, 'and plenty big enough for what he needs it for in the immediate future.'

'My husband the idiot,' Lorrie said affectionately. 'Jimmy, dear, the only baby boy ever going to be born with the equipment you expected will also have horns because he'll be the Antichrist.'

'Well, I'm glad he's not the Antichrist,' I said. 'I can just imagine what the load in *his* diapers would smell like.'

Even in that moment of joy, Beezo was in our minds. We weren't whistling through a haunted graveyard; we were laughing through it.

42

Having become the new chief of police, Huey Foster provided protection for Lorrie and baby Andy at the hospital. The guards — off-duty officers, out of uniform — were instructed to draw as little attention to themselves as possible.

A day and a half later, when I took my wife and newborn home, another policeman was already stationed in the house, waiting for us.

The chief assigned the officers in twelve-hour shifts. They came and went as unobtrusively as possible, through our garage, hiding in the backseat of Dad's car or mine.

Huey acted not solely out of concern for us but with the hope that he would snare Konrad Beezo.

After a nervous week, when the clown did not come, Huey could no longer justify the expense of providing us protection.

Besides, if his pastry-addicted men gained any more weight, they wouldn't be able to button their pants.

For the remainder of that first month, Dad and Mom and Grandma moved in with us from next door. Safety in numbers.

We relied also on out-of-town muscle from the Colorado Guild of Bread and Pastry Professionals. These guys put on weight, too, but being experienced bakers and lacking our family's thoroughbred metabolism, they were wise

320

enough to wear only pants with expandable waistlines.

At the end of the month, the Guild men had done as much as they could, and our gallant colleagues went home.

Dad and Mom moved back into their house with Weena.

We'd begun to think that Konrad Beezo might be dead. With his abiding rage against the world, his paranoia, his arrogance, and his propensity for homicidal action, he should have gotten himself killed decades ago.

If not dead, he might be residing these days in a cozy insane asylum. Perhaps he had assumed one too many false identities and now lived in a delirium of split personalities, believing himself to be Clappy and Cheeso and Slappy and Burpo and Nutsy and Bongo, all at once.

Although I feared that calamity would befall us as soon as we became convinced that Beezo was gone forever, we could not remain in a state of high anxiety for the rest of our existence. Even mere wariness eventually became an unsustainable burden.

We had to get on with life.

By July 14, 2001, when Andy celebrated his first birthday, we felt that we had safely crossed a divide between a world haunted by Beezo and a world free of him.

Life was good and getting better. Three and a half years old, Annie had long ago been potty trained. Lucy, over two years old, had just graduated from a potty to a potty seat on the grown-up toilet, and was enthusiastic about it.

Andy knew the purpose of a potty but thoroughly disdained it . . . until gradually he began to recognize the pride that Lucy took in her ascension to a real throne.

Annie and Lucy shared a room across the hall from us. Annie liked yellow, Lucy pink; so we had painted the room half and half, with a dividing line down the middle.

Already something of a tomboy, Annie sneeringly called Lucy's half of the room *girly*. Not yet having mastered sarcasm, Lucy judged her sister's half *stupid lemon*.

Both girls believed that a monster lived in their closet.

According to Lucy, this beast had a lot of hair and big teeth. She said it ate children and then vomited them up. Lucy was afraid of being eaten but more afraid of being vomit.

At only twenty-eight months, she had a preference for neatness and order that other toddlers not only didn't exhibit but didn't understand. Everything in her side of the room had its proper place. When I made her bed, she followed after me, smoothing the wrinkles out of the spread.

We figured that Lucy would be either a brilliant mathematician or a world-famous architect, or the subject of intense interest to psychologists studying obsessive-compulsive disorder.

To the extent that Lucy thrived on order, Annie luxuriated in disorder. When I made *her* bed, she followed after me, 'smunching' it to give it a more relaxed look.

According to Annie, the monster in the closet had scales, lots of tiny teeth, red eyes, and claws that it painted blue. Her monster, like Lucy's, ate children — not in a gulp, as did Lucy's terror, but slowly, savoring them nibble by nibble.

Although we assured the girls that no monsters lived in the closet, any parent knows that such assurances are not particularly effective.

Lorrie designed a fancy sign on her computer, printed it in red and black, and taped it to the *inside* of the closet door: MONSTERS, PAY ATTENTION! YOU ARE NOT ALLOWED INTO THIS BEDROOM! IF YOU CAME IN THROUGH A CRACK IN THE CLOSET FLOOR, YOU MUST LEAVE AT ONCE THE SAME WAY! WE DO NOT ALLOW YOUR TYPE IN THIS HOUSE!

This comforted them for a while. Irrational fears, however, are the most persistent kind.

Not just in children, either. In a world where rogue states ruled by madmen are seeking nuclear weapons, look at how many people fear a tad too much fat in their diets and one part per ten million of pesticide in their apple juice to a greater degree than they fear suitcase bombs.

To further reassure the girls, we stood Captain Fluffy, a teddy bear in a military-style cap, on a chair beside the closet door. The captain served as a sentry on whom they could depend to protect them.

'He's just a dumb bear,' Annie said.

'Yeah. Dumb,' Lucy agreed.

'He can't scare off monsters,' Annie said. 'They'll eat him.'

'Yeah,' Lucy concurred. 'Eat him and puke him up.'

'On the contrary,' Lorrie told them, 'the captain is very smart and comes from a long line of bears that have for centuries guarded good little girls. They have never lost one child.'

'Not one?' Annie asked dubiously.

'Not one,' I assured her.

'Maybe they lost some but lied about it,' Annie said.

'Yeah,' Lucy said. 'Lied about it.'

'Does Captain Fluffy look like a liar?' Lorrie asked.

Annie studied him. Then: 'No. But neither does Gran-gran Weena, but Grandpa says she didn't either know any guy blew himself up with a fart like she says.'

'Yeah,' Lucy said, 'blew up with a fart.'

I said, 'Grandpa never accused Gran-gran of lying. He just said she sometimes exaggerates a little.'

'Captain Fluffy doesn't look like a liar, and he isn't a liar,' Lorrie said, 'so you should apologize to him.'

Annie chewed on her lower lip for a moment. 'I'm sorry, Captain Fluffy.'

'Yeah. Fluffy,' Lucy said.

In addition to leaving on a Pooh night-light, we gave each girl a small flashlight. As everyone knows, a beam of light will vaporize either a vomiting or a nibbling monster.

Twelve months passed, another sweet year crowded with bright memories, without *real* terror.

Although three of the five dates on the back of the circus pass remained in the future, we could not assume that any of the ordeals ahead of me had anything to do with Konrad Beezo. Prudence required that we be more alert for threats that might come from sources having nothing to do with the clown or his imprisoned son.

Twenty-eight years had passed since the night of my birth. If still alive, Beezo would be nearly sixty. He might still be as insane as a maze-crazed lab rat, but time had to have taken a toll on him as it does on everyone. Surely he wouldn't be as passionate in his hatred, as energetic in his fury.

As the summer of 2002 waned, I felt that we had most likely seen the last of Konrad Beezo.

By September, when our Andy was twenty-six months old, he had a closet monster of his own. His was a child-eating clown.

Our apprehension at this revelation cannot be exaggerated. Although our house didn't easily lend itself to such retrofitting, we contracted to have an alarm system installed, wiring all doors and windows.

We hadn't told the kids about Konrad Beezo, Punchinello, or anything regarding the violence those men had perpetrated and the threats they'd made. Annie, Lucy, and Andy were far too young to understand any of that macabre history, too young to be burdened with it. The scariest thing they could handle at their age was a closet monster or three.

We considered that they might have heard

something of the story from a playmate. This was unlikely, because our kids never played with other children out of our sight.

We had never felt we could afford to assume for certain that Konrad Beezo was dead or moldering in a booby hatch; therefore, one of us always remained with the kids when they were at play, and often one or both of my parents were there, as well. We watched. We listened. Surely we would have heard.

Maybe Andy had seen a bad clown in a movie, on TV, in a cartoon. Although we monitored their exposure to packaged entertainment and tried to protect them from a media that seemed hell-bent on corrupting them in a hundred different ways, we could not be certain beyond all doubt that we had not slipped up and that impressionable little Andy hadn't glimpsed an evil clown with a chainsaw.

The boy provided no insight into the inspiration for his fear. From his perspective, the situation was simple:

There was a clown.

The clown was bad.

The bad clown wanted to eat him.

The bad clown hid in his closet.

If he fell asleep, the bad clown would munch on him.

'Can't you *smell* him?' Andy asked.

We couldn't catch a whiff.

We put a solemn sign on the inside of his closet door, warning off the cannibal clown. We presented Andy with a teddy bear named Sergeant Snuggles, his own version of Captain

Fluffy. He received his own special monster-vaporizing flashlight with an easy-on switch for small uncertain hands.

In addition, we put in the alarm system, purchased small aerosol cans of pepper spray and secreted them throughout the house in places high enough to be beyond the children's reach, purchased four tasers and distributed them in similar fashion. We added second deadbolts to the front door, the back door, and the door between the kitchen and the garage.

Because Grandpa Josef had not mentioned January 12, 1998, in his predictions — the night that Beezo had attempted to kidnap Lorrie, deliver our first child himself, and abscond with the baby — but had cited only January 19, when our house had been burned down, we could only assume that he might have also failed to warn us of another bad day closely associated with the upcoming third date on his list. For at least two weeks prior, we would need to work ourselves into a state of judicious paranoia.

We had enjoyed nearly four years of peace, of normalcy. Now, as the third of the five dates approached — Monday, December 23, 2002 — we felt a long shadow falling across us, a shadow out of time, with its origins in August 9, 1974.

43

I am a fool for Christmas and a cherished customer of every purveyor of seasonal tinsel and festoonery. From the day after Thanksgiving until early January, on our roof a life-size spotlighted Santa stands with his bag of gifts at chimneyside, waving to passersby.

The chimney, eaves, windows, and porch posts of our house are outlined with so many strings of multicolored lights that we are no doubt visible to astronauts in orbit.

In the front yard, to one side of the walk, stands an elaborate nativity scene with the holy family, wise men, angels, camels. One ox, one donkey, two cows. One dog, five doves, nine mice.

To the other side of the walk stand elves, reindeer, snowmen, carolers. They are all mechanical, motorized, in motion, producing a hushed symphony of ticking clockworks and humming transformers.

On our front door hangs a wreath that might be heavier than the door itself. Evergreen boughs twined with holly, decorated with pine cones, walnuts, silver bells, gold beads, baubles, bangles, spangles.

Inside, for those six weeks, I cannot tolerate an unornamented surface or a drab corner. From every door header and ceiling-mounted light fixture dangles mistletoe.

Although the eve of Christmas Eve, December 23, was supposed to be a day to dread that year, the decorations were unpacked, polished, hung, strung, and activated.

Life is too short, and Christmas comes but once a year. We were not going to allow the likes of Konrad Beezo to take the shine off our celebration.

On the evening of December 22, we intended to have Mom and Dad and Grandma to our house for dinner at nine o'clock. They would stay through the night, helping us stand watch after midnight, when the clock brought us to the third day in Grandpa Josef's list.

By seven o'clock, the table was set with Christmas china, emerald green cut-crystal goblets, gleaming silverware, and candles in glass chimneys shaped like chubby snowmen. In the center were miniature poinsettias tucked among clusters of white chrysanthemums.

At 7:20, the telephone rang. I answered it in the kitchen, where Lorrie and I were preparing dinner.

'Jimmy,' said Huey Foster, 'we've just got some good news about Konrad Beezo you'll want to hear.'

'This isn't much in the yuletide spirit,' I told the chief, 'but I hope the bozo turned up dead somewhere.'

'The news isn't quite *that* cheerful, but almost. I'm here in my office with an FBI agent name of Porter Carson, out of their Denver division. He needs to speak with you and Lorrie as soon as possible, and I know you'll want to hear what he's got.'

'Bring him around right now,' I said.

'Can't bring him but I'll send him,' Huey said. 'Tonight's the department Christmas party. The eggnog's nonalcoholic, but as chief, I've got the authority to spike it, and then I pass out year-end bonuses. I gave Porter directions, but he won't even need 'em if he just follows the glow of your Christmas display.'

When I hung up, Lorrie was frowning at me. 'Beezo?'

I told her what Huey had said.

'Better hustle the kids a little farther out of the way,' she suggested. 'We don't want them overhearing this.'

Our three elves were in the living room, sprawled on the floor with boxes of crayons and a six-foot Christmas banner that featured an extravagantly ornamented message — WE LOVE YOU, SANTA CLAUS — which Lorrie had designed on her computer. Their assignment: Color it with care and with love so that on Christmas Eve, the good Claus would be more disposed to leave them a truckload of gifts.

We are fiendishly clever at devising tasks to keep a trio of hyperactive munchkins occupied.

Annie was almost five that Christmas, Lucy three months short of four, and Andy two and a half. Frequently, I'm proud to say, they could play together in an atmosphere of civility with a chaos-meter reading of no more than four on a scale of one to ten.

That evening they were especially calm. Annie and Lucy had made a competition of the

330

coloring and were bent to it intensely, tongues pinched between their teeth. Having lost interest in the banner, Andy was crayoning his toenails.

'Let's move this project to your room, girls,' I said, helping them gather their materials. 'I've got to straighten up the living room. Grandpa, Grandma, and Gran-gran will be here in a little while. In fact, you have to change clothes and look pretty for them.'

'Boys don't look pretty,' Annie patiently informed me. 'Boys look handsome.'

'*I* look pretty,' Andy protested, thrusting out one of his feet and spreading his rainbow-hued toes for our appreciation.

'Daddy looks pretty, too,' said Lucy.

'Thank you, Lucy Jean. Your opinions on beauty matter a lot to me, seeing as how you're going to be Miss Colorado one day.'

'*I'm* going to be better than that,' Annie announced as we moved toward the stairs. 'When I grow up, I'm gonna be a bullshit artist.'

They *do* surprise me. Perpetually.

Halted by this proclamation, I said, 'Annie, wherever did you hear *that*?'

'Yesterday, the mailman told Gran-gran she looked foxy, and she told him, 'You're a real bullshit artist, George.' Then he laughed and Gran-gran pinched his cheek.'

You don't want to tell them that a word is taboo. If I made that mistake, all three of them would work *bullshit artist* into every third sentence out of their mouths, which would make this a memorable Christmas for all the wrong reasons.

Letting it pass with the hope that they would forget about it, I resettled them with crayons in the girls' room.

I had no concern about them being upstairs while Lorrie and I were on the lower floor because for one thing the house was locked tight; for another thing, the alarm system had been set in monitor mode. If any door or window opened, the alarm would not sound, but a digitized voice on the system chip would announce, through speakers throughout the house, the exact location of the breach.

Downstairs again, I went to the foyer and watched the street through one of the tall, narrow French windows that flanked the front door.

The police station lay less than ten minutes from our house. I intended to open the door before Porter Carson could ring the bell and alert the kids that we had a visitor.

Within two minutes, a Mercury Mountaineer pulled to the curb at the end of our front walk.

The man who got out of it wore a dark suit, white shirt, dark tie, and open topcoat. Tall and trim, he moved with purpose and shoulders-back confidence.

As he climbed the steps, the porch lights revealed that he was in his mid-forties, handsome, with dark hair combed straight back from his brow.

When he spotted me at the window, he held up one finger, as if to say *Wait a sec*, and withdrew a vertical-fold ID wallet from his coat. He held his FBI credentials to the glass so that I could read them and compare his face to the photo before I opened the door.

Obviously, Huey Foster had told Carson that we were security conscious, and if the agent knew Beezo's history, he must understand why paranoia was common sense.

44

Conditioned by Hollywood, I expected Porter Carson to speak with the clipped diction and cool detachment of a movie fed. Instead, he had a voice that I at once warmed to: friendly, all the sharp edges rounded off the words by a Georgia accent.

When I opened the door to him, the digitized voice of the alarm system announced, '*Front door open.*'

'We have the same feature on our home alarm,' he said as we shook hands. 'My son, Jamie, he's fourteen and a computer whiz. Dangerous combination. He couldn't resist teachin' the monitor more vocabulary. Suddenly it starts sayin', *Front door open, watch your ass.* That got him grounded awhile.'

I locked the door behind him. 'We've got three kids, five and younger. They'll be teenagers together.'

'Ouch.'

As I hung his topcoat in the foyer closet, I said, 'We're thinking about just locking them in a room and feeding them through a slot in the door until they're all twenty-one.'

He drew a deep breath, savoring the air. 'This house smells like the highest-rent neighborhood in Paradise.'

Garlands of deodar cedar, star-pine Christmas tree, lingering fragrance of peanut brittle made just that afternoon, popcorn balls, vanilla- and cinnamon-scented candles, fresh coffee, ham baking in a bath of cherries, chocolate marmalade cake in the second oven . . .

Taking in the dazzle of tinsel and lights and our ubiquitous collection of Santa figurines, Porter Carson cocked his head to listen to 'Silver Bells,' sung by Bing Crosby. 'You folks keep Christmas like almost nobody does anymore.'

'And isn't that a shame,' I said. 'Come along to the kitchen. My wife's peeling some Idaho beauties for scalloped potatoes.'

Actually, Lorrie had finished and was drying her hands on a poinsettia-patterned towel when I introduced her to Carson.

If the rest of the house had smelled like Paradise, the kitchen was an even higher realm, the fragrant palace of divinities.

The FBI agent appeared to be smitten with Lorrie, as all men are, and treated her with Southern courtliness. He remained standing while she poured three cups of rich Colombian blend, then held her chair for her as she sat.

I felt like a clueless primitive and reminded myself not to slurp my coffee.

Settling in his chair at the table, getting down to business, Carson said, 'I don't want to raise false hopes. God forbid anythin' I say might cause you to let your guard down too soon, but I think your troubles with Konrad Beezo may be drawin' to an end at last.'

'Don't worry,' Lorrie said, 'I won't believe he's dead until I see his body being fed into a crematorium and ashes coming out.'

Carson grinned. 'Mrs. Tock, you're my idea of a carin' mother.'

As far as I knew, the murders Beezo committed hadn't been under federal jurisdiction. 'What got the FBI on his case?' I wondered.

'This is great coffee, ma'am. What's that extra bit of taste in it?'

'A little vanilla.'

'Perfect. Anyway, Beezo took a page from his son's book, put together a little crew, started robbin' banks not long after he torched your house.'

Bank robbery is a federal crime. So is removing a stuffing-analysis tag from a mattress before selling it retail. Guess which offense gets the FBI's attention.

'Hasn't blown up one of 'em yet,' Carson said, 'but he doesn't mind shootin' guards and tellers and anyone else gets in his way.'

'Tell me his crew isn't more clowns,' Lorrie said.

'No, ma'am, it isn't. Maybe his son recruited all the thievin' clowns there are. One of his crew was a guy named Emory Ornwall, been in Leavenworth for bank robbery. The other two were roustabouts.'

'I've heard the term,' I said, 'but I'm not sure I know what it means.'

'Roustabouts are the guys who put up the circus tents and pull 'em down, plus they take care of the equipment, the generators, that kind of stuff.'

'How many banks have they hit?' Lorrie

wondered. 'Are they good at it?'

'Yes, ma'am, they were. Seven in 1998, four in '99. Then they hit big with two armored-car heists, August and September '99.'

'Nothing in the last three years?'

'The thing is, the second of those armored cars was such a rich score — six million cash, two million in bearer bonds — Beezo decided he could retire, especially if he and Ornwall killed the roustabouts and didn't split with 'em, which is what they did.'

'Hard to imagine guys who knew Konrad Beezo would turn their backs on him,' I said.

'Maybe they didn't. Both roustabouts were shot point-blank in the face with such high-caliber rounds their heads were hollowed out like Halloween pumpkins.'

Carson smiled, then realized that what was a simple fact to an FBI agent might be excess information to us.

'Sorry, ma'am.'

'So you've been after Beezo all this time?' Lorrie asked.

'We nailed Ornwall in March 2000. He was livin' in Miami under the name John Dillinger.'

'You're kidding,' I said.

'No, sir.' Carson smiled and shook his head. 'Ornwall knows end-all about banks and armored cars, but he's one bean short of a full spoon.'

'Maybe two beans.'

'He told us bein' Dillinger was like Edgar Allan Poe's story 'The Purloined Letter,' like hidin' in plain sight. Who would expect a wanted

337

bank robber to be livin' under the name of a famous dead criminal?'

'Obviously, you guys did.'

'Well, because first time we arrested Emory Ornwall and sent him to Leavenworth, he was hidin' under the name Jesse James.'

'Unbelievable,' I said.

'A lot of criminals,' Carson said, 'are dim bulbs.'

'More coffee?' Lorrie asked.

'No thank you, ma'am. I can see you've got a big dinner comin' up, so I want to get out of your hair soon as I can.'

'You're welcome to stay.'

'Can't, I'm afraid. But thanks for your kindness. Anyway . . . like I said, Ornwall . . . he knows end-all about banks and armored cars, but he's no strategist or tactician. Beezo planned the jobs, and he was brilliant at it.'

'You're talking about *our* Beezo?' Lorrie asked disbelievingly.

'I mean, ma'am, we've seen some smart guys gone wrong, but none the equal of him. We were in *awe* of Beezo.'

This surprised me. 'He's crazy.'

'Maybe he is, maybe he isn't,' Carson said, 'but he's a genius when it comes to executin' big-ticket stickups. They say he was on his way to bein' the greatest clown of his day, and for sure he found this other line of work he was also born for.'

'From our experience, he's all emotion and rage, no reason.'

'Well, the genius sure wasn't Ornwall or the

338

roustabouts, all second-raters. They would've screwed up most of their jobs if Beezo hadn't planned so well and kept them in line. Pure genius.'

'It did take some planning to bug our house that time and keep a watch on us from Nedra Lamm's place,' Lorrie reminded me. Then she turned to Carson and got to the quick of it. 'Where is he now?'

'Ornwall tipped us that Beezo had gone to South America somewhere. He didn't know where, and it's a big continent.'

'When I was trapped in the Explorer with him, out there in the woods, he told me he'd gone to South America in '74,' Lorrie said, 'after he killed Dr. MacDonald.'

Carson nodded. 'Back then he spent six months in Chile, two and a half years in Argentina. This time . . . took us a while, but we tracked him to Brazil.'

'You got him?'

'No, ma'am. But we will.'

'He's there now — in Brazil?'

'No, ma'am. He left the first of this month, thirty-six hours before we broke his cover, got his identity and address in Rio.'

Lorrie looked meaningfully at me.

'Almost nailed him there,' Carson continued. 'But he skipped to Venezuela, where we have some problems with extradition treaties right now. Just a hiccup. He won't get out of there except we take him out in handcuffs or in a box.'

Only fear for her family could tighten Lorrie's

face in such a way as to diminish her beauty. 'He's not in Venezuela anymore,' she told Porter Carson. 'Sometime tomorrow . . . he's going to be *here*.'

45

Chocolate marmalade cake, baked ham steeped in cherry juice, dark-roasted Colombian coffee, and the subtle sour scent of heart-piercing dread, which also manifested as a faint metallic taste . . .

Until this moment, I hadn't realized that I had been deeply invested in the hope that Konrad Beezo was dead.

I had told myself that I couldn't count him out, that prudence required me to assume that he remained alive.

Unconsciously, however, I had put a stake through his heart. I had stuffed a clove of garlic in his mouth, placed a crucifix on his breast, and had buried him facedown in a churchyard of the mind.

Now Beezo had risen.

'Sometime tomorrow,' Lorrie predicted, 'or as early as midnight tonight, he'll be here.'

Her cold certainty surprised and perplexed Porter Carson. 'No, ma'am, there's no chance of that.'

'I'd bet my life on it,' she replied. 'And in fact, Mr. Carson, that's exactly what I'll be doing, whether I like it or not.'

He turned to me. 'Mr. Tock, I came here to ask something of you, but please believe me, I didn't come to warn you that Beezo is on your doorstep. He isn't. I can assure you.'

By her eyes alone, Lorrie conveyed a question to me that I could read as clearly as printed text: *Should we share with him the story of Grandpa Josef and the five dates?*

Only the adults in our immediate family and a few close and trusted friends knew about the prophecy under which I lived: five swords of Damocles hung by five hairs, two of which had spared me, three of which still dangled.

Huey Foster knew, but I didn't think he would have shared it with Porter Carson.

Reveal such a thing to a hard-nosed FBI agent, and he would write you off as a superstitious fool. I could almost hear him: *So you believe that you're cursed, Mr. Tock? You mean like witches and voodoo?*

Grandpa Josef hadn't cursed me. He had not wished five terrible days upon me. By some miracle, in the last minutes of his life, he had been given the power of prophecy to warn me, to give me a better chance to save — not myself, perhaps, but — those whom I loved.

Inevitably, however, it would sound like a curse to Carson. Even if I could pierce his skepticism and make him understand the difference between a malediction and a *prediction*, he was no more likely to believe in fortune-telling than he was in the effectiveness of a shaman's evil eye.

As a responsible officer of the law, he might feel it incumbent upon himself to report to child-protective services that Annie, Lucy, and Andy were being raised by parents who believed themselves to be hexed, who felt oppressed by diabolists and necromancers, who shared these fears with their offspring and thus terrorized them.

Over the years, newspapers had carried numerous stories of false charges of abuse resulting in parents' loss of custody, families torn apart for years until the accusers admitted to lying or were beyond doubt proved malicious. By that time, lives were ruined, children traumatized beyond full recovery.

Because no one wished to put children at risk, authorities in such cases often believed the most transparent lies by people with obvious grudges to settle. An earnest FBI agent who had no history with us, no reason to malign us, would receive a respectful hearing and swift action.

Unwilling to risk calling down upon our heads a buzzing hive of misguided and self-righteous bureaucrats by telling Porter Carson about Grandpa Josef, I answered the question in Lorrie's eyes with a shake of my head.

Turning to Carson again, Lorrie said, 'All right, okay, listen to me, I can't tell you how I know, but I *know* the crazy son of a bitch is coming right here sometime between midnight tonight and midnight tomorrow. He wants — '

'But ma'am, that's just not — '

'I'm *talking* to you, I'm *begging* you, listen to me. He wants my little Andy, and he probably wants to kill all the rest of us. If you're truly serious about catching him, then forget Venezuela, he's not in Venezuela anymore if he ever was. Help us set a trap here, now.'

The fervor in her face and the adamancy in her voice unsettled Carson. 'Believe me, ma'am,

I can absolutely assure you that Beezo is not on your doorstep and will not be here tomorrow. He — '

Frustrated, gray-faced with anxiety, Lorrie pushed back her chair, rose to her feet, and, wringing her hands, said to me, 'Jimmy, for God's sake, make him believe it. I get the feeling Huey doesn't have enough manpower to protect us this time. We aren't going to be lucky like before. We need help.'

Looking distressed, too much a gentleman to stay seated when a woman stood, Carson rose, and I stood, too, as he said, 'Mrs. Tock, please let me repeat and explain what Chief Foster told your husband on the phone a short while ago.'

Carson cleared his throat and continued: ''Jimmy, we've just got some good news about Konrad Beezo you'll want to hear.''

The most peculiar thing wasn't that he repeated precisely what Huey had said on the phone but that he sounded exactly like Huey, not like Porter Carson.

No, that wasn't what *Huey* had said on the phone. I had not been talking to Huey earlier, but to this man.

To me, the FBI agent said, 'And your response, as I recall, was pointed.' A pause. ''This isn't much in the yuletide spirit, but I hope the bozo turned up dead somewhere.''

His voice was so similar to mine in timbre and in nuance that I felt fear like blood flukes twitching in every vein and artery.

From beneath his suit jacket, he withdrew a pistol fitted with a sound suppressor.

344

46

Porter Carson had assured Lorrie that he hadn't come to warn her that Konrad Beezo was on her doorstep.

He was sincere on two counts. First, he had no intention of warning her. Second, Beezo had already gotten past her doorstep and into her kitchen.

Likewise, he had been confident that Beezo wouldn't be here tomorrow — because Beezo was here today.

Konrad Beezo had hazel eyes. Porter Carson's eyes were blue. Colored contact lenses had been available for years.

Beezo was nearly sixty years old. Carson looked forty-five. Now I could see similarities in body type and bone structure, but otherwise they appeared to be two different men.

Some of the world's finest plastic surgeons have offices in Rio to serve the jet set from all over the world. If you are rich, if you will accept the medical risks of profound restructuring, you can be redesigned, rejuvenated, fully remade.

If you are paranoid and obsessed with vengeance, if you believe you were destined for greatness that others conspired to deny you, perhaps you have the motivation to endure the pain and the hazards of multiple surgeries. Madness is not always expressed in reckless action; some homicidal paranoids have the patience to spend years planning their revenge.

Listening to Beezo's uncanny imitation of me, I remembered that he had mocked Dad by imitating his voice, too, in the expectant-fathers' lounge over twenty-eight years ago.

In response to my father's amazement, Beezo had said, *I told you I'm talented, Rudy Tock. In more ways than you can imagine.*

In those words my father had heard only a boast by a vain and troubled man full of show, fond of flourish.

Nearly three decades later, I realized that it had not been a boast but a warning. *Don't tread on me.*

Now, as the three of us stood around the kitchen table, Beezo's smile was ripe with gloating. His hazel gaze, even filtered through blue lenses, burned with a vicious exultation.

In his own voice, not in the mellow Southern accent of Porter Carson but the rougher timbre of the man who had harried us in the Hummer, Beezo said, 'As I told you, I came here to ask something of you. Where is my compensation?'

My attention, and Lorrie's, moved on a short vertical track: from his hate-twisted face to the muzzle of the silencer-equipped pistol, to his face again.

'Where is my *quid pro quo?*' he demanded.

Pathetically, to gain time to think, we lamely pretended not to understand his question. Lorrie said, 'What *quid pro quo?*'

'My recompense, my makeweight,' Beezo said impatiently, 'my something for something, your Andy for my Punchinello.'

'No,' Lorrie said neither angrily nor with apparent fear, but with a flat finality.

'I will treat him well,' Beezo promised. 'Better than you treated *my* son.'

Anger and sharp terror throttled my voice, but Lorrie firmly said again, 'No.'

'I've been robbed of the fame that should've been mine. All I ever wanted was immortality, but I'm willing to settle now for a little secondhand glory. If I teach the boy what I know, he will be the greatest circus star of his age.'

'He has no talent for that,' Lorrie assured him. 'He's the descendant of pastry chefs and storm chasers.'

'Bloodlines don't matter,' Beezo said. 'All that matters is my genius. Among my gifts is mentoring.'

'Go away.' Having fallen nearly to a whisper, Lorrie's voice had the quality of an incantation, as though she hoped to cast some spell of sanity upon him. 'Father another child of your own.'

He persisted: 'Even a boy with a minimum faculty for clownery can be molded into greatness with me as his guide and his master and his guru.'

'Father a child of your own,' she repeated. 'Even a creep like you can find some madwoman who'll spread her legs.'

A cool scorn had entered her voice, and I could not grasp her purpose in further angering him.

She continued: 'For enough money, some drug-addled slut, some desperate whore, will gag

347

down her nausea and mate with you.'

Incredibly, instead of angering him further, her scorn clearly disconcerted him. He flinched more than once at her words and licked his lips nervously.

'With the right psychotic hag,' she continued, 'you could father another murderous little maggot as insane as your firstborn.'

Perhaps because he hadn't the courage to meet Lorrie's eyes any longer or perhaps because in my furious silence he sensed the greater threat, Beezo shifted his attention to me.

Trembling, the pistol in his right hand followed the interest of his eyes, and the muzzle offered me the dark bore of eternity.

The instant Konrad Beezo was distracted, Lorrie thrust a hand into a pocket of her cheerful Christmas apron, extracted a miniature pressurized cannister of pepper spray.

Realizing his error, Beezo turned away from me.

As he twitched toward Lorrie, she scored a bull's-eye. A rust-red stream of fluid splashed his face.

At least half blinded, Beezo squeezed off a shot — a hard muffled *thup* — exploding a pane in a windowed cabinet door, shattering dishes.

I snatched up a chair and thrust it at him as he squeezed off another wild shot. He fired a third as I drove him backward across the kitchen in the manner of a wild-animal trainer warning off an enraged lion.

A fourth shot drilled the chair between us. Splinters of pine and soft wads of foam padding flicked my face, but the bullet didn't find me.

When he backed into the kitchen sink, I rammed the legs of the chair into him.

He cried out in pain and fired a fifth shot that cracked the oak-plank flooring.

Cornered, the rat found a tiger in himself. He wrenched the chair from me, fired a sixth round that blew out an oven window.

He threw the chair. I dodged.

Gasping for breath, wheezing out the fumes of pepper spray, streaming tears from bloodshot eyes, waving the gun, he staggered across the kitchen, nearly cold-cocked himself with the refrigerator, slammed through the swinging door into the dining room.

Lorrie had fallen into a terrible silence, a perfect stillness on the oak. Shot. And oh, God, the blood.

47

I could not leave her there alone, yet I could not stay at her side with Beezo loose in the house.

This rending dilemma was in an instant resolved by one of the many tough equations of love. I loved Lorrie more than I loved life. But the two of us loved our children more than ourselves, which in the language of mathematics, you might call love-squared. Love plus love-squared equalled an inevitable choice.

Sickened by the prospect of an intolerable loss, terrified by the anticipation of another loss unendurable, I went after Beezo, desperate to stop him before he found the kids.

He wouldn't be content to escape and return another day. We had seen his new Brazilian face. Never again would he enjoy the advantage of surprise.

We were in the end game. He would have his compensation, his something for something, Andy for his Punchinello. He would murder the girls, too, and call it fair interest on the debt.

As I crashed through the swinging door into the dining room, he staggered out of there, clipping the frame of the archway with his shoulder.

In the living room, he shot at me. Pepper-blurred as his vision must have been, luck rather than skill guided the bullet.

Fire seared my right ear. Although the flash of

350

pain was not disabling, it scared me into a stumble, a fall.

I scrambled up.

Beezo had vanished.

In the foyer, I found him with the pistol in his right hand, his left hand clutching the bannister on the balustrade, doggedly climbing the stairs, with half of the first flight already behind him.

He must have thought that I had been head-shot and disabled, or even killed, because he didn't look back or seem to hear me in pursuit.

Before he reached the first landing, I seized him from behind and dragged him down.

Fear for family and the terror of a life alone made me not courageous, really, but venturous, even heedless.

We fell against the balustrade. Wood cracked. He dropped the gun, and we tumbled together to the foyer floor.

I had him in a choke hold, my right arm across his throat, pulling back hard on my right wrist with my left hand. Untroubled by the slightest compunction, I would have tightened the hold until I crushed his windpipe, would have listened with savage pleasure as he drummed his heels against the floor in death throes.

Before I'd been able to lock the hold, however, Beezo had gotten his chin down, wedging it against my arm, making it impossible for me to apply full killing pressure.

He reached behind his head, clawing with both hands, hoping to blind me. Those cruel hands that had strangled Nedra Lamm. Those merciless hands that had shot Dr. MacDonald, Nurse Hanson.

I strove to keep my face away from him.

He snared my bullet-grazed ear and twisted.

Pain flared so intensely that all breath flew from me, and I almost passed out.

When Beezo felt the choke hold relent for an instant and then discovered his fingers slick with my blood, he knew my weak spot. He bucked and wrenched this way and that in a bid to break my grip, all the while groping backward for my ear.

Sooner than later, he would snare it again.

Next time the pain would trigger a trapdoor, a plunge into unconsciousness, vulnerability, death.

The pistol lay a few feet away, on the bottom step.

Simultaneously, I released the choke hold and shoved Beezo away from me.

One roll carried me to the bottom of the stairs. I plucked the pistol off the step, turned, and fired.

At such close range, as he reached for me, the bullet tore out his throat. He flopped faceup, arms spread, the back of his right hand rapping spasmodically against the floor.

Assuming that my count proved correct, eight shots had been fired. If the weapon contained the usual magazine, two rounds remained.

Gagging, gushing, whistling air through his ruined throat, Konrad Beezo was dying in wheezes and spurts.

I wish that I could say mercy motivated me to shoot him twice again, but mercy had

352

nothing to do with it.

Death took his life, and something worse collected his soul. I could almost feel the chill of that collector stepping in to take what was owed to him.

His eyes — one blue now and one hazel — looked as round as those of a fish, glazed and senseless, yet filled with the mysteries of ten thousand fathoms.

My right ear was a cup full to the brim with warm blood, but I still heard Annie in the second-floor hallway, calling 'Daddy? Mommy?' I heard Lucy, too, and Andy.

The kids were not yet at the head of the stairs, but they were coming.

Frantic to spare them the sight of Beezo torn and dead, I thundered, 'Get in your room! Lock the door! *There's a monster down here!*'

We never teased them about monsters. We treated their fears solemnly and with respect.

Consequently, they took me at my word. I heard running feet followed by the boom of the girls' bedroom door thrown shut with such force that the walls shook, the windowpanes vibrated, and the sprig of mistletoe hanging from the foyer light fixture trembled on the suspending ribbon.

'Lorrie,' I whispered, hushed by the fear that Death, having come to gather Beezo, might linger for one more harvest.

I ran to the kitchen.

48

Love can do all but raise the Dead.

The mind is quicksand, letting nothing go, and even what is learned reluctantly in school, once thought to be forgotten, rises to the surface less when needed than when some dark spirit would mock us with the uselessness of all we know.

As I rushed to the kitchen, that line of verse — *Love can do all but raise the Dead* — returned to me from English studies, as did the name of the poet, Emily Dickinson. She had often written to comfort the heart, but these words tortured mine.

What we learn is not the same as what we *know*. Pushing through the swinging door into the kitchen, I knew that my love was so fierce that it could do what the poet said it couldn't.

Were I to find Lorrie dead, I would resurrect her by an act of will, by the power of my need always to be with her, and lips to lips would pour into her my own life through sweet resuscitative breaths.

Although I knew a conviction in my reanimating power was crazy, as insane as anything that Beezo had believed, a part of me remained certain of it nonetheless, because to believe that even my love could not raise the dead would be to collapse into hopelessness and a kind of living death.

In the kitchen, every moment mattered and

354

every action had to be taken not only quickly but also in its proper order. Otherwise all would be lost.

First, around the broken chair to the telephone, leaving Lorrie unexamined. The handset slippery in my sweaty grip, I keyed in 911 and endured two rings, each eternal.

When the police operator answered before the third ring, she was a woman I knew, Denise Deerborn. We had dated twice. We liked each other well enough not to waste each other's time on a third date.

I spoke urgently, voice raw and trembling: 'Denise, this is Jimmy Tock, my wife's been shot, Lorrie, she's been shot bad, we need an ambulance, please, now, *please*.'

Aware that our address had appeared on the computer in front of Denise the moment that the connection had been made, I wasted no more time with her, dropped the receiver, letting it dangle on its cord and bang against the cabinetry.

I knelt at Lorrie's side, in her spreading blood. Beauty this perfect and this pale usually could be found only in sculpture, on marble monuments.

She appeared to have been shot in the abdomen.

Her eyes were closed. No movement under the lids.

Pressing fingertips to her throat, I felt and felt, and feared the worst, then found a pulse — rapid and weak, but a pulse.

A sob exploded from me, and another, until I realized that even though unconscious, she might hear me and be frightened by my grief. For her sake, I controlled myself, and although my chest heaved with sobs unexpressed, I let out only the ragged sound of my panicked breathing.

Although she seemed to be unconscious, her respiration was rapid, shallow. I touched her face, her arm. Her skin felt cold and clammy.

Shock.

My shock was emotional, to the mind and heart, but she suffered physiological shock from the violence of the trauma and the loss of blood. If her wounds didn't kill her, shock might.

She was lying flat on her back, an ideal position for treatment.

After folding a dish towel, I eased it under her head merely to cushion her. Only her feet should be raised.

I pulled cookbooks from nearby shelves, made a pallet of them, and carefully elevated her feet about ten inches.

Combined with plummeting blood pressure, heat loss could prove deadly in her condition. I needed blankets but dared not leave her side long enough to sprint upstairs and get them.

If she died, I would not let her die alone.

The adjacent laundry served also as a mud room. I plucked winter coats from wall pegs.

Again in the kitchen, I blanketed her with coats. My coat and hers. Annie's, Lucy's, Andy's coats.

Lying beside her, heedless of the blood, I pressed my body against hers for what warmth I might provide.

As a siren rose in the distance, I felt her throat.

Her pulse wasn't any stronger than before, but I assured myself that it wasn't any weaker, either — and knew that I lied.

I spoke into the delicate shell of her ear, hoping that she would hold fast to my voice, that my words would tether her to this world. I said things I can't remember, assurances and encouragements; but soon I had been reduced to three words, the greatest truth I knew, repeated with urgency and passion: 'I love you, I love you, I love you, I love you . . . '

49

My father urged the worried neighbors to move back, off the front-porch steps, off the walkway, onto the lawn among the Christmas figures.

Immediately behind Dad came two paramedics, wheeling Lorrie out of the house on a gurney. She lay unconscious beneath a wool blanket, receiving plasma through an IV drip.

I moved at her side, holding high the bottle of plasma. The paramedics preferred the assistance of a police officer, but I trusted only myself with the task.

They had to lift the gurney down the steps. The wheels met the walkway with a clatter, rolled squeakily toward the street.

My mother was upstairs in the girls' room with all three kids, comforting them and making sure they didn't look out a window.

Half a dozen police vehicles angled along the street, engines idling, their arrays of emergency beacons painting the snow-crusted trees and the surrounding houses red, blue, red, blue. The ambulance waited curbside, behind the Mercury Mountaineer in which Konrad Beezo had arrived.

Kevin Tolliver, the paramedic who would treat Lorrie en route to the hospital, took the bottle of plasma from me and climbed into the back of the ambulance as his partner, Carlos Nuñez, shoved the gurney into the vehicle.

When I started to climb inside, Carlos stopped me. 'No room, Jimmy. Kevin's going to be busy. You don't want to make things harder for him.'

'But I've got to — '

'I know,' Carlos interrupted. 'But when we get to the hospital, she'll go straight to surgery. You can't follow her there, either.'

Reluctantly, I stepped back.

Closing the doors between her and me, closing the doors on what might be my last sight of her alive, he said, 'Your dad will drive you, Jimmy. You'll be right behind us.'

As Carlos hurried forward and got in the driver's seat, Dad appeared at my side and led me out of the street, onto the sidewalk.

We passed the manger where angels, wise men, and humble beasts watched over the holy family.

A small spotlight had burned out, leaving one of the angels in shadow. In the otherwise lighted tableau, this dark form with half-furled wings looked ominous, waiting.

In the driveway of my parents' house, crystallized exhaust vapor plumed from the tailpipe of Dad's Chevy Blazer.

Grandma Rowena had moved the SUV out of the garage and readied it for our use. She stood there, dressed for a ham dinner, coatless.

Although she was eighty-five, she could just about break your ribs with a hug.

Pumping the siren, Carlos swung the ambulance away from the curb. A policeman waved him through the nearby intersection.

As the siren rapidly receded, Grandma pressed

something into my right hand, kissed me, and urged me into the Blazer.

The policeman at the intersection waved us through, and as we drove toward the hospital, I regarded my clenched right hand. The fingers were crusted with my blood and the blood of my beloved wife.

When I opened my hand, I discovered that Grandma, who for a while had been upstairs with Mom and the kids, had retrieved from Lorrie's jewelry box the cameo pendant that I had given her when we were dating.

The pendant was one of only three things to survive the fire that destroyed our first home. As delicate as it was, it should have been lost. The gold chain and the gold-plated mounting should have melted. The carved white soapstone cameo of a woman in profile should have cracked, blackened.

The only damage, however, was a slight discoloration of a few locks of the woman's soapstone hair. Her features were as finely engraved as ever they had been.

Some things aren't as fragile as they appear.

I closed my bloodstained hand around the pendant, clutching it so tightly that, by the time we reached the hospital, my palm ached as if a nail had been driven through it.

Lorrie was already in surgery.

A nurse insisted on taking me to the ER. The bullet Beezo had fired at me in the living room had ripped the cartilage of my right ear. She cleaned the ear and flushed the clotted blood out of the eustachian tube. I refused to submit to anything more than a local anesthetic while a young doctor stitched me up as best he could.

For the rest of my life, that ear would give me the look of a battered boxer who had spent too many years in the ring.

As we were not permitted to stand watch in the hallway outside the operating room where they had taken Lorrie, and as she would be transferred to intensive care when the surgeon had finished, Dad and I waited in the ICU lounge.

The lounge was cheerless. That suited me fine. I didn't want to be coddled by bright colors, soft chairs, and inspiring art.

I wanted to hurt.

Crazily, I worried that if a numbness of mind or heart or body overcame me, if I admitted any kind or degree of exhaustion, Lorrie would die. I felt that only by the sharpness of my wretched anguish could I keep God's attention and be sure that He heard my petitions.

Yet I must not cry, because to cry would be to acknowledge that I expected the worst. By such an acknowledgment, I would be inviting Death to take what he wanted.

For a while that night, I had more superstitious rules than those obsessive-compulsives whose daily lives are governed by elaborate domestic rituals and codes of conduct devised with the intention of magically warding off bad fortune.

For a while Dad and I shared the ICU lounge with other haunted people. Then we were alone.

Lorrie had been admitted at 8:12. At half past

361

nine, Dr. Wayne Cornell, the surgeon tending to her, sent a nurse to speak with us.

First, she told us that Dr. Cornell — qualified for general surgery with a specialty in gastrointestinal work — was an excellent surgeon. She said the team with him was 'awesome.'

I didn't need this soft-spoken sales pitch. To stay sane, I had already convinced myself that Dr. Cornell was a genius with hands as sensitive as those of the greatest concert pianist, a nonpareil.

According to the nurse, although Lorrie remained in critical condition, the surgery was going well. But it would be a long night. Dr. Cornell's best estimate was that he would not be finished until sometime between midnight and one o'clock.

She had taken two bullets. They had done much damage.

Just then I didn't want more details. Couldn't bear them.

The nurse left.

With just me and Dad in it, the small ICU lounge seemed as big as an airplane hangar.

'She'll be fine,' he told me. 'Good as new.'

I couldn't remain seated. Had to move, burn off nervous energy.

This was Sunday, December 22, not one of the five dates on the back of the circus pass. At midnight, the third day on Grandpa Josef's list would begin.

What could happen after midnight that would be worse than what had happened this evening?

I pretended not to know the answer. I pressed

362

from my mind the dangerous question itself.

Although I had gotten up to pace, I found myself at one of the two windows. I didn't know how long I'd been standing there.

I tried to focus on the view beyond the glass, but there didn't seem to be one. Just blackness. A bottomless void.

I was holding tightly to the window frame. Vertigo had overcome me. I felt I would fall through the window, into a dark whirlpool.

Behind me, Dad said, 'Jimmy?'

When I didn't answer, he put a hand on my shoulder.

'Son,' he said.

I turned to him. Then I did what I had not done since I was a little child: I wept in my father's arms.

50

Near midnight, my mother arrived with a large tin of homemade cookies: lemon snaps, madeleines, Scotch shortbread, and Chinese sesame bars.

Weena followed close behind her in a yellow snowsuit. She carried two big thermoses of our favorite Colombian blend.

The hospital provided snacks and coffee from vending machines. Even in a crisis, however, we were not a family that ate from vending machines.

Annie, Lucy, and Andy had been moved to my parents' house. They were in the care and under the protection of a phalanx of trusted neighbors.

Mom had also brought a change of clothes for me. My shoes, pants, and shirt were stiff with dried blood.

'Honey, clean up in the men's room down the hall,' she said. 'You'll feel better.'

Leaving the lounge long enough to wash up and change seemed to be breaking the vigil, an abandonment of Lorrie. I didn't want to go.

Before leaving home, Mom had found her favorite snapshot of Lorrie and had inserted it into a small frame. She sat now with it in on her lap, studying it as if it were a talisman that would ensure her daughter-in-law's full recovery.

My father sat beside my mother, took her hand, held it fast. He murmured something to

364

her. She nodded. She stroked the photo with one finger, as if smoothing Lorrie's hair.

Gently, Weena took the cameo pendant from my hand, clasped it in both of hers, warming it between her palms, and whispered, 'Go, Jimmy. Make yourself presentable for Lorrie.'

I decided that the vigil would not — could not — be broken with these three remaining in attendance.

In the men's room, I hesitated to wash my hands, for fear that I would be washing Lorrie away with her blood.

We don't fear our own deaths as much as the deaths of those we love. On the cusp of such a loss, we go a little crazy with denial.

When I returned to the ICU lounge, the four of us drank coffee and ate cookies with such solemnity that we might have been taking Communion.

At 12:30, the surgical nurse returned to inform us that Dr. Cornell would need more time than originally projected. He now expected to speak with us at about 1:30.

Lorrie had already been in surgery over four hours.

The cookies and coffee soured in my stomach.

Still wearing his greens and cap, the surgeon arrived with our internist, Mello Melodeon, at 1:33. Dr. Cornell was in his forties, looked younger, yet had a comforting air of experience and authority.

'Considering how terrible her injuries were,' Dr. Cornell said, 'everything went as well as I could have hoped.'

He had removed her damaged spleen, which she could live without. More troubling, he removed a badly ravaged kidney; but, God willing, she would be able to enjoy a full life with the one that remained.

Damage to the gastroepiploic and mesenteric veins required much careful work. He had employed grafts using lengths of another vein taken from her leg.

Punctured in two places, the small intestine had been repaired. And a two-inch torn section of the descending colon had been excised.

'She'll be on the critical list for at least twenty-four hours,' Cornell told us.

With the intestinal damage, she faced some possibility of peritonitis, in which case he would have to operate on her again. She would be put on blood thinners to minimize the risk of stroke from clots forming where vein walls had been stitched.

'Lorrie's not out of the woods yet,' he cautioned, 'but I'm a lot more confident about her now than when I first opened her up. I suspect she's a fighter, isn't she?'

'She's tough,' Mello Melodeon said.

And I said, 'Tougher than me.'

After they brought her to the ICU and settled her, I was allowed to visit in her cubicle for five minutes.

She remained sedated. Even with her features relaxed in sleep, I could see how much she had suffered.

I touched her hand. Her skin felt warm but perhaps because my hands were icy.

Her face was pale but nevertheless radiant, like the face of a saint in a painting from a century in which most people believed in saints, artists more than anyone.

She was on an IV, hooked up to a heart monitor, with an oxygen feed in her nostrils. I looked away from her face only to watch the steady spiking of the light that traced her heartbeat across a graph.

Mom and Grandma spent a couple minutes with Lorrie, then went home to reassure the kids.

I told Dad to go home, too, but he remained. 'There's still some cookies need eating in that tin.'

In those pre-dawn hours, we would have been at work if we'd not been at the hospital, so I didn't grow sleepy. I lived for the brief visits that the ICU staff allowed.

At dawn, a nurse came to the lounge to tell me that Lorrie had awakened. The first thing she'd said to anyone was 'Gimme Jimmy.'

When I saw her awake, I would have cried but for the realization that tears would blur my vision. I was starving for the sight of her.

'Andy?' she asked.

'He's safe. He's fine.'

'Annie, Lucy?'

'They're all okay. Safe.'

'True?'

'Absolutely.'

'Beezo?'

'Dead.'

'Good,' she said, and closed her eyes. 'Good.'

Later, she said, 'What's the date?'

I almost didn't tell her the truth, but then I did. 'December twenty-third.'

'The day,' she said.

'Obviously, Grandpa missed it by a few hours. He should have warned us about the twenty-second.'

'Maybe.'

'The worst is passed.'

'For me,' she said.

'For all of us.'

'Maybe not for you.'

'I'm fine.'

'Don't let your guard down, Jimmy.'

'Don't worry about me.'

'Don't let your guard down for a minute.'

51

My father went home to take a three-hour nap, promising to return with thick roast-beef sandwiches, olive salad, and an entire pistachio-almond polenta cake.

Later in the morning, when Dr. Cornell made his rounds, he pronounced himself pleased with Lorrie's progress. Those woods she hadn't been out of the previous night were still around her, but hour by hour there were fewer trees.

People with tragedies of their own had come and gone from the ICU lounge. The two of us were alone when Cornell sat down and asked me to take a seat, as well.

At once I knew that he had something to tell me that might explain why my grandfather had identified the twenty-third as the day to dread.

I thought of bullets puncturing intestines, ripping up kidneys, tearing through blood vessels, and I wondered what other damage might have been done. Suddenly I thought *spine*.

'Oh, God, no. She's paralyzed from the waist down, isn't she?'

Startled, Dr. Cornell said, 'Good heavens, no. Anything like that I would have told you last night.'

I would not allow myself to feel relief, because clearly he had *something* to tell me that wasn't news you celebrated with fine champagne.

'I understand that you and Lorrie have three children.'

'Yeah. Annie. Lucy. Andy. Three.'

'The oldest will soon be five?'

'Yeah. Annie. Our tomboy.'

'Three kids under five — that's a handful.'

'Especially when they won't share one closet monster.'

'Is that Lorrie's ideal family?' he asked.

'They're darn good kids,' I said, 'but they're not ideal.'

'I mean, the number.'

'Well, she wants twenty,' I said.

He stared at me as if he'd just noticed that I'd grown a second head during the night.

'That's partly a joke,' I explained. 'She'd settle for five, might like six or seven. *Twenty* — that was just an exaggeration she came up with to express how important family is to her.'

'Jimmy, you know how fortunate Lorrie is to be alive?'

I nodded. 'And I know she's going to be weak for a while, going to need lots of recuperation time, but don't worry about the kids. My folks and I can handle it. There won't be a strain on Lorrie.'

'That's not the issue. Jimmy, the thing is . . . Lorrie won't be having any more children. If that's going to be a blow to her, I don't want her knowing until she's on her feet again.'

If I could have just Lorrie, Annie, Lucy, and Andy, I would thank God every morning and every night that I'd been given so much.

I didn't know for sure how she would take the

370

news. She is practical, but she is a dreamer, too, a realist and a romantic at the same time.

'I had to remove one of her ovaries and a fallopian tube,' he said. 'The other ovary is undamaged, but the trauma to the associated tube will inevitably result in scar tissue that'll close off the isthmus entirely.'

'It can't be repaired someday?'

'I doubt it. Besides, she has just one kidney now. She shouldn't get pregnant again, anyway.'

'I'll tell her. I'll know when the time is right.'

'I did everything I could, Jimmy.'

'I know. And I'm more grateful than I can ever put into words. You've got free baked goods for life.'

After Dr. Cornell left and as the day wound on, I kept my guard up, waiting for whatever unspeakable horror my grandpa had foreseen, but wondered if Lorrie's sterility might be it. To me, that would be an abiding sadness, yes, but nothing worse; to her, however, it might qualify as tragedy.

As it turned out, we would not fully understand for several months why that twenty-third of December had been almost as terrible a day in our lives as had been the evening of the twenty-second.

Looking rested, Dad returned with the roast-beef sandwiches, olive salad, and an entire pistachio-almond polenta cake.

Later, during another short visit with Lorrie in the ICU, she said, 'Punchinello's still out there.'

'In a maximum-security prison. No need to worry about him.'

'I'll worry a little anyway.'

Weary, she closed her eyes.

I stood beside the bed, looking at her for a while, then said softly, 'I'm so sorry.'

She wasn't asleep, as I had thought. Without opening her eyes, she said, 'Sorry for what?'

'For getting you into this.'

'You didn't get me into anything. You saved my life.'

'When you married me, my curse became yours.'

Opening her eyes, fixing me with an intense stare, she said, 'Listen up, muffin man. There's no curse. There's only life.'

'But — '

'Did I say 'listen up'?'

'Yes, ma'am.'

'There's no curse. There's only life the way it is. And in my life, you're the greatest blessing I could have hoped for. You're my every prayer answered.'

On a subsequent visit, when she *was* asleep, I gently slipped the cameo pendant around her neck, fastened the catch.

Delicate but indestructible. Beauty enduring. The profile of love everlasting.

52

On January 11, 2003, Lorrie was discharged from the hospital. For a while she stayed at my parents' house, next door to ours, where there would be more hands to help her.

She slept on a roll-away bed in Mom's art alcove, adjacent to the living room, under the watchful gaze of an unfinished portrait of Lumpy Dumpy, someone's pet turtle.

By Sunday, January 26, Lorrie had been on a regular diet long enough and with sufficient success that we deemed her ready for a holiday dinner, Tock style.

Never had our Christmas table been so heavily laden. Serious discussions were held as to the possibility of the table cracking under the burden of so many delectables. After calculations in which the kids contributed their unschooled but imaginative mathematics, we concluded that we were two dinner rolls shy of the weight required to trigger a collapse.

Eight of us gathered around the table for the postponed feast, the children boosted on pillows, the adults lifted higher by good wine.

Never had the Christmas candles painted our faces so warm, so bright. The children glowed like blithe spirits, and when I looked around at Mom, at Dad, at Grandma, at Lorrie, I felt that I was in the company of angels.

During soup, Grandma Rowena said, 'The

wine reminds me of the time Sparky Anderson uncorked a bottle of Merlot and found a severed finger in it.'

The kids squealed as one, grossed out and delighted.

'Weena,' my father warned, 'that's not an appropriate story for the dinner table, especially not for the Christmas dinner table.'

'Oh, on the contrary,' said Grandma, 'it's the most Christmasy story I know.'

'There's nothing whatsoever Christmasy about it,' Dad said exasperatedly.

Mom came to the defense of Grandma: 'No, Rudy, she's right. It is a Christmasy story. There's a reindeer in it.'

'And a fat guy with a white beard,' Grandma added.

Lorrie said, 'You know, I've still never heard the story about how Harry Ramirez boiled himself to death.'

'That's a Christmasy story, too,' my mother declared.

Dad groaned.

'Well, it is,' Grandma agreed. 'There's a midget in it.'

Dad gaped at her. 'What makes a midget Christmasy?'

'Haven't you ever heard of elves?' Grandma asked.

'Elves aren't the same as midgets.'

'They are in my book,' Grandma said.

'Mine, too,' said Lucy.

'Midgets are people,' Dad persisted. 'Elves are fairies.'

'Fairies are people, too,' Grandma scolded him, 'even if they do prefer going to bed with their own gender.'

My mother remembered: 'And wasn't the midget's name Chris Kringle?'

'No, Maddy dear,' Grandma corrected, 'he was Chris *Pringle*, with a P.'

'Boy, that's Christmasy enough for me,' Lorrie said.

'This is nuts,' Dad said.

Mom patted him on the shoulder and said, 'Don't be such a Scrooge, dear.'

'So,' Grandma began, 'Sparky Anderson pays eighteen dollars for this bottle of Merlot, which was a lot more money in those days than it is now.'

'Everything's gotten so expensive,' Mom said.

'Especially,' Lorrie said, 'if you want something with a severed finger in it.'

The next of the five terrible days was ten months away, which that night — bright with tinsel, fragrant with roast turkey — seemed like forever.

PART FIVE

JUST LIKE PONTIUS PILATE, YOU WASHED YOUR HANDS OF ME

53

Nine miles from Denver, the Rocky Mountain Federal Penitentiary, a maximum-security facility, stands atop a foothill stripped of trees and flattened into a plateau. The higher slopes behind it and the slopes below are thickly forested, but the grounds of the prison are barren, offering no obstacle if searchlights are needed, no cover for escapees trying to dodge gunfire from the guard towers.

No inmate has ever escaped from Rocky Mountain. The two ways they get out are on parole or dead.

The stone walls soar high, punctured only by barred windows too small for any man to squeeze through. The steeply pitched slate roof beetles over every rampart.

Above the main gate to the walled parking lot, carved in stone are the words TRUTH ★ LAW ★ JUSTICE ★ PUNISHMENT. From the look of the place and considering the class of hardened criminal housed therein, the word *rehabilitation* was probably not an inadvertent omission.

On that Wednesday, November 26, the fourth of my five fateful days, the lowering sky pressing down on the prison looked as bleak as any inmate's future. The icy wind bit to the bone.

Before we were admitted through the gate to the parking lot, the three of us had to get out of the Explorer while two efficient guards searched

379

the vehicle inside and underneath for larger objectionable items such as suitcase bombs and rocket launchers.

'I'm scared,' Lorrie admitted.

'You don't have to go in with us,' I told her.

'Yeah. I do. Too much is riding on this. I've got to be there.'

Approved for entry to the lot, we parked as near the walk-in gate as possible. The bitter wind turned even the shortest walk into an ordeal.

The staff had the privilege of a heated underground garage. This surface lot served visitors.

On the day before Thanksgiving, you might expect a stream of loved ones. Instead, there were nine empty spaces for every vehicle.

Considering that the prisoners were drawn from all over the Western states, perhaps the distance was too great for many of their relatives to visit regularly. Or perhaps their families didn't give a damn about them.

In some cases, of course, they had killed their families and couldn't reasonably expect holiday reunions.

Even in this sentimental season, I was unable to work up any sympathy for the lonely men in those drab cellblocks, their hearts heavy and their eyes turned longingly toward birds winging across the ashen sky beyond their mean windows. I've never understood the weird Hollywood mind-set that romanticizes convicts and prison life. Besides, most of these guys had TVs, subscriptions to *Hustler*, and access to whatever drugs they needed.

Inside the main entrance, in a short reception corridor staffed by three armed guards — one with a shotgun — we identified ourselves, produced photo IDs, and signed in. We passed through a metal detector and submitted to fluoroscopic examination. Ceiling-mounted cameras watched us.

A handsome German shepherd, trained to detect drugs, lay at his handler's feet, chin cushioned cutely on one paw. The dog raised his head, sniffed in our direction, and yawned.

Our stash of aspirin and antacids was insufficient provocation to cause him to spring to his feet, snarling. I wondered how he might respond to visitors with legitimate Prozac prescriptions.

At the end of the corridor, we were examined remotely by another camera. Then from the farther side, a guard opened another steel door to admit us to a holding chamber.

Because our visit had been arranged through Huey Foster and because of the unusual nature of our business, we were given VIP treatment. The assistant warden himself, accompanied by an armed guard, led us from the holding chamber to an elevator, up two floors, along a series of halls, and through two additional gates that released after reading his fingerprints when he pressed his right hand against a wall-mounted scanner.

Outside the conference room, we were required to take off our coats and hang them on a wall rack. We read a short list headlined RULES OF CONDUCT posted beside the door.

Initially, only Lorrie and I went into the room, which measured approximately twenty feet by fifteen. Gray vinyl floor tiles, gray walls, low acoustic ceiling with fluorescent panels.

The sullen light of a dismal sky seemed barely able to penetrate the glass-and-wire-sandwich windows.

Centered in this space was an eight-foot-long conference table. On the farther side of the table stood a single chair; four chairs waited on the nearer side.

In the lone chair sat Punchinello Beezo, who did not yet know that he possessed the power either to grant our family a reprieve from tragedy or to condemn us to nearly unendurable suffering.

54

Welded to Punchinello's side of the table were two steel rings that had been wrapped with electrician's tape for sound attenuation. Each of his wrists had been chained to one of those rings. The length of these shackles allowed him to get up from his chair and stretch his legs in place, but didn't provide him with enough slack to move away from or around the table. The legs of the table were bolted to the floor.

Usually visitors spoke with prisoners through a speaker grille in a bulletproof-glass partition, in a communal lounge that served several parties simultaneously. Conference rooms like this one were used most frequently by attorneys who required privacy with their clients.

We had requested a private meeting with Punchinello not because we wished to discuss something confidential with him but because we felt that in a more intimate atmosphere, we'd have a better chance of persuading him to grant the request we had come here to make.

The word *ambience* was too highbrow to describe the stark and forbidding mood of the conference room. It didn't feel like a place in which a hardhearted man could be persuaded to do a goodhearted thing.

Remaining in the hallway, the guard who had escorted us now closed the door through which we had entered.

Punchinello's guard departed by a connecting door to another room. He stood at a window in that door, out of earshot but watchful.

We were alone with the man who would have killed us more than nine years ago if he'd had the chance, and who had been sentenced to imprisonment for life based in part on our testimony.

Considering the likelihood of his responding with hostility to any request we made, I wished that prison rules had permitted us to bring cookies.

Nine years behind bars appeared not to have left a mark on Punchinello. His haircut was less stylish and less well executed than it had been when he had blown up the town square, but he was as handsome as ever, boyish.

His movie-star smile seemed genuine. His dazzling green eyes gleamed with lively interest.

As we sat across the wide table from him, he wiggled the fingers of his right hand at us, a gesture most commonly made by grandmothers and accompanied by the word *toodle-oo*.

'You're looking well,' I said.

'I *feel* well,' he replied.

'Hard to believe it's been nine years.'

'Maybe for you. Seems like a hundred to me.'

I found it difficult to believe that he harbored no grudge toward us. After all, he was a Beezo, therefore marinated in umbrage and steeped in resentment. Yet I wasn't able to detect any animosity in his voice.

Inanely, I said, 'Yeah, I guess you have a lot of time on your hands in here.'

'I've put it to good use. I earned a correspondence degree in law — though being a felon, I'll never be admitted to the bar.'

'A law degree. That's impressive.'

'I've filed appeals on my behalf and for other prisoners. You wouldn't believe how many inmates here were wrongly convicted.'

'All of them?' Lorrie guessed.

'Nearly all of them, yes,' he said utterly without irony. 'At times it's difficult not to despair over the amount of injustice in this society.'

'There's always cake,' I said, and then realized that without having heard my dad's favorite saying, Punchinello would think that I was spouting gibberish.

Taking my puzzling comment in stride, he said, 'Well, I like cake, of course, but I'd rather have justice. In addition to getting the law degree, I've learned to speak fluent German because it's the language of justice.'

'Why is German the language of justice?' Lorrie wondered.

'I don't really know. I heard an actor say that in an old World War II movie. It made sense to me at the time.' He spoke to Lorrie in what sounded like German, then translated: 'You are quite beautiful this morning.'

'You always were a charmer,' she said.

He grinned at her and winked. 'I've also learned to speak fluent Norwegian and Swedish.'

'I've never known anyone who studied Norwegian *and* Swedish,' Lorrie said.

'Well, I thought it would be polite to address

them in their own language when I accept the Nobel Prize.'

Because he seemed dead earnest, I asked, 'A Nobel Prize in what category?'

'I haven't decided. Maybe a peace prize, maybe for literature.'

'Ambitious,' Lorrie said approvingly.

'I'm working on a novel. Half the guys in here say they're working on a novel, but I really am.'

'I've thought about writing nonfiction,' I told him, 'sort of biographical.'

'I'm on chapter thirty-two,' Punchinello said. 'My protagonist has just learned how deeply evil the aerialist really is.' He spoke in what might have been Norwegian or Swedish, then translated: 'The humility with which I accept this award surely is equal to the wisdom of your decision to give it to me.'

'They'll be in tears,' Lorrie predicted.

Though he was as looney as he was homicidal, I was nevertheless impressed by his apparent accomplishments. 'A law degree, learning German and Norwegian and Swedish, writing a novel . . . I'd need a lot longer than nine years to do all that.'

'The secret is, I'm so much more able to make the most of my time and to focus my energies without the distraction of testicles.'

I had expected that we'd get around to this sooner or later. 'I'm sorry about that, but you really didn't give me any choice.'

With a wave of his hand, he dismissed his loss as if it were of no consequence. 'There's plenty of blame to go around. What's done is done. I don't live in the past. I live *for* the future.'

'I limp on cold days,' I told him.

He wagged a finger at me, rattling the chain that tethered his hand to the table. 'Don't be a whiner. You didn't give *me* any choice, either.'

'I suppose that's true.'

'I mean,' he said, 'if we're going to get into a blame game, I hold the trump card. After all, you killed my father.'

'It's even worse than that,' I said.

'And you didn't name your firstborn son after him, like you promised. Annie, Lucy, Andy, no Konrad.'

A chill traveled my spine as I listened to him recite our children's names. 'How do you know their names?'

'They were in the newspaper last year, after all the hoo-ha.'

Lorrie said, 'By 'hoo-ha,' do you mean his attempt to kill us and kidnap our Andy?'

Making a patting motion with his hand, as if to gentle Lorrie, Punchinello said, 'Relax, relax. There's no Hatfield-and-McCoy thing between us. He could be a difficult man.'

'Maybe 'difficult' isn't descriptive enough,' Lorrie suggested.

'Tell it like it is, girl. And who would know better than me? Maybe you remember, nine years ago, when we were in the subcellar of the bank, when everything was fun and hadn't turned ugly yet, I told you that I had a cold and loveless childhood.'

'You did,' I agreed. 'You said exactly that.'

'He tried to be a good father to me, but it

wasn't in him,' Punchinello said. 'Do you know all the years I've been in here, he never sent me a Christmas card or a little money for candy?'

'That's hard,' I said, and actually felt a faint flutter of sympathy for him.

'But surely you haven't come here just so we could tell one another what a bastard he was.'

I said, 'Actually — '

He held up a hand to halt me. 'Before you tell me why you're here, let's agree upon terms.'

'What terms?' Lorrie inquired.

'Obviously, you want something important from me. You didn't go to all this trouble just to apologize for castrating me, though I appreciate that you did. If you get something from me, it's only fair that I be compensated.'

'Maybe you better hear what we want first,' I suggested.

'No, I'd prefer to get the basic terms established,' he said. 'Then if I feel I'm getting the short end of the trade, we can revise the deal.'

'All right,' Lorrie said.

'First, I'd like to receive a birthday card every August ninth, and a Christmas card every year. Most of the guys here get cards now and then, but I never do.'

'Two cards,' I agreed.

'And not junk cards or those ones that are supposed to be funny but are really just mean,' he qualified. 'Something from Hallmark with a nice sentiment.'

'Hallmark,' I agreed.

'The library here is underfunded, and we can

388

only receive books directly from a publisher or a bookstore, not from individuals,' he explained. 'I'd very much like you to arrange for a bookstore to send me every new paperback by Constance Hammersmith.'

'I know those books,' I said. 'She writes about a detective with neurofibromatosis. He goes all around San Francisco wearing a hooded cloak.'

'They're *fabulous* books,' he declared, and seemed delighted to discover that we shared this literary enthusiasm. 'He's like the Elephant Man and nobody ever loved him, he's always been ridiculed, an outcast, so he shouldn't give a crap about anyone, but he *does*. He helps people in trouble when no one else will.'

'She writes two books a year,' I said. 'You'll get them both as soon as thcy hit paperback.'

'The last thing is . . . I'm allowed to have a cash account. I'd like a little money for candy, gum, and now and then Cheez Doodles.'

In the end, he had become such a pathetic monster.

'The money's going to be a problem,' Lorrie said.

'I don't want much. Like fifty dollars a month or forty. And not forever, just as long as seems fair. Life in here without money is hell.'

'When we explain why we're here,' I said, 'you'll see why we can't give you money. But I'm sure we can arrange for a third party to send you an allowance, if we're all discreet about it.'

He brightened. 'Gee, that would be wonderful. When you're reading Constance Hammersmith, you've got to have Hershey's bars.'

The deformed, cloaked detective in her books has a passion for chocolate. And for the harpsichord.

'We can't get you a harpsichord,' I warned.

'That's all right. I'm not musically talented, anyway. Just what we've already agreed — that would make a world of difference. Life in here is so . . . limited. It's not right, being made to live with so many restrictions, so few pleasures. The way they treat me, you'd think I'd killed a thousand people.'

'You did kill several,' Lorrie reminded him.

'But not a *thousand*,' he said. 'And the courthouse tower fell on that old lady. I didn't *intend* to waste her. Fair punishment ought to be proportionate to the crime.'

'If only it were,' I said.

Leaning forward with keen interest, clinking his chains as he folded his hands on the table, Punchinello said, 'So I'm just dying to know. What brings you here?'

I said, 'Syndactyly.'

55

Syndactyly.

He flinched at the word as if I'd slapped him. His prison pallor faded from cream to milk to chalk.

'How do you know about that?' he asked.

'You were born with five fused toes on your left foot,' I said.

'The bastard told you, didn't he?'

'No,' Lorrie said. 'We didn't learn about your syndactyly until a week ago.'

'Three fingers were fused on your left hand,' I said.

He raised both hands, spreading the fingers wide. They were nice hands, well formed, though at the moment they trembled violently.

'Only the skin was fused, not the bone,' he said. 'But he told me there was nothing to be done about it, that I would have to live with it.'

His eyes filled with tears, which he shed copiously, silently. He made a bowl of his hands and poured his face into it.

I looked at Lorrie. She shook her head.

We gave him time. He needed several minutes.

Beyond the windows, the sky had darkened, as if some celestial editor had cut the day from three acts to two, eliminating afternoon, splicing morning to twilight.

I had not known what to expect from Punchinello when we made these revelations, but of all the reactions that I had anticipated, this misery was not among them. The sight of him in this condition shook me.

When he could speak, he revealed his sodden face. 'The great Beezo . . . he told me the way I walked, hobbled by five fused toes on one foot, gave me a natural advantage as a clown. When I did a funny walk, it was *authentic*, he said.'

The guard at the observation window watched, expression curious, no doubt astonished to see the ruthless killer weeping.

'People couldn't see my foot, just the funny way I walked. But they could see my hand. I couldn't always keep it in a pocket.'

'It wouldn't have been ugly,' I found myself assuring him. 'Just different . . . and damn inconvenient.'

'Oh, it was ugly to me,' he said. 'I hated it. My mother had been perfection. The great Beezo showed me photographs of her. Many photographs of her. My mother had been perfection . . . but I was not.'

I thought of my mother, Maddy. Although lovely to the eye, she falls short of physical perfection. Her kind and generous heart is perfect, however, and worth more than all the glamor in Hollywood.

'From time to time, as I grew older, the great Beezo took photographs of my deformed foot and hand. Without a return address, he mailed them to the swine of swines, the old syphilitic weasel, Virgilio Vivacemente.'

'Why?' Lorrie asked.

'To show Virgilio that his most beautiful and

talented daughter had not produced an aerialist, that the next generation of circus stars in the Vivacemente dynasty would have to come from his other and less promising children. How could I, with my foot, walk a high wire? With my hand, how could I switch from trapeze to trapeze in midair?'

'When did you have the surgery?' I asked.

'When I was eight, I came down with a bad case of strep throat. The great Beezo had to take me to a clinic. A doctor there said that with the bone not involved, separating fused digits would be easy. After that, I refused all instruction in clowncraft until I was made whole.'

'But you had no talent for clowning.'

He nodded. 'After the surgery, I tried hard to keep my end of the bargain, but I was a lousy clown. From the moment my toes and fingers were separated, I *knew*.'

'You were born an aerialist,' Lorrie said.

'Yes. Secretly I took some instruction. Too late by then. One has to begin practicing even younger. Besides, in the eyes of that talking sewer sludge, Virgilio, I was tainted with clown blood. He'd pull all the strings in his web to prevent me from performing.'

'So eventually you decided to throw your life away in a frenzy of vengeance,' I said, pretty much quoting him from the night we had met him in 1994.

He repeated what he had told us almost a decade ago: 'Might as well die if I can't fly.'

'The crazy story he told you about the night of your birth, the assassin nurse and the doctor

393

bribed by Virgilio to kill your mother — that was all a grotesque lie,' I told him.

Punchinello smiled through his tears and shook his head. 'I sorta suspected it might be.'

This admission chilled me. 'You sorta suspected it might be? But you still came back to Snow Village to kill a bunch of people and blow things up?'

He shrugged. 'It was something to do. The hatred was something to hold on to. I didn't have anything else.'

Something to do. It's a slow Friday night, so let's blow up a town.

Instead of giving voice to that thought, I said, 'You seem to have a facility for foreign languages. You could've become a teacher, a translator.'

'All my life, I'd never been able to please the great Beezo. And there was no one else who *wanted* me to please them. Being a teacher wouldn't have impressed him. But taking extreme vengeance for my mother's death — I know that made him proud of me.' An almost beatific smile overcame him. 'I know my father loved me for that.'

'Really?' I asked with scorn I could not entirely conceal. 'You know he did? He never even sent you a Christmas card.'

A little knife of sadness whittled at his smile. 'I'll grant you he was never a good father. But I know he loved me for what I did.'

Lorrie said, 'I'm sure he did, Punch. I think you did what you had to do.' With those words, she reminded me that we had come here to win

394

him over, not to alienate him.

Her approval, insincere to my ear but genuine to his, restored Punchinello's faltering smile. 'If things hadn't gone all wrong that night in Snow Village, you and I might have had a future together, instead of you and him.'

'Boy, that's something to think about, isn't it?' she replied, and matched his smile.

'Syndactyly,' I said again.

He blinked, and his witless smile morphed into puzzlement. 'You never said how you knew about that.'

'I wasn't born with hand problems, but I had three fused toes on my right foot, two on my left.'

More appalled than astonished, he said, 'What in God's name kind of rotten hospital *was* that?'

I marveled that he could seem sometimes so sane and sometimes so flat-out crazy, that he could be smart enough to earn a law degree and learn German but could say something as stupid as what he'd just said. 'It had nothing to do with the hospital.'

'I should have blown it up, too.'

With a glance, I consulted Lorrie.

She took a deep breath and nodded.

To Punchinello, I said, 'We both had fused digits because we're brothers. We're twins.'

He favored me with a look of amazement, then gave some of it to Lorrie. Next came a slow crooked grin, a squint of amused suspicion. 'Try that one with some dope who's never seen himself in a mirror.'

'We don't look alike,' I said, 'because we're fraternal twins, not identical twins.'

56

I didn't want to be his fraternal twin, not only because that made me the brother to a homicidal maniac, but also because I didn't want to put Konrad Beezo's picture in the family album and label it FATHER. Natalie Vivacemente Beezo might have been beautiful beyond imagining, perfection of the flesh, but even she was not welcome in my family tree.

I have one father and one mother, Rudy and Maddy Tock. They — and only they — raised me to be the person I am, gave me the chance to become who I was meant to be. I was destined for baking, not for the big top. If their blood does not run in my veins, their enduring love does, for they have all my life given me transfusions of it.

Other possibilities — that Natalie might have lived, that even if she had died, I might have been raised by Konrad — did not bear contemplation.

Besides, those other possible lives all fall in the category of never-could-have-been. Think about it. Grandpa Josef — not my true grandfather — made predictions not about his real grandson, who was stillborn that night, but about *me*, the infant that Rudy and Maddy would incorrectly believe was their own. Why would he have psychic visions of events in the life of a 'grandson' to whom he wasn't in fact related?

I can only believe that some higher power,

aware of the quirk of fate that was about to occur, used my grandfather not solely or perhaps not even primarily to warn me of five terrible days in my life, but also, and more important, to ensure that Rudy would believe with all of his heart that this infant with fused toes, who would grow up to have no resemblance to his parents, was the child that Maddy had carried for nine months. Grandpa Josef told Rudy that I would be born at 10:46 P.M., measure twenty inches in length, weigh eight pounds ten ounces, and have fused digits. By the time I was handed to him, wrapped in a delivery-room blanket, Dad already knew me and accepted me as the son that fulfilled *his* father's deathbed predictions.

Some guardian angel didn't want me to wind up in an orphanage or to be adopted into another family. He wanted me to take the place of Jimmy Tock, who had died on the way into the world.

Why?

Maybe God thought the world was short one good pastry chef.

Maybe He thought Rudy and Maddy deserved a child to raise with the love, the sweetness, and the selflessness that they lavished upon me.

The only full and true answer lies in mysteries so deep that I will never plumb them — unless they're revealed to me after my own death.

One thing I said is wrong. Jimmy Tock did not die on his way into the world: a nameless infant perished. I am the only Jimmy Tock, the only one who was meant to be, son of Rudy and Maddy regardless of the loins I sprang from. I was destined for pastries and for Lorrie Lynn Hicks and for Annie-Lucy-Andy, destined for more that I do not yet know, and every day of my life I fulfill the plan even if I cannot comprehend it.

I am profoundly grateful. And humble. And sometimes afraid.

In 1779, a poet named William Cowper wrote: *God moves in a mysterious way, His wonders to perform.*

Way to go, Bill.

From behind his slow crooked grin and his squint of amused suspicion, Punchinello said, 'Tell me about it.'

'We've brought along someone who might be more convincing,' Lorrie said.

I went to the door, opened it, leaned into the corridor, and asked Charlene Coleman, the earthly instrument of my guardian angel, to join us at the table.

57

Charlene Coleman, maternity-ward nurse on the night that I was born and still on the job at fifty-nine, has not entirely lost her Mississippi accent after all these years in Colorado. She's as sweet-faced now as she was then, and certainly as black.

She has gained some weight, which she attributes to years of free pastries from my father. But as she says, if you want to get to Heaven, you've first got to get through life, and you need some padding for all the hard knocks along the way.

Few women have more presence than Charlene. She is awesomely competent without being smug. She is determined without being bossy, morally certain without being judgmental. She likes herself but is not full of herself.

At the table, Charlene sat between me and Lorrie, directly across from Punchinello.

She said to him, 'You were a red-faced, pinch-faced, fussy little bundle, but you turned out the kind of handsome that breaks hearts without trying.'

To my surprise, a blush brought color to his prison pallor.

Punchinello seemed pleased by the compliment, but he said, 'Not that it's done me any good.'

'Little lamb, never question the gifts God gave

399

you. If we don't make anything of our gifts, that's our fault, not His.' She studied him a moment. 'What I think is you never really knew you were a good-looking boy. You don't quite believe it even now.'

He stared at the hand that had once been cursed with syndactyly. He spread the fingers, worked them independently of one another, as though they had been separated only yesterday, as though he were still learning how to use them.

'Your mama was beautiful, too,' said Charlene, 'and as sweet as a child, but fragile.'

Looking up from his hand, he returned by long habit to the mad fantasy that his father had concocted: 'She was murdered by the doctor because — '

'None of that,' Charlene interrupted. 'You know crazy when you hear it, as sure as I do. When you pretend to believe things that aren't true, just because it's easier than dealing with the facts, you turn your whole life into a lie. And where's that get you?'

'Here,' he acknowledged.

'When I say your mama was fragile, I don't mean just because she died giving birth, which she did, though the good doctor tried everything to save her. Her spirit was fragile, too. Someone seemed to have broken it. She was a frightened little thing, afraid of more than just child-birth. She grabbed my hand and didn't want to let go, wanted to tell me things, I think, but was scared to hear herself say the words.'

I sensed that if Punchinello had not been chained to the table and that if the posted rules of conduct had permitted it, he would have reached out to Charlene, as his mother had done. He stared at her, transfixed. His countenance was a pool of sorrow, with drowned hopes in his eyes, and on the surface floated a childlike longing.

'Though your mama died,' Charlene continued, 'she gave birth to healthy twins. You were the smaller. Jimmy was the bigger.'

I studied him as he gazed at Charlene, and thought how different my life would have been if she had scooped him up to save him instead of scooping me.

The possibility of our lives exchanged, his for mine, should have made it easier for me to see him as my brother, but I could not get my heart around him. He remained a stranger to me.

'Maddy Tock,' Charlene told Punchinello, 'had difficult labor, too, but it turned out opposite from what happened to your mother. Maddy lived, and her baby died. Her final contraction was so painful she passed out — and never knew her child was stillborn. I took the precious little bundle and put him in a bassinet in the crèche, so she wouldn't see his tiny body when she woke . . . and wouldn't have to see him at all if she decided not to.'

Curiously, when I thought of that stillborn infant, I mourned him as a lost brother, as I could never mourn Punchinello.

Lorrie said, 'Then Dr. MacDonald went to the expectant-father's lounge to console Konrad Beezo for the loss of his wife, Rudy Tock for the loss of his child.'

'We were shorthanded that night,' Charlene recalled. 'A mean virus had been making the rounds, people were out sick. Lois Hanson was the only delivery nurse available besides me. When we heard Konrad Beezo shouting at the doctor, so bitter, accusing, and such shameful profanity, we both thought of the twins, but for different reasons. Lois, she figured the sight of his babies would calm Konrad, but I'd come off a marriage to a cruel man, and I knew I heard the same violence in this one, rage that can't be put out by kindness, that could only burn itself out in fury. My only thought was to get the babies safe. Lois took you down the hall toward the lounge and got herself shot to death, but I went the other way with Jimmy here, and hid out.'

I had worried that in spite of the revelation that we had both been born with syndactyly, Punchinello would receive Charlene's story with skepticism if he didn't reject it outright. Instead, he appeared not merely to believe it but to be enraptured by her account.

Perhaps he warmed to the romantic notion that he had much in common with the betrayed title character in Alexandre Dumas's *The Man in the Iron Mask*, that he was the equivalent of a heroic peasant while I, his twin, had ascended to the throne of France.

'When I discovered that sweet man, our lovely Dr. MacDonald, had been murdered, and Lois Hanson, too,' Charlene continued, 'I realized I was the only living soul who knew Maddy's baby was born dead and Natalie Beezo had given birth to twin boys. If I did nothing, Maddy and Rudy would have a tragedy at the center of their lives, an awful thing to get around. And the baby I saved would be put at the mercy of the state, sent to an orphanage or foster homes ... or maybe claimed by relatives of Konrad Beezo every bit as crazy as he was. And all his life people would point and say, *That's the son of the murderer.* I knew what good honest people Rudy and Maddy were, and I knew the love they would shower on their boy, so I did what I did, and Lord Jesus forgive me if He thinks I played God.'

After closing his eyes and absorbing the nurse's tale in silence for a half minute or so, Punchinello turned his attention to me. 'So what happened to the real you?'

I didn't at once understand what he meant. Then I realized that 'the real you' was Mom and Dad's lost infant.

'Charlene had a huge straw purse,' I said. 'She wrapped the dead baby in a soft white cloth that night, put him in the straw bag, and took him from the hospital to her minister.'

'I'm Baptist born and raised,' Charlene told Punchinello, 'one of the joyful denominations. I'm a Sunday-go-to-meetin' girl dresses better for church than for Saturday night, from a family likes to praise the Lord in gospel songs. If my preacher had told me I'd done a wrongful thing, I would have undone it, I suppose. But if he had his doubts, compassion swamped his judgment. Our church has its own graveyard, so my preacher and me, we found a pretty corner there for Maddy's baby. Buried him with prayer, just the two of us, and about a year later, I bought a little headstone. When the spirit moves me, I go there with flowers, tell him what an admirable life Jimmy here is living in his place, how proud he'd be of the fine brother Jimmy has become to him.'

I had been to the cemetery with my mom and dad, and had seen the headstone, a simple two-inch-thick rectangle of granite. Carved in it are these words: HERE LIES BABY T. GOD LOVED HIM SO MUCH HE CALLED HIM HOME AT BIRTH.

Maybe it's our free will misdirected or just a shameful pride, but we live our lives with the conviction that we stand at the center of the drama. Moments rarely come that put us outside ourselves, that divorce us from our egos and force us to see the larger picture, to recognize that the drama is in fact a tapestry and that each of us is but a thread in the vivid weave, yet each thread essential to the integrity of the cloth.

When I stood before that headstone, such a moment took me like a swelling tide, lifted me, turned me, and brought me back to shore with greater respect for the unmappable intricacy of life, with more humility in the face of mysteries unresolvable.

58

Bitter cold compressed the snow from flakes to granules that clicked against the prison windows as if the ghosts of the inmates' victims haunted the day and tapped for their attention.

With Charlene having told all that she had to tell and having returned to the hallway, Punchinello leaned toward me and asked with apparent earnestness, 'Do you sometimes wonder if you're real?'

The question made me nervous because I didn't understand it, because I worried that he would take us off on some crazy tangent from which we could not comfortably approach the request that had brought us here. 'What do you mean?'

'You don't know what I mean because you've never doubted that you're real. Sometimes I'm walking down a street, and it's like no one sees me, and I'm sure I've become invisible. Or I wake up in the night convinced there's nothing out there beyond my window, nothing at all but darkness, a vacuum, and I'm afraid to open the drapes and look, afraid I'll see a perfect emptiness, and that when I turn from the window, the room will be gone, too, and I'll cry out but won't make a sound, just float there with no sense of touch, no taste or smell, deaf and blind, the world gone as if it never was, me with no body that I can detect, no heartbeat I can

405

feel, and yet unable to stop thinking, thinking, furiously and frantically thinking about what I don't have and what I want, about what I do have but want to be free of, about how I am nothing to anyone or anyone to me, never real and yet all these memories, these churning, insistent, hateful *memories*.'

Despair is the abandonment of hope. Desperation is energized despair, vigorous in action, utterly reckless. He was telling me that everything he had learned from the use of guns and explosives to the German language, from the rules of law to Norwegian grammar, had been learned in desperation, as if in acquiring knowledge he would acquire substance, reality. But still he woke in the night, certain that a devouring void lay beyond his window.

He had opened a door on himself, and what I saw within him was both pitiful and terrifying.

His words revealed more than he realized. He had shown me that after the deepest self-analysis of which he was capable, he still did not understand the most important thing about himself, still lived a lie. He presented himself to me — and to himself — as one who doubted his own reality and therefore the meaning of his existence. In truth, it was the existence of the world he doubted and only himself that he believed to be real.

They call it solipsism, and even a pastry chef like me has heard of it: the theory that only the self can be proved to exist, extreme preoccupation with and indulgence of one's feelings and desires. He would never be capable of seeing himself as one thread in a tapestry. He was the universe, and all the rest of us were his fantasies, to be killed or not, as he saw fit, with no real consequences to us or to him.

This kind of thinking did not begin as madness, though it might end up indistinguishable from insanity. This kind of thinking began as a choice — it was taught as a philosophy worth consideration in the finest universities — which made him a more formidable figure than he would have been as a poor lost boy driven mad by circumstances.

More than ever, he scared the crap out of me. We had come here hoping — *needing* — to touch his heart, but we could no more move him than we ourselves could be moved to make a sacrifice by the mumblings of a phantom in a dream.

This was the fourth of my five terrible days, and I knew now why it would be the worst of the five to date. He would refuse us, and by his refusal we would be condemned to endure an unendurable loss.

'Why did you come here?' he asked.

Not for the first time, when words failed me, Lorrie knew the right thing to say. She played to the fundamental lie by which he convinced himself that he was a victim rather than a monster.

'We came,' she said, 'to tell you that you're real and that there's a way to prove it to yourself once and for all.'

'And what way would that be?'

'We want you to save our daughter's life. You're the only one who can, and that's as real as anything can get.'

59

From her purse, Lorrie withdrew a photograph of Annie and slid it across the table to Punchinello.

'Pretty,' he said but did not touch the picture.

'She'll be six years old in less than two months,' Lorrie said. 'If she lives that long.'

'I'll never have children,' he reminded us.

I said nothing. I had apologized once for effectively castrating him, although a surgeon eventually completed the job that I had not quite finished.

'She had nephroblastoma,' Lorrie said.

'Sounds like a grunge band,' Punchinello replied, and smiled at his weak joke.

'It's cancer of the kidneys,' I explained. 'The tumors grow very rapidly. If you don't catch them early, they spread to the lungs, liver, and brain.'

'Thank God she was diagnosed in time,' Lorrie said. 'They took out both kidneys and followed up with radiation, chemotherapy. She's free of cancer now.'

'Good for her,' he said. 'Everyone should be free of cancer.'

'But there's a further complication.'

'This isn't as interesting as all the baby-switching stuff,' Punchinello said.

I didn't trust myself to speak. I felt as though my Annie's life hung by a thread, a filament so fine that I could cut it with one word too sharp.

Lorrie proceeded as if he hadn't spoken. 'Without kidneys, she's been on hemodialysis, four-hour sessions three times a week.'

'Six years old,' Punchinello said, 'she doesn't have a job to go to or anything. She's got plenty of free time.'

I couldn't decide whether he was merely as graceless as he was uncaring or whether he was needling us and enjoying it.

Lorrie said, 'At the center of the dialysis machine is a large cannister called a dialyzer.'

'Could that Charlene person get in trouble with the law because of what she did?' Punchinello asked.

Determined not to be baited into losing my temper, I said, 'Only maybe if my folks wanted to press charges. And they don't.'

Soldiering on, Lorrie said, 'The dialyzer contains thousands of tiny fibers through which the blood passes.'

'I usually don't like black people,' he informed us, 'but she seemed nice enough.'

'And there's a solution, a cleansing fluid,' Lorrie continued, 'that carries away the wastes and excess salts.'

'She's quite a tub, though,' Punchinello said. 'The amount of food she must pack away each day, you gotta wonder if she ate that baby instead of burying it.'

Lorrie closed her eyes. Took deep breaths. Then: 'It's very rare, but sometimes the dialysis patient is allergic to one or more of the chemicals in the cleansing solution.'

'I'm not prejudiced against black people. They should have equal rights and everything. I just don't like the way they aren't white.'

'The dialysate, the cleansing solution, contains a number of chemicals. Only the most minute quantities of those chemicals ever return to the body with the blood, infinitesimal amounts that are usually harmless.'

Punchinello said, 'I don't like the way their palms are pale and the tops of their hands dark. The soles of their feet are pale, too. It's like they're wearing badly made black-person disguises that weren't too well thought out.'

'If the doctor prescribes a dialysate that isn't working as well as it ought to,' Lorrie explained, 'or if the patient is sensitive to it, the formula can be adjusted.'

'One of the ways I know the world is wrong,' he said, 'is black people being in it. The design would be more convincing if everyone was white.'

Perhaps without realizing it, he had come as close as he might ever get to admitting that he thought the world was merely a stage, an illusion crafted to deceive him, and that he himself was the only piece of good design in it.

Lorrie looked at me, her face placid but her eyes feverish with frustration. I nodded to encourage her.

By the minute I saw less chance of reaching him, but if we gave up, Annie had no hope at all.

'Once in a great while, hardly ever,' Lorrie said, 'a dialysis patient is so violently allergic to even the most minute quantities of an array of

410

chemicals essential to dialysates that no adjusted formula will work for her. The allergic reactions grow worse each time until she's at risk of anaphylactic shock.'

'Well, Jesus, give her one of your kidneys, why don't you?' he asked. 'You have to be an acceptable match for her.'

'Thanks to your father,' she reminded him, 'I only have one.'

To me, he said, 'Then one of yours.'

'I'd have been on the operating table already if I could,' I told him. 'When they tested me to do a transplant compatibility profile, they discovered I have hemangiomas of both kidneys.'

'You're going to die, too?'

'Hemangiomas are benign tumors. You can live with them all your life, but they make me unsuitable as a donor.'

The last thing Grandpa Josef had said on his deathbed was *Kidneys! Why should kidneys be so damned important? It's absurd, it's all absurd!*

My father thought that my grandfather at the end lapsed back into incoherence, that those last words were of no importance.

We know what the poet William Cowper would say about that if he hadn't died back there in 1800.

In addition to waxing on about God's mysterious ways, Old Bill also wrote, *Behind a frowning providence, God hides a smiling face.*

I had always believed the same. But lately there were times when, I must confess, I wondered if His smile was as screwy as some with which Punchinello had favored us.

411

Now my murderous brother suggested, 'Sign the kid up on a transplant like everyone else does.'

'We could wait a year,' Lorrie said, 'maybe longer, to get a suitable match. Lucy and Andy are too young to donate.'

'A year isn't so long. I didn't get surgery for syndactyly until I was eight. Where were you then?'

'You're not listening to me,' Lorrie said tightly. 'Annie has to be on dialysis in the meantime — but she can't be. I explained already.'

'I might not be a suitable match.'

'Almost certainly you will,' I disagreed.

'It'll be a head-in-the-bucket thing again,' he predicted. 'It always is.'

Trying to force an emotional connection between him and Annie, Lorrie said, 'You're her uncle.'

'And you're my brother,' he said to me. 'But where were you for the past nine years when the justice system crucified me? Just like Pontius Pilate, you washed your hands of me.'

The irrationality of his accusation and the delusional grandeur implied by his comparison of himself to Christ allowed no response.

'Another thing that's all wrong with the black-people idea,' he said, 'is a black man's semen ought to be black if a white man's is white. But it's white, too. I know, I've seen enough porno.'

There are days when it seems to me that in literature the most convincing depiction of the world in which we live is to be found in the phantasmagorical kingdom through which Lewis Carroll took Alice on a tour.

Lorrie attempted to persevere: 'Sooner than later, anaphylactic shock will kill Annie. We can't risk it again. We're in a corner now. She's literally got only . . .'

Her voice broke.

I finished for her, 'Annie's literally got only a couple days.'

Putting it into words, I felt a garrote of dread cinch my heart and could not for a moment inhale.

'So it always comes down to good old Punchinello,' my brother said. 'The greatest clown in all history will be Punchinello Beezo. Except I wasn't. But, oh, the greatest aerialist of his age will be Punchinello Beezo! Except I was not allowed to be. No one will ever have avenged his mother's death as Punchinello will! Except I didn't get away with the money and had my testicles cut off. Now again — only Punchinello of all the people in the world, only Punchinello can save little Annie Tock — whose name rightly should be Annie Beezo, by the way — only Punchinello! But in the end she'll die anyway because this is, like all the other times, just a setup for the rug to be pulled out from under me.'

His speech had devastated Lorrie. She rose from her chair and turned away from him, stood trembling uncontrollably.

All could say to him was 'Please.'

'Go away,' he told me. 'Go home. When the little bitch dies, bury her in the Baptist cemetery beside the nameless baby whose life you stole.'

60

When we stepped out of the conference room and into the hall, Charlene Coleman knew the awful truth the moment she saw our faces. She opened her arms to Lorrie, and Lorrie fell into them, and held tightly to her, weeping.

I wished that I could turn back time while remembering all that had happened in the past half hour, and go at him again with greater finesse.

Of course I knew another session with him would not achieve anything more than the one just ended, as neither would ten sessions, a hundred. Talking to him was talking to the whirlwind, words wasted as surely as cease-and-desist commands shouted into a monsoon.

I knew that I had not failed Annie, that coming here had been a hopeless gamble from the start. Nonetheless, I *felt* that I had failed her, and I found myself in a despair so enervating that I didn't think I had the strength to walk back to the parking lot.

'The photo,' Lorrie suddenly remembered. 'The rotten bastard has Annie's photo.'

She didn't need to elaborate. I understood why the skin around her eyes turned livid, why her mouth tightened with revulsion.

I couldn't bear the thought of him alone in his cell with my Annie's photo, drinking her in with his eyes and slaking his thirst for cruelty with the thought of her painful death.

Bursting back into the conference room, I found him with the guard, who was about to unshackle him from the table.

Reaching out to him, I said, 'That photo belongs to us.'

He hesitated, held it toward me, at arm's length, but would not release it when I tried to take it from him.

'What about the cards?' he asked.

'What cards?'

'On my birthday and at Christmas.'

'Yeah, right.'

'Real Hallmark. Our deal.'

'We don't have any deal, you son of a bitch.'

His face flushed. 'Don't call my mother names.'

He was serious. We had been here before.

The anger receded from him, and he said, 'But I forgot . . . she's your mother, too, isn't she?'

'No. My mother's at home in Snow Village, painting an iguana.'

'Does this mean no candy money, either?'

'And no Cheez Doodles.'

He seemed genuinely surprised at my attitude. 'What about the Constance Hammersmith paperbacks?'

'Give me the photo.'

Releasing it to me, he said to the prison guard, 'We need a few more minutes of privacy, please.'

The guard looked at me. 'Sir?'

Afraid to speak, I merely nodded.

The guard retreated from the room and

415

watched from behind the window.

'Did you bring a medical release for me to sign?' Punchinello inquired.

From the threshold of the drab room, where she had been holding open the hallway door for me, Lorrie said, 'I have three copies in my purse, drawn up by a good attorney.'

'Come in,' he said. 'Close the door.'

Lorrie joined me on the sane side of the table, though I'm sure she suspected, as I did, that he was playing us for fools, setting us up for one more cruel reversal.

'When would we do it?' he asked.

'Tomorrow morning,' I said. 'The hospital in Denver is ready for us. They just need twelve hours' notice.'

'The deal we made . . . '

'It's still yours if you want it,' Lorrie assured him, removing the medical forms and a pen from her purse.

He sighed. 'I *love* those detective stories.'

'And Hershey's bars,' I reminded him.

'But when we negotiated,' he said, 'I didn't know I'd be giving up a kidney, which is a lot to ask, considering you've already gotten both my testicles.'

We waited.

'There's one more thing I want,' he said.

Here's where he would surely hit us with the punch line and laugh at our devastation.

'This is a private room,' he advised us. 'No listening devices because inmates usually meet here with their attorneys.'

'We know,' Lorrie said.

416

'And I doubt the moron at the window can read lips.'

'What do you want?' I asked, certain that it would be a thing beyond my power to grant.

'I know you don't trust me like you should a brother,' he said. 'So I won't expect you to do this *before* I give her my kidney. But once she has it, you're obligated.'

'If it's something I can do.'

'Oh, I'm positive you can do it,' he said cheerfully. 'I mean, look what you did to the great Beezo.'

I couldn't read him at all, didn't know whether this was leading to a vicious joke or to a genuine proposal.

Punchinello said, 'I want you to kill that scab on Satan's ass, Virgilio Vivacemente. I want you to make him suffer and let him know I'm the one who sent you. And in the end, I want him deader than any man has ever been dead.'

This was no joke. He meant it.

'Sure,' I said.

61

The white fluorescent panels in the gray ceiling, the white documents on the gray steel table, the granular snow blowing white out of a gray day, tapping the windows as the pen described his signature with the faintest whisper of ballpoint on paper . . .

Punchinello's guard and the one who had accompanied us from the holding chamber stood witness. They signed their names under my brother's.

Lorrie left one copy of the document with Punchinello and returned the others to her purse. The deal had been sealed, though the conditions of it were not on paper.

We didn't shake hands. I would have if he'd wanted to, a small unpleasantry in exchange for Annie's life. But he didn't seem to feel that a handshake was required.

'When this is all done and Annie's well,' he said, 'I'd like it if you'd bring her here to see me once in a while, Christmas at least.'

'No,' Lorrie replied bluntly and without hesitation, though I would have said anything he wanted to hear.

'I'm her uncle for one thing,' he said. 'And her savior.'

'I won't lie to you,' she told him. 'And neither will Jimmy. You'll never be the smallest part of her life.'

'Well, maybe the smallest part,' Punchinello said, reaching back as best he could, in chains, to indicate the position of his left kidney.

Lorrie stared him down.

He grinned at last. 'You're some piece of work.'

'Right back at ya,' she said.

We left him there and brought the news of his change of heart to Charlene Coleman in the hallway.

From the prison, we drove into Denver, where Annie had been undergoing just-in-case prep at the hospital and where we were staying at the Marriott.

The bruised sky spat granular snow like bits of broken teeth.

In the city, patches of fresh icc mottled the pavement. Wind whipped the coattails of pedestrians on the sidewalks.

Charlene had met us at our hotel that morning. Now, after hugs and thank-yous and God-blesses all around, she drove back to Snow Village.

In our Explorer again, just the two of us, with Lorrie behind the wheel, on the way to the hospital, I said, 'You scared the hell out of me when you told him Annie would never be a part of his life.'

'He knew we'd never allow that,' she explained. 'If we had agreed, he'd have known we were lying. Then he'd have been sure you were lying about killing Vivacemente, too. But now he thinks you'll really do it — because, like he said, look what you did to the great Beezo. If he thinks you'll do it, he'll keep his end of the bargain.'

We were silent for a block or two, and then I said, 'Is he crazy or evil?'

'The distinction doesn't matter to me. Either way, we have to deal with him.'

'If he was crazy first and found his way to evil, there's some explanation for him. And almost some sympathy.'

'None here,' she said, for she was a lioness with an endangered cub and would give no consideration to the predator.

'If he was evil first, and being evil made him crazy, I don't owe him anything that one brother would owe another.'

'You've been thinking about this for some time.'

'Yeah.'

'Give yourself a pass. Forget it. The courts already settled the issue when he was judged mentally fit to stand trial.'

She braked to a stop at a red traffic light.

On the cross street, a black Cadillac hearse glided past. The windows were tinted for privacy. Maybe it was transporting a dead celebrity.

'I'm not actually going to kill Vivacemente,' I assured Lorrie.

'Good. If you ever decide to turn homicidal, don't just run around offing people at random. Talk with me. I'll give you a list.'

The signal light changed to green.

As we passed through the intersection, three laughing teenage boys on the corner gestured obscenely at us. They were wearing black gloves from each of which the middle finger had been cut away to add emphasis to insult. One of them threw an ice-riddled snowball that cracked hard against my door.

A block from the hospital, still brooding about Punchinello and worrying about Annie, I said, 'He'll back out.'

'Don't even think it.'

'Because this is the fourth of my five terrible days.'

'It was already pretty terrible there for a while.'

'Not terrible enough. There's worse coming. There's got to be, judging by the past.'

'The power of negative thinking,' she warned me.

In spite of the defroster, ice began to crust on the windshield wipers, and the blades stuttered across the glass.

This was the day before Thanksgiving. It looked like the frozen heart of January. It felt like Halloween.

62

Captain Fluffy, brave guardian bear who prevented night monsters from creeping out of the closet and nibbling on children, shared the hospital bed with Annie. This was the most difficult assignment of his career.

When we arrived, we found our daughter sleeping. Always tired, she slept a lot these days. Too much.

Though Annie didn't know how close her mother had come to dying eleven months earlier, she knew the story of the cameo pendant, that it had survived an all-destroying fire, that her mother had worn it in the ICU. She had asked for it. She wore it now.

My beautiful little Annie had withdrawn into a gray disguise of sallow skin and brittle hair. Her eyes were mascaraed with mortality, her lips pale. She looked tiny, birdlike, old.

Neither magazines nor TV, nor the view from the window, had any interest for me. I could not stop staring at my little girl, seeing her in my mind's eye as she had been and as she might be again.

I was reluctant to look away from her or to leave the room, for fear that when I returned, I would not have Annie to look at anymore, only photographs as she had once been.

Her indomitable spirit, her courage through these exhausting months of illness, pain, and decline, had been an inspiration to me. But I wanted more than inspiration. I wanted *her* — healed, healthy, full of life once more. My tomboy. My little bullshit-artist wannabe.

My parents didn't raise me to ask God for blessings or benefits. For guidance, yes. For the strength to do the right thing, yes. Not for a winning lottery number, not for love or health, or happiness. Prayer is not a gimme list; God isn't Santa Claus.

As they have taught me, I believe that without asking, we are given all we need. We must have the wit and wisdom to recognize the strengths and tools at our command, and find the courage to do what must be done.

In this instance, however, we seemed to have done all that we humanly could. If her fate had been in the hands of God now, I would have rested more easily. But her fate seemed to be in the hands of Punchinello Beezo, and anxiety, like swarms of something winged, flew around and around in my stomach, fluttered in my bones.

And so I prayed to God to give me back my tomboy, and asked Him to ensure that Punchinello did the right thing if even for the evil reason of buying Virgilio Vivacemente's murder.

Even God himself might need a fancy calculator to compute the mathematics of *that* morality.

While I sat with Annie, immobilized by anxiety, Lorrie was all motion, making phone calls, coordinating things between the hospital and the penitentiary officials.

When Annie was awake, we talked of many things, of cabbages and kings, of next year at Disney World and the year after in Hawaii, of learning to ski and bake, but never of now and here, never of the dark what-if.

Her brow was warm to the touch, her delicate fingers cold. Her slender wrists had grown so slight that it seemed they might snap if she risked lifting a hand from the sheets.

Philosophers and theologians had spent centuries debating the existence and the nature of Hell, but I knew there in the hospital that Hell existed and I could describe its streets. Hell is a child lost and the fear of never being reunited.

Healthcare and prison bureaucrats proved extraordinarily helpful and expeditious. During the afternoon, Punchinello Beezo arrived in a prison van, handcuffed, fettered ankle to ankle, under the watchful eyes of two armed guards. I did not see him, only heard reports.

Tests were done. They said he was a match.

At six in the morning, the transplant would be performed.

Midnight of this terrible day still lay hours away. He could change his mind before then — or escape.

At 8:30, my father phoned from Snow Village to fulfill Grandpa Josef's prediction in an unexpected fashion. After lying down for a nap before dinner, Weena had passed away peacefully in her sleep at the age of eighty-six.

Lorrie drew me against my will into the corridor to share this news, lest Annie hear.

For a while I sat in a chair in an empty

hospital room, so Annie wouldn't see my tears and become anxious that they were shed for her.

On a cell phone, I called Mom, and we talked for a while about Grandma Rowena. You feel grief for a mother and a grandmother, of course, but when the life was very long and happy, and when the end came without pain or fear, it would almost be blasphemous to grieve too hard.

'What surprises me,' my mother said, 'is that she would go just before dinner. If she'd known what was going to happen, she wouldn't have laid down for a nap until after we'd eaten.'

Midnight came. And Thanksgiving morning.

Considering that Annie's deteriorating condition might have made her too weak for surgery in another day, the transplant procedure began none too soon at six o'clock.

Punchinello didn't welch.

I visited him hours later in his room, where he was chained to his bed and watched over by a guard. The guard stepped into the hall to give us privacy.

Although I knew well the nature of this beast, my voice broke with gratitude when I said, 'Thank you.'

He conjured that movie-hero smile, winked, and said, 'No thanks necessary, bro. I'm looking forward to birthday cards, candy, mystery novels . . . and one snake-hearted aerialist tortured with red-hot pliers and dismembered alive. I mean, if it works for you to do it that way.'

'Yeah, that sounds about right to me.'

'I don't want to cramp your creativity,' he assured me.

'Don't worry about me. What you want is all that matters.'

'Maybe you could nail him to a wall before you really start on him,' Punchinello suggested.

'Nails don't hold in drywall. I better buy a stud finder.'

He nodded. 'Good idea. And before you start cutting off his fingers and hands and stuff, take his nose off. He's a vain bastard, the great Beezo told me, very proud of his nose.'

'All right, but if there's anything more you want, I better start taking notes.'

'That's everything.' He sighed. 'Gosh, I sure wish I could be there with you.'

'Wouldn't that be wonderful,' I said.

Annie came through the surgery as smoothly as a hot-air balloon sailing, sailing.

Unlike its donor, the kidney was neither crazy nor evil, and it was such an ideal match for his niece that not one serious post-operative complication arose.

Annie lived. Annie bloomed.

These days, she charms, she shines, she dazzles, as ever she did before the cancer dragged her down.

Only one of the five days — April 16, 2005 — remained ahead of me. Life would seem strange thereafter, with no dreaded dates on the calendar, the future unclouded by grim expectations. Assuming that I survived.

PART SIX

I Am Moonlight Walking, the Love of Every Woman, the Envy of Every Man

63

Between baking cakes and taking additional instruction in the use of a handgun, between perfecting my recipe for chestnut-chocolate terrine and negotiating murder-for-hire contracts with insane kidney donors, I wrote the previous sixty-two chapters of this book during the year preceding the fifth of Grandpa Josef's five dates.

I'm not entirely sure why I felt compelled to write.

To the best of my knowledge, no pastry chef has ever had a memoir on the *New York Times* best-seller list. Celebrity tell-alls, hate-mongering political tracts, diet revelations about how to lose weight eating nothing but butter, and self-help books about getting filthy rich by adapting the code of the Samurai to business dealings seem to be what is wanted by contemporary readers.

Ego has not motivated me. If by some miracle the book were to be a success, everyone would still think that I am biggish for my size, a lummox. I am not a James, and if I wrote an entire library full of books, I still would not be one. I was born a Jimmy, and I will be a Jimmy when they lay me in my grave.

In part I wrote the book to tell my children how they got here, through what stormy seas, past what dangerous shoals. I want them to know what *family* means — and what it doesn't. I want them to know how loved they were, in case I don't live long enough to tell each of them a hundred thousand times.

In part I wrote it for my wife, to be sure she will know that without her, I might as well have died back there on the first of the five days. Each of us has his or her destiny, but sometimes two destinies twine, becoming so tightly braided that if Fate cuts one, she must cut both.

Also I wrote this to explain life to myself. The mystery. The humor, dark and light, that is the warp and weft of the weave. The absurdity. The terror. The hope. The joy, the grief. The God we never see except by indirection.

In this I have failed. I am less than four months short of my thirty-first birthday, have endured much, have piled up all these words, yet I can explain life no better now than I could have done when Charlene Coleman spared me the fate of Punchinello.

I can't explain the why of life, the patterns of its unfolding. I can't explain it — but, oh, how I love it.

And then, after seventeen months of peace and happiness, came the morning of the fifth day, April 16.

We were prepared in all the ways that experience had taught us to prepare, but we also knew that we could not properly prepare at all. The design can be imagined but not truly foreseen.

Because we lived by baker's hours and didn't want our kids to live by a different schedule, they were home-schooled. Their classes started at two o'clock in the morning and ended at eight,

430

whereafter they had breakfast with us, played in sun or snow, and went to bed.

Their usual school was the table in the dining room, with occasional field trips to the table in the kitchen. Their mother served as their teacher, and served them well.

Annie had celebrated her seventh birthday the past January, with a kidney-shaped cake. In a few months, Lucy would be six, while Andy confidently cruised toward five. They loved learning and were demon students in the best sense of the adjective.

As usual on my special days, I stayed home from work. If I had thought it would have done any good to tether crocodiles around the house and board up all the windows, I would have done so. Instead, I helped the kids with their lessons for a while, then prepared breakfast.

We were at the kitchen table, halfway through our waffles with strawberries, when the doorbell rang.

Lucy went directly to the phone, put her hand on the receiver, and prepared to dial 911.

Annie took the car keys from the pegboard, opened the door between the kitchen and the laundry room, and opened the door between the laundry room and the garage, preparing the route for an escape by wheels.

Andy hurried into the half bath off the kitchen to pee, so he would then be ready for flight.

After accompanying me as far as the archway between the dining room and the living room, Lorrie gave me a quick kiss.

The doorbell rang again.

'It's midmonth, so it's probably just the newspaper boy,' I said.

'Right.'

Less in honor of the day than to conceal a shoulder holster, I was wearing a handsome tweed sport coat. In the foyer, I slipped a hand under the coat.

Through the tall French window beside the door, I could see the visitor on the porch. He smiled at me and held forth a silver box tied with red ribbon.

He appeared to be about ten years old, handsome, with jet-black hair and green eyes. His trimly tailored pants were of a metallic-silver material; the red shirt silk had sequined silver buttons. Over the shirt he wore a sparkling silver jacket with silver-and-red buttons in a spiral pattern.

He looked as if he were in training to be an Elvis impersonator.

If ten-year-old boys were coming around to kill me, I might as well die and get it over with. I certainly wasn't going to shoot a little boy, regardless of his intentions.

When I opened the door, he asked, 'Jimmy Tock?'

'That's me.'

Holding out the box, smiling like a band mascot marching at the head of a Happiness Day parade, he said, 'For *you*!'

'I don't want it.'

The smile widened. 'But it's for *you*!'

'No thanks.'

The smile faltered. 'From me to *you*!'

'It isn't from you. Who sent you with this?'

The smile collapsed. 'Mister, for God's sake, take the freakin' box. If I have to go back to the car with it, he'll beat the shit out of me.'

At the curb stood a sparkling silver Mercedes limousine with red racing stripes and tinted windows.

'Who?' I asked. 'Who will beat you?'

Instead of going pale, the boy's olive complexion turned taupe. 'This is taking too long. He's going to want to know what we talked about. I'm not supposed to *chat* with you. Why are you doing this to me? Why do you hate me? Why are you being so *mean*?'

I accepted the box.

At once the boy broke into the band-mascot smile, saluted me, and said, 'Prepare to be *enchanted*!'

No need to brood about where I'd heard *that* phrase before.

He turned on his heel — literally swiveled 180 degrees as smoothly as a pivot hinge — and crossed the porch to the stairs.

I noticed that he was wearing peculiar shoes, similar to ballet slippers, supple with thin soft soles. They were red.

With uncanny grace, he descended the steps and seemed to float rather than walk to the Mercedes. He got in the back of the limo and closed the door.

I couldn't get a glimpse of the driver or any other passengers.

The limousine drove away, and I took the gift-wrapped bomb into the house.

64

Sparkling, intriguing, the box stood on the kitchen table.

I didn't actually believe it was a bomb, but Annie and Lucy were certain that it could be nothing else.

With smirky disdain for his sisters' powers of threat analysis, Andy said, 'It's not a bomb. It's somebody's head cut off and stuffed in a box with a clue in his teeth.'

No one could ever doubt that he was Weena's great-grandson by temperament if not by blood.

'That's stupid,' Annie said. 'A clue to what?'

'To a mystery.'

'What mystery?'

'The mystery of who sent the head, dummy.'

Annie sighed with theatrical exasperation and said, 'If the guy who sent the head wants us to figure who sent it, why doesn't he just write his name on the thing?'

'On what thing?' Andy asked.

'On the thing, whatever it is, that's between the teeth of the stupid head,' Annie clarified.

Solemnly, Lucy said, 'If there's a head, I'm gonna barf.'

'There's not a head in the box, sweetcakes,' Lorrie promised. 'And there's no bomb, either. They don't deliver bombs in flashy silver-and-red limousines.'

'Who doesn't?' Andy asked.

'Nobody doesn't,' Annie said.

Lorrie got a pair of scissors from a kitchen drawer and snipped the red ribbon.

Studying the box, I figured it was just about the perfect size to hold a head. Or a basketball. If I had to bet on one or the other, I'd put my money on the head.

As I was about to lift the lid from the box, Annie and Lucy put their hands over their ears. They were concerned more about the noise of an explosion than about the shrapnel.

Under the lid was a layer of folded white gift-wrapping tissue.

Having climbed onto a chair, kneeling there to get a better view, Andy warned me as I reached for the tissue paper, 'Could be snakes.'

Instead of snakes, packed into the box were banded packets of twenty-dollar bills.

'Wow, we're rich!' Andy declared.

'This isn't our money,' Lorrie said.

'Then whose is it?' Annie wondered.

'I don't know,' Lorrie said, 'but it's bad money, for sure, and we can't keep it. I can smell the evil on it.'

Sniffing at the treasure, Andy said, 'I don't smell nothin'.'

'All I smell is Andy's beans from yesterday dinner,' Annie announced.

'Maybe it could be my money,' Lucy suggested.

'Not as long as I'm your mother.'

Together, the five of us took all the money out of the box and piled it on the table so we could smell it better.

There were twenty-five packets of twenty-dollar bills. Each packet contained a hundred bills. Fifty thousand bucks.

The box also contained an envelope. From the envelope, Lorrie extracted a plain white card with handwriting on one side.

She read the card and said, 'Hmmm.'

When she passed the card to me, the six eyes of three children followed it with intense interest.

Never before had I seen handwriting as meticulously scripted as this. The letters were bold, elegantly formed, flowing as precisely as if a machine had penned them: *Please accept this as a token of my esteem and as proof of my sincerity. I request the honor of a most cordial meeting with you at seven o'clock this evening at the Halloway Farm. The precise location will be obvious upon your arrival.*

The note was signed *Vivacemente*.

'This,' I told the kids, 'is evil money. I'm going to put it back into the box, and then we're all going to wash our hands with a lot of soap and water so hot it hurts a little.'

65

My name is Lorrie Tock. I'm not the goddess Jimmy said I am. For one thing, I've got a pinched nose. For another thing, my teeth are so straight and symmetrical that they don't look real.

And no matter how meticulous the surgeon has been, once you've been shot in the gut — well, when you wear a bikini, you turn heads but not always for the same reason that Miss America does.

Jimmy would have you believe that I am as tough as one of those acid-for-blood bugs in the *Alien* movies. That is an exaggeration, though it's a major mistake to piss me off.

On the night that I was born, no one made predictions about my future, and thank God for that. My father was chasing a tornado in Kansas, and my mother had recently decided that snakes would be better company than he was.

I have to take over this story for reasons that will become clear and that you might already have deduced. If you let me take your hand, metaphorically speaking, we'll get through this together.

So . . .

Near twilight, under a fiery sky, we took the kids next door to stay with Jimmy's parents. Rudy and Maddy were in the living room when we arrived, taking practice swings with the

437

Louisville Sluggers they had bought in 1998.

Immediately after us, six of the most trusted neighbors on the block came to visit, ostensibly for an evening of cards, though all of them had brought baseball bats.

'We play an aggressive game of bridge,' Maddy said.

Jimmy and I hugged the kids, kissed them good-bye, kissed them again, but tried not to make such a big deal of it that we might scare them.

After returning to our house, we dressed as seemed suitable for a 'most cordial meeting.' In preparation for the fifth of the five days, we had added to our wardrobes. We had shoulder holsters, pistols, two little cannisters of pepper spray for each of us.

Jimmy made a pitch for me to wait with the kids while he went alone to meet with the aerialist, but I presented a convincing case for accompanying him: 'You remember what happened to Punchinello's testicles? If you try to keep me from going with you, you'll discover that Punch got off easy.'

We were mutually agreed that going to Huey Foster and bringing in the cops would be a bad idea.

For one thing, Vivacemente had done nothing wrong thus far. We would have a difficult time convincing a jury that a gift of fifty thousand bucks in cash constituted a threatening gesture.

Besides, we worried that whatever Vivacemente's intentions, he would clam up in front of cops and later would go after whatever he wanted more discreetly. Even alerted by his first approach, we would most likely be blindsided. Better that everything remained out in the open between us.

The weather was surprisingly mild for an April evening in high-country Colorado. That doesn't tell you much, because sometimes in April, below freezing is considered mild. To Jimmy, facts are like recipe ingredients, so he would research the temperature in the *Snow County Gazette* before he wrote about it. Me, I'd guess it was maybe fifty degrees.

When we arrived at Halloway Farm, we debated where Vivacemente expected to meet with us. We decided that the giant red-and-white circus tent might be the place.

In this large flat meadow, adjacent to the highway, the circus had set up for business that week in August 1974, when Jimmy had been born. Since then, they had played no return engagement, most likely because they figured that ticket sales would be adversely impacted by the fact that during their previous visit, one of their clowns had killed two much-loved locals.

Neither Jimmy nor I had heard anything about the circus coming to town here in April. For sure, the kids hadn't heard about it, or they would have been in full didja mode: *Didja gets tickets, didja, didja?*

Andy would have begun having clown-in-the-closet dreams again. Me, too, probably.

On second look, we realized that the entire circus wasn't here. An operation of their size involved scores of trucks, motor homes, massive portable generators, and other vehicles. Lined up along the lane to the distant Halloway farmhouse were just four Peterbilts, a VIP bus, and the limousine in which the costumed boy had delivered the fifty thousand smackers.

Emblazoned on the flank of each huge silver truck, festive red lettering announced *VIVACE-MENTE!* In small but still bold lettering: BIG TOP! BIG SHOW! BIG FUN!

'Big deal,' I said.

Jimmy frowned. 'Big trouble.'

66

Only the single enormous tent awaited Jimmy and me. No smaller tents for the customary array of lesser attractions, no animal cages, no roach wagons offering hot dogs, snow cones, popcorn.

Standing alone, the big top made a greater impression than if it had been at the center of the usual bustling medieval fair.

Four poles marked the high ridge line of the tent. Atop each, in the glow of a spotlight, flew a red flag with a silver circle at its center. In each circle were an italicized red V followed by an exclamation point.

Regularly spaced strings of festive, low-voltage lights dropped from the ridge line to the sidewall, red bulbs alternating with white. Twinkling white lights surrounded the main entrance.

One of the four Peterbilts housed the power source. The only sound in the night was the rhythmic chug-and-growl of gasoline-fed generators.

Above the twinkling lights of the main entrance, a banner warned *PREPARE TO BE ENCHANTED!*

Heeding that warning, we drew our pistols, checked to be sure the magazines were fully loaded — though we had checked them before leaving home — and eased them in and out of our shoulder holsters a few times to assure ourselves nothing would inhibit a quick draw.

No one had come forward to greet us when we parked and got out of the car. In spite of the tents and the lights, the meadow seemed to be deserted.

'We're probably misjudging Virgilio,' Jimmy said.

'If Konrad Beezo thought he was a monster, then he's probably a saint,' I reasoned. 'Because when was anything Konrad said ever less than full-on nuts?'

'Exactly,' Jimmy agreed. 'And if Punch thinks he's a festering canker on Satan's ass — '

' — swine of swines — '

' — animated sewage — '

' — worm from the bowels of a syphilitic weasel — '

' — spawn of a witch's toilet — '

' — then he's probably a sweetheart,' I concluded.

'Yeah.'

'Yeah.'

'Ready?'

'No.'

'Let's go.'

'Okay.'

We had tied shut the silver box. Jimmy carried it by the new red ribbon, and together we crossed the meadow to the tent. We went inside.

Under the big top, the meadow grass had been mown short, but no sawdust had been spread.

The bleachers to accommodate the paying public had not been assembled. This was meant to be a show for an audience of two.

At each end of the tent, they had erected the sturdy frames that supported platforms and trapezes for the aerialists. Rope ladders and loop lines provided access to the heights.

Aimed toward upper realms, banks of footlights revealed flyers in the air. The men looked like capeless superheroes in silver and red tights. The women wore one-piece, legless, silver-and-red gymnast uniforms, their bare limbs fetching.

They hung by their hands from trapeze bars, hung by their knees. They arced, they somersaulted, they twirled, they flew, they snared one another out of thin air.

No circus band played; no music was necessary. The performers themselves were music — elegant harmony, exquisite rhythm, symphonic in the complexity of their routines.

Jimmy put down the box of money.

For a few minutes we stood entranced, still aware of the weight of our wardrobes, pistols heavy in our holsters, but all thought of danger relegated to the backs of our minds.

They concluded with a particularly amazing series of midair exchanges during which aerialists flew from trapeze to trapeze with stunningly precise timing, three in flight at any time, only two trapezes available, collision and catastrophe always a possibility.

Out of this bedazzlement of wingless birds, one of the men soared high off a bar, twirled in midair, folded into a somersault position, and tumbled down, down. At the last moment he spread his arms like wings, came out of the ball position, and landed on his back in the safety net.

He bounced high, bounced again, rolled to the edge of the net, and dropped to the ground, on point like a ballet star, his arms raised above his head, as though he had just completed an entrechat.

From a distance of thirty feet, he appeared to be handsome, with bold features, a proud Roman nose. His barrel chest, broad shoulders, slim hips, and trim figure made him an imposing man, lionesque.

Although his hair was coal black and though he appeared to be no older than forty-five, I knew this must be Virgilio Vivacemente, for from him radiated the pride of a king, a master, a paterfamilias.

Because even in 1974 he had been the patriarch and the brightest star of a famous circus family, father of several children, including his twenty-year-old daughter Natalie, he must have been seventy or older this night in April. He not only appeared much younger, but had just proven himself to be athletic and extraordinarily limber.

The circus life seemed to be his fountain of youth.

One by one, the other performers dropped from high flight into the net. They bounced, descended to the ground, and lined up in a crescent behind Virgilio.

When they were all earthbound, they raised their right arms high overhead. Then, theatrically lowering their arms to point at me and Jimmy, they said in unison, 'The Flying Vivacementes fly for *you*!'

Jimmy and I started to applaud, but caught ourselves, and also stopped grinning like children.

Members of the troupe were male and female, all good-looking, including a girl who appeared to be eight or nine and a boy of ten. They bounded out of the tent like gazelles, gamboling together as though the demonstration high in the big top had required no serious effort, had been mere play.

Through the performers' entrance where the group made their exit came a tall muscle-bound man with a scarlet robe over his arm. He went to Vivacemente and held this garment while the star slipped his arms into the sleeves.

The carrier of the robe had a brutal, scarred face. Even at a distance, his eyes seemed as menacing as those of a viper.

Although he departed, leaving us alone with his boss, I was glad we were carrying pistols. I wished we'd thought to bring attack dogs.

The heavy yet beautifully draped robe was of a luxurious fabric, perhaps cashmere, with padded shoulders and wide lapels. In it, the aerialist had the air of a 1930s movie star, when Hollywood still had glamor instead of glitz.

Smiling, he approached us, and the closer he drew, the clearer it became that he had taken measures to stave off the effects of time. The glossy black shade of his hair was too inky to be real; it had come from a bottle. Perhaps he had earned his physique with vigorous and relentless exercise — and with steroids for lunch every day — but age had been trimmed from his face by battalions of scalpels.

We have all seen unfortunate women who began having extensive face-lifts much too young and who submitted to subsequent surgeries too frequently, until by their sixties — sometimes even sooner — their faces have been stretched tight to the point of snapping. Their Botoxed brows look like plastic. They cannot completely close their eyes even to sleep. Their nostrils have a permanent flare, as though they are perpetually testing the air for an offensive odor, and their enhanced lips are pulled and puckered into a permanent pouty half-smile that inevitably reminds us of Jack Nicholson playing the Joker in *Batman*.

But for the fact that he was a man, Virgilio Vivacemente looked like one of those unfortunate women.

He came so close that Jimmy and I involuntarily backed up a step or two, which elicited a sharky smile from our host. Apparently, part of his manipulative style was to invade the space of others.

When he spoke, he had a baritone voice closer in register to bass than to tenor. 'Of course you know who I am.'

'We've got a pretty good idea,' Jimmy said.

Because the ten-year-old boy who delivered the box of money had been terrified of having the crap beat out of him by this man, and because of the offensive implications of the money itself, we refused to extend to him

446

courtesy that he had not earned. He'd chosen to play a game called Who's the Big Dog? — and we could bark as loud as he could.

'In every corner of the world,' said the patriarch, 'everyone knows who I am.'

'At first we thought you were Benito Mussolini,' I said, 'but then we realized he'd never been an aerialist.'

'Besides,' Jimmy said, 'Mussolini's been dead since the end of World War II.'

I said, 'And you don't look like you've been dead nearly that long.'

Virgilio Vivacemente smiled more broadly, and his smile even less resembled a smile than it did a knife wound.

Although the tightness of his face made the nuanced meaning of his various smiles impossible to read, I recognized the glaze that came over his eyes as he listened to Jimmy and me. He was a man who possessed no sense of humor whatsoever. Zero. Zip. Zilch.

He didn't realize that we were joking between ourselves, and because he didn't grasp our tone and intent, he also didn't realize that we were insulting him. To his ear, we were talking gibberish, and he was wondering if we might be mentally retarded.

'Many years ago, the Flying Vivacementes became stars of such worldwide renown,' he said with sonorous self-importance, 'that I was able to buy the circus of which I had once been an employee. And now today there are *three* Vivacemente circuses playing at all times in every significant venue in the world!'

Pretending suspicion, Jimmy said, '*Real* circuses. You even have elephants?'

'Of course we have elephants!' Vivacemente declared.

'One? Two?'

'*Many* elephants!'

'Do you have lions?' I asked.

'*Prides* of lions!'

'Tigers?' Jimmy asked.

'Snarling *hordes* of tigers!'

'Kangaroos?'

'What kangaroos? No circus has kangaroos.'

'No circus is a circus *without* kangaroos,' Jimmy insisted.

'Absurdity! You know *nothing* of circuses.'

I said, 'Do you have clowns?'

Vivacemente's stiff face froze entirely. When he spoke, his baritone voice issued between teeth set edge to edge like the jaws of a nutcracker: 'Every circus must have clowns to draw the weak-minded and silly little children.'

'Ah,' said Jimmy. 'So you don't have as many clowns as other circuses do.'

'We have all the clowns we need and more. We are *infested* with clowns. But no one comes primarily for clowns.'

'Lorrie and me, all our lives, we're crazy about clowns,' Jimmy said.

'Or is it,' I proposed, 'that all our lives, clowns have been crazy about us?'

'Crazy is in there somewhere,' Jimmy said.

The aerialist blustered on: 'Our biggest draw is *always* the immortal Flying Vivacementes, the greatest circus family in all of history. In all three of my shows, every member of every aerialist troupe is a Vivacemente, related by blood and by talent that makes lesser performers weep with jealousy. I am the father of some, the spiritual father of all.'

To me, Jimmy said, 'For a man who has achieved so much, you might expect his pride to be overweening, but how wrong you'd be.'

'Humble,' I agreed. 'Remarkably humble.'

'*Humility is for losers!*' Vivacemente thundered.

'I've heard that somewhere,' Jimmy said.

'Gandhi?' I suggested.

Jimmy shook his head. 'I think it was Jesus.'

Eyes glazing again with the conviction that we were idiots, Vivacemente said, 'And of all the Flying Vivacementes, I am supreme. On the trapeze, I am poetry in motion.'

Jimmy said, ''Poetry In Motion,' Johnny Tillotson, top ten, back in the early '60s. Good beat, you could dance to it.'

Ignoring him, Vivacemente boasted, 'Transiting the high wire, I am moonlight walking, the love of every woman, the envy of every man.' He drew a breath, expanded his big chest, and continued: 'And I am rich enough and determined enough always to get what I want. In this case, I am certain that what I want is what you will want, because it will bring wealth and great honor to you as you otherwise would never have known.'

'Fifty thousand dollars is a lot of money,' Jimmy said, 'but it isn't *wealth*.'

Vivacemente winked to the extent that his

449

trimmed eyelids were capable of completing a wink. 'Fifty thousand is just earnest money, proof that I am sincere. I have calculated the full sum to be three hundred and twenty-five thousand.'

'And what do you expect in return for that?' Jimmy asked.

'Your son,' Vivacemente said.

67

Jimmy and I could have left the big top and driven home without another word to the maniac aerialist. Having walked out, however, we would not have understood his reasoning, and we would not have had peace, wondering what his next move might be.

'His name is Andy,' said Vivacemente, as though we needed to be reminded of our only son's name. 'But I will create a better name, of course, something classic, less plebeian. If I am to shape the boy into the greatest star of his generation, I must begin instructing him before his fifth birthday.'

As darkly funny as all this might be, it had also become too scary to play his game any longer.

I said, 'Andy, which will *always* be his name, has no talent as an aerialist.'

'He must. He has Vivacemente blood. He's my Natalie's grandson.'

'If you know about that, then you also know he's Konrad Beezo's grandson, too,' Jimmy reminded him. 'Surely you'll be the first to admit he's too much clown for the high wire.'

'He is not tainted,' the patriarch said. 'I've had him watched. I've studied the films of him. He is a natural.'

Films of him.

Although the night was mild, my heart had gone cold.

451

'People do not sell their children,' I said.

'Oh,' Vivacemente assured me, 'people *do*. I myself have bought the children of certain Vivacemente cousins in Europe, whose family lines were strong enough to produce fine aerialists. I have bought some of them from the cradle, some at the age of two and three, but always before the fifth birthday.'

With revulsion that no doubt eluded our host as much as did our humor, Jimmy pointed to the box on the ground. 'We brought your money back. That's the end of it.'

'Three hundred *seventy*-five thousand,' Vivacemente offered.

'No.'

'Four hundred thousand.'

'No.'

'Four hundred fifteen thousand.'

'Stop it,' Jimmy demanded.

'Four hundred twenty-two thousand five hundred, and that's my final offer. I must have this special boy. He's my last chance, my best chance, to create another like me. The blood of aerialists is *concentrated* in him as never before.'

As Vivacemente's tucked and tightened face tried to express the operatic emotions that raged in him, I half expected it to crack at every corner and peel up from the bone.

He pressed his hands together as if in prayer, and he began to beseech Jimmy instead of bullying him: 'If I had known in 1974 or any time during the years immediately after that Natalie had given birth to twins, that you had been given to the *baker* and his wife' — the word

452

baker issuing from him with the acidic disdain of a blue-blood snob — 'I would have come for you, I swear. I would have bought you back or rescued you one way or another. I *always* get what I want. But I thought I had only one son and that the vicious Beezo had fled with him.'

Icily, Jimmy rejected this bizarre protestation of fatherly love: 'You aren't my father even in the sense that you might call yourself the spiritual father of everyone in your troupe. Punchinello and I aren't in your troupe, and we're not your sons in any sense. We're technically your grandsons, God help us. But I don't accept even that relationship. I deny you the right to be my grandfather, I refuse you, I renounce you, I *repudiate* you.'

The beseeching hands that had been pressed together abruptly separated. They formed into white-knuckled fists.

Although Vivacemente had no sense of humor, he had a rare capacity for hatred, which sharpened his eyes into knife points and which expressed itself unmistakably in the tightly screwed features of his carved face.

The old man's voice was hypodermic, his words poisonous: 'Konrad Beezo never had a child with any woman he ever laid with. He was the husk of a man, sterile.'

With a jolt, I remembered — and I'm certain Jimmy did, too — Konrad Beezo in our kitchen, the Porter Carson identity cast aside, just before he shot me. He wanted Andy as recompense for our sending Punchinello to prison, as 'something for something.' He hadn't known that Jimmy was

Punchinello's twin, hadn't realized that Andy might be of his bloodline. He just wanted *quid pro quo*, his 'makeweight.' When I had asked Konrad why he didn't lie down with some desperate hag who might have him and make a baby of his own, he flinched from my words and could not meet my eyes. Now I knew why.

This venomous filth before us, this walking worm in a scarlet robe, drew himself to his full height and with demented pride said, 'I wanted to *concentrate* the aerialist genes as they had never before been concentrated. And my dream was *conceived* in the biblical sense. But she fled me for Beezo, and denied me what was mine. Natalie was my daughter, but I am your grandfather *and* your father.'

Whoa.

Having adjusted to the creepy discovery that he was Konrad Beezo's son and Punchinello's brother, poor Jimmy — sweet Jimmy — now had to get his mind around the even creepier idea that he was still Punchinello's brother but was in fact Vivacemente's son *and* grandson, the product of incest.

Move over, Johnny Tillotson. The hits just keep on coming.

68

Movement at the perimeter of the tent drew our attention. From outside, the muscle-bound brute with the cobra eyes stepped into the main entrance and stood there with his legs wide apart, looking as if he could deflect a runaway elephant. He was armed with a shotgun.

Another man spookily like the first — except that he had keloid scars across his face and neck, as if he had been cobbled together by Victor Frankenstein — appeared in the performers' entrance. He, too, held a shotgun.

Three others had slipped under the sidewall canvas where it hung loosest between stakes. They were spotted around the big top, beyond the footlights, in shadows but visible. I suspected they had weapons, too, but I couldn't see them well enough to be sure.

'And so you see,' Vivacemente continued, 'your son Andy is my Natalie's grandson. He is also my grandson *and* great-grandson. My dream has been delayed one generation, but now it will come to pass. If you don't sell me young Andy for four hundred twenty-two thousand five hundred dollars, I will kill the two of you. I will kill Rudy and Maddy, and I will take *all three* of your children at no cost to me whatsoever.'

Clearly Jimmy didn't want to risk taking his eyes off Virgilio Vivacemente any more than he would have turned his back on a coiled rattlesnake, but he nevertheless looked at me.

Most of the time, I could tell what my Jimmy was thinking. The terrain inside his wonderful head was my backyard; I felt at home there.

This time, his lovely eyes were not windows to his thoughts, as previously they had always been. His expression remained flat, enigmatic.

A lesser man might have been so hammered by these revelations that he would have been paralyzed by shock, revulsion, and despair. He might be shocked and revolted, but Jimmy never despaired.

He said, 'Does this blow or does it blow?'

'It blows,' I said.

Sensing triumph, his face *crafted* for the smug expression that overcame it, Vivacemente put his hands in the pockets of his scarlet robe, rocked back and forth in his red slippers, back and forth. 'If you think I can't kill all of you and get clean away with it, you're wrong. When the two of you and Rudy and Maddy are dead at my feet, I will dismember the four of you, marinate your remains in gasoline, burn them, urinate on the ashes, put the wet ashes in a bucket, take them to a lovely farm I own, and stir them into the muddy wallow in the corner of a pigpen. I've done it before. There is no vengeance equal to the vengeance of Virgilio Vivacemente.'

His gaze still locked on me, Jimmy quietly said, ' "With the right psychotic hag, you could father another murderous little maggot as insane as your firstborn." '

Vivacemente cocked his head. 'What did you say?'

456

I recognized Jimmy's words. He had quoted what I had said to Konrad Beezo in our kitchen on that December night in 2002, just before the clown had shot me.

I had been trying to rattle Beezo with attitude and insults, and to some extent, I had succeeded. He had flinched at my verbal assault, had looked away from me to Jimmy, giving me the opportunity to draw the pepper spray and squirt him in the face.

Jimmy was proposing a similar tactic with Vivacemente.

He saw that I understood.

Pushing us harder, the maniac said, 'When you are nothing but urine-soaked ashes in a pig wallow, I will take your three children to an estate I maintain in Argentina. There I will train Andy and perhaps Lucy to be the finest aerialists of their generation, and perhaps Annie, as well. If she is too old at seven . . . well, she will, have other uses. Lose your lives and *all* your children, or sell Andy to me. Only a *clown* could not make the right choice between those two options.'

'It's a lot of money,' Jimmy told me. 'The better part of half a million, cash, no taxes.'

'And we'd still have Annie and Lucy,' I said.

'We can always have another son,' Jimmy proposed.

'With a new baby, we'd forget Andy in no time.'

'I'd forget him in three months,' Jimmy said.

'Might take me six.'

'We're young. Even if it takes us *eight* months

457

to forget him, we've got a lot of good life ahead of us.'

Vivacemente was smiling, or appeared to be, as best anyone other than his surgeons could tell.

Incredibly, he seemed to be buying what we were selling. His credulousness did not entirely surprise me. After all, Jimmy and I had enormous experience talking to maniacs in their language.

'But, hey,' Jimmy said to me, 'wow, that gives me an even *better* idea.'

I crafted a mask of bright-eyed curiosity. 'What's that?'

Turning to Vivacemente again, Jimmy said, 'Would you buy two?'

'Two what?'

'Two boys. If we had another, you could buy him early, right out of the cradle.'

I said, 'Jimmy — '

'Shut up, honey,' he warned me. 'You've never had a head for finances. Leave this to me.'

Jimmy had never before told me to shut up. I knew he meant to convey that *he* would distract our target to give me the opportunity I needed.

'I'm a bull in the baby-making department,' Jimmy told the crazy aerialist, 'and the little lady here, she can really pump them out. She could take a fertility drug, too, and maybe we could have them in batches.'

Jimmy and I were *both* going to die. We understood that we were cold meat standing. With all the firepower in the tent, we couldn't escape. But in dying, we could take Vivacemente with us. When this beast lay bullet-riddled and

458

dead, our kids would be safe with Rudy and Maddy.

Expanding upon his proposal with enthusiasm, Jimmy held the old man rapt, and when the moment seemed ideal, I went for my pistol.

I don't believe Vivacemente saw me from the corner of his eye. I think instead that like a champion poker player, he caught some subtle tell from Jimmy.

Without taking his hands out of his cashmere robe, he opened fire on Jimmy with a handgun concealed in the deep right pocket. He squeezed off two rounds as I was drawing, both of which hit Jimmy in the abdomen, fired two more as I brought my pistol to bear on him, and those two slammed Jimmy in the chest. By the roar of them, these were high-power rounds. The first two knocked Jimmy backward, and the second two knocked him down.

Intending his fifth bullet for me, Vivacemente turned my way but not fast enough. I shot him in the head once, and he dropped.

Screaming like a Valkyrie, possessed of a fury that only the righteous sane can know, that never can be matched by madmen in their moral confusion, I shot him three more times, this *thing* who raped his own daughter, this *monster* who bought children, this *demon* who would make me a widow.

Beyond the damage to his face, I glimpsed in it an expression of surprise. He hadn't thought that he could die.

I should have saved my ammunition, because the thuggish-looking roustabouts came toward me at a run. I couldn't take out all of them, however, and in fact I wasn't hot to shoot any of them, not as long as I could be sure that Vivacemente was down for good, forever.

When I swiveled toward the first of the approaching men, he threw down his shotgun. The second had already discarded his.

The other three came out of the shadows, past the footlights. One had an ax, and dropped it. One had a sledgehammer, and pitched it aside. If the third had been armed, he had chucked his weapon far back near the sidewall of the tent.

Gasping equally with amazement and astonishment, with terror and horror, I watched those five brawny men gather around the corpse of Virgilio Vivacemente. They regarded it with shock, with awe . . . and suddenly broke into laughter.

My sweet Jimmy, my muffin man, lay flat on his back, silent on the ground, and the roustabouts laughed, and one of them cupped his hands around his mouth and called out in circus lingo that made no sense to me.

As I collapsed to my knees at my Jimmy's side, the troupe of aerialists burst into the tent, still dressed in their costumes, shrieking like birds.

69

For a few days, my chest and stomach hurt so bad that I could almost believe the four bullets had not flattened against the Kevlar vest under my shirt, but had penetrated and done major damage. The hideous bruises didn't fully fade for weeks.

As Lorrie told you, after leaving the kids at my parents' house, we had dressed as seemed suitable for a 'most cordial meeting' with a possible lunatic. We'd gotten the two vests a year earlier through Huey Foster.

Okay, we yanked your chain again, like we did back in chapter twenty-four. How much fun would it have been, there in the big top, if you'd been absolutely certain that I had survived?

The Kevlar stopped all four rounds, but the impact, even spread across the surface of the vest, knocked the breath and consciousness out of me. I experienced a brief and not unpleasant dream about chocolate amaretto cheesecake.

When I came to, some people were laughing robustly. Others were shrieking with what at first might have been shock and fear but which quickly changed to giddy delight.

The adults and the teenagers and the children alike came to the body of Virgilio. None seemed to be either angry about his death or grossed out by his condition.

Instead, each regarded the cadaver with

stunned disbelief that gradually brightened into an awareness of their freedom.

Vivacemente had not believed that he could die — and neither had any of the troupe that snapped to the crack of his whip. The collapse of the Soviet Union surely had not surprised them a fraction as much as this did.

With belief, the aerialists found themselves virtually exploding with energy, with joy. They scampered up rope ladders and loop lines, into the higher reaches of the tent, to their platforms and trapezes.

As sirens rose in the distance, as Lorrie helped me to my feet, the flyers flew in exaltation, in rhapsodies.

70

Earlier, in a windy moment, I wrote that revenge and justice are twin braids in a line as thin as the high wire that an aerialist must walk, and if you can't keep your balance, then you are doomed — and damned — regardless of whether you fall to the left or to the right of the line. A restrained response to evil is not moral, but neither is excessive violence.

The only anguishing moral dilemma that Lorrie carried out of that big top was related to whether she should have shot to wound and disable Virgilio Vivacemente or whether blowing him to bits with four well-placed, hollow-point rounds might have been justified.

She agonized over this for about twenty-four hours, but during a parade of desserts after dinner at my parents' house on the evening of Sunday, April 17, as Vivacemente still lay in a morgue drawer, she achieved a satisfying catharsis. She decided that if she had shot the crazy son of a bitch *five* times, including four times after he was already dead instead of just three, *that* would have been an excessive and unjustifiable response. As it was, she had no doubt — nor did I — that she was on the side of the angels.

In any moral dilemma, as one strives to analyze one's motives and actions, a speedier and usually satisfying resolution can be reached

463

if one consumes abundant quantities of sugar.

As for me, I came out of the experience with no knotty moral issues. The truth of my conception didn't change who I had become, who I was. I declined to dwell upon it.

More important, the fifth of my five days had come and gone. I had survived. Every member of my family remained healthy and alive, except for Grandma Rowena, and she had died in her sleep.

We had suffered a great deal en route to this safe harbor, but who does not suffer in life? When the pain passes, there is always cake.

Life insurance companies price their policies on the basis of many factors, including actuarial tables. They have arcane formulae to predict your life expectancy, and if they didn't they would soon be out of business.

I do not define life expectancy by the length of life, however, but by the quality of it, by what I *expect* from it and by how well my expectations are met. What I have learned from my true father, Rudy, and from my true mother, Maddy, and from my glorious wife, and from my beloved children is that the more you expect from life, the more your expectations will be fulfilled. By laughing, you do not use up your laughter, but increase your store of it. The more you love, the more you will be loved. The more you give, the more you will receive.

Life proves that truth to me every hour, every day.

And life continues to surprise:

Fourteen months after the incident in the big

top, Lorrie became pregnant. She had been told that she could never conceive again, and her doctors had been so certain of her barrenness that we took no precautions.

Considering the grievous wounds that Lorrie had survived and the fact that she had one kidney, Dr. Mello Melodeon counseled us to terminate.

In bed the night after receiving this news, Lorrie said, 'We'll never have the five. Four is the most there's any hope of. This will be the last chance. Maybe it's risky. Maybe it's not.'

'I don't want to lose you,' I whispered in the darkness.

'You can't,' she said. 'I'll haunt you in this life and kick your ass for dawdling when you finally join me in the next.'

After a silence, I said, 'I'm paralyzed by this.'

'Question.'

'What?'

'Once we were together and knew it was for always, after each of us had the strength of the other to rely on, when were we ever gutless?'

I thought about it awhile. Finally, I said, 'When?'

'Never. So why start now?'

Months later, when little Rowena arrived, she popped out as easy as bread from a toaster. She was eighteen inches long. She weighed eight pounds even. She did not have syndactyly.

While we were still in the delivery room, as Charlene Coleman (on the eve of her retirement) handed our swaddled infant to Lorrie for the first time, a young redheaded nurse stepped into the doorway and asked to speak to Mello.

He conferred with her in the hallway for a few minutes, and when he returned, he brought her with him. 'This is Brittany Walters,' he told us. 'She works ICU, and she has a story you need to hear.'

According to Brittany Walters, an elderly woman named Edna Carter had been admitted to the ICU forty-eight hours earlier, after a massive stroke paralyzed her and left her unable to speak. Suddenly this evening Edna had sat up in bed — minutes before Lorrie delivered, as it turned out — no longer paralyzed. She had spoken clearly, too, and with urgency.

By the time Nurse Walters reached that point in her story, I dared not look at Lorrie. I didn't know what I would see in her eyes, but I was afraid of the terror she would see in mine.

The nurse continued: 'She insisted that a baby named Rowena would be born in this hospital in minutes. That Rowena would be eighteen inches long and weigh eight pounds on the nose.'

'Oh my,' said Charlene Coleman.

Nurse Walters held out a sheet of notepaper. 'And Edna insisted that I write down these five days. When I'd done it . . . she fell back in her bed and died.'

My hand shook as I took the paper from her.

When I glanced at Mello Melodeon, he didn't have as grim an expression as I thought a friend should have at a moment like this.

Reluctantly, I scanned the dates on the paper and murmured strickenly, 'Five terrible days.'

'What did you say?' Nurse Walters asked.

'Five terrible days,' I repeated, but didn't have the strength to explain.

'That's not what Edna Carter said,' Nurse Walters told me.

'What did she say?' Mello urged her, but I could see that he knew the answer to his question.

Puzzled by our reactions, Nurse Walters said, 'Well, she told me these were five glorious days, five especially joyful days to come in a blessed life. Isn't that odd? Do you think it means anything?'

At last I met Lorrie's eyes.

'Do you think it means anything?' I asked.

'My hunch is yeah.'

Folding the paper, tucking it in a pocket, I sighed. 'It sure is spooky this side of paradise.'

'But lovely.'

'Mysterious.'

'Always.'

'Sweet.'

'Oh, yeah,' she agreed. 'Sweet.'

Gently, reverently, I took tiny Rowena from Lorrie. So small she was, but in spirit and in potential, no smaller than any of us.

Holding her so that she faced away from me, I turned in a full circle. Even if her eyes were as yet unfocused, perhaps she could see the room in which she had been born and see the people who had been present for her entry. Perhaps she wondered about them and about what waited beyond this room.

Turning with her, turning, I said, 'Rowena, this is the world. This is your life. Prepare to be enchanted.'

THE TAKING

Dean Koontz

On the morning that will mark the end of the world they have known, Molly and Neil Sloan awaken to the drumbeat of rain. They find an eerily luminous and silver downpour that drenches their small Californian mountain town. As hours pass, they hear news of extreme weather phenomena across the globe. An obscuring fog turns once familiar streets into a ghostly labyrinth. By evening, the town has lost all communication with the outside world. The young couple gathers together with some neighbours, sensing a threat they cannot even imagine. The night brings strange noises, and mysterious lights drift among the trees. At dawn, the small band will encounter something that reveals in a terrifying instant what is happening to the world.

ODD THOMAS

Dean Koontz

Odd Thomas takes pride in his work as a fry cook. His fame has spread, bringing strangers to the restaurant in Pico Mundo. Odd cannot say what it is that disturbs him about this particular stranger, but his sixth sense is alert . . . This is a man with an appetite for terror. He craves extreme violence: multiple untimely deaths, spiced with horror. Odd's fears are first for Stormy Llewellyn, his one true love. Stormy believes that our passage through this world is intended to toughen us for the next life — that the terrors we know here are an inoculation against worse in the world to come. But Odd Thomas knows more than Stormy about this world. He sees the restless dead, those with unfinished business and, sometimes, plenty of post-mortem rage . . .

DATE DUE FOR RETURN WV